Praise for *City of Broken Magic*

"This debut builds a fascinating setting that readers will want to keep coming back to."

—*Publishers Weekly* (starred review)

"A fascinating debut . . . Readers will be antsy for the next installment."

—*Library Journal*

"With complex characters, political intrigue, and discussion of feminism and the caste system . . . readers will enjoy *City of Broken Magic* and its fresh spin on the fantasy genre."

—*Booklist*

"*City of Broken Magic* shines most brightly in the interactions between the three Sweepers, and fantasy fans will hope for more exploits in Amicae."

—*Shelf Awareness*

"Incredible attention to detail."

—*BookPage*

"Full of enough action and intrigue to keep you on the edge of your seat all night long."

—*The Arched Doorway*

"Fantasy fans will hope for more exploits in Amicae."

—*Infinite Reads*

"Terrifying shadow monsters haunt a vividly rendered working-class present with the sins of generations past. A thrilling ride, with promise of deeper mysteries to come."

—Max Gladstone, Hugo Award finalist

"*City of Broken Magic* explores what happens after the familiar heroes have gone, and the importance of those who remain to begin again."

—Fran Wilde, Hugo and Nebula finalist,
award-winning author of the Bone Universe series

ALSO BY MIRAH BOLENDER

City of Broken Magic

THE

MONSTROUS

CITADEL

※

MIRAH BOLENDER

A TOM DOHERTY ASSOCIATES BOOK ◣ TOR NEW YORK

THE MONSTROUS CITADEL

Copyright © 2019 by Mirah Bolender

Edited by Jen Gunnels

Designed by Greg Collins

A Tor Book
Published by Tom Doherty Associates
120 Broadway
New York, NY 10271

www.tor-forge.com

Tor® is a registered trademark of Macmillan Publishing Group, LLC.

The Library of Congress Cataloging-in-Publication Data is available upon request.

ISBN 978-1-250-16929-7 (trade paperback)
ISBN 978-1-250-16928-0 (ebook)

Our books may be purchased in bulk for promotional, educational, or business use. Please contact your local bookseller or the Macmillan Corporate and Premium Sales Department at 1-800-221-7945, extension 5442, or by email at MacmillanSpecialMarkets@macmillan.com.

First Edition: November 2019

Printed in the United States of America

0 9 8 7 6 5 4 3 2 1

DEDICATED TO MY MOTHER,

WHOSE LOVE OF

Masterpiece Mysteries

IS PARTIALLY TO BLAME FOR WHY MY STORIES

TURN OUT THE WAY THEY DO.

ACKNOWLEDGMENTS

Publishing a second book is a whole different beast from the first. It took about five years of tinkering for *City of Broken Magic* to emerge. While drafts for *The Monstrous Citadel* have been around almost as long, the changes to book one and the sudden influx of publishing knowledge have affected it greatly. The real work of it has been crammed into about a year. Quite frankly, I kitchen-sinked it. This completed version is thanks to the tireless work of my editor, Jennifer Gunnels, who helped me find the most important pieces and helped me polish them into the narrative they were meant to be. My sincere thanks also goes to my agent, Peter Rubie, who helped guide me through this literary version of the "sophomore slump," and called to make sure I was okay when he saw the sheer amount of edits on draft one.

There's also a crowd of people I didn't know well enough to thank in book one, so I'll remedy that now: Thank you to June Clark, who steered me through author presence and helped me build my website; thank you to my publicist, Lauren Jackson, who focused on book presence and helped me make my first real appearance, at the Wisconsin Book Festival; thank you to Natalie Naudus and the Macmillan Audio team, who turned *City of Broken Magic* into an audiobook and therefore fulfilled a wish I've had since my childhood road trips (now if only I could connect it to my old car radio!); thank you to cover artist Tony Mauro, because it's one thing for the debut book you've worked so long on to have a cover, but it's a dream to have a cover that looks so fantastic; thank you to my copyeditor, whom I didn't interact with directly but who saved me from phrasing mistakes I hadn't even noticed; thank you to the Tor team at large, for all the work they've put into pitching and delivering this series so far; thank you to my grandmother, who immediately went out and bought twelve copies of book one; thank you also to Boswell Book Company in Milwaukee, for giving her the opportunity to buy those twelve books, for listening to her bragging about the author, and for earlier introducing said author to fantastic independent bookstores.

Last but not least, thank you, reader. Every writer has a fear that their work isn't good enough, or that the only people who'll end up reading it are their family members. You've proven my worries wrong in the best way.

It's been a long and exciting road to *The Monstrous Citadel*. I hope you enjoy it.

THE

MONSTROUS

CITADEL

AMICAE RIOTS

The friendly city of Amicae descended into chaos following a massive infestation. Amicae has long believed that infestations cannot penetrate their city walls, but these delusions were rudely swept away on November 5th by a damaged Pit and ensuing swarm. With their Sweeper department crippled and consisting of only three persons—now only two—Amicae was ill-equipped to handle the event. Assistance from Puer and Terrae Sweepers allowed them to repel the infestation, but not before the city was evacuated and many lives were lost. The death toll is yet unknown but growing as citizens sweep through the streets and protests for truth become violent. Lux head Sweeper Olga Verbaun says that while painful to hear, this protest is necessary. "Amicae has lied to itself for too long," she explained yesterday morning, after a routine safety demonstration at a local school. "Ignorance of a problem is not safety. With its location Amicae can't afford to pretend invulnerability. It's a miracle the city hasn't been destroyed already." Verbaun is a crusader for public awareness to locate and minimize damage done by infestations. When asked if she had any advice for the Sinclair Sweepers of Amicae, she replied, "I hope that they're able to recover quickly. Even with Amicae finally aware of the danger, two is a very small number for Sweepers. If even one falters, the city will fall."

EYES OPENED

This past week Amicae's Council was forced to come clean regarding the existence of infestations. "The wall policy" has been the bane of city relations for decades, but with its demise Canis and surrounding cities hope for better communication and trade with our befuddled neighbor. Despite this, Canis's head Sweeper has misgivings. He advises that Canis businessmen stay on their toes and, if possible, handle any Amicae dealings remotely. Sweepers warn that infestation activity is rising fast again, and who would wish to be stranded in a doomed city?

Avis *Wings*, November 19, 1233

SWEEPERS IN MOURNING

Last evening Sweepers gathered at the reflection pool to grieve for those lost to Amicae's Falling Infestation. Amicae's tragedy has one of the highest death tolls in recent memory. Avis's head Sweeper stresses the importance of recognizing the losses of other cities, not only as an act of compassion, but to impress upon our own citizens the danger we face. He wishes Amicae, especially new head Sweeper Laura Kramer, the best of luck.

Amicae *Dead Ringer*, November 26, 1233

SWEEPERS RIDICULED, BUSINESS AS USUAL

Despite destroying an infestation running rampant in the First Quarter, Head Sweeper Laura Kramer has been lambasted by the general populace for "gross negligence." For what, one may ask—for not responding to no less than 3,000 telephone calls from paranoid citizens in a single day? Only one of these proved valid and the police department has investigated every other call. For property damage, perhaps? Testimony from foreign Sweepers and even previous Amicae records show that damage goes hand in hand with Sweeping. You are pleased if a roof caves in on mobsters during a fight, but if the same happens during the eradication of a monster that would destroy other buildings, eat any who cross its path, and spread its offspring through the city until it can feed on everything you love from the inside out—this is where you draw the line? At least a mobster will leave you a body to bury. The Ringer bids you review your priorities immediately.

Amicae *Sun*, November 28, 1233

HEAD SWEEPER FIRED

Amid the turbulence of recent events, the Council has chosen to remove Laura Kramer from the head Sweeper position. At 20 years old she was not the youngest head Sweeper in Amicae's history—see Clae Sinclair's 15—but citizens expressed doubt in her ability to uphold the office. Many push for her to be removed from the Sweepers altogether, claiming that she should have done everything in her power to spread the truth. Councilwoman Victoria Douglas pointed out to these protestors that the situation was beyond Kramer's, or even Sinclair's, control. She further stated that we must bolster our Sweepers in any way we can; to fire Kramer would mean our only Sweeper is not yet 20 and not yet employed for four months, a recipe for certain disaster. Efforts are under way to recruit more Sweepers, and Juliana MacDanel of Puer has been appointed as new head Sweeper. MacDanel, 35, has worked as a Sweeper since her school days and came highly recommended by her city.

Amicae *Dead Ringer*, November 28, 1233

AMICAE NEVER LEARNS

Once again the public bends its ear to the very problem. Who will you trust, Amicae: the Council who deliberately chose not to warn you and caused the very destruction you're screaming over, or the person who risked life and limb to save you from your nightmares? Congratulations. You've thrown your hero to the wolves.

1

BACKLASH

Laura's dismissal had been a shock, initially. It came on the tail end of an infestation, just as reported in the Amicae *Sun*. Damage had been done, yes, but it hadn't been anywhere near as bad as what she'd done to the army barracks in September, or even what she and Clae had done to a residence in August. Where those incidents had been either picked at or overlooked entirely, stories about this one had ballooned. It couldn't be blamed on mobsters or another far-fetched reason, not now in Amicae's "age of truth." As good as it was to have people who knew about infestations, in this instance it proved extremely annoying. When infestations came up now, the public reacted in hysterics. Citizens wrote to the papers, bemoaning her ineptitude: Why couldn't she have just not damaged anything? Why couldn't she have prevented the infestation from coming at all? Why hadn't she done her civic duty and shared the truth with everyone from the start? Okane suggested that maybe she should avoid the papers for a while, but she ignored him. If she was head Sweeper, she'd do this right. She needed to know what everyone was saying, so she could give them a proper and well-educated *fuck you* in case she ever met one of these idiots in person. ("- - - sound like Clae," he'd informed her, and even his lack of "you" sounded exasperated.)

Part of her was viciously pleased when the *Dead Ringer* newspaper rose to her defense, but mostly she felt squeamish. Anyone with a brain knew that the *Dead Ringer* was run by the Mad Dogs mob. The Mad Dogs helped Sweepers during the Falling Infestation, but that had been basic self-preservation. With their own fleet of Sweepers far outnumbering the Sinclairs, there was no need for them to dig in their heels like this. Laura had a bad feeling that the Mad Dogs would come knocking on her door with a debt she'd never asked for. Furthermore, the obvious new link between Sweepers and Mad Dogs was a nightmare in publicity. Albright had since redirected any phone calls to the shop, but after the first *Dead Ringer* article a woman called the Sweepers and accused Laura of assisting the Mad Dogs in bombing a business on the east side and killing her son. Adding insult to injury, the bombing in question had been undertaken by Blackwater, a completely different mob. The very next day, the *Dead Ringer* churned out a page reading, *You don't even know which mob you hate! Why do you think you know enough to judge an organization you didn't even know existed?*

Laura had braced herself for a rebuke from the Council. Sure enough, she received a letter with the Council's phoenix stamp. Inside it simply read:

Due to recent circumstances, we have agreed that you are no longer suitable to hold the position of head Sweeper.

Below it were signatures from multiple Council members. Councilwoman Victoria Douglas hadn't graced the letter with her signature or approval, but majority ruled. Laura was demoted. She might have been biased, but she was still convinced this was a petty dismissal. There was no benefit for Amicae in removing the most veteran member of such a small Sweeper department, and Clae had remained in power for twelve years under the same tactics. Worse, there was no one to replace her with. The only Council-approved option was . . .

"Juliana MacDanel's been authorized for full citizenship."

In the here and now, December 5, 1233, Okane paged through another newspaper. It still took him a while to read everything, but he took in all the words with eyes she vowed never to compare to silver coins. "The *Sun*'s done a highlight on her in celebration."

Laura's head lay in the middle of a newspaper halo. She turned to look at him, scrunching the pages of today's *Dead Ringer*.

"A highlight? Like they do for film stars?"

"Yes. I don't see how they had the opportunity to do this kind of interview unless they paid for the telephone call," said Okane. "It says she enjoys dogs, playing Aces, and eating Ralurian potato peels. When advertisements listed that as a delicacy, I thought it was a joke."

"I'm still not convinced it isn't." Laura felt tempted to sink lower in her slouch, but there wasn't anyplace lower to go when one's face was plastered to the counter. She had no doubt this interest in Juliana MacDanel was engineered: a way to soothe the public, make Amicae feel like the Council was answering their call, all while endearing the Sweepers to them like the friendly entourage of a film star. "If they're trying to make the head Sweeper into a mascot, I'll admit I'm not a good fit for the job."

Okane eyed her reproachfully. "There's no way she would know the job better than - - - do."

"With twenty years on the job, she would," said Laura. "Knowing layout isn't everything. She'll probably learn quickly."

"I still think - - -'re more suitable," said Okane.

Laura snorted. "Look at it this way. If the head Sweeper's going to be a media darling, that cuts back on her Sweeping time. She'll be in an interview, and I'll be on the extermination. I won't have the title, but I'll still be the real power here. So long as I can keep Sweeping, that's enough for me."

It was a lie, but admitting that felt petulant. She'd reach for any silver lining she could at this point. Okane seemed to be even more upset about this than she was, but luckily she was spared any additional arguing by a knock at the door. While strange during business hours, the gesture meant it must be one of two people. Okane waved at the large windows, and the visitor creaked the door open.

The police chief, Heather Albright, stepped in. She carried her black helmet under one arm, freeing dark red hair to fall in a frazzled braid down her back. Her glasses half hid the dark circles under her eyes, the sheaf of paper under her other arm presumably to blame. At one time her presence might've been odd, but ever since the disaster she dropped by to check on them multiple times a week. Whether this was because she worried over losing a vital cog in the city machine or actually felt concern for their personal well-being Laura didn't know, but she appreciated the attention. She'd expected Albright to drop by, but the man who sidled in behind her, hands in the pockets of his overcoat and a pipe held loosely between his teeth, wasn't familiar. He stood behind and off to Albright's side, close enough to observe but not in the way, and seemed very used to this spot. Albright didn't so much as look at him, instead fixing her tired gaze on the Sweepers.

"Good afternoon. Has business been well today?"

"Not really," said Laura. "No one came in, even for recycling."

"After the incident I didn't think we'd need so many warnings printed, but I'll ask for another round in the papers," Albright muttered. "That should send them hurrying in."

Laura smiled. "Did you need something today, Chief Albright?"

"Just giving you some news." She brandished the papers. "For one thing, we've got the politics hammered out on this problem of yours. Might want to thank Douglas. She nearly turned the case into a crusade."

The idea of the stern, elderly councilwoman charging into battle surprised Laura, but then again she'd never met Victoria Douglas. "How did it turn out?"

"Clae Sinclair's will is going to be carried out as intended. Whether or not it was used for public service, all Sweeper equipment is privately owned, so the Council and city can't claim it." She muttered something about a gray area of whether Pits were considered private property, something the Council had argued over in the process. "And whoever inherits his estate gets all of it, since Sweepers are tax-free. The Council *loved* that. Bottom line: there's a lot more up for grabs and possibly yours, but that's all up to the estate administrator carrying it out."

"Good. I wouldn't trust the Council with it," said Laura. She'd read more than enough about the early days when the Council had used Gin to pay off any small debt, and her personal experiences with their orders hadn't been enjoyable. "Do you know how long an administrator should take?"

"I wouldn't know. I've never had to deal with them." Albright turned to look at the man, who'd drifted toward the counter to inspect the Kin. "Rhodes, how much time does it take for them to do their job?"

The man straightened up from squinting at a flask, pushing his hat back on thick auburn hair. "Depends," he said, in a slow drawl. "If there's organized documentation, they could be in and out in no time. If there's not, you may have to deal with them for a while. Don't worry, though. They don't take nearly as long as people seem to think."

Albright nodded her approval before plucking a small page from her papers and setting it on the countertop. Laura leaned over to see it better and recognized it as a telegram.

"In addition, your new boss is coming soon." The mention made Laura's stomach twist; half shame for her horrendously botched job and following dismissal, half dread for the newcomer. "Personally, I think it's unnecessary. As far as I'm concerned you did the right thing. Clae Sinclair certainly wouldn't have done any different. You prevented a massive loss of life, and—"

"And the Council doesn't want another Clae," said Laura. "I'm not happy about it, but there's nothing I can do. Besides, I have faith in whoever Puer's head Sweeper picks out."

Albright pursed her lips but didn't argue. "That man was in contact with us about her, and had a lot of good things to say. The Council sent someone to properly interview her and they were impressed, so she's been accepted. This"—she tapped the telegram—"was sent yesterday. There was a mix-up in the mailroom so it only reached me today, but it says she's eager to start and left for Amicae already. If the trains run on schedule she'll arrive tonight, and if she's as enthusiastic as I believe, she'll swing by to look at the shop as soon as she does. You may meet her before I do."

Laura wasn't sure what to think. She thought they'd have a little more warning before the replacement swooped in to usurp the job. Time to mentally prepare themselves, time to hide the Sinclairs. She almost wished no one had been picked as head Sweeper.

She folded her hands, bit her lip. She glanced at the man before whispering, "Should we tell her about, um, *those two*?"

Albright leaned back and regarded them a moment.

"I think that's up to you. I don't know the extent of politics and rivalry between Sweepers, but I know nothing's free of corruption. Wait awhile and judge whether you can trust her first. For the moment, I'd keep it secret. That said, I've shared information about the Sinclairs with Rhodes."

Laura froze. "You what?"

"Rhodes, come over here."

The man sauntered over to their group. He stood next to Albright, easily taller than all of them, though he had a slouch and his eyes were droopy in a friendly kind of way. If she'd met him any other time Laura would've thought he was harmless, but now she felt on edge.

"This is Byron Rhodes, a private investigator," said Albright. "I've asked him to keep an eye on you. With the news and the recent riots, criminals have been getting bold. There's been an upsurge in crime rates, mob and otherwise, so I won't have the time to check on you. He'll be monitoring you in my stead. He's currently investigating the events leading to the disaster and evacuation, so in order for him to have a full understanding I gave him the whole story. What I know, anyway. If you have any other information I urge you to share it with him."

So a stranger was free to know about Clae and Anselm while the head Sweeper wasn't? That didn't make much sense, but if the chief of police put so much faith in this investigator, Laura supposed she could trust him to an extent.

"It's nice to meet you, Mr. Rhodes," she said, trying her best to look unruffled.

"Just call me Byron," he replied, tipping his hat. "No need to be nervous. I'm here to support you, same as Heather here." Strangely enough, Albright didn't look remotely concerned with the use of her first name. "Quite a few strange pieces in motion around that infestation. There's no telling who's behind it, but if they attacked Amicae on such a grand scale, I'm sure their next attempt will be just as vicious. I'd like to make sure you don't become casualties."

Laura blinked. "Next attempt? I thought Sullivan was the one behind it all, and he's in jail now. It was his pipes, right?"

"Maybe, but the man himself couldn't have done the deed," said Byron. "Takes a lot of workers. We've got false IDs on what's left of the interior record and no matches in his workforce. I'd say there's another group at work here."

It couldn't have been the Mad Dogs mob. The Mad Dogs had a disagreement with Sullivan before, and their Sweepers had come to fight off the infestation rather than evacuate. That left another city, Rex: they'd sent a small infiltration force, and their crest was blatantly painted under the ruined bulwark tree. But they'd only had three men, two captured. Surely one man couldn't manage all that. But Rexian rumor was worse than ghost stories, and Laura had to quash her unease.

"You'll find out who did it?"

"He's more capable than his looks suggest," said Albright, "which is one of the reasons I'm assigning him to you. If you have any immediate problems, go to him."

Laura nodded but said nothing. Byron seemed to understand her reluctance. He pulled a card from his pocket and set it on the counter before her.

"Here's my information if you need it. You probably won't see me often, but I'm there if you need me. Until then I'll try to stay out of your way."

"Thanks," Laura mumbled, while Okane slid the card closer and squinted at the type.

Albright checked her watch and let out a short, angry sigh. "I'll have to be going now. Good luck with your new boss."

Business finished, Albright inclined her head and left. Byron followed close behind, and their forms flitted past the right-hand window as the door clicked shut. The pair stared after them, silence unbroken for a while before Okane gave a shuddering sigh.

"So what do we do?"

"We keep Clae secret." Laura shrugged. "I guess we move him."

"Now?"

"If the new head Sweeper comes by tonight she'll want to get in, right? Best move them now. Just to make sure."

"To where, though?" He gestured at their surroundings. "It's almost closing time. There's no way we can get anywhere without people seeing them. This is all the space we have."

"What about upstairs?"

The second floor of the Sweeper shop was a living space, Clae's—now Okane's—home. Other Sweepers would have no reason to go up there, boss or not.

That was how they found themselves hauling Clae bodily up the stairs. It occurred to Laura that there was a reason they'd left him on the ground floor in the first place. The stairs were steep and he was extremely heavy, not to mention slippery after being stuck in a tub of water. Laura couldn't get a good hold on his feet without losing grip, having to lurch sideways and hug his boots to her side. Okane didn't fare much better, but at least he could grab Clae under the arms. Clae's face was enraged, as it had been the past few weeks, but if he'd been aware of the proceedings she thought he'd make the same expression. She stopped a third of the way up the steps.

"I don't remember these stairs being so much like a ladder," she panted.

"It's an architectural disaster," Okane wheezed.

"How did the Sinclairs get any furniture up there in the first place?"

"Magic?"

Laura panted some more before heaving Clae's feet up again and staggering. They went three steps before the crystal slipped in their grip and they scrambled to a halt. Clae's form hit the steps with a loud thunk, and Laura sucked in a breath, horrified.

"Oh, shit. Is he okay?"

Okane squinted down and nodded. "This crystal must be tougher than it looks."

Somewhat reassured, Laura steadied herself and they lurched up again.

"Why did we start with him?" Okane groaned.

"Anselm will be a piece of cake in comparison."

"Where are we putting him?"

"I don't know. You live up there, you tell me!"

"Bed?"

"Just lead the way."

It took an eternity, but they reached the second floor and hauled Clae down the hall, into the back room with the twin beds. They deposited him none too gracefully, and turned back to the stairs.

Anselm was, luckily, a hell of a lot lighter. Okane hefted the crystal into his arms and took him up alone. Laura watched from the bottom and called up when he stumbled.

"You're leaning left again! Don't slip!"

He made a frustrated noise and disappeared into the second floor. Eventually he emerged again with a pensive look on his face.

"What do you think they'll say about me? About the '- - -' thing?"

"They won't notice it." Laura noticed, but she'd trained herself for it. Okane shook his head. "And the eyes?"

"If they give you trouble at all, I'll back you up. Nothing like the Sullivans will ever happen to you again."

Okane rubbed at his covered arms, and the scars there. "Thanks."

A clattering sound made Laura jump and look back at the shop. There was someone by the windows, headed straight for the door. Could that be the new boss? She gestured madly for Okane to come down, hissing, "She's here! I think she's here!"

Okane sped down the stairs while Laura straightened, heart jumping into her throat. The door creaked open, admitting two people.

The first was a woman with long brown hair twisted into a knot at the back of her head. Her hazel eyes and upturned nose reminded Laura of a film star, and her expensive coat and fur stole only enforced the idea. She gave them a smile both excited and bashful. Laura was immediately distracted by the man behind her: tall, reedy, with the same coloring and upturned nose, though the rest of his face was long, thin, and gaunt, and he'd opted for a plain overcoat.

"Hello," the woman said breathlessly. "I'm Juliana MacDanel. This is Sinclair Sweepers, right? It's hard to read the sign."

Laura forced a smile. "Are you our new head Sweeper?"

Juliana's face brightened. "Yes! I was sent over from Puer. So you're—Oh, I know this, they sent the information. Laura Kramer, and Okane Sinclair?"

At each name she went to shake their hands. She had a strong grip, and Laura needed to rub her hand to get the feeling back when the woman turned. Okane's reluctance to touch ended up being interpreted as something completely different, and Juliana pulled back.

"Sinclair. So you were a relative of the previous head Sweeper? I'm sorry I'm not him, but I'll try my best to carry on his great reputation." She put a hand over her heart and said this sincerely. Okane shuffled and ducked his head.

"Did you know Clae?" Laura asked.

"Not personally, but he was something like a Sweeper celebrity: the youngest head Sweeper in recent history, worked almost solo most of his career, and still somehow managed to be the most effective fighter in Terual. Even Rex could see he was talented."

A smile tugged at Laura's lips. If the new boss had a healthy respect for Clae, she couldn't be too bad.

"And, since my companion doesn't seem interested in introducing himself, I'll do it for him. This is my brother, Lester. He's also a Sweeper. Once I heard how small Amicae's force was, I begged him to come along. I hope you don't mind?"

"Not at all!" Laura hadn't expected more than one new member, but the help would be welcome.

Juliana shrugged off her coat and hung it up on the coatrack, revealing a dress underneath. She looked ready for an evening party. Had she dressed up to meet them, of all people? It was almost flattering.

"What do you say, you want to give us the grand tour?"

"Tour?"

"Of course!" Juliana laughed. "The Gin, the weapon construction, the storage areas, what have you."

"Well . . . this is it." Laura waved around at the room. "Everything is on this floor. We've got the Kin," she gestured at the hissing setup behind her, "storage," she tapped the glass of the counter, "and the Gin is in the next room."

"It looked like there was a second floor."

"That's a home."

"*My* home," Okane piped up. "I'd prefer - - - didn't go up there."

"Of course! We've got no reason to pry."

Thank goodness they didn't press the matter. Laura slipped off the stool and led the way to the black drapes. The newcomers followed, Juliana with a distinct spring in her step. Laura held the curtains aside and scrutinized them as they passed. She startled when she realized Lester was scrutinizing her right back.

"Is there a problem?" Juliana glanced from one to the other. Had Laura made a noise without realizing it?

"It's nothing," she said quickly. "Sorry, I'm just not used to letting people in here. Clae was protective of the equipment."

"Was he?" Juliana sounded interested.

"Amicae has a long history of taking away Sweeper inventory and selling it off," said Laura. "The Sinclair family had to purchase most of their equipment from the city to keep it from being destroyed. Okane, wasn't there something about the Pits, too?"

"Functioning Pits are city territory, but sunken ones are private property," said Okane. "Otherwise the mining would've disturbed them."

"A grave concern," said Lester, and his voice sounded grave too.

"We'll have to keep that in mind during our future dealings with the Council," said Juliana, stepping through the curtains.

Laura leaned to watch as the pair inspected the Gin room. Without Clae or Anselm present it looked innocent enough. But rather than checking the water basin, the rocks, or the tubing, they turned to the shelves. Juliana's hands sifted through the empty Eggs, moving the glass shapes in search of something while Lester did the same on the other side.

"Are you expecting something else?" Laura asked.

"Oh, nothing," Juliana replied, even as she tilted her head to see the back of one shelf. "I'm a little surprised is all. Excelling the way he did, I thought Mr. Sinclair would've had a few more tricks up his sleeve."

Laura leaned against the doorway and crossed her arms. "No. He was just talented."

"You're sure? There's nothing else?"

"No."

Juliana looked disappointed but moved on quickly. "Who's the weapons supplier?"

Laura blinked. "The what?"

"Weapons supplier." She held up one of the Eggs. "Who makes the Egg shells? The bullets? The Bijou?"

Laura didn't have a clue.

"Her name's Amelia." Okane peered around Laura, content to use her like a shield. "She used to be a Sweeper, but now she works with companies to get equipment."

Juliana perked up again. "That's wonderful! Where's her office?"

"I don't know. We've only talked over the telephone."

"Other Sweeper buildings?"

"None."

"Our Council contact?"

"Clae harassed them on his own."

Juliana gave a perplexed sigh. "How did you function with so few resources?"

"Clae." Laura shrugged as if his name should explain everything.

"We haven't had experience with larger operations, so we have nothing to compare this to." Okane ducked further behind Laura as Lester turned around.

"In any case, we've got a lot of work to do," Juliana announced, folding her arms. "Sad as it is, that big infestation should've rattled your Council. Now that they've got some fear in them, they'll be willing to pump up defenses. We can get away with a lot of demands, so long as we pitch it right."

"Demands like what?"

"Like more funding, more equipment, more space." Juliana gestured around the cramped room. "We can get this place back into shape and working properly."

Laura decided she liked the sound of that; she'd given thought to such a plan during her brief stint as head Sweeper, but had no idea how to follow through with it. "How do we begin?"

"Tomorrow morning, as soon as shops open, we're making phone calls."

An hour later the MacDanels left. They needed to find their new lodgings and unpack their luggage. Juliana wished them a cheery good evening as she left, while Lester gave a solemn farewell of his own. The shop was quiet again. Laura sat heavily on a stool and looked at Okane. He lurked behind the inactive Kin with an expression like a kicked dog.

"Well?" she asked.

The single word implied more. Opinion? Trustworthy? *Will this work?* Okane gave a halfhearted shrug and wandered farther down the counter.

"That's enlightening," Laura grumbled.

"Well, what do - - - think?"

Laura paused, leaned back to look at the ceiling. Her mouth twisted. "I think . . . I think this might turn out okay. They—Juliana at least—seem like they're going to put a lot into this. She's a proper Sweeper."

Okane peered around the tubing of the Kin, his eyes darker, brooding. "And?"

"And I don't think they need to know about Clae or Anselm. Not yet, anyway."

He nodded his approval, very slowly. "That sounds like the best plan. I don't like them."

"That's a pretty quick decision."

"They were snooping." Okane circled all the way around the counter and sat on another stool. He looked very moody.

Laura sighed. "So we'll keep Clae and Anselm a secret permanently? How can we manage that? The house works for now, but it seems too close. If anyone ever goes up there, they'll find them."

"Can we take them to - - -r house?"

Laura burst out laughing. Okane kept looking at her, and she realized he was serious. Her mirth died into uneven giggles.

"Okane, I live on the eighth floor. There's no elevator, and Clae might be lighter than he was as a normal person, but if he is, it's not by much. I can't carry a grown man up all those stairs. Besides, I live with people. Should I stuff him in a closet to keep my cousin from finding him?"

"Maybe? I could help carry them."

"We can't set up the Kin in my house, either!"

"The Kin?"

"Well, yeah." She avoided his gaze, staring at the toe of her boot. "We can't pull Anselm out of the Kin without losing all our power, can we?"

A long pause.

"I thought - - - didn't want to include him."

Right after the fact, Laura was very opposed to the idea of using either Sinclair in the Kin. It felt like desecration. But the more she thought about it, the more she wondered. Clae hadn't liked using Anselm, but he'd kept doing it. It was the only way to get through the onslaught of monsters at the time. While there were more Sweepers now, nothing guaranteed they'd do well or even if they'd survive the first infestation that came along. Besides, another spike of stronger monsters would hit soon; Clae had said it himself. They couldn't afford to lose any power. It was logical, but the more she thought about it the guiltier she felt. She'd barred Clae from being used. Would she feel the same about Anselm if she'd ever seen him alive?

Okane exhaled slowly. "So we need somewhere for the Kin."

Laura rubbed her face, suddenly tired as she thought over their options. Their only Sweeper building was now off-limits. Albright couldn't take them. Even if Morgan and Cheryl happily accepted the presence of crystal people—doubtful—they might talk and the information would get around the whole city in an awful game of telephone. Perhaps they could create a space. She had some savings squirreled away with the idea of funding herself later in life: emergency money, college fund, rent for her own apartment. Whatever half-baked plans she had were flying out the window.

"Should we rent someplace?" she suggested, but her voice was forlorn. She was stingy and apartments were expensive these days.

Okane tugged at his hair some more, frowning at the floor. "I don't like the idea of them being far away. I want someone to keep an eye on them."

"That might be impossible."

"Still."

They lapsed into silence. After a while, Laura heaved a sigh.

"Tomorrow we can start looking at options."

The next day was Saturday. Laura would typically be on call on weekends and not go in to the shop at all, but since today was Juliana's first full day she felt obligated to go. Laura left at her usual time, arrived at the shop at eight in the morning, to find the blinds down on the windows. Strange. She rolled her bicycle up the steps and knocked on the door. A long pause followed. She started to wonder if Okane was even awake this early on a Saturday, but a muffled voice called through the door.

"Who is it?"

"Laura."

A shorter pause, a clacking and shuffling at the lock, and the door opened. Okane blinked at her, very much awake.

"Good morning?" He sounded confused. "What are - - - doing here?"

"I thought I'd come over before the MacDanels do. What are you sneaking around for?"

He glanced around, then opened the door wider and beckoned her inside. Raising an eyebrow, she hauled her bicycle over the threshold.

The room felt hot and humid as if the Kin equipment had been going, but none of the usual gold could be glimpsed inside it. The floor of the shop, however, was cluttered: green Puer Eggs, more Bijou, more guns and bullets, along with bags, straps, masks, goggles, and tens of other things she couldn't identify. Okane sat on one of the stools and resumed his earlier activity, trying to load one of Clae's old pistols with Puer bullets. He'd gone through three varieties, and the fourth didn't fit either.

"Juliana said we can take what we want," he said.

"So she did show up," Laura muttered. "I'm sorry. I wanted to get here before she had a chance."

He shrugged. "It was uncomfortable, but it's not as if I expected them to hurt me."

"Will they be coming back soon?"

He shook his head and pointed; a note had been left on the Eggs.

Hi, Laura! Sorry if it feels like we've ditched you. Lester and I are on our way to the Council to get a full report of the city and what's expected of us. With the situation as is, I expect we'll be gone most of the day. In the meantime feel free to look through these presents from Puer! All this equipment is top of the line. Our kin formula and accompanying devices are all the product of years of scientific refinement; even cities as far south as Canis swear by it. I recommend giving them a try and seeing just how strong Sweepers can be!

"The first full day of the job and she's already avoiding us." Laura caught sight of his expression and snorted. "That was a joke."

"I know," he mumbled. The fifth bullet slid in clean and he popped the cylinder back into place. Almost immediately he hastened to get it out again. "Not good!" he squeaked. "Very much not good. That's a disaster."

"Didn't it fit?"

"I get the distinct feeling that it won't when it needs to. It feels like . . . like standing on the Quarter wall and looking down." He eyed the bullet once it was out, expression defeated. "I don't think our equipment's compatible with Puer assembly lines."

No, Laura agreed, it wasn't. When she finally selected a sturdy supply bag, it was only to find that its compartments were designed for Puer's rounder Eggs, with their greenish kin; the yellow, Amicae variety were too oblong and threatened to spill right out of the slots. Cursing, she went upstairs to raid the old sewing basket for stitch rippers and new thread. She set it all down before her and paused. Yellow Eggs on the right, green on the left. Dusty material worn soft but sturdy, versus the glossy reddish sheen of something new off the assembly line. Somehow she felt lost. She looked up at Okane, only to see him looking back.

"It's different," he said simply.

"Alien," she agreed. "It's better quality. I don't know why I'm hesitating."

"I like things staying the same," he said, spinning the cylinder. "When they're the same, they're predictable. They're safe. I don't . . . I don't really want to switch the gun, even if Puer's is supposed to be better."

"'Better' may apply to some things, but not others." Laura stood and buckled on the new bag. There were four different buckles and chains, and by the end of it she was sure that not even a typhoon could pull it all off. "What do you think? We can mix the equipment and make it work. There's more than enough bullets in storage to cover that gun."

He perked up a little. "- - - think so? I don't think we have the budget to replace them."

"Even if the office itself doesn't, once you get your share of Clae's estate, there should be more than enough to cover anything you need."

"My share?"

Why did he sound so surprised?

"Yes, your share. Albright was just talking to us about it."

He grunted in disbelief. "Clae didn't look like he was rolling in money. If he couldn't replace his stove, what makes - - - think he had anything in his estate to cover anything?"

"His family owned Gin underground, and charged people to power amulets from it," she pointed out. "That's expensive, and he didn't have to pay income tax on that."

"But the stove—"

"Maybe he was a miser."

Okane gave a short huff of laughter. "I could see that. Still, I don't think he left me money, or if he did, not a lot. So we shouldn't count on it."

Laura frowned. "Why do you think that?"

"I'm not important enough." He folded his hands in his lap as he said this, expression sad but earnest. He believed it.

"Okane. Okane." Laura mimicked Morgan's pitying tone as best she could. "*Okane.* You're not that stupid."

"Excuse me?"

"He gave the time and effort to get you out of trouble. *You have his name.* Of course you were important!"

"But—"

"But nothing." She crossed her arms and frowned, daring him to question her. "I guarantee it. He left you a lot."

"Hmm."

Still unconvinced. Laura rolled her eyes.

2

FOOLS, WARY

She'd never said anything about it to anyone, but Laura was still bitter about schooling.

Part of her blamed Morgan and Cheryl. Being a nearly fulltime babysitter on limited funds did nothing to help her studying or obtaining supplies; her best friend in middle school always brought extra pencils and extra notebooks, and took notes religiously on the days Laura couldn't go to class. She remembered many mornings standing grumpily by the door with Cheryl in her arms, uniform on but schoolbag abandoned while Morgan rushed out the door, apologizing for another last-minute job. None of the neighbors then would even speak to such a disreputable woman, let alone take care of an "angelina's" child for the day. It might've been different if the job paid better—"day care" was a mythic place out of reach—but to earn higher pay one needed a higher education. Few women had one, leaving them to the whims of their bosses if they wished to climb the pay chain or even keep their jobs. It took Morgan eight years of clawing her way up the ladder to get steady hours and decent paycheck.

This, like many things her poor aunt went through, showed Laura very well that she had no interest in the "traditional woman" box.

At the time the existence of Sweepers seemed just as dubious as the prospect of day care, so she had to find her own way to break out. University seemed like the best choice. She liked school, liked learning new things and piecing them together, so additional years in a classroom didn't bother her. University streamlined someone for the grander parts of the workforce, and even if a graduate didn't go into their studied field, the simple fact that they had a degree ensured good pay and reasonable hours. She just needed to study hard, place into the right graduating class in high school, and get a scholarship.

Simple.

Except it failed.

She still had all the old university pamphlets and flyers tucked away in her closet under her Coronae Sweeper book and the Sinclair journal. Back then she'd told herself she could apply properly once she'd amassed some funds. After the recent events, she knew it would never happen.

"Good-bye, Royal Academy of Sciences," she said dully, picking up the pamphlet from the uneven pile on the table. With a swish and clunk, it landed in the trash bin with a pack of similar papers.

"Good-bye, Arbor Branch."

Swish, clunk.

"Good-bye, Prima College."

Swish, clunk.

"Good-bye, Amicae Grand University."

She paused at this one. The Grand University's magnificent façade looked back at her from a state-of-the-art brochure. This had been her favorite prospect. With its sprawling museum and top-notch faculty, it was the destination for many history majors, alongside multiple other distinguished courses. History had been her favorite subject; after all, it was only a step removed from fairy tales and myth, and learning the exploits of Terulian queens and their current impact on Orien was so much more interesting than adding up numbers. She sighed, fingering the dog-eared corners.

The front door rattled open, making her jump. Cheryl charged into the kitchen, a single mitten stuck in her mouth. As she attacked the bread box, Morgan hurried after her, waving the other mitten.

"I'm serious! It's cold outside, you have to take your scarf! And what's wrong with your old coat?"

"It's got too many holes," Cheryl replied, in the brief moment of swapping mitten for food.

"I just mended them!"

"Well, it ripped again."

Morgan slumped over the table. It took a moment for her to take in the stack of paper, but when she did she brightened.

"Rutherford University? Isn't that Charlie's school?"

"No." Laura slapped the Grand University's brochure back over it.

"Yes, it is! Were you considering a job there?" Morgan shone like the sun. Charlie had been making every effort to get into Morgan's good graces. Laura had called him out on his behavior not long ago, so this might've been an attempt to prove her wrong. It made Laura's blood boil, but redoubled Morgan's matchmaking schemes. "I've heard there are secretary positions open, and even a school switchboard! It should be easy for you to get into, and then you'd get to see Charlie every day!"

"No. Not happening."

Laura scooped up the whole pile and dumped it in the bin. Morgan plucked the offending item back out and flipped to the next page.

"Look, see? They have plenty of opportunities for the enterprising young woman! Oh, but this one's a few years old. Twelve twenty-nine? Have you been thinking of it that long?"

"I haven't been thinking about any of it," Laura snapped. "That's why they're going in the trash, where they belong."

"It's nothing to be ashamed of."

Morgan hummed, eyes still fixed on the pamphlet as she trailed back to her room. Laura groaned and buried her head in her hands.

"Of all people, why'd she have to get hung up on Charlie?"

"Because he's going to be rich," said Cheryl. "Plus he's nice to her."

"Maybe to her face," Laura grumbled. She still hadn't forgiven Charlie for the nasty way he'd spoken about Morgan, as if their near decade of acquaintance and all the times she'd helped him meant nothing. What kind of ass called their most helpful neighbor a worthless whore?

"She should give up. It's obvious you don't like him," said Cheryl.

"Exactly! How long do you think it'll take her to realize?"

Cheryl's face scrunched, and Laura took that to mean *never*.

"I'm leaving before she comes up with another grand matchmaking scheme," said Laura, standing and grabbing her bag. "If you get the chance, ditch that pamphlet for me."

Maybe Laura would use her funds to rent a new apartment after all. Gain some distance from Charlie and Morgan's ridiculous plots, and keep the Sinclairs there for safekeeping. She'd have to check the newspaper listings when she got to the shop.

"You're going already?" Morgan ducked back into the kitchen and followed her toward the door. "I hope you'll be working hard and, of course, thinking hard."

Laura turned, giving her a flat look as she buttoned up her coat. Morgan completely ignored it and fluffed up Laura's scarf, the smile still glued to her face.

"Make a good impression with your new boss, okay? If you end up moving jobs they could give you a good recommendation."

As if any new employer could see the name "Laura Kramer" and think anything positive.

"Cheryl's going to be late for school if you take much longer."

"Of course! Cheryl, honey, I'm serious about the scarf. If your coat's got holes, that's all the more reason—"

Morgan hurried away, prompting a loud, annoyed noise from Cheryl. Laura rolled her eyes and pushed the door open. Chill morning air blew against her face, but she barely felt it. She was too focused on the woman standing directly in front of her. Laura didn't recognize her, but the woman certainly knew her. She pushed herself up from her previous recline against the banister and smiled.

"Good morning."

"Good morning," said Laura. "Sorry, are you here for Morgan? I can get her, it'd be just a moment—"

"I'm here for you, Miss Sinclair."

The tone rang sweet, but the words felt loaded. God, could this be one of her critics, come to badger her in person since they couldn't get her on the telephone?

"Miss Sinclair?"

Laura's trepidation shattered at the new voice. Charlie had stepped out of his apartment—presumably leaving for university—and now looked at them both with a sullen expression.

"I'm a Sinclair Sweeper," Laura said icily. "If you expect me to remember every boring detail of your life, you could at least try to do the same for me." She turned on her heel, bared her teeth at the woman. "Why don't we talk as we walk? I'll buy you coffee."

She'd rather deal with someone screaming half-truths than an outright backstabber. Luckily the woman followed without further prompting.

"This isn't about titles and you know it," said Charlie.

"Why not? Titles are all you care about, you buzzard."

His face went red in anger and embarrassment, but it kept him quiet long enough for Laura to escape.

"I'm sorry you had to see that," Laura fretted, one floor down. "I'm not usually so—" On second thought, that was a lie. She backtracked. "I have a personal problem with him."

"Enough to call him a buzzard," the woman laughed. "Oh, that's such a pity. I came here to hate you and you've made yourself personable."

Laura raised a brow. "I didn't think that went over as a pleasant appearance."

"I never said *pleasant*. You've just revealed your humanity is all."

"I'm not sure I understand," Laura said slowly. "You seem very positive for someone who hates me."

"I'm a wonderful actress."

That answered nothing.

"So, why'd you come calling so early? It would've been easier to catch me at the Sweeper shop, and probably more appropriate if this is about the job."

"It's about Sweeping, but on the other hand it's not. Follow me?"

Baffled, Laura did so.

Upon leaving the Cynder Block, the woman led her down one of the nearby roads. It was a route Laura knew well, even if she no longer frequented it. She'd taken this path for three years of high school. She knew where other children came in off the branching streets, knew which stores opened earliest to entice students who'd skipped break-fast, knew which canal-spanning bridges were steepest. School was in session today, so they were soon crowded by high schoolers and book bags. A pair of girls walked in front of them, whispering the same ghost story about the Sylph Canal that Laura had gossiped over in her time on this path. Between this and the discarded brochures, she was in a bittersweet, nostalgic stupor and almost missed it when the woman spoke again.

"Have you been following the *Dead Ringer*?"

The familiarity of this place no longer comforted her.

"Of course," said Laura. "It would be stupid to ignore what people are saying about me."

"And does it please you to see what they write?"

"Not really. I never agreed to any sort of mob alliance, so if they come knocking for favors, they'll be disappointed." The woman hummed, thoughtful. Laura sucked in a breath, gathered her courage, and contin-ued, "That being said, I don't think anything they've printed is wrong. Petulant maybe, but still. The Council *is* making weird decisions for Sweepers, and citizens *are* focusing on the wrong things. I don't care whose authority steers the Sinclairs, if it's me or Juliana or even some-one else, but I do care about it all functioning well and being sure we can protect against infestations. As far as I can see, the *Dead Ringer* and Mad Dogs have the same priorities."

She'd meant to make a critic think deeper. She clearly made the wrong decision. The woman's expression plunged into something en-tirely chilling.

"So you do ally with them."

She said nothing more but kept walking. It wasn't enough of a dismissal for Laura to feel comfortable leaving, so she kept walk-ing too. Before them loomed the Naia Canal bridge. The canal and accompanying Naia Street were an industrial thoroughfare. Small boats chugged up and down the waterway, and the bridge rose high to accommodate them; its height gave a good view over the cars of Naia, and it was this that made Laura pause. Students complained and circled past her on the bridge, but she didn't pay attention. One of the buildings on Naia was a tall, unassuming office complex, but she'd seen its façade printed in a newspaper: the *Dead Ringer*'s headquarters. Police surrounded it, but they weren't raiding it. Their backs faced the building and they looked out into the crowds as if searching for something.

The woman stopped. The chill hadn't left her, but a smile returned to her face. "Is something wrong, Miss Sinclair?"

"Are you a mobster?" said Laura. "Because if you're a Mad Dog, I just said—"

"A Mad Dog? Don't insult me." The woman turned entirely and stepped back toward her. It was a slow movement, deliberate and slinky and very much predatory. "But you're decently fast on the uptake. No, I'm not a Mad Dog, and neither are you. We'd like it to stay that way."

We. Laura's eyes jumped about, trying to pick out any kind of mobster tag, and alighted on a metallic gray hair clip. It could easily be nothing, easily be coincidence, but—

"Silver Kings?"

"Good guess," said the woman. "Now, you're familiar with the MARU? Of course you are."

Anyone who'd lived in Amicae knew about the Mob Action Resolution Unit. The roughest members of the police force, they'd been turned loose on the lower Quarters with the sole mission of breaking up the mobs. They'd attacked anyone remotely connected, and used any tactic—coercion, torture, outright murder—to take someone off the scene. They ruled with an iron fist until the Silver Kings rallied all the mobs under their banner. The MARU could fight scattered mobsters, but the united front overwhelmed them. Mobsters made the MARU's actions look like child's play. They hunted down every last member, picked them off one by one with increasingly gruesome tactics, and everywhere they went they left circles. A circle like a target.

A circle like a noose. They drew it on victims splashed by acid, slapped it on cars and along the MARU's frequent routes, hung it over baby cradles and gifted wreaths to unwitting wives. For months Amicae had been tormented by circles on every street, and the MARU broke under it. Most died by the mobs' hands; some took their own lives; the few who survived were either too injured or too afraid to return to the force. The mobs dispersed quickly afterward, but the point was made. Amicae knew who held true power.

For a long time the Council had spread the rumor that Sweepers were the current incarnation of the MARU, but as far as Laura knew, the mobs knew better. She and Clae had never been drawn into their fights, and circles never appeared at their door.

"We're not the MARU," Laura said anyway. "We're not involved with your politics."

"So you say, but the Mad Dogs have you in their pocket," said the woman. "I don't know what kind of agenda the Mad Dogs are pushing, but there's a delicate balance to this city. We've lost too much protecting that balance to let it be broken now."

"I'm not allied with them!" Laura snapped.

"But you will be, and that can't be allowed."

Fire and glass burst from the upper floor of the *Dead Ringer* office, with force enough that the very air trembled. Students screamed and ducked.

Back, whispered something far away in her mind.

Back, she thought in reply.

The amulet on her belt activated. She was thrown back so fast she felt as if she'd been shoved. Her rear hit the low railing, and her head reeled to keep up. She'd dodged something. A knife. The woman pivoted, slashed her little blade upward now. Laura canted sharply back. The knife missed her chin by an inch. She tried to catch the rail and heave herself back up, but it was too smooth. Her hands slipped. With nothing else to catch her, she fell over the side. Partway through the tumble she snapped her arms to her sides and cried, "Straighten!"

The amulets in her shoes answered this time, catching gravity so she hit the water in a pencil dive. The canal closed over her head, muffling the shouts and the crackling of the bombed building. She didn't have time to do more than thrash before something caught her under the arm and towed her upward. She broke the surface, coughing and spitting out canal water. She'd been caught with a curved metal pole, something used to hook fallen cargo from the little boats. The man wielding it didn't look used to reeling in fallen humans, but reached out a hand and called, "Here, missy!"

He hauled her onto the deck. She stood fast and looked back up at the bridge; would the woman have a gun, too?

The woman stood at the rail, knife still in one hand. The students fled, tripping in their haste to get away from her, but she remained totally calm.

"You should work on your escapes. That lacked any sort of grace," she called.

"You're the one who just tried to stab me!" Laura retorted. "What kind of grace is that?"

"The best kind." She put the knife away and rummaged in her purse. "Remember what I said about balance. A single floundering Sweeper I can let go, but if it gets more than that, you won't be the only one suffering. Remember the MARU."

She pulled an object out of her purse and threw it. It spun and fell with a clunk at Laura's feet. It was a wreath of flowers woven tight against a painted backing, like the ones used at graduation ceremonies or funerals. As pretty as the flowers were, Laura could only see the circle now. She glowered at the woman, snatched up the wreath, and snapped it in half. The woman threw back her head and laughed. Another bomb went off on the *Dead Ringer*'s second floor. Laura flinched on instinct. When she opened her eyes again, the woman was gone.

"Miss Kramer!" A policeman teetered at the canal's edge. "My god, it is you! Are you all right? Are you hurt?"

She'd recognize that man anywhere. "I'm fine, Officer Baxter!" she replied.

"Can you get back up here?" said Baxter. "Really, this is no place for you, miss!"

The boatman steered her to the canal's side, where she caught the metal rungs and pulled herself back up to street level. This done, she gave a salute and the boat happily chugged away from this mess.

"Please tell me this isn't a Sweeper job," she said, grimacing at the burning building.

"What? Oh, no," said Baxter, ushering her away. "This is regular mob warfare, no infestations. They tipped their hand, too, so no one was actually in the building, but—" A third blast shook the area, and the building groaned. Baxter hurried her faster. "But that doesn't mean they won't show up to retaliate! Let's get out of here!"

The other officers had moved out, herding the remaining students away from the danger zone and waving in reinforcements. Baxter stopped alongside a parked automobile and groaned. Another circle had been painted over the door, obscuring Amicae Police Dept with crimson.

"Should you use that, or is it a trap?" said Laura.

Obviously they had no time to waste on worrying; Baxter climbed in without hesitation, explaining simply, "They're painting it on everything these days."

Laura took a seat, tossing the ruined wreath in the back, and he started the engine. They peeled away from the curb just as another vehicle sped past, siren blaring.

"Are you sure you should be leaving?" said Laura, craning her neck to see the billowing smoke. The sight made her feel sick.

"Ensuring your safety is more important," said Baxter. "They clearly targeted you on the bridge, and led you here to begin with. If they want you around, the chief wants you as far away as possible. If something happened to you, the only Sweepers in the city would be mob-employed. It would be disastrous."

Laura sucked in a shuddering breath and closed her eyes. "How long have the Silver Kings and Mad Dogs been at each others' throats?"

"We don't know for sure. It came out into the open the same time the truth came out about the wall."

Maybe the wall policy had been part of the Silver Kings' balance.

That was a hell of a change for their regime, and the Mad Dogs had pushed for its collapse the whole time. No wonder they were angry enough to bomb each other.

No one died, though, and they could've tried much harder to be rid of Laura. This wasn't a real attack. It had to be a warning.

They stayed quiet all the way up until trundling to a stop on Acis.

"Well, here we are. I apologize for all of this. It's a frightful business."

Laura frowned, eyes closed. She still felt off, like something was about to spring at her. "It's fine," she said distantly.

The sound of a wind chime made her look up. Okane leaned out of the shop door, squinting at them. Once he realized who it was he came out.

"Laura? What's going on?"

"I got caught up in something," she replied. "Don't ask what. Even I don't know."

"Don't worry, though, we'll be increasing security on your shop and home," said Baxter, clambering out.

Okane gave Laura a horrified look, and she sighed. "I'll tell you inside."

Laura turned, readying herself to leave the vehicle. On a whim she glanced at the backseat. The wreath's flowers had withered. A white blossom trembled and fell, revealing something pitch black beneath. The painted backing had split so easily because it contained a hollow.

"Get away from the car!" she screeched, leaping out.

Baffled, Baxter followed, and not a moment too soon. The blackness made a rattling sound and expanded. The vehicle doors shuddered as it slammed against them, and the horn honked as feelers slipped up over the controls.

"An infestation?" said Okane. "But I didn't sense it at all!"

"It must've been hibernating," said Laura, cursing her own carelessness. "They knew any damage would get it moving."

"They? Was it planted?"

"Classic mobsters," Laura spat, pulling an Egg from her bag. She wound up to throw but hesitated. The memory of her single job as head Sweeper sprang back to mind, the seemingly obvious target and the following damage. She couldn't do that again. "How likely is that vehicle to blow up if I throw an Egg at it?"

Judging by Baxter's expression, very likely.

She snatched up a rock from the ground instead. It hit the door hard enough to dent. With a blur of motion, the infestation snatched it into its bulk before it could hit the ground. It otherwise seemed unwilling to budge from the seats, content to hide under the roof. They'd have to drive it out another way.

She pulled on her goggles, swapping the Egg for a flash pellet. Okane copied, circling to the other side. Laura crept closer. At first the infestation milled, oblivious, but it came to attention as her steps grew louder. It swelled to fill the entirety of the vehicle, clicking and clattering. The horn blared again, only to cut out as the vehicle wrenched and shuddered. Inky hands slithered out, hissing when they met the weak sunlight. Not a very smart creature, she decided, and threw in the pellet. It ricocheted off an arm and stuck by the door before going off. Baxter yelped and tumbled at the sudden harsh light. Laura leapt back as the infestation flailed, feelers swinging far too close.

"Any idea where we can find a broom?" she called.

"What?" said Okane. He spooked at another swipe of feelers and tossed his own pellet. The infestation squealed in fright and sucked back into the vehicle.

"If we can't hit it in the car we need to get it out. Drive it into the amulet and maybe we can flip it out!"

"Are - - - crazy? It would eat - - - along with the broom!"

"Not if we get it fast enough."

She hoped, anyway.

She stepped in close, arm raised to sling another pellet, and stopped short. Nothing was there. The seats were discolored, a few petals scattered on the cushions, but there was no monster and no wreath.

"Down!" Okane shrieked.

She caught a flicker of movement by her feet and retreated fast. More arms stretched from under the car, faster and farther than be-

fore. Too fast. She threw her pellet on the road to spook it into slow-
ing and only then escaped to the sidewalk. The infestation squirmed
before withdrawing. It bubbled like water around the vehicle's wheels,
and the road beneath it bled black.

The door behind Laura opened. The pawnshop owner peered out,
irritation fading quickly to fear before she pulled the door almost shut
again.

"What in hell—"

"Stay inside," Laura ordered. "Don't worry, we'll take care of it."

"Try not to break my shop," the woman snapped, and the door
closed.

So other people had heard of her track record. Hardly surprising,
since it had been published in Amicae's largest newspaper, but still.
Anger burned hot in her throat. *I didn't sign up to be sneered at.* She
clenched her teeth and focused on the infestation again.

The bubbling solidified about the tires, and without warning it
moved. The wheels spun, sending the whole thing careening forward.
Laura swore and ran, but she couldn't outrun it. She dodged into the
thin alley between two derelict houses. The vehicle hit the entrance
hard enough for its front wheels and hood to buckle, and the headlights smashed. The infestation slithered out into the shadowed walkway even faster than before. Laura tried another flash pellet, but the
infestation had realized they were harmless; it slid up the walls on
either side. Laura rolled a Bijou between her fingers but didn't throw
it—she'd taken out the majority of a building with some before, and
now was hardly the place for a repeat performance. But what else
could she do?

The infestation knit together overhead. Something winked behind
it, a moment before a blast shook the ground. The infestation reeled
away, studded with glass and debris from the smashed car; kin glinted
bright alongside shards of metal and glass, sucked fast into the black
body. The infestation swirled back toward the street, trilling angrily as
it sought the more dangerous threat. She saw it lash out once, twice,
and a furious cracking sound made it flinch back each time. Okane
slung another Egg at the infestation, but it batted this aside to smash

somewhere in the vicinity of Brecht's bookshop. It was properly angry now. It smoked again in the sun, clawing out of the alley. Blackness wrenched at tires and the vehicle jerked back. It changed targets.

Laura ran out again as the ruined automobile leapt back into the street. Okane backed away fast on its other side, switching out for flash pellets again. The infestation didn't so much as flinch. It whipped two more long arms at him. He ducked the first just barely, so it hurtled through a shop window. Screams came from inside but he didn't have time to look before the other arm smashed into the road beside him. He scrambled on hands and knees now as the first arm swung down in his way, barring his escape. His magic crackled. The nearest arm flinched, but the entire black surface of the main mass bubbled. The arms dug deeper, hauling the vehicle straight at him. His face paled. He sprang at the arm blocking him, accompanied by a particularly loud snap of magic, but stopped short. His magic wasn't enough to drive it out of the way. When the interior of Amicae had been covered in infestations, it had worked. When Laura had been caught by an infestation, he'd defied five hundred years of fact and driven it off with his magic. And now, on an infestation not even a fraction of the last foe's size or strength, it wasn't working?

Laura gritted her teeth, clacked an Egg against her amulet, and threw as hard as she could. It sailed straight into the backseat, its flashing eclipsed briefly before it exploded. The roof blasted off and sparks danced over cobblestone. The infestation shrieked. Its arms liquefied and Okane leapt over them, stumbling over the curb just in time. The vehicle slammed into the shop. Laura met him near the door.

"You okay?"

"In one piece," he said.

"Good. Fall back for now, okay?"

He didn't need telling twice. She wrenched the shop door open. Five people were inside, one with his legs crushed under debris, three others pulling him out; the last one had been caught by the infestation's charge.

"Hurry and get out of here!" she called. "It won't be long before the infestation recovers!"

Sure enough, the black ooze on the floor was drawing back together. It pooled over the counter, slipped over the last person, and dragged the silent body into its bulk. The other four hurried outside and toward Baxter. Laura ducked back outside and threw another Egg.

The infestation reeled. The vehicle lurched back again, scraped to face her now, and sped forward, spitting infestation covering its every surface. Laura stood her ground.

"Okane! Bijou!" she shouted, rapping another Egg against her belt.

This one hit and burst on the hood, spewing gold and clearing the windshield. An inactive Bijou flew past and bounced just off the side, but it was close enough. The heat of the Egg blast set it off, and the Bijou veered back into the vehicle with a scream. The infestation seeped inward to protect itself, but sparks ripped through it. The whole mess wove past Laura, and she tossed in two more Bijou. This done, she tore off after the others.

"Three?" said Okane, shaking. "But how many did it take to—"

"Not important. We're getting rid of this before it can grab anyone else," she retorted. Louder, "You up ahead, don't look back!"

"Yes, ma'am!"

The two other Bijou caught. Within seconds they were all howling, spitting light, and burning enough that thick, roiling clouds billowed off the creature's body. The infestation lashed, tossing this way and that so the car veered erratically. One swing of feelers sent a Bijou flying back out, but it curved in midair; once it hit the ground it raced along the cobblestone and under the vehicle. The glow dimmed for a moment. Next came a thundering *bang*. The vehicle burst into flame. Fire licked high, vivid but smudged at the edges. The wreckage rattled as the infestation thrashed. It seemed smaller now, less solid. Laura didn't arm her Egg this time, simply lobbed it in. Its break wasn't audible but the fire stained vividly yellow. The infestation curled up so it was completely invisible. The familiar black cloud issued, snuffing the fire and shadowing the entire street. Laura pressed her bandana close against her face. Some smell still got through, and her eyes watered.

"It's dead. Is everyone okay?"

The shop victims crowded further down the street, but Baxter hovered over them like a fretful hen.

"Rattled but whole," he reported. "And you? You weren't harmed?"

"It'll take more than that to take me out," said Laura.

"Glad to hear, Miss Kramer."

Okane all but collapsed onto the sidewalk. Laura knelt beside him. "What's wrong? It didn't touch you, did it?"

"No, nothing like that." He knit shaking fingers together and attempted a smile. "I'm just—Back in the interior, after Clae—I could touch infestations and they'd leave me alone. This one wasn't afraid of me at all. Is it—was I not scared enough? Am I not that strong anymore? Was *it* stronger than months-old swarms?"

Laura didn't know, and she didn't like the idea. "This one could've been a lot older," she suggested. "Mobs plant hibernating infestations all the time."

His nose wrinkled. "Since when do they hibernate?"

"Since always. It's a defense mechanism. If an infestation reaches a point when it eats everything alive around it and can't sense movement, it pulls back into the amulet and goes dormant. It resurfaces to check the surroundings and starts up again if it senses anything. If not, it just keeps sleeping. It can go weeks, or years. Decades, even." She paused. "That's the reason we even have the wilds. Infestations eat nonliving things too, so if there was no dormancy they'd eat the trees, the *ground*. There'd be nothing left."

Okane shuddered. "Scary."

"Most dormant infestations are from the wilds, so mobs buy from the idiots who harvest them. God knows how they keep from being eaten themselves."

"Or maybe it's not older at all," said Okane.

"What else could it have been?" said Laura.

Okane's brow furrowed. "The hive mind learns. Maybe it's already adapted past my abilities, after seeing us in November."

A distant wail reached them, coming closer by the second. Another police car tore around the corner, followed close by a white-canvased ambulance. One of the local shopkeepers must have called for help during the ordeal. Baxter waved them down, and soon medics fussed over all of them. While most stuck to the victims, one jogged over to the Sweepers.

"Are you hurt at all?" she asked, looking them up and down.

"Rattled but whole," Laura echoed.

Okane nodded slowly. "I'll be okay."

Once the medical personnel attended to all the victims, the Sweepers quickly retreated into the shop. It felt good to be there, safe, in a place completely saturated with the smell and feel of magic.

"I don't understand what they were trying to do," Laura said once they were inside. "I mean, at first that woman was trying to convince me of something, then she threatened me to stay on the right path, and then she doesn't even give me a chance to follow her advice?" She threw her hands up in frustration. "What was the point? If you're going to kill me in a flashy way, why not do it with the backdrop of a burning building?"

"Maybe it was just emphasis," said Okane.

"On what?"

"They can catch - - - off guard." He peered through the window, up the street at the damage. "They can catch us even in a place we thought was safe. If she was handling infestations so easily, it could also be emphasis on their own Sweepers."

Every mob had a Sweeper force, rarely seen. In the past, most mob-related incidents were settled quietly or specifically left for the Sinclairs to clean up. With all the talk about one of the Mad Dogs being an ex-Sinclair, Laura had always imagined the Mad Dogs being Sweeper-heavy, but of course the Silver Kings would have their own.

"So what, they're saying we're not needed?" she grumbled, joining him at the window.

"I wouldn't know," said Okane. "Sullivan never met with Silver Kings. The few Mad Dogs he invited to the mansion didn't talk much about Sweepers, but then again he never cared about such things."

They were startled from their thoughts as the door banged open. The wind chime downright clanged, and in came Juliana.

"Are you two all right?" she cried, before she was even over the threshold. "We got a call from the police about some kind of mob hit on the shop, and came as soon as we could. You're not injured, right? They didn't actually catch you?"

Laura was too overwhelmed to respond as Juliana caught her by the shoulders and gave her a critical once-over. Finding nothing, Juliana simply stared at her.

"It was an infestation, not a bombing," Laura said once she finally found her tongue. "We were able to take care of it, but you probably saw the damage outside."

Juliana nodded solemnly. "Were any people caught up in it?"

"One dead, multiple injured," said Laura. "We had a policeman already on-site and more arrived fast. They'll have the official numbers."

"I'm just glad you two weren't caught up in it."

Lester entered far more slowly. "Juliana, the officer out here says it was a mob hit."

"A what?" Juliana looked aghast.

Laura winced. "I think they were after me. One faction got upset over all the newspaper articles and decided to make a stand. It doesn't make sense to me, though. I don't see what they'd gain from it beyond public backlash."

Juliana's expression became thunderous. "Of all the ridiculous—If this is how they'll be, fine. We'll teach you to defend yourselves more. Lester, let's move up the training schedule."

3

THE SUNDOWN SHOWDOWN

The popping and cracking of the shooting range made Laura flinch.

"Terrible, isn't it?" said Juliana, smiling sympathetically. "I could never stand it myself."

"Guns aren't your specialty," said Lester, as he returned from the check-in desk. "You're all the running and throwing type. More athletic."

"You're just as athletic as we are," Juliana chuckled. She turned to Laura and Okane to elaborate, "Lester's Sweeper training was just as rigorous as mine, but he focused more on guns after the apprentice stages. He likes keeping his distance."

"Clae was the same way," said Laura.

"Probably for different reasons," said Lester. He held out what looked like a pair of metallic earmuffs. "Put these on. It'll help with the noise."

Hesitantly she set them over her head. Juliana set to work adjusting the settings so it fit snug, and soon all sound was gone. Laura's ears felt hot against the cloth padding. A buzzing sound echoed in her head, the world so quiet her brain had to imagine noise. This time Juliana twisted a dial on the earpiece. Her mouth moved and Laura simply stared. Two more turns. Juliana spoke again and this time came a faint echo.

"What?" said Laura.

Six turns forward, one turn back, and Juliana said, "How's this?"

"Muffled," Laura replied.

Another gunshot came from the range, but this time it was so dull, the sound didn't hurt her ears at all.

"Wonderful," said Juliana. She handed Laura a set of goggles, then moved on to fix similar equipment on Okane.

"Usually we'd have to purchase all of our ammunition here at the range, but that wouldn't work with our equipment, and that's what we're trying to drill into you," said Lester. "Back in Puer, ammunition wasn't regulated the same way it is here. It was the gun itself that was hard to get hold of."

"Puer's might be the better system," Laura sighed. "Ammunition is limited here, but somehow the mobs come up with more than enough of their own."

Lester smiled sympathetically. "Nothing's perfect. I've brought the less powerful kin bullets this time, so we don't end up burning down the building."

"It's not like the range can argue about our brands. They make our equipment already," said Juliana, nodding up at the wall.

The entry room they stood in was wood paneled, the entire wall opposite the desk covered in guns of every type. A bold red sign hung at the top, marked with the same flower logo and the words CHERRY CO. AMICAE-MADE FIREARMS FOR ALL OCCASIONS. Cherry Co. produced Amicae's Sweeper bullet supply, but Laura had never been under the impression they'd looked favorably on Sweepers.

"Don't be nervous," said Juliana, misreading her expression. "I'll walk you through it all."

Once equipped with ear protection, the four Sweepers filed through the door to the range proper. The place was huge. A wide section stretched ten feet before being cut off by a waist-height wall, beyond which lay the no-man's-land, dead-ended with targets. Most targets were basic: a sheet of paper with the outline of a man. At the very end, however, two shooting stalls used very different targets—robots fitted with cloth skin, faces, and clothes painted in a mockery of a person.

The nearest one had been graced with a white tie, implying a mobster from the Silver Kings. The doll lurched up and down, stump arms waving as if for mercy while the teenagers at the stall jeered. Juliana stopped short.

"What is that?" she said, voice carefully flat.

"Moving target practice," Lester answered reluctantly. "It got popular here after that MARU group disbanded. It's a petty revenge on the mobs, since the city couldn't enact punishment."

"It's teaching them to shoot people," said Juliana.

"What else do you expect them to shoot, in a city?" said Lester.

"It's not the target so much as the mentality," said Juliana. "If it were someone shooting to practice self-defense, or preparing for real danger, I'd have no problem, but look at that. Look at the way that doll's moving. That's not a threat, it's a plea for help. These people are just here to get their kicks murdering something, like a great exercise in destroying their own empathy. That's the type of person who'd shoot first and leave an innocent person to die."

"Is it?" said Lester.

Most shots had missed the dancing doll, but one finally hit. A great hole opened in its torso and reddish sand poured out. The teenagers whooped.

"Our stalls are right next to it," said Lester. "If you want, I'll go on that side."

Juliana took one look at Okane's green-tinged face. "No need to coddle me. I can handle some bloodthirsty boys."

Lester didn't look convinced but didn't argue. They took up their positions in the stalls. While brick dividers hid the neighboring shooters from view, the no-man's-land had no barrier, and Laura could see the doll floundering, more sand pouring from another hole in its gut.

"I'm sorry," said Juliana. "Back in Puer the shooting range is a lot more . . . professional. They'd never allow something in such bad taste." She looked genuinely upset.

"Don't worry about it," said Laura. "We've seen a lot of messed-up things these days."

"Amicae's out of control, isn't it?" Juliana murmured.

In Laura's mind, Clae had been the only thing holding the city together. It was a silly thought—far more than Clae had been lost and tarnished—but if he'd been here he would've controlled it. No newspaper could make a fool of him, no Council could've ripped him away, and he'd have a plan for post-"enlightenment" Amicae; he'd probably dreamt of that day his whole life. But no, now the city lay in shambles with a stranger at the helm of the Sweepers. She couldn't wish him back. She'd tried.

"It used to be better," she said. "Well. Maybe not better, but peaceful."

Juliana smiled ruefully. "Ignorance is bliss, isn't it? But you know, that's what we're here for. Once we can prove ourselves to the city, to the media, that we're vigilant and capable, they'll start to breathe easier. We're not hobbled like Sinclair was. We can do this."

Laura's mouth quirked. "You sound confident."

"I am. I figure I've got a wealth of knowledge and the Sweeper city at my fingertips. Determination can get me anywhere here." She winked. "And I fully intend to make you my second-in-command."

On the one hand Laura wanted to say, *Of course you will,* because she was the obvious choice, the most veteran local Sweeper. On the other hand, the media had been none too pleased with her, and the Council couldn't have given Juliana any recommendation for it. Juliana could just as easily have named Lester to the position.

"Thank you," said Laura.

Juliana nodded, pleased. "Sure, you made a mistake and got fired for it. But most mistakes in this line of work get you or someone else killed, and not only did you avoid that, you learned a lesson that'll stick. I want smarts and guts, and you seem to have a fantastic blend of it. Now! First things first. Have you ever used a gun?"

"No."

"Show me how you think you should shoot."

Laura tried to line herself up the way Clae had. It was difficult; most memories seemed tied to *running* and shooting, and while Clae had frequently managed one-handed shots in all the twisting and pivoting, that couldn't possibly be good form. The Puer gun felt ridiculously heavy and awkward in her hands, but she held still and tried to relax as Juliana looked her up and down.

"You're on the right track, but not quite there," she said, and began adjusting Laura's position.

Wider stance, unlocked elbows because apparently the recoil was a doozy. As Juliana fussed over hand placement, Laura asked, "You've been a Sweeper for twenty years, right? Why did you join?"

"My heart has always belonged to Sweepers," Juliana chuckled. "Being able to come in and work with magic in its purest form . . . I've never gotten over it. It sings, you know?"

"It does." Laura had heard kin sing, laugh, and scream. She'd never expected magic to do that before she'd joined the Sweepers, but Juliana probably understood it better than anyone.

"What made you want to leave Puer?" said Laura.

"Ah, that," said Juliana. "It's such old news, even the gossips in the Puer guild don't talk about it."

Laura raised a brow. "You admit the Puer Sweepers are gossips?"

"You'd have to be an idiot not to notice," Juliana snickered, but became solemn again. "Two years ago, one of my friends died fighting an infestation. Her name was Eliza. She was a very talented Sweeper, but in this business you can't just rest on your laurels. Infestations are always learning, and always growing, and this one caught her. I was there, but I didn't react in time to save her. You know in your head that Sweepers die, but when it's someone you know personally, it affects you in ways you don't expect. Lester took it particularly hard. The three of us were close, you see. I worked harder after that, promised myself I'd never let any other friends die, but." She shrugged. "Passing the place she died, day after day . . . it wore on me. I needed to get out of there or I'd go crazy."

Laura could relate to that. Death had felt somehow distant from her until Clae died.

"I'm sorry for your loss," she said.

"No need to be. I've gotten over it." Juliana stepped back. "So, now that I've fixed your stance, how do you feel?"

"Foolish," Laura admitted.

"Practice makes perfect," said Juliana. "Now, remember, this bullet leaves the barrel at tremendous speed, and it's going to exert a lot of force and make a *really* loud noise. Make sure you've got a good grip."

"I know."

"Just a reminder. Pull the trigger."

Laura took a deep breath. She looked down the sight of the gun, down toward the target, and squeezed the trigger with her finger pad. The flash of light from the gun registered first, then the *bang,* then the fact that said gun seemed determined to launch backward into her face. She managed to keep hold of it but staggered back a step. Juliana stepped with her, arm out as if to save her from swooning.

"There you go! How do you feel?"

"I didn't expect it to be that strong!" said Laura. How had Clae ever shot one-handed with such backward force?

"Words can't really describe it," said Juliana. "But you're feeling okay?"

"Yeah, I just need a minute."

"No hurry. You're actually taking it pretty well. A lot of first-time shooters I've seen refuse to pick it up again or actually start crying."

"I thought this was supposed to be enjoyable. Aren't there hobbyists?"

"Some people love guns from the start. First reactions aren't logical, you know? And just because you get scared the first time doesn't mean you can't progress to the point you're comfortable with them." Still, she gave Laura a conspiratorial wink. "Personally I still hate them, but you don't want to end up stranded with the one piece of equipment you don't know how to use."

Laura nodded but frowned at the target. The bullet had left a dark smear two feet under the place she'd been aiming for.

"Juliana?" Lester leaned around the divide, looking pained. "Could we have them swap guns?"

Juliana cocked her head. "Why?"

"He brought the Amicae gun, and he's very adamant that we can't use the bullets I brought." Lower, he said, "I don't think he likes me. Perhaps a feminine touch . . . ?"

Juliana frowned at Laura. "Did I spring this on Okane too fast? He doesn't seem terribly open to team bonding."

"He has trust issues, and good reason for them," said Laura. "I could go over and show him what I just learned."

"That would be the blind leading the blind," said Juliana. "And I hate to say it, but he can't just use you as a crutch for the rest of his life. What would happen if you're not there? I want to make sure he can trust us in an emergency. No, not even an emergency. I want to be able to share his burden. That's what Sweepers do."

It made sense, not that Laura wanted to admit it. She stuck behind them as the pair circled to the next stall. Okane looked frazzled, but thankfully his magic hadn't started acting up. He gave Laura an expression of hopelessness.

"I don't like it," he told them all flatly.

"You don't have to handle them all the time, just know how to use them in a pinch," said Juliana. "How about you try our gun?"

Laura handed over her gun and took Okane's instead. The Amicae model was a subtly different shape; while it still felt foreign, it felt a little more right. She held it up to get a better look at the pictographs, and was startled when a hand rested on hers and guided it right back down.

"Rule one of gun safety," Lester said sharply. "Always consider the gun loaded, and always keep it pointed somewhere safe."

Laura jumped at his tone. "Right. Sorry."

Lester sighed and forced himself to relax. "I've seen accidents happen, both on and off the shooting range. Let's not add you to the list of injuries."

She backed off while the MacDanels concentrated on Okane's form. In the corner the doll slumped entirely and a buzzer sounded for the end of the session. The teenagers laughed as they toted their rented guns back to the front. Another man stepped in as they left. He looked up and down the range before walking straight to Laura's stall.

"Excuse me," she said, annoyed. "That one's taken."

He looked at her. There were no words, no scowl, but Laura felt suddenly rooted to the spot. He didn't look like much—tall, reedy, with unkempt red hair, a gaunt face, and eyes with dark bags under them but bright as if he'd gone days without sleep on sheer mania. He looked like a breeze could blow him over, but those eyes held something deep and dark as pitch. He watched her a moment before smiling, and this was worse than the menacing blankness.

"I can't say I've seen a Sweeper here before. What's the occasion?"

"Practice," she forced out.

His eyes dragged from her face to the gun in her hand. "Practicing for Sinclair's memory, I see."

Her curiosity piqued. Hesitant, she asked, "Did you know Clae?"

"Know him? My dear, we hated each other. Of course I knew him." The man pulled out his gun, fit in a dummy round. "It's a shame he passed. We would've made spectacular coworkers, but he never knew when to say yes."

Now prepared, he raised his weapon. The gun was distinct. She'd seen the model in a hundred mob films, knew its white enamel handle better than she knew Gustave's Moon. Worse, there was a tattoo on his hand: a savage red dog scrambling from wrist to knuckles, jaw open in a snarl. A Mad Dog.

"I think I see why Clae didn't like you," she said evenly.

He pulled the trigger and the paper target tore, directly in the middle of the silhouette's head. The noise made Laura's hair stand on end, and as much as she willed herself to calm she couldn't.

"Guns aren't so satisfying," the mobster sighed. "Give me a grenade any day."

"What do you want?" said Laura.

The mobster looked at her again, grin widening. "How blunt. What makes you think I want something from you?"

"You're the ones raving about me in the *Dead Ringer*," she scoffed. "You don't really think you can play this off as a coincidence, do you?"

He laughed. "Of course not. But don't worry, I'm not here to interview you. I just thought I'd check up on a few things. Investigate some *rumors*."

He looked to her right, and Laura glanced back. Lester had leaned around the divide to investigate the noise, and the blood drained fast from his face.

"What do you think?" said the mobster. "So much glory in the *Sun*'s pages, how about you and your sister set up an appointment for our own little highlight? The public would rave over it."

"I'm sorry, but I don't know who you are or what you want," said Lester.

"And yet you're scared." The mobster looked amused. "What deep, dark secrets are you hiding, MacDanel? The public has a right to know."

Laura had no idea what was going on or why the Mad Dogs would develop an interest in Lester of all people, but this was her department. Maybe she didn't have the boss title anymore, but she was fully willing to throw her weight around regardless.

"The MacDanels just got here," Laura snapped. "They've got nothing to do with your mob wars or any of your articles. Leave them alone."

The mobster's smile looked positively manic. "If they wanted to stay neutral, they should've watched their step for the past few years. Oh, *yes*, MacDanel, we heard about that."

Was he talking about Eliza's death?

"If something happened to them in Pucr, that's none of your business, is it?" said Laura.

"Isn't it?" said the mobster.

Lester stepped close to him. The Mad Dog stood his ground, expression darkening as if he was ready for a fight. That expression smoothed out as Lester pressed a wad of bills into his hand.

"Please, leave my sister alone."

"Oh? Is this protection money?" the Mad Dog snickered, flipping through the cash. "Usually there has to be an incident before people think of paying us."

Oh, hell no. Laura made to step forward, to argue because this was the absolute worst idea she'd ever seen carried out in front of her, but Lester held out an arm to stop her.

"Please," he said again.

The Mad Dog paused halfway through counting. His eyes remained fixed on the money, but one brow rose. "I knew you were an odd one, MacDanel, but you're even surprising me."

"What's going on?"

Juliana stepped around the divide now too. Her brow furrowed at their expressions, but smoothed out again as she faced the mobster.

"Hello," she said brightly. "I hope we haven't disturbed you. I'm the head Sweeper, Juliana MacDanel."

She held out a hand. For a moment they all stared at her. She wanted to shake his hand? Him, an obvious mobster reeking of danger? Eventually the mobster settled into amusement. He pocketed the money and shook her hand, ignoring Lester's tenseness.

"A pleasure, Miss MacDanel. I've heard of you already."

"We'll be making great strides in protecting the city," said Juliana. "I daresay we won't even need your mob Sweepers in a year's time."

"Hubris," the mobster chuckled. "Do what you will. We'll carry your slack as long as we care to."

"I appreciate your frankness."

Juliana went on smiling as he put his gun away, and to Laura's amazement he actually went to leave. He paused in the doorway, looked over his shoulder, and said, "Oh, *Head Sweeper*? Just a fair warning. Mob factions are at war in this city. Once you pick a side, there's no switching over. We're monogamous in that sense." With that he was gone.

"You just chased off a Mad Dog," Laura whispered.

Juliana's cheer buckled, and only worry remained. "He didn't threaten you at all, did he?"

"No," said Lester, and he shot Laura a look that pleaded for her to agree.

"No," she said slowly. "Those parting words were definitely the most foreboding."

They were on edge afterward, and while Laura finally managed to hit the target, she felt little excitement. To her relief, the buzzers finally rang over their stalls.

"That wasn't so bad," said Juliana, seemingly determined to stay positive. "I think you've picked up some valuable lessons for the future."

"Thanks for bringing us here," said Laura, and Juliana beamed.

They paused in the entryway as Lester conferred with the clerk, and Juliana launched into her training plans. Apparently Puer had entire buildings dedicated to Sweeper training equipment, and she'd been scouting out locations to mimic the exercises. Laura found herself wondering how any Sweeper could possibly keep up with the numerous exercises Juliana listed off and do their job. But Puer had many Sweepers; they probably had a system rotating teams into the field, with others training in the meantime. Amicae barely had enough for one team. There was no way it would work.

"Juliana," said Lester, and she broke off from her explanation of tumbling lessons. "Someone's on the phone for you."

The clerk offered the earpiece. Juliana circled the desk and took it.

"Hello, this is Juliana." A moment later she brightened. "Oh, yes, the police chief! How can I help you?"

Her brow furrowed deeper as the other person—it had to be Albright—explained the issue. She waved her hand at one point, and Lester pulled a pen and scrap of paper from his pockets. She scribbled something down and promised to be there shortly. Once finished, she hooked up the earpiece and announced, "We have an infestation. Do either of you know where to find Sundown Hill?"

As they were already in the trashier entertainment section of the Fourth Quarter, it wasn't far to reach Sundown Hill. The "hill" of its name came from the location, set snug around one of the less-frequented ramps from Fourth to Third Quarter with the outer wall of the ramp painted all up the slope like a massive mosaic sun. Fiery paint and broken glass made a luminous halo around the bold red lettering declaring its name, races held, and festivals of general tomfoolery. In the sun's shadow stretched racetracks, most meant for bicycles or automobiles, but a special one set aside for horses. Wooden stands encircled them, and around these were the Sundown parlors, gambling dens held by the mobs. As a holdover from the MARU incidents, it was owned by the Silver Kings but ran on a strange schedule, rotating to "Blackwater Night" or "Mad Dogs Night," and each time they gave the namesake mob the lion's share of the night's winnings. Mobsters always tried to lure in customers on their particular nights, but somehow it remained peaceful, its business booming. It was one of the few places rival mobsters could meet without bloodshed, and the Silver Kings upheld a strict no-violence policy. Never before had Laura heard of it being swarmed with police, but today it was.

Albright waited for them near the entrance.

"It was a mob hit," she told them, as soon as they were in earshot.

"How?" said Laura. "This is mob-held territory! Why would they attack themselves?"

"Inter-mob war," said Albright. "They've moved on from focusing entirely on police to menacing each other."

"What's the point? And of all places, Sundown Hill?"

"I'm not sure I understand," said Juliana.

"This is a no-fighting zone," Laura told her. "Even if two mobs are at odds in other parts of the city, they never bring it here."

"Does this have anything to do with the attack at our headquarters?" said Juliana.

Albright nodded grimly. "Now that Sinclair Sweepers have stepped into the spotlight, you've become a topic in mob politics, and a hotly debated one at that. From what we hear, the two largest voices talking about you are the Silver Kings and Mad Dogs, and they're forcing all the other mobs to take sides. Silver Kings wants you to be left alone and do your job, but Mad Dogs? We don't know what they want. Today's attack is probably meant as a warning to other mobs that there's no neutrality in this subject."

"Did the Mad Dogs attack this place, or was it a smaller mob?" said Laura. "Mad Dogs are dramatic, but would they go this far?"

"We don't know. All they left here are circles," said Albright.

"Circles?" Juliana echoed.

"Targets," said Okane. "A fear tactic."

"The MARU was brought down by circles," said Albright. "Whatever you do, keep them off your backs."

"What's the situation with the monster?" said Juliana.

"It's in the middle building, the nightclub. The infestation was sighted in the bar area, but we haven't located its root amulet."

"Any casualties yet?"

"Yes, but there's no telling who or how many. The people who'd been there scattered as soon as we showed up, and the few we caught are keeping their mouths shut."

An impossible headcount.

"Was there anything special about it that we should keep in mind?" said Laura.

"At this point, no. All we know is that the infestation is there. The bartender described it as 'watery.'"

"Then we'll get started if you have the perimeter," said Juliana. She turned to the other Sweepers. "Do we all have the equipment? Guns?"

"Check," said Lester.

"I, um—Check?" said Okane.

"No?" said Laura.

"This soon after learning how to use one, it's not a good idea anyway," said Juliana. "How about Eggs?"

"Check," Laura said quickly.

"Check," said Okane.

"Check," said Lester.

They went through every single item. On the one hand Laura could appreciate being prepared, but she'd checked herself over en route to this place; she knew she had everything she'd ever needed on previous infestations, along with a little blue capsule she simultaneously hoped and dreaded to use. She glanced at the building, hoping the creature inside wasn't doing too much damage while they were standing around.

"We could stand to have a little more equipment next time, but that's okay." Juliana clapped her hands and regained Laura's attention. "We have enough material and four people. Even if it's a close fight, we'll come out on top."

"Then let's get started," said Lester.

Immediately they shifted stance, from tall and easy to crouched and prowling. Strange to show such dedication in broad daylight, but Laura followed their lead.

The building they approached had walls of yellow stucco, patterned just like the outer walls of the Quarters to match the overarching sun. The heavy door opened easily under their touch. Lester peered in, eyes roving around the hallway before nodding his head. At this signal they moved in.

The hallway they strode through was bright with electric lights and spaced all the way down with framed photographs of famous patrons. Laura spotted a few Council members and even Amicae's famous actor Barnaby Gilda, frozen in black-and-white. She tore her eyes away from Gilda's smile to look at Okane. Okane was quiet and slow, which she took to be a good thing. There wasn't nearly enough white showing in his eyes for there to be an incoming monster.

"Thoughts?" she whispered.

Okane opened his mouth to answer but Juliana spoke first: "None yet. With no sound or visuals there's no way to get a good prediction of its age or strength."

Okane shrugged. *What she said.*

Near the end of the hall Lester paused again. It opened into a wide room scattered with tables, with a large stage on the far side. Music stands and instruments had been abandoned in the rush to get out. Food remained on tables, and chairs lay overturned.

"I guess it's a good thing the infestation chose now to appear," Juliana murmured. "Lunch at a nightclub is a scant affair, as far as I know."

"The gambling parlors go all day," said Laura. "There's no way it was empty."

But this room did appear to be vacant of all life, so they passed through it. Another branching hallway led to a second seating area, this one with a grand stone fireplace.

"Are you sensing anything?" Laura whispered to Okane.

"It's close, but not focused," he replied. "At least not on us."

"Maybe we can sneak up on it."

"Doubtful."

Juliana shushed them, and Laura snapped her mouth shut. Since they didn't see a bar in here, they went to the dance room. Nothing big or fancy—few things in this Quarter were—but it looked well-frequented. The scuffed hardwood floor must've been there for decades. A few tables ringed the edge of the dance floor, but the most prominent feature was the long wooden bar stretched across one end of the room, polished to perfection. Lester groaned at the sight of it.

"Of all things to sacrifice to an infestation, it has to be a work of art."

"Better the art than us," said Juliana. "Any eyes on the infestation?"

None, as far as Laura could see. She looked up just in case, but no telltale trail of black marred the ceiling. In their sudden silence, they heard a crash. A long, drawn-out pause, and it happened again.

"Storage room?" Laura guessed.

"Check around the bar," said Juliana.

They circled in. Laura pulled out an Egg, hoping the weight in her hand would calm her nerves. All of the Eggs she carried were the Puer variety, with no Clae or Anselm added into the mix. She'd been happy with it before, but now she felt oddly alone, the kin's color foreign. She felt more like she'd carted around containers of lemonade than weaponized magic.

That's fine, she told herself. *We've got two more experienced Sweepers here, and this kin mix is the pride of Terual. We'll be fine.*

Okane reached the edge of the bar. He peeked over the side, studying the taps and glasses, before reaching over. A flick, and one of the glasses fell. The shattering sound split the quiet like a crack of thunder, but worse followed. Thudding and crashing and tearing, and suddenly a portion of the wall broke away as a hidden door smashed off its hinges. More glass shattered in the aftermath, hardly audible as blackness seethed from the door.

It came in a wave, with a sickly pseudo-splashing sound. It cascaded onto the floor, roiled up as it hit the bar, and spattered outward in a poisonous spray.

"Get down!" Juliana shouted.

Laura and Okane lurched out of the way, and the MacDanels

opened fire. A single bullet burst in the spray and sent green energy zigzagging amid the droplets, zapping them from existence before hailing down on the beast itself. The infestation swept up again, surged over the top of the bar, and rolled down the other side, heaving all the bar's contents with it. Bottles, glasses, rags, and a pencil clattered on its back like a turtle's shell. It flattened to the floor and spread outward. Laura jumped onto one of the tables. The blackness seeped underneath, causing the structure to lurch, and an ugly noise rose from below. Laura slapped her amulet, ordered weightlessness, and jumped. She caught one of the low chandeliers in one hand and swung herself to a further table; the previous one quickly sank, then overturned so the legs bristled like spikes.

What the bullets had done to the spray didn't work on the main infestation. Juliana and Lester fired shot after shot into the incoming creature, but it barely smoked and it didn't slow at all. As it came within ten feet of them, they dismissed this method and split.

"Bullets aren't working!" Juliana called. "We'll try regular Eggs next!"

Laura rapped her Egg against the amulet on her belt and slung it down into the mess. It flashed and sank with a plop into the darkness near the table legs, then blew. Light burst from the spot. Blackness went flying, singeing into smoke midair. It barely dented the thing. Laura was used to entire swaths of infestation ripped and singed in a single Egg attack, but this didn't even register as a hiccup. It only affected a patch a foot wide. They might as well be attacking a canal with a stone. The infestation jittered a little, sounding more like inhuman laughter than fright. It plowed faster, toward Okane, and slammed up the wall when he leapt away.

"Egg isn't working either!" Laura said, panicked. "That should've worked! It always works!"

"This creature might be older than you're used to."

Juliana armed one of her own Eggs, then lobbed it into the air. This sank into the middle of the mass, blew, and did even less than Laura's had. That was a bad sign. That was a very, very bad sign.

"No panicking!" Juliana shouted. "We'll wear it down! Keep hitting it!"

Okane threw an Egg. Lester threw an Egg. Anything they threw did little more than scratch the surface and shatter what glass it clung to. The monster eddied, churning near the center of the room as if waiting for something. The hive mind had probably told it Amicae's strengths and weaknesses. It operated under the idea that they still had Clae's level of magic, and waited, sniffing out a trap. Amicae's forces wouldn't be this weak. It was sad that the infestation had more faith in them than they did, but Laura took advantage of its stillness to keep throwing Eggs. She'd already thrown three and couldn't see any damage.

At last, it realized that this was all it would be getting, and it seemed downright delighted. With a shrilling sound, the infestation pulled itself up into a column, twisting and spinning before throwing itself out in a wide wave. The Sweepers scattered, but just because the blackness missed them didn't mean they went unscathed. The infestation flipped and launched the debris from its back. Okane ducked, and the pencil slammed half its length into the wall where his head had been. The jagged base of a glass caught Lester as he was running, and with a yelp he crashed to the ground.

"Lester!" Juliana cried.

"I'm fine!" he snapped. "Look out before it—"

Juliana ran to his side. Sensing a man down, the infestation swarmed toward him too. She stood firm in front of him, armed another Egg, but it wouldn't be enough. Not with that magnitude. As the black tide reeled in, Laura jumped back to the floor and dashed for the bar. The source was somewhere back there. From her bag she pulled wire and two Bijou. A flick, and the wire sparked. As soon as the Bijou caught, she lobbed them over the side and went sprinting back the way she'd come.

"Get down!" Okane yelled, and Laura hit the floor without question.

The infestation was a foot from cascading over the MacDanels when the Bijou shrieked. The initial blast rocked the dance floor, smashed the bar apart so wood and metal flew and embedded splinters into the walls. The infestation gave a hideous wail, and it fell apart into ash.

One of the keys to fighting standard infestations was figuring out the location of the source amulet and how the infestation reacted to disguise it. The infestation howling and whirling to take up all the space it could made this difficult, but sometimes it got full of itself and focused too much on a point, leaving its connection to the amulet in full view. This one had stretched thin, lending all its bulk to removing the MacDanels while leaving the trail only inches wide. In this state the Eggs might not have any impact on it, but the Bijou Laura carried were old, and they sang with Anselm's influence. They had no qualms about shredding this infestation like tissue paper. She hoped they would eat it right down to the roots, but that wasn't to be. While damaged, the infestation wasn't dead by any means. It had merely lost a limb. The body resurged from beyond the hidden door, a great cloud of seething, shining awfulness. The Bijou shrieked. The infestation roared. They railed at each other, and heavy smoke billowed around the room.

"Good thinking!" said Juliana.

"I'm not sure how long it'll last!" Laura replied. "Got any plans to snuff it out?"

"Keep hitting it with whatever does damage."

She dug in her own bag and pulled out more Bijou. They looked very similar to the kind Laura used, but when thrown they did little more than sparkle; they vanished fast into the black cloud, and the only light visible came from the Amicae variety. Juliana bit back a curse.

"Was our equipment damaged in transport?" said Lester, wincing as he tried to pull himself up.

"It can't have been," Juliana snapped, putting an arm under him to help steady his stance. "I was sure to take the ones properly matured. Unless someone specifically tampered with them in the shop . . . Okane, has there been any sign of a break-in?"

"None," he said, and quickly ducked.

It wasn't immediately obvious why he did that, but Laura copied the motion. Seconds later, the infestation lashed out. The Bijou spun through the air like screaming comets, close enough for Laura to feel the heat. One hit the wall and embedded itself, only to shriek and shudder in place. The last zipped past Lester and into the hallway. The infestation bubbled and snapped, spilling out and over the bar again, and Okane aimed the gun at it.

Bang!

This bullet definitely did damage. He'd only hit the edge, but a chunk of the creature two feet across sizzled and crackled to nothing, the edge falling to ash and the main body sparking gold. The infestation squealed. It rolled sideways and slipped off the bar, pooling tight and concentrating its remaining debris to bristle like spines as it tried to figure out what had happened.

"Old bullet?" Laura whispered.

Okane nodded. "Very."

Juliana had taken advantage of the distraction to heave Lester back into the other room. She came striding back here, reaching for Okane.

"Okane, give me that gun."

"What?" he spluttered.

"I've got better aim than you right now," she said. "I'll do the shooting, you go back there and help get Lester to safety. If the infestation decides to expand its territory, he'll be a sitting duck and I'm not going to risk his life on faith in a flimsy wall. Get him into sunlight and then get back in here."

"I—But—"

"Are you questioning your head Sweeper?"

In response, he held up the gun and popped open the cylinder. Six spent shells dropped and clattered on the floor.

"I'm out," he said hopelessly. "I used the others at the range."

"I'm not," she snapped. "Hand it over."

"But Puer's bullets don't fit properly! The gun will backfire!"

"Puer's bullets are the finest stock in all of Terual!"

They didn't have time to argue over it. The infestation snarled and snapped. It swirled out along the ground, reeled, and rose. Juliana shoved Okane toward the doorway with one hand, the other flying to the sheath on her thigh as she bared her teeth.

"Get out there and help Lester! We'll hold it back!"

As Okane went, he nearly tripped on a Bijou rolling back in. Juliana yanked a long dagger from its sheath. Laura had never seen a blade imbued with magic before, but knew as it caught the meager light that it had been forged strangely. It had something like the reliable-dog feeling of Laura's amulets, but faded. Like the negative of a photograph.

"What are you going to do with that?" said Laura.

"Fight, obviously," said Juliana.

As the infestation whirled toward them, she stepped toward it too. They came to a head in a flash of light. The infestation shrieked. A hazy glow followed the knife's trail as Juliana slashed again, and more of the infestation billowed into nothingness. Laura armed an Egg and threw it to the other side, hoping to distract the creature while Juliana struck again and again. The action didn't do much beyond anger it. Howling and twisting, the infestation brandished its table legs and broken glass. Juliana hopped back and in again, far too close, but the knife only had so much reach. While she focused on the mess at eye level, the creature branched left and right, swarming in on her sides. Laura had nothing in hand that could stop it, but one Bijou still spun by the door. She stomped one foot and cried, "Here!"

She gave the amulet's command at the same time. The Bijou reacted immediately, spouting sparks as it shot straight for her. Juliana and the infestation stood directly in its path. It sped between them, careening through inky darkness. Its sparks caught and multiplied, searing over the creature's surface. This time its concentration shattered, and the branches dropped into black puddles on the floor. The infestation snarled in frustration and turned to follow the Bijou, slamming one spattering arm after another in its sparking wake. The little bead sped faster than a bird could fly, right past Laura before swooping back to circle her. The infestation careened after it, and Laura threw her last Egg. The grenade's light fizzled out like a candle on its back.

"This is such bullshit," said Juliana, coming level with her. "How is it so strong?"

"Amicae's home to a lot of mavericks," said Laura, too busy watching their enemy to glance at her. "Look out!"

They ducked again as a black scythe swept overhead. Broken glass and debris chewed up the floor, forming gouges that made the Bijou jump erratically and slow in speed on its orbit. If the terrain got too damaged it could stop moving entirely. Juliana lashed out again with her knife. It did little good. The infestation surged closer, braving the smoke and searing light to grab at her. Juliana pulled back in time, but her weapon wasn't so lucky. The creature latched on to the blade and yanked it out of her hands. She screamed in frustration.

"Do you have another one?" said Laura, panicked.

"No," Juliana seethed. "Those blades are rare, it's a miracle I even had one."

She stepped back fast as the Bijou hit one of the gouges and veered. With its aim off, the infestation surged in. Laura grabbed Juliana by the shoulders and yanked her away without thinking. Juliana fell with a shriek, but the infestation missed her, and the Bijou righted itself. The blackness churned in a full circle around them. It hummed and clattered on the same frequency as the amulets. The creature was enjoying them now.

Laura wished desperately that Okane would come back and break an escape route for them, but what could he throw that they hadn't already done? Nothing would work.

"I should've known," Laura hissed.

Clae would never have kept Anselm in the Gin mix if he could survive with regular magic. Puer's Eggs held nothing but Gin energy, held none of the potency they needed to take down an infestation. They didn't have anywhere near the supplies or manpower to bring this monster down.

The Bijou was still going strong, but to do any damage it would have to leave them undefended, and even the limited shield it provided left their survival in question. The only thing Laura hadn't tried was the blue capsule. It had some kind of effect, obviously, but the only time she'd seen it in action visuals hadn't been clear. Was it worth attempting now? Yes, she decided, as another wave crashed high enough to curl up and cross the ceiling, tearing at the rafters; yes it was. She clacked the capsule against her amulet and threw it upward.

She watched it as if in slow motion. The capsule rose, reached its peak. It dropped, tumbling end over end. Halfway through its fall, the contents flared brighter blue. It changed course in an instant, shrilling sideways, and plunged into the infestation with force enough to leave a smoking hole in its wake. The creature withdrew, seeping and squirming wildly in its confusion. For a split second the tangle of black thrashed everywhere; the next, it had all folded in and vanished from the room.

"What just happened?" said Laura.

"I don't know," said Juliana. "What was it that you—"

A catastrophic bang echoed from beyond the door, and the entire building shuddered. The damaged rafters buckled, and down came the ceiling, the roof, in a thunder of wood and brick and shingles. Laura leapt back, and Juliana rolled. It was over in seconds. Soon half the room fell in, nothing but a heap of rubble in its wake. The bar was completely gone under it, no door in sight. Laura stayed frozen, braced for the infestation to lunge again. One second. Two seconds. Three. The dust settled. Slowly, acrid black smoke filtered through the debris. Nothing moved. Laura pulled out a flash pellet. It couldn't do damage, but it would at least chase anything out of hiding. It landed in the heap and ignited, sending more debris scattering. One of the pieces hit the ground a few feet away, and Laura backed up fast from the smoking shard of blackness. She stepped closer to the flickering piece and realized that part of this material had been stained vivid blue, just like the capsule. The smoke had the telltale stink of a dead infestation, so she felt secure as she knelt down and picked it up. She turned it over in her hands, studying the smooth surface, how only one side was blue and how that sang with warmth and a deadly hum while the rest was smooth stone. Not glass. It wasn't the capsule at all.

It was the root amulet, smashed to bits. She looked up, horrified, at the mess.

What remained of the amulet was somewhere beneath all that rubble, scattered and easily host to new infestations. Where this monster died, she'd just ensured that five more could take its place. The capsule could only be a last-ditch destroyer. She bit her lip, fisted her hand around the shard, and turned back to Juliana.

"The infestation's destroyed. So is the amulet."

Juliana had propped herself up, but now the fight went out of her. She pressed her forehead to the ground and exhaled deeply. "Thank god."

They remained still for a moment, not quite relaxed enough to move on but calming enough to catch their breath.

"Are you okay?" said Laura. "I didn't really think when I pulled you over. If you got hurt—"

"I'm fine."

Still, Laura went to help her up. Juliana let her heave her to her feet and blinked dazedly at the wreckage.

"That was . . . well, I suppose Puer's further north. Amicae's brand of infestation would be stronger. Closer to the hive mind."

"I'm sorry," said Laura. "I don't know if it's the spike or if we're out of practice, or—It didn't look like our weapons made any dent in it at all. Usually our Eggs do so much damage, but this time it just shrugged them off."

"And the weapons were strong when Clae Sinclair was around?"

"Yes." With Anselm's influence, but Laura wasn't going to let his afterlife serve as little better than a potion ingredient. "But it might have been that better hands wielded them. Clae had a lot of experience."

"Better hands," Juliana murmured. "And yet, the second-best hands had to save my life."

Laura bristled. "Helping each other is what we do. You keep saying that's the Sweeper way."

"It wasn't an insult," Juliana said quickly. "It was just that—" She paused, regarded Laura with a strange, sad solemnity before whispering, "I'm supposed to be the one helping you."

"You have," said Laura.

"Not enough." Juliana turned back to the damage. "Though somehow I'm doubting that tool caused all of this destruction. It's only supposed to affect amulets."

She strode for the rubble, and Laura followed half a step behind. She wasn't familiar enough with building materials to recognize much beyond bricks and shingles and maybe plaster, but Juliana toed through the pile and unearthed something.

"Glass?" Laura wondered. "That's big, considering the bottles it was carrying around. We broke those down to little pieces."

"It's curved," said Juliana.

She stooped and eased it out. It was indeed curved, long and gentle like an ornamental vase but completely transparent. In the bottom-most bend the dust had caked weirdly, half wet and sparkling gold. Laura dipped a finger inside it, tracing a trough in the grime.

"Kin," she said.

"Yours?" said Juliana.

"No, ours burned on impact. This . . ." This felt different. Like an off brand of vanilla, technically the same thing but the wrong smell, and the flutter of energy she felt was downright dull—something she doubted was caused by its dusty state. "Someone was storing kin here."

"Or producing it," said Juliana.

They kicked aside more and more of the debris, and the theory proved right. Tubing, fasteners, more broken glass and glittering, evaporated remnants caught the light.

"A distillery," said Juliana. "But why in a gambling den of all places?"

"Where safer for Silver Kings to store it, than the place no one would attack?" said Laura. "Really, no wonder we did damage. We lit an entire vat of kin at once. That should kill any infestation."

Juliana nodded, but her eyes grew hungry. "Where's the rest?"

"What?"

"The rest of the components."

Laura looked over it all, trying to place what she meant, and then realization dawned. "The Gin stones?"

If kin had detonated nearby, the air would be choked with magic and the heavy scent of vanilla. She saw no additional light, and the blast hadn't been enough to send something as large as Gin careening out of their range. Unless the mobs had only amassed small pieces?

"We should tell the police," said Laura. "They know who handles cleanup on these cases. They can search for the amulet fragments and the Gin all at once. We're not exactly equipped for searching right now."

Juliana didn't appear pleased with the idea, but a few more kicks at the rubble and she admitted defeat. "We need treatment for Lester anyway."

"Is he all right? I didn't get a good look at him."

"He says he was only grazed. I'm not sure why he'd drop the way he did in that case, but—"

"He likes distance, right?" said Laura. "If you're used to that, having an infestation get close and personal would be a nasty surprise. Maybe it was shock."

Juliana's brow furrowed. "I didn't think he was still susceptible to that."

Soon the police entered, and Juliana reported the details of the infestation to Albright. The chief nodded along as another man called for a medic, and yet another man ordered the presence of a cleaning bot. Lester was brought to an ambulance to be treated.

"It's not bad," he informed her, even as two medics loaded him on a stretcher. "It wasn't even that deep a blow. I'll heal fast."

Laura would take his word for it. She stood by with Okane near the parlor doors as the cleaning bot finally arrived. It wheeled around the side of the building and set to work pulling apart the debris with its many hands. As Juliana continued to speak with Albright, her eyes remained fixed on the bot's undulating movements.

"Her intensity is a little creepy," Laura mumbled.

"She told Albright she wanted to claim this Gin," said Okane.

Laura almost asked *why* to the obvious. Any additional Gin in their combination would lend power to their mix, and they'd just shown that their current blend was horrendously weak. If they could get more Gin, she wouldn't have to think about resorting to using Clae or Anselm.

"Did you sense any Gin around here?" she asked. "When they're active, I've been able to pick up on their presence, but I don't think I felt or smelled anything like Gin here."

Okane shrugged. "It may have already been stolen. A mob wouldn't sacrifice something so valuable if they could help it."

"An inside job?" Laura guessed.

"Who knows?" Okane pondered a moment, then said, "There might be far more than one amulet delivered to us. From what I understood, mob Sweepers kept their growing infestations in the same areas they stored their Kin."

Laura's heart plummeted. "What? Why?"

"Easy containment. A monster won't come out of its hiding place when a threat is so close. This one, though. It came out anyway. It started breaking glass before we even attacked it."

"So?"

"So, it directly attacked the Kin machine. The hive mind knows how to sabotage us now."

It was a chilling thought.

Almost half an hour later, a policeman came up to Albright and saluted.

"Chief, we've pulled apart the larger debris. We've found no large stones, Gin or otherwise. Evidence of several broken amulets."

Albright nodded. "Continue with the smaller debris. We can't afford to let any of those amulet pieces remain unaccounted for." She glanced at Juliana. "Do try not to blast these apart in the future. Killing one isn't worth the spread unless it's easily collected."

Laura winced. Juliana nodded, but she seemed to have deflated.

"Of course," she said. "I'll be sure to speak with my Sweepers about that. Is there anything else that you need from us?"

"Not at the moment. We'll deliver the amulet pieces to your shop tomorrow."

"We'll be sure to store them as soon as possible."

Juliana turned. Laura and Okane were directly in her line of sight but she didn't look at them at all, instead making a beeline for the ambulance. It made sense for her to first check on her family, but Laura still felt snubbed.

"I didn't like the look on her face," said Okane.

"What look? She didn't even look at us," said Laura.

"The face she made at the robot," said Okane. He pulled the collar of his coat tighter. "She's scheming something."

Laura frowned at him. "Is this a feeling, or is it something they've specifically done?"

"- - - trust my feelings when it comes to infestations."

"I trust you in general, I just want to know if there's something I should be looking out for."

She still wanted to believe that Juliana was trying to do this all right. She'd resented the idea of a new head Sweeper, sure, but if they could have a comrade supportive and tough as nails, then even if it wasn't Clae she'd appreciate them. She craned her neck to get a better look at the ambulance. Juliana scolded Lester there. She didn't look like the sort of person who'd hurt them. Then again, Sullivan didn't look like the type of man who'd carve money symbols into a child's skin on superstition.

Please, please be a good person, she thought. *I want this to succeed too much for you not to be.*

4

EXECUTRIX

When Laura reached the Sweeper shop two days later, the shop itself was dark, the street deserted. A few buildings down the street were stained black by infestation and fire, though the wreckage had been towed. Okane teetered on the edge of the roof. Laura stopped her bike in front of the shop and craned her neck to get a better look at him.

"What are you doing up there?"

"Practicing," Okane replied, far too innocently.

"Practicing what?" Laura said suspiciously. "What can you practice up there that you can't do in the road?"

"Things."

"You'll have to elaborate a little more here."

"Oh, - - - know."

Was that "you" lapse on purpose? Laura puzzled over amulet specifications before realizing he meant a different form of magic. She dropped her bike in horror.

"Tell me you're not going to jump off the roof!"

"I'm not going to do that *yet*," said Okane.

"Why would you do it at all?" said Laura. "You'll break your neck, or your legs at the very least!"

"I didn't do that last time."

"Last time," Okane miraculously fell five stories, landed on his feet, and gained no injuries from it. Clae had proceeded to panic over security blankets and overworked magic, and while Laura hadn't understood the urgency then, she more than understood it now.

"But we don't know if it'll react the same way!" she said. "And even if it does, what if you overdo it? What if you turn out like Clae and Anselm?"

Okane fisted his hands. "That's what I'm afraid of."

"Then why risk it?"

"Because I need to understand what I can do," he said. "As a Sweeper, and even beyond that, no one's been able to tell me what I can do or how to keep myself safe. Clae tried, but he wasn't like me. He could—But he wasn't—" Frustrated, he looked up and down the street for eavesdroppers. "- - - can't understand the root cause if - - - don't experience it. I don't want to live uncertain anymore."

"I know I'd live a lot more certainly if you could back away from the edge right now," said Laura.

Okane coughed out a laugh and stepped back.

A bell rang from down the street as the bakery door opened. Mrs. Keedler stepped out with a large basket balanced on her hip. Laura waved at her with one hand, trying to gesture Okane out of sight with the other. Unfortunately Okane had no qualms about being seen.

"Hello, Mrs. Keedler," he called.

"Good morning, you two." Mrs. Keedler didn't seem to know whether to be worried or not as she came alongside Laura. "Okane, dear, what are you doing up there?"

"Checking the chimney," he lied. "I think I'll need it cleaned soon."

"Do be careful up there," said Mrs. Keedler. "Even with amulets, you're not safe at that height. That poor apprentice died up there while practicing with them."

Okane stiffened. "Oh?"

"Poor Alf Jackson," said Mrs. Keedler. "He was a rude boy, but he didn't deserve to break his neck."

Apparently the idea of injury hadn't crossed Okane's mind if he had magical assistance; he eyed the roof's edge with more trepidation. "Did he, now?"

"Yes, a tragedy."

"How about you go inside?" said Laura. "We'll meet you in there."

"Exactly! I brought some food to help welcome your new head Sweeper!" said Mrs. Keedler, lifting her basket. "I'm almost a week late, but—"

Okane perked up again. "Will - - - be staying? Would - - - like some tea?"

"How gracious! I'll take up that offer if you're not bothered."

"Not at all," said Okane, and vanished from the roof.

"It takes a little while to break through his shell, but he's very sweet," Mrs. Keedler chuckled. "Has everything been going well for you so far?"

"As well as can be expected," Laura sighed, picking up her bike. "You know, I don't think Clae ever mentioned an Alf, and he was pretty fond of bringing up dead apprentices."

"That was a little white lie." Mrs. Keedler winked. "Alf sprained his ankle while fooling around and quit immediately after."

"You sly fox."

"A little healthy caution never hurt anyone."

Laura laughed as she opened the door. She parked her bike in the usual place, pulled over a stool for Mrs. Keedler to sit on, then climbed upstairs to check on Okane. He was already heating up the kettle, and looked up at the sound of her approach.

"Does Mrs. Keedler come over often?" said Laura.

He cracked a smile. "Usually she and her husband try inviting me over for dinner. I think they're trying to adopt every business owner on the street."

"Really?"

"The only reason she hasn't roped - - - into it is because - - - live so far away."

Laura laughed and turned away. The upper floor looked just as she remembered it from the time Clae had lived here, but she hadn't investigated it much. Rosemarie's room she knew from having napped there; the twins' room she knew from carrying Clae here. The only one she hadn't looked into was the master bedroom. A folding screen separated this from the rest of the flat, but it had been pulled aside; a little table sat like an island there, and she stepped around it to get a look. Newspaper clippings and photographs were pinned to the wall above a dresser, opposite a metal-framed bed with a patchwork quilt. A dusty-colored coat hung on one of the bedposts, long enough that it brushed the ground.

Laura leaned in to inspect the pictures. She saw photographs of the twins, their grandmother, and their parents; Helen Blair smiled from one of them, an arm around both Clae and Anselm, her expression so out of place on her that Laura was almost unnerved. Dotted in between were faces Laura didn't recognize, though she spotted her own and Okane's on the far right. The articles nearby featured Sweepers or random locations in Amicae; most predated Clae's time as head Sweeper.

Looking at them, Laura felt almost hollow. Someone belonged here, and it certainly wasn't her. Did Okane feel the same, staying in his home? Or worse, she thought, tracing a finger down newsprint that predated even Clae's birth, had Clae felt like an intruder in his own home?

Behind her, the kettle whistled. Okane pulled cups from the cupboard and put dark, shriveled leaves in them.

"Could - - - bring these down if I get the kettle?"

"Of course."

They descended the stairs and set up the tea while Mrs. Keedler set out an arrangement of scones. As they worked, a shuffle and clack announced the arrival of mail through the slot on the door.

"That's early," Mrs. Keedler observed. "Doesn't the postman come in the afternoon?"

Laura picked up the envelopes. There were four: the first two were things Laura had no interest in, what looked like a bill and another clearly addressed "To the New Head Sweeper" (still a fresh wound), but the others had no return address and were written in a semi-familiar script.

"Weird." She turned the one with her name over to examine the back, as if expecting a wax seal.

"What is it?"

"Letters addressed to us." She held the second out to Okane, who accepted it with a baffled expression.

"Who's it from?"

"Hell if I know."

"Maybe you have secret admirers," Mrs. Keedler chuckled.

More like not-so-secret critics.

Laura slapped the other mail down and sat to inspect the envelope. Her name and the address of the shop were written in a neat blend of print and cursive. She ripped the envelope open to find multiple pages folded inside. *Laura,* it started, and she felt a bit resentful that this person addressed her so casually, but upon reading the next sentence, she realized who it was.

Laura, if this is sent, I'm dead. Took me long enough. If you receive this letter you're still working as a Sweeper, hopefully higher than apprentice status. At the time I'm writing this you're the only other Sweeper working, so you're the one I'm leaving instructions to. You should have gotten a key or will soon. It doesn't look like a master key, but it is. It opens the contents of 684 and the armory. Clear it with the executor first, but 684 will be left to you. The executor will have to look at the armory, but I don't have many debts so nothing should be seized. Amelia Huxley, an ex-Sweeper, lives nearby. Ask her if you need help with equipment or startup in general. Her number is 3-212-6341-3312. For 684, go to the Central Security Bank in the Second Quarter. The safe-deposit-box key is in the sewing box upstairs. Forewarning, the contents will be heavy. Take care of them—they're irreplaceable. Also take care of the Kin, and particularly Anselm. I've seen you snooping around the curtains, so you've probably seen him already. The kid's name is Anselm Sinclair. He's my brother. He was reduced to a magic strain several years ago, and functions as a third Gin for

Amicae. He's the only reason we've been staying afloat over the past 20 years. DO NOT TELL ANYONE ABOUT HIM. If word gets out, there could be disastrous results. Sweepers are far more ambitious than you realize. People may try to break in to steal him, either to use him or sell him. I don't want the Council trying to sell him off to pay for some goddamn project. Worse, someone might try to turn people into Gin on a larger scale. By the time I die I hope you're knowledgeable about the job, but if you don't know how to do something or if you're not sure about a procedure, refer to the other pages here. The list may not be lengthy, but it should give you the right idea. If there are other problems, Amelia is well versed in these things. Good luck.

—Clae Sinclair.

Laura gripped the paper so tight the other pages crinkled under her grip.

"Are you all right?" Mrs. Keedler looked from Laura to Okane (still engrossed in his own letter, face getting paler by the second), but leaned toward Laura in the end, worry on her face. "What is it? You look like you've seen a ghost."

"We got a letter from a ghost." Laura tipped the letter so she could glimpse the handwriting. "Clae had letters sent to us after he died."

"He what?" Mrs. Keedler rested a hand on her breast and leaned back in shock. "What did he say?"

"It's information for the job, mostly." Laura shuffled through the papers, finding a description of the Kin workings, the Egg production, listings of other Sweeper contacts.

"You too?"

Okane put down his letter quickly. "I—yes. Job things."

"That man." Mrs. Keedler put her hand on her cheek now and shook her head. She didn't seem sure what to say, so just repeated, "That man."

Another knock pulled them from their reverie. Laura rose again with a groan and pulled the door open. A woman stood on the steps, slim with a close-fitting gray skirt and matching coat. A brassy decorative pin kept her curled hair in a tight bun at the back of her head, and she turned to look at Laura through spectacles that would have made Albright's glasses seem clunky in comparison. Her very presence exuded authority. Laura straightened unconsciously.

"Hello. Can I help you?"

"My name is Elinor James." The woman's tone was formal but not entirely unkind. She pulled a business card from the pocket of her coat and held it out. LYMAN AND JENSEN FIRM, it read, in stark black ink; the format and the insignia of a banking guild on the side gave away her true identity before she finished talking. "I've been appointed estate administrator for the will of Clae Sinclair. Is there an Okane Sinclair here?"

Laura stood aside for the woman to enter, mind racing. She hadn't thought the will would be carried out so soon. Okane stood, face pale.

"You're Okane?"

"Yes, ma'am."

Elinor walked straight forward and shook his hand. "We talked on the phone. Is this a good time to begin inventorying?"

"I think so," he said. "What exactly do I have to do?"

"I'll be recording larger assets left in Mr. Sinclair's possession. I may have to refer to your knowledge if I can't identify something, but otherwise I'll work alone during this process."

"Do I have to leave?"

"No."

Relief washed over his face. "Thank goodness."

"There's no point in making you leave, in this case," Elinor told him.

"Why not?"

Elinor glanced at the others. "May I speak with you privately?"

Okane blinked at her, then the other two. Laura shrugged and Mrs. Keedler gestured toward the stairs. He nodded jerkily and stepped toward the door.

"We can talk upstairs? Is that all right?"

"Of course."

She followed him up, and the first floor went quiet again. Laura sat next to Mrs. Keedler.

"What do you think she needs to talk about privately?" she asked.

"It's probably to do with the will," said Mrs. Keedler. "Maybe talking about Okane's share. I'm sure Clae wanted to support him, after all. She doesn't know us, so she's trying to protect them both. Don't worry, dear. It'll be fine."

Fifteen minutes later Okane came back downstairs, unsteady as if in a haze.

"Okane? Are you okay?" Laura called.

Okane turned to face her, stared, then tottered over. A foot away, he whispered, "Everything."

"What?"

"Everything but a box. He left everything else to me."

Mrs. Keedler smiled and nodded as if she expected this, but he still looked baffled. Laura laughed.

"What did I tell you?"

Elinor stayed upstairs to begin the inventory process. When he recovered, Okane explained that, since he was the heir, she wasn't afraid he'd make off with anything (it was his, why bother stealing it?), but otherwise he would've had to find somewhere else to live in the meantime. Of course, just because his name was in the will didn't mean he'd get everything. If Clae had any outstanding debts, some things might need to be sold to settle them. He informed them of this in a mechanical tone. Laura suspected he was regurgitating what Elinor told him. As it was, he'd claimed all things in the twins' room as his instead of Clae's, so Elinor had agreed to close the door and ignore everything inside; the crystals would escape notice easily.

"It feels like things are going too well," he said, actually bouncing on the balls of his feet. "Does that make sense?"

"Sometimes you should just accept the good," Mrs. Keedler chuckled.

Okane didn't look convinced. "I feel like I should be making tea for her or something. Is that—But if I give her some now, then I won't have any tea leaves left for when Juliana and Lester show up."

"They have been gone awhile," said Laura, squinting at the windows. "Usually they're early. Of all the days to be late, they're missing out on scones."

She almost wished they wouldn't come at all. Ever since the Sundown infestation, Juliana had seemed . . . off. She kept smiling, kept up the motions, but where she'd been encouraging and almost oversharing before, she became abruptly distant. Lester's graze didn't impede his movement or personality, so that hadn't caused it. Was it frustration over the lack of recovered Gin stones? Had Laura somehow caused it? She'd agonized over it to Morgan, who'd told her that any boss with more talented underlings was on the road to success; a jealous boss who punished talent would only get themselves killed in the Sweeping game, and hadn't Juliana been so eager to do well? Wasn't she a good boss?

"I'll get more tea," said Okane. "The grocery store isn't far."

"But isn't that woman expecting to deal with you?" said Laura.

"She said she'd be upstairs for a while. Just make sure no one else goes up there, and it'll be fine."

"But—"

"Think of this as training. I'm going to run *really* fast."

So he was still hooked on figuring out magic. Better this than flinging himself off rooftops.

Laura sighed. "Do what you want."

Okane made for the door. He leapt from the front stoop with enough force that his magic gave an audible pop. Laura hadn't heard his magic like that except in infestations, so she jumped almost as badly as Mrs. Keedler.

"Oh, dear." Mrs. Keedler blinked down at her teacup. "Did I really hear that?"

"It must've come from upstairs," said Laura.

The MacDanels arrived around ten o'clock, laden with stacks of papers. Almost every day they'd gone in person to appeal to various offices and track down elusive contacts to get things back on track. Juliana's claim to get going as soon as stores opened had been anything but a lie.

"Good morning!" Juliana beamed. "Good weather, isn't it?"

"Sure is," Laura agreed.

Mrs. Keedler looked thrilled. "You're the new Sweepers! I'm Georgia Keedler. It's a pleasure to meet you!"

Juliana looked pleasantly surprised and shook the other woman's hand with gusto. "It's good to meet you too! I'm Juliana MacDanel, the new head Sweeper."

"You're the *head* Sweeper! Good to see another woman in charge," Mrs. Keedler laughed.

"Oh? What are you in charge of?"

"The bakery just up the street. I suppose we're neighbors now!"

They seemed to get along well. Laura watched their conversation with mixed feelings. Juliana wormed her way in everywhere, to the point it was almost scary. No, "intimidating" would be the better word. Good social skills. Lester drifted to the side, still holding the papers. Only one stool remained open but he didn't take it—perhaps he was waiting for Juliana to do so. Mrs. Keedler noticed the seating problem quickly.

"Oh!" She leapt up. "I've taken your chair. There aren't enough in here, I always told him—"

"It's fine!"

"No, I need to be heading back anyway. You know that husband of mine," she added to Laura, rolling her eyes.

"Helpless, that one," Laura drawled.

"Give it another five minutes and he'll be captain of a sinking ship. I'd best get back before the noon crowd comes in. It was good to see and meet you. Thank you for the tea, dear."

Juliana hummed as the door closed behind their guest. "She seems nice enough."

"She's our most sociable neighbor," said Laura. "Have you met the others yet?"

"Only in passing," said Juliana. "Mr. Brecht is . . . a character. And I'm under the impression that the pawnshop owner doesn't like me."

"I get the same impression about myself," said Laura. "They're very supportive of Sweepers, though. If you ever need a hand, they're willing to help."

"Pardon my saying so, but it's a miracle they would be, considering Clae Sinclair's attitude," said Juliana.

Laura shrugged. "He was a surprising person."

"I'm sure he was." Juliana set down her smaller stack of papers and looked around. "Speaking of Sinclairs, where did Okane go?"

"Just down to the grocery store," said Laura. "He ran out of tea."

"Hopefully he'll be back soon. I wanted to check with you two about—Lester, what are you looking at out there?"

Lester started guiltily and looked away from the window. "Nothing."

"It's not nothing if it's caught your attention." She walked to the window and squinted out of it. "Who is that?"

Curious, Laura joined them. Across the street stood a man in a long coat and bowler hat. The style wasn't exactly distinctive, but she was sure she'd seen that exact hat somewhere, and it wasn't Byron's.

It was the Mad Dogs negotiator, who'd spoken to them after the Falling Infestation. He'd brought his mob's Sweepers down to help them and left without any other acknowledgment. More than likely he had something to do with the *Dead Ringer*.

"I've seen him before," said Laura. "I'll take care of him."

She left before the MacDanels could protest. The negotiator looked up as she approached. Laura crossed her arms and hoped she looked properly intimidating.

"Are you the one I have to thank for the media attention?" she asked. "Because if you were looking to help me, all you've managed to do is tarnish my reputation and land me in trouble with the Silver Kings."

"We don't mean to make things difficult for you, Miss Kramer," said the negotiator. "If involvement with the Silver Kings could've been avoided we'd have done it. In fact, I'm not even supposed to be involved here. I'm meant to come and go again rather quickly. If you'd like to chat, you'll need to make an appointment."

She raised a brow. "Really? You're loitering and claiming you're on a tight schedule, all at once?"

The negotiator smiled. "Think of this as a pre-appointment. I'm here to set up a meeting with Lester MacDanel."

Oh, hell no. Laura widened her stance.

"Sorry, but whatever nonsense your coworker at the shooting range implied, there's no connection here. Lester's got no ties to mobs, and I'm not about to let you sink your claws into him."

"Such authority, and no title to back it up," the negotiator chuckled. "Regardless, there's no attempt at recruitment here. Lester's the one who requested I come out."

She faltered. "What?"

"What a mess," the negotiator sighed, checking his watch. "I've been here thirty minutes already. When he walked past earlier he completely ignored me, and now he's peeking out windows but not coming out. Whatever setup this is, it's not very well done."

"What do you mean, Lester set this up?"

"My esteemed colleague came to monitor you at the shooting range. You remember, right? In that 'payoff,' Lester passed him a message asking for us to drop by and wait. No explanation why. We thought this might be the bridge to speaking with you." He looked up and feigned surprise. "Oh, dear. Didn't Mr. Sinclair leave the building not long ago? I wonder who's left inside."

Laura's insides froze. She'd been so focused on the obvious mobster, she hadn't thought about what she was leaving behind. She dashed back in, ignoring his call of "We'll speak with you soon, Miss Kramer!" Juliana wasn't in the main shop. Lester made a noise and moved as if to block her, but Laura was faster. She raced up the stairs, and stopped short in the flat's entryway.

Juliana was in the wider area of the kitchen, smiling. Elinor had placed herself to block the hallway, five feet and three inches of determination, unknowingly protecting the man whose estate she was handling. The pair of them looked alien here. This was a place dominated by the past, by Sweepers; the only people who belonged up here were Okane and Clae. Juliana shouldn't be anywhere near the place where Clae had done headstands and drilled Laura about upcoming jobs, but there she was, usurping his home like she'd done his title. Laura's blood boiled.

"What's going on here?"

The sharpness of her tone made them both jump.

"Oh, Laura!" said Juliana. "Just in time! I was just looking to see if there was some tea left after all."

"And I was asking her to leave," said Elinor. "I believe I made it clear that I was inventorying Mr. Sinclair's estate? Okane Sinclair I'll allow to be here, given that this is his home, but other people coming and going would disrupt the process."

"I'm sorry to interrupt you," said Laura, but she was glaring daggers at Juliana. "*I* believe I made it clear that this isn't Sweeper property, and that Sweepers aren't allowed up here."

Elinor took a step back; she obviously sensed that this was personal territory, and wanted nothing to do with it.

Juliana, on the other hand, looked completely unrepentant. "Sorry! I'm just so used to Puer, I forget Amicae's so much smaller. We always had extra tea or coffee supplies in the back room, but yours is dedicated to the Kin, so I thought perhaps it would be upstairs. Puer had multiple floors, of course."

Of course, because Puer was supposedly better in everything. But how could Juliana, who picked up on the smallest details in her meetings with the Council, have possibly missed such a glaring fact about her own office space? The only conclusion was that she hadn't. Had the MacDanels seriously gone so far as to trick a Mad Dog into playing distraction so they could poke around for whatever Clae left behind?

Laura clenched her hands. She tried to focus all her anger there, leaving her voice calm as she said, "As far as I'm concerned, I should still be head Sweeper, but I think I've handled the Council's decision pretty well. I do appreciate you being here, I recognize you're talented, and I do recognize you as the new boss, but if you keep on with petty little lies, that respect won't be around much longer."

For a moment, absolute loathing flashed over Juliana's face. It was so different from the usual smiling mask that Laura's anger wavered. The smile was back so fast, it seemed almost as if it had never changed.

"What a shame!" Juliana said brightly. "And here I thought we'd begun a wonderful partnership." She kicked the cupboard door closed behind her. "I think it's obvious that I won't find what I'm looking for here. I hope Okane brings back that tea quickly."

She stepped past Laura and headed downstairs.

"I'm sorry you had to see that," Laura muttered.

"I'm not involved, and I have no wish to be," said Elinor. Still, she seemed to relax now that Juliana was gone.

Going back downstairs, Laura found Juliana and Lester bent over their new paperwork. They acted totally normal, as if the whole episode were commonplace. Laura wanted to sit down and start demanding answers. If the negotiator had been so transparent and the *Dead Ringer* so supportive, surely there was some truth in the mobster's words, back at the shooting range? *What deep dark secrets are you hiding? Oh, yes, MacDanel, we heard about that.* In the next moment she scolded herself. Since when did she consider mobsters a trustworthy source of information?

Calm down, she thought, rubbing at her temples. *You're making a bigger deal of this than it needs to be.*

So what if Juliana went upstairs? She hadn't seen anything, hadn't stolen anything. If she'd truly forgotten once, today would reinforce the fact that the Sweeper shop began and ended on one floor. Lesson learned. Time to move on.

Little changed. Okane returned eventually, some conversation was had, and Juliana remained distant. Okane knew immediately that something had happened, and eyed Laura for most of the day. She told him what had happened when the MacDanels and Elinor finally left. Predictably, he didn't like the idea of strangers going upstairs. Laura assured him that she'd made it clear Juliana was unwelcome.

"A little too clear," she grumbled. "I think I overreacted."

Okane scoffed. "They called in a Mad Dog for a distraction. If they had a day and time scheduled for that, obviously they meant to go up there on purpose. They counted on - - - confronting him, but they didn't count on him being so agreeable, or on Elinor already being there. It was premeditated, just poorly executed."

"But that only takes care of me," said Laura. "They couldn't have counted on you running to the grocery store on a whim! What would they have done, if you were still—"

"Why would I be in the shop if - - - were outside?"

"What?"

"- - - have to admit, I tend to follow - - - around," said Okane. "They probably counted on me following - - - to face off with the mobster."

At least they weren't outright belligerent. Still, the entire ordeal left Laura with a sour taste in her mouth.

"I don't even understand why they'd go to such lengths," she said. "What's the point of going behind our backs? We've kept Clae and Anselm totally secret. No one else but Albright and that Byron Rhodes would know about them. From the MacDanels' perspective, there's nothing to chase. Nothing to gain."

"- - - don't know that," said Okane. "Remember what Juliana said that first night? She was positive Clae had a secret weapon. She doesn't know Anselm's form, but she knows something like him exists. Depending on how sure she is, and what she plans to do with it, she could go to great lengths. We can't really guess what she'll do unless we know what she does, though."

"I could ask her," said Laura.

Okane gave her a wary look. "Right after - - - called her out on being a lying, subpar Sweeper?"

Laura flushed. "I'd be worming my way into her good books first, obviously!" Okane remained unconvinced, and she continued, "Give me a chance. Look, tomorrow morning, Elinor will probably show up early, right? And the MacDanels have been late all this week. You stay upstairs with Elinor, and I'll see what damage I can undo with Juliana."

Somehow, she got him to agree. The next morning he led Elinor upstairs again, asking questions on what else estate administrators did beyond inventorying. She didn't seem completely pleased by the distraction, but took it in stride. She likely thought his presence was meant to dissuade any more potential trespassers. It would, of course, but that wasn't the plan. Laura remained in the shop, eyes trained on the windows. She planned to confront Juliana nonchalantly: start by looking up from the newspaper, move into meaningless conversation to warm her up, then act the part of the contrite apprentice. This plan didn't happen.

Juliana burst into the shop almost before Laura even saw her. She came out of breath, totally devoid of paperwork and somehow missing Lester's usual shadow.

"Are they here yet?" she demanded.

"Who?" said Laura.

"The reporters," said Juliana. "We got a call at our apartment this morning, saying they wanted another spotlight. And it's—Oh, goodness, I'm not prepared at all."

She hurried in and tried arranging the stools into a nicer pattern. Laura threw her newspaper in the trash and rushed to clear off the rest of the counter.

"Do you know who? When?"

"The *Sun*," said Juliana. "I told them I'd only be available after nine, so that means they could come through at any minute. Do I look all right? Everything in place? Is there a mirror anywhere?"

Laura had been attempting to stow the largest of the extra Kin flasks under the counter, but paused. She scrubbed at the flask with her sleeve until it shone again and said, "Will this work?"

Juliana stooped lower to see it and sighed in relief. "That'll do nicely. Do you have any experience with the *Sun*'s reporters?"

"A little," said Laura. "The reporter I met was supportive of Sweepers even before it was popular. They've been here before, back when it was all cluttered, so you don't have to worry about them accusing you of being unorganized. You're still in the process of moving in. They can't expect you to have everything whipped into shape already."

For a moment Juliana was silent, but then she gave a soft laugh. "Of course. I keep thinking I have to put my best foot forward, but some things just aren't physically possible."

"I wouldn't worry about it too much. The papers already love you," said Laura. "But I thought you'd already had a spotlight in the *Sun*. Didn't you speak with a reporter then?"

"Not directly. The Amicae representative who interviewed me had the list of questions with him, and brought it back to Amicae when he left."

Still, she seemed to have calmed down significantly. Laura watched her re-pin her hair, debating before finally asking, "Why did you really go upstairs yesterday?"

Juliana's hands stilled. "Haven't I said it already? I got a little turned around. Puer's second floor is a storage area."

"If this one was Sweeper property, we'd have given you a tour."

Juliana's mouth quirked. "Really? Because it sounds as if there's an armory I haven't been to."

Laura winced. "Honestly, not even Clae talked about it. I didn't know it existed until just yesterday."

Juliana huffed and went back to smoothing out her hair. "You didn't expect him to keep all his gear in a tiny office like this, did you?"

"Well."

Juliana looked up at her, wide-eyed. "Oh my god, you really thought that."

"I thought he brought equipment here as soon as factories produced it," Laura admitted. "In retrospect it doesn't make sense, and he did talk about storage once, but I never put much thought into it."

"So he didn't tell you everything," said Juliana, pensive.

"There wasn't much time to. I only joined Sinclairs in May."

At this, Juliana straightened very slowly. "Eight *months* ago? Not years?"

"You don't have to sound so scandalized."

"Eight months," Juliana repeated, as if in a daze. "I'm . . . I'm impressed. I'm sure you met some of the apprentices in Puer when you visited. Some of them have come from long-established Sweeper families, and you easily outshine them."

She fell into contemplative silence. While not in the plan, that exchange served well enough as "small talk." Laura didn't have her answer yet, but maybe . . .

"I'm sorry for what I said yesterday."

Juliana's head tilted. "What?"

"For accusing you of lying and everything. It was rude and uncalled for. I just get really protective over this place. Amicae practically crushed Sweepers out of existence, and Okane . . . well. We've got good reason not to trust people. It's not easy to put that behind me, and I didn't think before I acted. You are a fantastic Sweeper—if you weren't, you wouldn't have this position. And I know you're very intelligent, and dedicated to doing the job right. You've already lost someone, so you know the gravity of this work, and it's easy to tell that you're dedicated to not letting that happen again. I want to trust you, but I can't do that if you're not honest with me and I don't know what you're doing."

For a while they simply looked at each other. The longer time dragged on the more Laura wanted to take back what she'd said. It had come out more honest than anticipated. Juliana sighed. She pushed the glass flask aside and took Laura's hand in both of hers.

"Tell me, Laura, why did you become a Sweeper? You were old enough not to be wheedled into it, and Amicae is hardly the place to glorify the job."

"I've wanted to be a Sweeper since I was little." Laura shrugged self-consciously. "It just took a while before I realized it was something I *could* do."

Juliana paused again, regarded her solemnly before saying, bluntly, "Clae Sinclair had some kind of secret to his Sweeping. Unless he was literally birthed from the heavens, there's no other explanation. Before he died, your kin was a hell of a lot stronger, wasn't it? And once he died, it faded. It was obvious just by your reactions in that fight. Did he ever tell you what that kin secret was?"

Do not tell anyone about him. Disastrous consequences.

"No," said Laura.

"Was there anything here that he was particularly protective over?"

"Everything," Laura snorted, but gestured back at the black drapes. "Mainly he obsessed over the storage room, since that's where the Gin is stored. The setup hasn't changed since he died, though. Okane walked me through the system and he didn't think anything was missing."

Juliana's eyes glinted. She leaned closer and said, "Perhaps it's something the family itself keeps close? A Sinclair secret?"

"As far as Clae was concerned, any of his Sweepers were Sinclair enough to be in his good books."

Juliana waved a hand. "That doesn't mean much. Some of these well-established guilds are built around families, just like the upper class, and just like the upper class they see their core members as the only real heirs to their secrets. Dea's Sweeper family won't even let in-laws handle their kin recipes. If Amicae's Sweepers go so far as to slap their name over the office, then surely they're believers in the bloodline?"

"Clae was the last Sinclair left, and he knew it. He wouldn't jeopardize the city by sitting on that kind of information."

"Wall," Juliana said simply.

"That had punishment of death if we talked," Laura snapped. "Sinclairs tried. Sinclairs failed. Clae did everything he could within his boundaries."

"I don't doubt his intentions or yours. But if there were boundaries set by the city, maybe there were boundaries that existed in his mind and not in yours. I thought if there was a family secret, it would be located in a place only the family had access to. That's why I went upstairs yesterday."

"I've been up there a few times, and Clae was never protective of the house," said Laura.

Juliana's eyes flicked up toward the ceiling as a board overhead creaked. "Then perhaps it's a secret held by a person instead of a page. An oral tradition."

"Okane's never mentioned—"

"He's a Sinclair. Of course he wouldn't have given that information freely. But if you asked him directly . . ."

Laura drew back, frowning. "Me?"

"He trusts you, doesn't he? More than anyone else. If I asked he'd never answer, but you? If you wanted to I'm sure you could make him tell you anything. Could you do that for me?"

A chill ran down Laura's spine, but she pretended to laugh. "Are you telling me to manipulate Okane?"

"You've got him wrapped around your finger! And don't worry

about thinking you're taking advantage of him. We're going to use that secret to protect this city, and protect him too. He's still our teammate. He doesn't risk losing that by talking."

Juliana smiled warmly, and Laura did her best to mimic the gesture. She felt sick.

"I'll ask him," she said. "But for the record, I'm positive that he has no idea what the secret is either. If he did, he would've implemented it already."

Juliana clapped a hand on her shoulder. "That's my girl. We'll get this office in shape, just you watch."

And now someone was calling her "girl" again. Laura barely had time to feel frustrated before footsteps sounded on the stairs. Juliana drew back as Okane appeared on the landing.

"I just looked out the window," he said. "Is there a reason Lester's leading someone with a camera?"

"The reporter!" Juliana gasped. She straightened and patted down her clothes, as if they'd somehow come out of place during that short conversation. "We're expecting them. Come on out, Okane! They'll be happy to see other Sweepers."

The door creaked open. Lester entered first, carrying a paper bag and chatting amiably with the two people behind him.

"Oh!" Laura leapt to her feet. "Annabelle!"

Reporter Annabelle Kilborn paused in the doorway. "Good morning! It's good to see you again."

"Likewise," said Laura. "I knew a reporter was coming, but I wasn't expecting you. I didn't realize you did spotlights."

"My coworkers decided I had the most experience with positive Sweeper articles," said Annabelle.

"Well, we're glad to have you," said Juliana. "It's a pleasure to meet you."

She and Annabelle shook hands, and Annabelle turned to introduce her cameraman. Lester stepped to the counter. Out of the bag came several bottles of vividly orange Fezziwig soda.

"Sorry for the surprise," he told Laura and Okane. "It was a last-minute offer and Juliana's eager to get on the public's good side right now. It'll give us more sway in negotiations. I hoped delaying them a little would give you some time to prepare."

"I appreciate it," said Laura, taking one of the offered sodas.

She popped off the cap and took a long drink as the others settled themselves. The cameraman snapped a picture of Juliana before pulling back. Annabelle and the MacDanels took the remaining stools, and Annabelle began reading out a prepared list of questions.

"So," Okane whispered, eyes still fixed on the interview, "did - - - find anything out?"

"Not much beyond what we already knew," Laura replied. "She knows something's here, and she thinks you, as the last remaining family member, have the secret. Like an oral tradition. She wants me to trick it out of you."

"I figured as much. What do - - - want to do from here?"

"Carry on?" Laura shrugged. "I don't know that there's anything we can do. I'll tell her you didn't know anything, she'll suck it up, and we'll move on. Hopefully for the better."

She refocused on the interview. Annabelle had moved on from the basic introduction, and gone on to ask about Juliana's previous Sweeping experience. Juliana had laughed through the tale of her and Lester signing up as apprentices at age fifteen, and now went into Amicae's selection process.

"You know, I wasn't even the person they were supposed to interview that day. It was totally luck."

Annabelle paused. "You weren't Puer's recommended choice?"

"No, the head Sweeper there was very intent on sending you someone named Joan," said Juliana. "Joan's good, but I wouldn't call her fantastic. If you put her in power she wouldn't know how to use it. She ran so late for her interview, the Amicae representative almost left, but my brother caught him in time and asked if I could interview instead. They were so eager to talk to me, I was flattered! And when they said my old boss spoke so highly of me, I almost cried. Some men in charge are determined never to compliment you to your face, so hearing that—"

Okane glanced at Laura. "Joseph Blair didn't strike me as someone who withheld compliments."

"No," Laura murmured. "I don't think I heard him speak badly of anyone, even when he was stuck between the Sinclairs."

Even at Clae's wake, Puer's head Sweeper had admitted his wife's guilt but tried to defend her at the same time. Laura thought back, trying to match any instance to Juliana's statement, and something occurred to her. Joseph had said he'd send a Sweeper to help them keep up basic training. Laura had assumed he meant Juliana, but it must've been Joan. Laura pulled one of the *Dead Ringer* pages back from under the counter and uncapped a pen.

Meanwhile, Annabelle had taken this in stride. "So you outshined even your city's first pick. How does it feel to be the top Sweeper in Amicae?"

"It's been a whirlwind so far," Juliana chuckled. "It's very different here than Puer. Clae Sinclair left little more than a shell of what a proper department should be."

Blame the goddamn Council, not Clae, Laura wanted to rage, but kept her mouth shut and focused harder on her writing.

"We're in the process of putting things back together and making improvements, so the citizens of Amicae won't have to fear anymore. Their safety won't be determined by a capricious head Sweeper or the whims of the mobs. It will be done professionally, promptly, under the Council's authority."

Words couldn't describe how much Laura wanted to kick over Juliana's stool. She jabbed her note extra hard at the end and tore the piece off its page. She slid this toward Okane. He squinted down at the message:

To Melody Dearborn—Are MacDanels approved?

"What's this?" he whispered.

"A telegram I want you to send," she replied just as quietly. "This whole situation stinks, and I want to understand what's going on. I trust Melody to give us a straight answer."

"I suppose if Juliana suspects - - - of sending messages, that wouldn't go over well." He slipped the note into his pocket. He paused, and she raised a brow.

"What's wrong?"

"I just wondered whether she's really the one to worry about."

Laura looked back at the others. On the other side of the room Lester sat in silence, a pack of notes resting on one knee. If he'd tried using the Mad Dogs as a harebrained distraction once, there was no telling what else he'd do to support Juliana. Laura hoped he wasn't stupid enough to involve himself deeper in the mobs, but he was like Juliana's shadow, almost impossible to get a read on. Even now there was little trace of emotion or individuality on his face. He simply watched, with frightening intensity, as Juliana chatted her way through her next answer.

5

THE KEY KEEPER

The armory was located on a street called Fortore. The wide paved road and well-kept sidewalks marked it as a frequented route, but it held none of the clamor and traffic of a thoroughfare like Tiber or Acis. The quiet street hugged closer to the interior wall of the Third Quarter, its upscale location reflecting this in the form of tidy buildings, mostly residential but dotted with quaint shops. The armory building, obvious due to polished metal numbers on the front, stood three stories tall, three buildings in from a corner whose crossing street bore the lines of a trolley route.

The armory looked nothing like what Laura had pictured. It wasn't in the Gothic style, of brick and barred windows, and it sat unassumingly between an apartment building and an upscale restaurant, perfectly painted a dark charcoal color with windows made of multicolored glass. The bottom level had no door but a garage wide enough to hold two automobiles. The proper door to the second floor required climbing a flight of decorative metal stairs on the outside of the building, between it and the rosy brick apartments. Small gingerbread patterns lined the edge of the sloped roof.

Laura surveyed this all from the other side of the street, studying the windows, then the apartments, then the restaurant's sign advertising the best teccinia in the city, then looking back at the armory.

"It looks like a weird house," she commented at last.

"It's nicer than the shop." Okane scratched his nose as he took in the sight. "Aren't satellite locations supposed to be lesser quality?"

"You'd think."

They eyed the building a while longer. Laura knew from frequent checking of her pocket watch that it was 10:00 A.M. Okane had arranged for them to meet with Elinor here any moment now; with Laura holding the only key to the premises, there was no other way for their estate administrator to continue her job. Laura felt around in her coat pocket and turned the key over in her fingers. No modern keys had hooks or spirals, but it matched the shape drawn in Clae's letter, and Okane had confirmed that it was a key of some sort. A key for the armory and whatever was in that box.

"So how does this work? Just like a normal key?"

Okane shrugged. "I only remember people carrying them, not how they work. Maybe it turns the other way? Or maybe it doesn't even turn?" He muddled this over, and Laura spotted the last person of their group.

Elinor turned the corner and walked along the path, past the restaurant. The Sweepers crossed the street to meet her.

"Hello," Laura greeted.

"Hello." Elinor didn't face her; instead, she squinted up at the building in question. "This is the armory?"

"Judging by the numbers, yes."

"Haven't you been here before?"

"Actually, I never even knew this place existed."

"It's in his name," Elinor muttered, opening her folder to check the print inside. "Someone else has been helping pay for expenses on it. It's been repainted in the time since his death."

"It has?" The paint looked immaculate, so Laura shouldn't have been surprised.

"We'll have to track that person down eventually. In the meantime, let's see the inside."

No one moved. Elinor had no key but looked to Okane, Okane watched Laura for what to do, and Laura came to the conclusion she'd have to play leader.

"Come on, then," she grumbled.

The metal staircase was black, the railing wrought with designs of blooming flowers and curling vines that shone dimly in the morning light. Despite the spring décor, the metal chilled Laura's hand as she climbed the stairs. Every step produced a loud retort, and the trio made a racket all the way up to the door, which loomed vaguely purple though a coat of black had been painted over it, bronzy knob and strangely shaped keyhole glinting bright in contrast.

Laura pulled out the key, eyed the curl, and leaned in to inspect the keyhole on the door. Thin, rectangular, looked the same size. She tried to fit the key, and it slid in easily. As soon as it fit, a click sounded from inside. The key froze in place, then wrenched ninety degrees to the right, one-eighty to the left, one-eighty right again, and back to its original position. At the first twist Laura tried to jerk back, but her fingers stayed glued to the key. She couldn't let go. Groaning and clicking came from the door, as if tumblers moved throughout its entire structure. Eventually an odd pop sounded, and the door bounced ajar as if bumped off its threshold. Laura snatched her hand away as soon as she felt the pressure vanish.

"What kind of freakish machine is this?"

Okane had been eyeing the door dubiously, but looked at her in concern. "What do - - - mean?"

"It grabbed my hand or something. I couldn't let go of the key." She rubbed the hand in question, rueful.

"Is it okay?"

"Fine."

Embarrassed, she kicked the door open further. It swung open with a groan. The room beyond was mostly dark, though pale blue and yellow lights glowed in its recesses. They squinted in.

"Do - - - think there's a light switch?"

"Probably. Where are the windows, though? I swear there should be windows."

"If you go inside, you might find the lights," Elinor pointed out.

Laura stepped in, reaching to the right in search of a switch. She found a wooden shelf laden with glass objects she realized were Eggs. While she pondered this Okane walked farther in, and everything brightened dramatically. A multitude of tiny, circular glass lanterns of various colors spanned the ceiling, each slightly bigger than an Egg, so densely packed they hid the ceiling entirely with their glass, metal, and chains. The scattered colors illuminated reinforced shelves upon shelves of Eggs both empty and full that reached from floor to ceiling. Most bore Eggs in rows, though one set of shelves on the left wall contained Pit Egg–size equipment, the parts not yet fit together, along with tiny capsules filled with blue. Laura approached this shelf and picked one up.

"These again," she murmured. "What are they?"

"They're called Sinkers."

Everyone jumped. Laura scrambled not to drop the capsule, Okane backed up into a shelf and rattled the Eggs, and Elinor gasped and clapped a hand to her chest. The newcomer snickered at their reaction. A woman stepped farther into the room—a brunette with gray eyes, a skinny frame, and a limp that made her skirt swish more than normal. Her hair hung longer on the left side of her face, and she pulled this back to reveal nasty scarring along her cheek, just missing the eye and reducing the ear to little more than a shriveled lump. These scars crinkled as she grinned.

"Wondered when you two would stop by."

She spoke as if they were familiar, and she *looked* familiar. After a moment Laura recognized her as the one-eared woman who'd been at Clae's wake.

"Who are you?" Elinor demanded.

"Name's Amelia. Amelia Huxley, ex-Sweeper. I'm the armory's warden these days. And you two—" She stepped closer. Laura happened to be nearest of the two Sweepers, so she reached her first to shake hands with a firm grip. "You're the ex-apprentices! Congrats on the promotion! And the un-promotion. Wow. Shame about the circumstances."

"I think I saw you at the potluck?" Laura smiled weakly. Was this one of Clae's apprentices? As far as she could tell, it was a rare one that hadn't died on the job.

"I knew the Sinclairs pretty well. I was his dad's apprentice, so I've known Clae since he was tiny. It's weird thinking he trained some fully fledged Sweepers of his own."

She ruffled their hair with the kind of fondness Morgan used. Laura wasn't sure what to think of it. Okane immediately leaned away from the woman's hand. Amelia snorted.

"Sorry." She pulled her hands away and folded them together. "I'm a touchy person. Most people are used to it, so I keep forgetting around strangers. Anyway, I'm not officially a Sweeper but I'm counted as part of the department and I know the lingo. If you need help with anything, be it advice, equipment"—she tilted her head toward the Sinkers—"you name it, feel free to call me. My number should be pinned up next to the telephone back at the shop. If that doesn't work, throw something at my window. It's right next to the door here."

True enough, there was an open window in the apartment building, directly on the level of the railing. Had Amelia jumped over?

"Are you the one who had this building painted?" asked Elinor.

"It was due for a repaint. Got to keep up to a certain image in this neighborhood. Besides, I thought we might want to impress the new head Sweeper."

"And you paid for the painting yourself?" Elinor frowned.

"That was the deal: I get to store things in here, but I have to pay for upkeep."

"You store things here?" Laura echoed, confused.

"I've got an automobile downstairs, some furniture upstairs. More incentive to keep an eye on the place."

Elinor looked annoyed; this probably made everything more complicated. "You'll have to list your possessions in detail."

While not the politest person in the world, Amelia seemed very genuine, and the simple fact that she'd been mentioned in Clae's letter put Laura more at ease. She held up the blue capsule and prompted, "You said this was a Sinker?"

"Yep." Amelia tapped it lightly with her finger. "I'm not surprised you don't know about it. It's a last-resort type of thing because it smashes the root amulets to bits. We don't want Sweepers smashing amulets all over the place, so apprentices get regular Eggs drilled into their heads so they don't just rely on Sinkers. Some other cities don't even make them, they're so dangerous."

Elinor's frown deepened. "Do you not know about all the equipment?"

"Apparently not," Laura mumbled, somewhat ashamed. Some expert she turned out to be.

"She still knows a lot more than I do," Okane pointed out.

"That won't help determine the value of anything."

"You're trying to put a price on this?" Amelia laughed.

"That's my job," Elinor retorted. "I'm inventorying the estate of Clae Sinclair, so I need to know the value of his possessions."

"Then I'm your girl!" Amelia laughed. "I know everything in here. What was his, what was city property, what's mine. I can give you a rundown on anything you're not familiar with, too."

"That'd be wonderful." Laura cracked a smile, which Amelia returned enthusiastically.

"Please do so," Elinor sighed, rolling her eyes in resignation.

"Right! Well, this building is Sinclair family property. So are the lights"—she pointed at the lantern-strewn ceiling—"and the door and built-in mechanics. Those are specially worked in with Gin amulets, so they're useless unless you sell the whole shebang, in which case it's priceless."

"Priceless?" Okane gave the lanterns a skeptical look. They did look cheap.

"This is actually a complex system to keep the armory secure. You have the key and you're authorized. Otherwise you'd get nasty magic backlash and the building would go into lockdown, in which case it seals itself up and gets impossible to crack. If somebody unauthorized with the key gets in, it goes on semi-lockdown and sends a distress signal to registered Sweeper rings."

"Is that a spell?" Laura asked.

"One of the very few that can be utilized, and only by certain people," Amelia replied.

Okane shifted his weight uneasily, and she decided that "certain people" meant Magi.

"And the other objects in this room?" Elinor was writing on a pad.

"The Eggs are all city-owned. Council money pays for them. If you'll follow me."

Amelia led them through another doorway, into a much larger room that took up the rest of the floor. As they entered, a grand rectangular lantern flared bright pink in the middle of the ceiling, flanked by miniature versions in the corners. On the far wall were doors to two staircases, left one going down, right up. The left wall bore shutters for the windows, and strewn all over in a vaguely organized mess lay Sweeper weapons. Guns, cases of bullets, Bijou, empty Eggs, staffs of varying sizes with patterns carved into them, more staffs topped with enormous nets, bows and arrows, lightweight armor with intricate designs, bandoliers, bags and belts and straps, and worn trunks whose weathered locks hid smaller troves of gear. All of this lay scattered over tables and floor, though many staffs were propped up in a rack. Pinned to the walls between framed pictures Laura could see scraps of paper, articles, more photographs, stray leaves and ribbons from events over the years.

"I'm sure this is what you're most interested in." Amelia leaned over a table full of gauntlets to yank the shutters open.

Colored light spilled in, brightening the room further, glinting over the metallic pieces and lending a festive atmosphere. Even full of weapons the place seemed bright and welcoming. Okane wandered to the middle of the room and turned slowly in place, taking it all in.

"This is amazing," he breathed.

"The Sinclairs got to be pack rats when it came to supplies. I could've sworn at one point I saw old Rosemarie stockpiling food, too," Amelia laughed. "I haven't seen half of this used, but they clung to it all just in case. Maybe they expected a Sweeper revival?"

Laura picked her way around spools of wire to inspect the rack of staffs. She lifted one and found it lighter than expected, though top-heavy with the gnarled end.

"I saw one of the Puer Sweepers using this. What is it?"

"It's a staff. Pretty self-explanatory, right? It's got Gin on top so you can use it like a spear, and then there's the fog it creates when active. That protects you, since you have to get up close and personal to use it. The nets work the same way," Amelia explained.

"There are a lot of them."

"Used to be a Sinclair specialty. Clae and Anselm—you know he had a brother, right?—they had their own staffs, and Clae used his until he got to be head Sweeper. It's the little one on your right, with the crappy writing on it. After Anselm died he got skittish and wanted distance, so he switched over to guns. Speaking of which, these rifles—"

She kept going, but Laura turned away to look for Clae's staff. She found it easily, as it happened to be one of the two smallest and actually had his name sloppily carved into it. She picked it up in one hand and raised it to get a better look at the carvings.

"How do - - - think it works?" Okane lifted the one with Anselm's name and weighed it in his hands.

Laura pursed her lips and angled her staff so it clacked against the other like a wooden sword. "Like that?"

"They're in good condition for that kind of treatment."

Amelia kept talking to Elinor, who drank in all the information and jotted notes. Laura gleaned from the chatter that nothing in here would be easy to price, and once you gave a price, that could easily be changed: the whole was far more than the sum of its parts, but to Amicae citizens it would only be junk, and if you tried selling it to other Sweepers they'd pretend it was all garbage and only pay a fraction of its real value. With no way to sell them fairly, they were most valuable to Amicae as they were.

Laura drifted over to the doors. The left-hand door wouldn't open, but the right one swung open easily and soundlessly. Laura started up the stairs.

"Should - - - really be doing that?" Okane whispered.

"He gave me the key, didn't he?" said Laura. "And it's your building now. Why not check it out?"

He glanced back at the others before shaking his head. "Fine, but let's be fast. I don't want them to think we're sneaking."

The next floor had no walls or separate rooms, but the entire expanse stretched open for the length of the building. More lanterns lit the room, illuminating scattered mounds of covered furniture. Laura looked around, a smile slowly forming.

"Hey, Okane. Don't you think the Kin could fit in here?"

It took a moment for him to catch her drift, to understand that yes, this was a Sweeper building with limited access and a potential ally already keeping guard. He began to nod. "Yes. . . . Yes, I think it would."

6

CHIMNEY SMOKING

"How much for a paper?"

A paperboy looked up from his stack and said flatly, "Five argents."

"That's almost double the old price," Laura grumbled, but dutifully searched through her coin purse. "Why the increase?"

"It's getting dangerous." He shrugged. "Did you hear the *Dead Ringer* got bombed by the mobs? Most papers are hiring more protection, and need some way to pay for it. The little papers would've closed up entirely, but our news got popular in other cities. Bigger market than we've ever had before."

"What's gotten other cities so interested?" said Okane.

"Probably the fact that the walls don't do shit. Boss says Amicae's reactions are better than films these days. Maybe it's entertainment. Maybe they're waiting for more monsters."

"I don't suppose Sweepers are buying these?" said Laura.

"Some of our biggest customers. You know Vir Sweepers? Awful people. Their head Sweeper called and just about bit Boss's head off because the train didn't bother to keep their papers out of the rain."

The extra audience was daunting, but Laura still felt comforted. If Sweepers monitored Amicae, they'd be ready to jump into action at the slightest hint of trouble. Amicae could avoid another Falling Infestation.

"Speaking of Sweepers . . ." The paperboy squinted from her payment to her face. "Have I seen you before?"

"Sure you have," said Laura, unfolding her new paper. "Haven't you heard? I'm a Sweeper myself. Apparently I'm a problem child."

"- - - sound a little too pleased about that," said Okane, as they turned away from the stall.

"I just did a little remembering. Wasn't that Clae's favorite expression? It's better to be a pain than a comfort."

"I don't think Juliana will appreciate that sentiment."

Laura snorted, flipping the page. Her mood plummeted as she found the headline: REXIAN FORCES SIGHTED EAST OF VIR.

"Oh, great. They're still on the move."

"We never did find that last Rexian Sweeper," Okane murmured. "You know, the one from the infestation?"

"The mobs sheltered him, but they also actively worked against his goals," Laura recalled. "I doubt they're helping him now. He might be dead in a gutter." Okane made a disbelieving noise and she raised a brow. "What, do you know something?"

"I—well—no. I've just been looking into Rex more, since they're supposedly targeting us. Reading's slow, but Brecht has filled me in on some of their history and politics. They're a bit more than a boogeyman."

Rex wasn't simply scary because of its frequent attacks on neighbors, though stories and pictures coming out of ransacked satellite towns made even the toughest men wince. A deeper problem wound through these stories and twined deep into the city like a disease. Few outsiders glimpsed Rex's interior, and fewer escaped to speak of it.

To Laura's knowledge only a couple of Carmen citizens, lured in to discuss some treaty, had ever made it out again. But, Carmen being a city dedicated to films, it was only a matter of time before it depicted the event. Laura had asked Clae to see the film with her. Rex supposedly had the biggest, toughest Sweeper force in Orien; being starved of any Sweeper content in current media made her eager for anything, and surely seeing a film with an expert on the subject could be fun. She expected him to at least gripe about whatever effects they used for the Sweeping. He'd looked at her a long time without saying anything before finally agreeing. In retrospect she really should've expected what she got; no one could watch anything related to Rex and expect *entertainment.* The film had been given a tame rating, but just because it showed no blood didn't mean it wasn't horrifying.

It followed the tale of the treaty, with Carmen's mob-run officials arriving in Rex, and it seemed at first that these schemers were the villains and Rex was a paradise. The entire city gleamed, triumphant with great arches and statues and beautiful people who greeted them with songs and gifts.

"Is this a single family they've turned out?" wondered a Carmenian, the first man in the film to notice strangeness. "All these people look remarkably similar."

The others laughed at him and brought the delegates to a lavish hotel, where still more smiling Rexians waited on them hand and foot. One of the servers related to them the history of Rex: how it was among the first cities fortified after the spread of infestation, meant for the king of Zyra to live in, but how that king had spurned them to live in Litus instead. From there they delved deeper, uncovering more and more truths that cracked their perfect image. They met a pregnant twelve-year-old with no husband, who proudly told them that her child belonged to none but glorious Rex itself. Shopkeepers smiled to their faces but washed down anything they touched or even threw the offending item in a fire after they'd passed. The Black Guard constantly followed them, spiriting away anyone not *properly accommodating.* It became clear that all the beauty and hospitality was a façade. Their hosts offered prostitutes, ten women all identical, and here the Carmenian broke and demanded an explanation. Where were the other people? Where were the Ralurians, the Ashain, the Kalu, the natives? The Rexians replied that there weren't any. Why should they allow such trash within their walls? Only Zyrans mattered. Zyrans were the only true human species. Any others were accidental, subhuman offshoots that could only smother the blossoming of glorious Zyrans. Glorious Rex.

The film continued to explain how, back when the walls had gone up and the people clustered together for protection, they'd sought to purge weakness. They attacked the natives with a vengeance, and at that time the Ralurians, Ashain, and Kalu did the same. But then they turned to the Ralurians, denounced their supposed weakness, threw them, too, into the fires, into the mines, into the gaping maw of infestations. Then came the Ashain. Then came the Kalu. Until it was only Zyrans, and then they had to seek out new cities to "convert." *You should be honored,* they spat at the Carmenians, *that we stooped low enough to tolerate your filth.* Because the Carmenians were Zyran, but not Zyran enough. They fled, and lost three of their number before escaping the gates. The film ended with an aged professor, tapping his finger atop an ancient skull.

Many people fall into the trap of sympathizing with Rex, he said. *Perhaps they feel threatened by other nationalities or beliefs, either due to city policy, or even the simple and silly matter of race. They think it better to repress another group to bolster their own. A classic tactic of power is to unite a group against another, because it's easiest to impress rules on a willing public under such "wartime" conditions. I ask you, though, is unification against true monsters not enough? Furthermore, once you have eradicated the so-called lesser group, will you be satisfied, or will you insist on continuing to eat yourself?*

Allow me to be frank. This is not a matter of race. This is a matter of irrational hatred. There has never been any kind of scientific proof or reasoning to suggest that any race is anything less than human. Indeed, the mere notion only originated in cases where one group wishes to feel validated in their mistreatment of another. We are all human, and the hallmark of humanity is empathy. Embracing our diversity is not only the key to advancement, but the key to survival.

For Orien to be truly great, all cities must stand together. If any group can be viewed as subhuman, it is Rex itself, but not for any reason of race. It is their ideology. They know no peace, and bring only pain and hatred to others. They have rejected empathy and rejected survival. They have become their own destruction.

In the here and now, Laura couldn't condense all of that into something simple beyond, "They're scary."

"They are. It makes me doubt they'd die so easily," said Okane.

By now they'd reached the Sweeper shop. The windows were dark; as hoped, the MacDanels hadn't arrived yet this morning. Laura unlocked the door and gathered the mail, tossed the paper down and sifted through the envelopes.

Over half were addressed to "Head Sweeper Laura Kramer," from various Sweeper guilds. The Vir contact had actually written it in capital letters. It made a lump form in her throat. In the short time she'd been head Sweeper she'd sent letters out to all of them after pawing through every newspaper she could get her hands on to determine how each city stood. The letters had been specially tailored. She'd been proud of them. She hadn't gotten to read a single reply since being booted from the position. Anything labeled "Head Sweeper" was for Juliana. God, there was even one from Coronae. She wanted more than anything to open it. Her fingers held tight enough to crinkle the return address, but she forced herself to discard it. She searched through the rest, and was discouraged to find absolutely nothing from Puer, to "Head Sweeper" or otherwise.

Meanwhile, Okane had pulled the newspaper closer and now studied the Rex article, brow furrowed. A long lock of hair slipped into his face. His eyes remained fixed on the print, but he gave a puff of air. The lock buffeted some before sliding still further into his vision.

"Your ponytail's loose," she pointed out.

"I'm aware."

He seemed dead set on reading his way through the article's entirety, which would take a while. Laura sighed.

"Can I braid your hair?"

"What?" He blinked at her.

"Braid."

Okane jerked his head in a nod and turned back slightly, not enough to let her leave his sight, but enough that she had easy access to his hair. She gathered it up and combed her fingers through. She encountered snarls and tugged lightly to work them out. He winced.

"Sorry."

"It's fine."

Laura studied the hair in her hands as she worked out the knots and separated it into three parts. As she began braiding, she asked, "I've been wondering, why do you keep this so long? It's not exactly uncommon, but—Is it a Magi thing? Clae's letter was about Magi, right?"

"It was. I don't know anything about Magi fashion, though," said Okane. "I just feel better with it. My hair is the one thing Sullivan never got interested in. It was the only thing I had full control over. I'm still a little loath to let go of it."

"Don't hurry on my account," said Laura. "I was just curious. What about the 'you' thing? Did Clae's letter mention that?"

"The what?" Okane questioned, tilting his head to see her better.

"You know, why you don't say it. Clae said something about it being your magic, but isn't that a waste? Why that of all things?"

"We *can* say it, just a different way," said Okane.

"But physically?"

"I've never tried. I never felt the need to. Mama said the word is stronger this way. More . . . more personal." He dropped off into silence. Laura hummed to show she got the idea, pinching the end of the braid with one hand while she dug into her pocket for a spare hair tie. Okane's hair twisted as he turned his head again to blink at her. She met his eyes, waiting for him to say something, but he didn't.

Realization crossed his face, and his brow furrowed. "- - -'re not listening to it."

Had he been saying "you" without her notice? "Once I knew about it I started paying more attention, and now I just don't hear it at all."

Okane changed direction to face her fully.

"(*You*)."

His mouth didn't move, but the word rang in Laura's ears. It was strong, loud, authoritative and direct, with a timbre that reverberated in her core. She inhaled sharply.

"What the—"

"Sorry." Okane leaned back again, concentration melting into surprise and some shame. "I was afraid - - -'d ignore it otherwise."

"What did you *do*?"

"I focused. I suppose it was kind of like yelling?"

"You yelled at me?"

"I wanted - - - to hear it."

"I definitely heard it." Laura put a hand over her heart, still unsettled.

"Sorry," he repeated. "But do - - - get what I mean? How it's personal? Special?"

When he put it that way, she supposed it did feel kind of special. Some weird emotional power directed entirely at her.

"I think?"

"Mama said it was genuine. People treasured it, from what I remember. The emphasis gives respect and sincerity. It's the sound of honesty. It's impossible to lie through the implication."

After a moment of hesitation she took up his hair again, sighing, "I wish there was a tip-off like that in regular speech. I'd love to know for sure what Juliana's thinking."

Of course, the MacDanels came in at this exact moment. Luckily they were already talking, so they didn't catch Laura's comment.

"We've got reports from the Council," Juliana said, stumbling in with five massive books. "I'll tell you all ab—oh, what have we here? I hope we haven't interrupted?"

"- - - haven't," said Okane.

"We're just discussing new ways to keep his hair out of his face," said Laura. "What were you saying?"

"Just more dealings with the Council." She set the books down, and Lester pulled one aside and opened it. It wasn't a book at all but handwritten notes, and Laura found herself gaping. Had Juliana written all of that? "We've finally got them to agree to raise the Sweeper budget."

"You don't sound happy with that," said Laura.

Juliana grimaced. "It's something, but they're not raising it by much. The way I see it, we have to double the budget or we'll fail. There's barely enough to pay all four of us as is. They're raising it by . . . how did you put it, Lester?"

"One-twenty-fifth," said Lester. "Something like zero point zero four percent."

"That's bullshit," said Laura, finally tying off the braid.

"They seem to think it's perfectly reasonable," said Juliana, shaking her head. "Every time I try to tell them it's madness, they come back saying 'the Sinclairs managed it like this,' and I keep having to tell them—god, it sounds so heartless—that their refusal to help strangled Clae Sinclair, and if he had the proper resources we'd never have this mess to start with. In the interview they were excited about what I had to say, but when it came to implementing ideas they shot everything down. Literally none of them had anything good to say about Sinclair beyond 'he could work on a limited budget.' And you know the worst of it? They kept addressing all their questions to him!"

She gestured violently at Lester.

"Seriously?" said Laura.

"Every time I said something, they replied to him, too," said Juliana, voice gradually rising. "It was like I wasn't even there. What do they think I am, a puppet? I can speak for myself! He's not the brains behind this! I'm the head Sweeper here! I got the interview! I'm the one they hired! I deserve this!"

"We know that," said Lester. "You're in charge."

Juliana had been working herself into a frenzy, but at his words she paused.

"Yes," she said distantly. "I'm in charge."

She slowly deflated, and while the redness didn't totally leave her face, it receded to a healthy flush.

"Do you have another plan?" Laura asked hesitantly. "We can tell you as much as we know about how we worked in here, but budget—"

"I'm hoping to get information from the police about previous exterminations," said Juliana. "An idea of how much equipment was used, damages, lives taken, anything I can build into a graph and put prices on. That way I can slap those councilmen in the face with hard facts."

Laura might not have trusted her with the Sinclair secret, but she wanted the Sweepers to succeed just as badly. "Is there anything I can do to help?"

"Could you call the police department and set up a meeting for me with their records department? The sooner the better."

"Of course." Laura sprang up to do so.

"Actually." Juliana paused, drummed her fingers against her chin. "Before you call, fill me in on something. What's the likelihood of the police seizing Gin from the mobsters here?"

"None," Okane said immediately.

Juliana scowled. "You answered that fast."

"Messing with mobsters even on their more obvious operations is a bad idea," he said. "It's what brought Sullivan down, and he just had a disagreement over prices. Actively sabotaging one of their vital businesses isn't something they'll take quietly. It's not worth the backlash."

"We can't mess with the mobs, but the police—"

"The police and Council still aren't over the MARU incidents," said Okane. "They'll talk big, but they won't lift a finger. I don't know everything about Amicae, but I do know mobs. Trust me on this one."

"We need Gin from somewhere," said Juliana. "What about the sunk Pits? You mentioned them the day we arrived. Do we have Gin around those?"

Okane recoiled. "Those are sunk for a reason, and they're not city property. They're private Sinclair property."

"All the better! And the Gin?"

"Will not be moved."

The conversation echoed one Clae had with Henry Sullivan, what seemed an eternity ago. But Sullivan always denied the existence of infestations and therefore the Pits' function; for any Sweeper, let alone the head Sweeper, to speak so lightly of this fragile defense made Laura uneasy.

"I'd think the fact that these Pits have sunk makes it all the more important for their Gin to stay as is," said Laura. "They're not otherwise accessible. We can't monitor them. We can't stop any infestations that would take root there. It would be like arming a bomb."

Okane nodded. "Take the Gin away, and we'd end up with another, more deadly version of the Falling Infestation."

The incident had been officially named such, as of that morning.

Juliana made an aggravated noise. "We have to make our equipment stronger! If a few things need to be sacrificed—"

"Remember what you're sacrificing, here," Laura snapped.

Juliana looked ready to snap right back. Lester hurriedly stepped in.

"This Council meeting is just the first of many. Once you have the facts, we'll be able to convince them to see reason," he said. "We could even bring in other Sweepers to back us up. Melody could—"

"I'm not giving that woman a word edgewise," Juliana spat. She only realized her vehemence after saying this, and visibly tried to calm herself. "Sorry. I never got along well with Melody. Girlish fights, you know."

Laura raised a brow in disbelief.

"I need to clear my head," said Juliana. "Lester, come with me. Show me where you got those sodas. I could use a refreshment."

She left the shop without waiting for an answer.

"The meeting was that bad?" Okane whispered.

"Very bad," Lester sighed. He shifted through his stack of papers before gingerly lifting a package from their midst. "I'll step out with her, but before I forget, I wanted to give you this. I got a candle for Eliza, and the store had these ready for you. I thought I'd save you the trip."

"Oh!" Laura took the package, just as delicately. "I didn't think they'd be ready yet. Was the store busy?"

"Exceedingly so." Lester glanced at the windows. "I should get going. Sorry for the commotion."

As the door closed again, Laura and Okane shared a troubled look.

"Should we be worried?" said Okane.

"Only if she decides to act on her own," said Laura. "I mean, she had some reasoning in there. She knew she couldn't take on the mobs herself. At the very least, she'd talk to us about whatever she's planning, right?"

Okane didn't look convinced, but didn't seem interested in pursuing the argument either. His gaze dropped to the package. "What is that, by the way?"

"Candles, of course. One of them is for you."

She sat down and gingerly pulled the item out of her bag. It was a long taper candle, sea green with dapples of brighter blue. Okane accepted it with reverence, but still looked confused. He'd probably understand if he saw hers, so she drew that one out too. It was pale brown like a dusty coat, flecked with shining yellow. Two words were emblazoned in black along its length.

"'Clae Sinclair,'" Okane read aloud, and gave her a perplexed look. "Is this to serve as his gravestone?"

"Sort of? It's traditional in Spiritualist churches to light a candle or incense for loved ones who've passed on. During Underyear, people buy special candles and light them at home, in memory of their family and friends. Light them when it gets dark, and let them burn all the way through till morning. I heard it began with the infestations. Since monsters don't leave bodies, people wouldn't know if someone was alive or not. They lit candles hoping loved ones would see the light and follow it out of the darkness."

Okane turned the candle over in his hands, studying the color. "This one doesn't have a name."

"I didn't know what to put on it," she admitted.

"Is it meant to represent multiple people?"

"No, it—It's for your mother."

His fingers stilled. "Mama?"

"You talked about her before. Was it—Should I not have?"

Okane didn't respond immediately. He blinked furiously. "It's a nice color. She would've liked it, I think."

Laura exhaled her nerves. "I'm glad."

"Thank - - -."

7

WINTER JAMBOREE

Trumpets and flutes had been blaring since 4:00 A.M. Being off the beaten path, the Cynder Block escaped most of the din of December 21. A loud crescendo of brass startled Laura awake around 4:45, but otherwise the festivities remained a distant echo. Now, in the midst of the party at 10:30 A.M., the noise was deafening.

The Tiber Circuit held twice as many people as usual—spilling into the road, as cars had been banned from this street today. The drab, muted colors of everyday fashion had morphed into blazing hues in fanciful form. A woman nearby cavorted in a ragged dress of red and purple, gold bells stitched along patched sleeves and jangling at her ankles so she created a racket of her own with every movement. Underyear being a time of strange and vivid fashion, no one gave her a second glance.

Cheryl had bells, though not as many. Hers were sewn onto the fabric belt around her waist, a bright green matching the rest of her dress so she looked like a little forest spirit. That dress was one of Morgan's labors of love many years ago; Laura had worn it when she was little, too. Now she and Morgan wore dresses in shimmering gold fabric, with multicolored patterns down the front in mimicry of stained-glass windows. Laura's dress smelled of mothballs, and the

stitched back bunched weirdly; these were given to her mother and
Morgan before Cheryl was even born, and Morgan dug them out for
every Underyear celebration.

Gold décor draped from the buildings along the Tiber Circuit,
mingling with red ribbons and electric candles above the heads of vendor stalls, which stood flush against the buildings with room between
them left only for the doors of businesses. The vendors sold candles,
charms, celebratory figures, and knickknacks, but mostly food. The
smell of fried and baked delicacies wafted in the air above them, and
Laura mentally counted through the contents of her coin purse. She
planned to drop money on the ever-popular kinral on a stick.

"Cheryl, stay close," Morgan chided, reeling her daughter in. "Let's
look at all of it before you buy something. Maybe there's something
better up ahead!"

"And we're supposed to meet Okane," Laura reminded them.
She'd arranged to meet Okane by the stand with the shooting game,
but while she saw a gaggle of preteens squealing over mock rifles up
ahead, she didn't see him. "He should be around here somewhere."

"Maybe he's looking for a signal?" Morgan suggested. "It's hard to
pick out anyone like this."

That was true. Laura couldn't see over the heads of the crowd,
which put a bit of a damper on her vision.

"I should've been more specific," she muttered.

Morgan leaned down, using both hands now to grab Cheryl's arm.
"Honey, didn't I just say not to run off?"

"But he's right there!" Cheryl pointed.

Okane was in the clock shop just to the side of the game stall. The
shop's windows, normally huge and bright with *Seeley's Sellers of Clocks,
Watches, and Timekeepers* painted across the panes, were mostly obscured by a vendor's banners. Through a gap between stall and banner,
Laura spotted her coworker turning over a small clock in his hands,
glancing up every so often to check the outside. She waved furiously.
To her relief this caught his attention. He left the shop and made his
way to them. The whole way he recoiled from the raucous crowd. He

had no Underyear garb of his own save for a thick sash belted around his waist, bearing a multitude of coin decorations that clanged as he walked; otherwise he wore his everyday clothes, even if he sported the brightest of his kin-treated vests.

"Happy Underyear," said Laura.

"Happy Underyear to - - -, too." He glanced around furtively. "Is it always so crowded?"

Laura laughed. "The fact that you even have to ask . . . Underyear's one of the biggest holidays in Orien. They call it the sleepless season. It's *eternally* crowded."

"You don't know about Underyear?" Cheryl leaned forward in Morgan's grip, eyes wide.

"He's been excessively sheltered," Laura offered wryly. "Have you done anything yet?"

"No," he admitted. "I was more under the impression that this would be a solemn holiday, what with - - -r stories about the candles. What I've seen so far is . . . uniquely irreverent."

"That's the spirit of Underyear," Morgan chuckled. "What you can't do normally, you can do this week."

"Like eat dessert first," said Cheryl.

"Not that," said Morgan.

"I'll explain on the way," said Laura, hooking their elbows and leading Okane down the street. This gave her an opportunity to lean a little closer, hopefully so Morgan couldn't catch her words; Okane got easily flustered over his lack of knowledge, so the last thing she wanted was her aunt making a big deal of it.

"Should I be expecting mob attitudes from everyone on the street?" said Okane.

"No," Laura scoffed. "We say 'anything goes,' but Amicae's still made up of stuffy traditionalists. On the main streets you'll get 'scandalous' fashion trends, lawful things happening in not-so-lawful places, and a hell of a lot of noise."

"And how does that tie into candles?"

"Underyear doesn't have a single origin story. It's a hodgepodge of five different holidays. They all had similar themes, so one way or another they ended up merging into the same week. The basic trend is that we're waking up spring and breaking out of winter. Some people do that solemnly, through praying, but that's not the popular method. These days it's just the loudest, brightest party you can manage. Lots of music, lots of light, and anything fun you can legally accomplish."

"Hence the candles," said Okane, eyeing the nearby vendors; wax dripped from almost every tabletop.

"It's the sleepless season because the noise and the light has to keep going for the full week," Laura continued. "The parties go on for days. You celebrate until you drop, take a nap, and come right back as soon as you wake up. You can probably tell it's Cheryl's favorite time of year: no school, and no bedtime."

"And no one takes advantage of it?" Okane marveled.

Laura winced. "If you look harder, you can see darker things happening behind the scenes, but all sorts of work and regulations fall apart during the holiday. I'd be surprised if there are even three policemen on duty in this Quarter today."

"Should we expect mobsters in the open? Like the Silver King - - - came across before?"

"Even they don't fight during Underyear."

"That's what - - - said about Sundown Hills."

True enough. Still, Laura tried to give him a confident smile. "Just stay where the light's brightest. Mobs won't touch you any easier than an infestation would."

A deafening crack echoed ahead of them, accompanied by a sparkling red flare that danced over the décor and sent a shudder through Laura's amulets. Okane startled so hard his elbow jabbed Laura's ribs, and she winced. Cheryl gave a delighted shriek, lost in the cheering of the crowd. In reply a salvo of colors showered after it, amulet-powered blues and greens that threatened to catch the streamers. Even farther along, someone whooped and fired a distress flare. An ugly white cloud arced over them.

Morgan clicked her tongue. "Light is one thing, but I'm not sticking around for them to set the street on fire. There's a concert near the old courthouse. How about we go there?"

"I was actually hoping to take Okane to one of the churches," said Laura.

"But that's *boring*," said Cheryl.

"We wanted to light more candles," said Laura.

Cheryl made to argue more, but Morgan thankfully caught her.

"You can join us again after the service," she said, already leading Cheryl toward a side street. "First one to find Lady Spring wins. Oh, and light a candle for Charlie, won't you? His uncle passed away this year."

Laura made a face. "Charlie can light his own candles."

"That's not very Underyear of you," Morgan scolded. "See you later!"

Okane eyed Laura skeptically. "Lady Spring?"

"There are about three hundred of them," said Laura, rolling her eyes. "Underyear is meant to wake up spring, right? So we have symbols of spring. They usually lead the parades, but kids like to track them down. It's like a game."

"And - - -r family is fine with - - - not participating?"

"I told you, it goes all week. I'll find Lady Spring and catch another concert later on. They go almost constantly."

He didn't look satisfied with this answer, but he hadn't seemed entirely comfortable at all today. "- - - don't have to lead me around. I may not be familiar with the holiday, but I'm not entirely ignorant. I don't want to spoil it for - - -."

"What would you be doing otherwise?" said Laura. "Sitting at home and waiting out the week?"

She'd wondered before what he'd do, and could only picture him sitting in the dark with that one blue candle. Quiet. Alone. The very idea drained her excitement, and judging by his silence now, she'd hit the nail on the head.

"Spiritualist churches are the ones who uphold candles," she said. "It's calm in there. Crowded, sure, but you might feel more at home.

Morgan catered to one of them last year, it's got fantastic architecture. Let's head over there, and we can get some food on the way. Honestly, the food's my favorite part of Underyear."

They wormed through a particularly large group of people, who shrieked about upcoming fireworks, orchestral concerts, and holiday drama series in the Second Quarter. A radio had been pulled out and balanced on a vendor table, where it blasted still more music over the roar of the crowd. A fiddler nearby competed with this for attention and clarity, and the furious movements of his bow threatened to injure passersby. More lights popped and crackled overhead, mingling with the cheers from game booths. They passed one of the Battle Queen squares, where people climbed the usually sacred plinth and equestrian statue; a shirtless man had seated himself behind the bronze queen, and now drunkenly waved sparklers while his fellows cheered. Okane gawked at this so long Laura had to practically drag him away. Shortly after, they found food vendors, and Laura finally got her kinral on a stick.

"Meals don't really happen at Underyear," she said, as they stopped again; on this side street, their progress had stalled due to an unorganized dance blocking the entire road. "It's sort of like the parties. Eat what you can at vendors and get right back to partying. I've heard it's different in upper Quarters, though."

"I wouldn't know," said Okane. He'd made short work of his baked potato, and held the last of it protectively. "Sullivan never stayed in the house around this time of year. He had other parties to go to, and never threw his own."

"Is that why you didn't know about Underyear?" said Laura.

"It explains why the other servants didn't come in," said Okane. "It wasn't bad, though. That first year, it was the only time I could be with my mother without someone yelling at us. We had the run of the house." His expression softened, his voice still quieter with the memory. "It was fun. I . . . I jumped on Frank Sullivan's bed, because even his son was never allowed to do that. She laughed at me."

A smile tugged at Laura's mouth. "Your mother sounds like she was a lot of fun."

"She was." He watched the dancers as if in a daze before coming back to the present. "What about - - -r mother? She wasn't with Morgan. Didn't - - - say she and - - -r father were on break now?"

"They've been on break for weeks, but I haven't seen them yet," said Laura. "They do that."

"Wouldn't they want to visit their daughter?"

Laura shrugged. "I don't really feel like their daughter. I think they only had me because they felt obligated to have a child after marriage, but they never had time for me, and never had the drive to take an interest. If they saw me right now, they wouldn't recognize me." She caught sight of his expression and snorted. "Don't make that face. I'm more than used to it. Morgan and Cheryl are all I need."

"Still—"

The dancers had been hopping along to the tune of a tuba, and either the performer got spooked by something or just wanted to keep them on their toes; an extra long, extra loud note roared over them, and what little organization the dancers had fell into chaos. A woman tripped straight into Okane. She giggled and tottered back into the dance, but she'd managed to knock the potato out of his hands. The devastated look on his face made Laura burst into laughter.

"Don't worry," she wheezed. "There's more than enough vendors between us and the church!"

"Church or temple?" A mobile vendor had appeared behind them, laden with marionettes and ribbons. "If you're going to the temple, they're giving out free ribbons. Want one?"

"Sure," said Laura.

The vendor beamed, pulling two ribbons from the bunch. "You can tie them onto any of the statues you please. I'm sure the Immortals will grant you their favor."

That done, the vendor moved off. Laura blinked down at the ribbons—one orange, one pink—and held them wordlessly out to Okane. After some consideration he took the pink one and scrutinized it.

"Temple means Immortalists, right? Like the place we practiced at, back when Clae was alive?"

"That's right. We're actually right in that area." Laura hadn't realized how far they'd detoured to avoid the concerts, and was struck with a sudden wave of nostalgia. The temple couldn't be more than a few blocks away. "Do you want to visit? It should be another quiet place."

"It would be nice to go there again," said Okane. "Without an infestation, it should be calm. I'd like to see that place as it's meant to be seen."

"Calm," however, was out of the question for Underyear. They found the temple's street packed with people, the stone canir by the door decked out like parade horses, and extra banners on the outer walls. More vendors handed out ribbons, directing curious passersby inside.

"That's a much bigger crowd than I was anticipating." Laura squinted at the doorway, where a throng gathered. She didn't remember this temple being very spacious; how were they fitting so many people? "Do you want to come back later? We do have the whole week."

"More people might come by that time." He wrapped the pink ribbon around his fingers only to unravel it and loop it differently over the digits. "Besides, I said I wanted to see it as it's meant to be. This might be it."

The entry hall of the temple echoed even when no one was around, so the clamor as they entered was almost deafening. The streamers overhead swayed with the air currents, but Laura ignored that as they emerged into the main room with its wide staircase and statue-filled alcoves. The stairs had no railing, so the pair kept to the walls as best they could. Laura focused so hard on navigation that she almost passed their destination entirely. Okane had to tug lightly on her sleeve to stop her. They stopped in front of the alcove with its familiar statue, where three months ago an infected amulet had been hidden. The idol had lost its old wreath and some of its ribbons, though the fruit offerings and horse statuettes at its feet had been replenished. No one else had stopped here, too busy with what must be more important statues.

"This is a sight for sore eyes," she joked.

"It's been a while," Okane agreed. He reached out to touch one of the horses.

"Kind of bizarre to see it again."

He held up the ribbon, unraveling it one last time. "Do we just tie these on?"

"I think so."

Laura dug out her own ribbon, and they leaned into the alcove to tie these around the statue's arms. The scraps of fabric blended in with the rest of the décor, but Laura felt a small amount of pride at the sight. The statue remained static and pale, faintly smiling like their amulets.

Okane's head swiveled around sharply. The speed made *infestation* spring to mind, and before it even properly registered Laura tensed, alert for any threat. Was this another attack by the mobs? Here of all places, now of all times? But no disturbance could be seen. No one looked so much as perplexed. Okane's focus rested on a specific person, who leaned against the wall between this alcove and the next.

The stranger was a young man, perhaps an inch taller than Okane. His dark hair hung in long bangs over his face, the rest falling back over his shoulders in a loose ponytail; thin braids and red beads could be glimpsed intermingled there, the red matching his simple robe perfectly. The overall look was reminiscent of native fashions, though not nearly as complex. A silver pendant in the shape of a cross potent lay on his exposed collarbone.

The man noticed their attention and gave a crooked smile. "Hello."

"Hello," said Okane.

When it came to strangers, Okane typically let Laura do the talking first. Even with the MacDanels, Laura tended to lead conversations unless he had a specific point. He'd fixed on this man now—obviously a point had to be made—but there was no urgency in his posture. Just . . . interest.

"Happy Underyear, sir," said Laura.

The man's smile widened by a fraction and he agreed, "A happy Underyear it is."

It looked like he'd say more, but he had to press further against the wall as more people shuffled past on the walkway. The same gaggle forced Laura and Okane closer to the alcove, so they almost knocked elbows with the statue. The crowd came to a standstill there, trapping the Sweepers. The man came to this conclusion as well.

"Seems we'll be stuck here awhile. May as well get to know each other. I'm Theron. And . . . ?"

"I—" Okane piped up immediately, but seemed to realize his own odd behavior and stopped short. After a moment he continued, softer, "I'm Okane. This is my friend, Laura."

"A pleasure," said Theron. "And how is Okane and Laura's day going?"

Strange phrasing, but Laura shrugged it off. "Bright, of course."

"It's my first Underyear celebration," Okane supplied, and immediately winced.

Theron's eyes widened. "Oh?"

Okane obviously regretted having mentioned it, and forced out, "I've been . . . apart from society around this time. Excessively sheltered."

Despite Okane's attitude, Theron continued smiling. Nothing about him hinted at anything dangerous—his posture stayed lax, and surely Okane would've recognized another mob negotiator—but he'd locked on to Okane the exact same way Okane had done to him. Full interest. Laura didn't trust it.

"What a shame!" he said. "Then it may be a first trip to the temple as well?"

"We've been here before, just . . . not with it so crowded," said Okane.

Theron hummed a note of appreciation, sliding to get a better look at the alcove they stood in front of. "Is this statue special, then?"

"It has memories for us."

"What kind?"

Okane glanced at Laura. His interest was colored by unease, as if even he had no idea why he was being so forthcoming. She replied for him, "Our old boss had an attachment to it, and he died recently."

"My condolences." Theron inclined his head, right hand brushing against his sternum in what must be a sympathetic gesture. He glanced at the alcove again. "Are Okane and Laura familiar with this Immortal?"

"Not really." Laura shrugged. "The priest said something about a light in the dark, that was all."

"A light in the dark, and gatherer of the lost." Theron ran a finger over a ceramic horse's mane. "Aster rides into the dark and soothes those he finds. Niveus is his sacred stone, so he's associated with the calm and mental healing it brings. He is the stars, immovable and unshakable in every season. One would think he'd be the focus of Immortalist Underyear, but he tends to only be popular in certain sects."

"Most of our visitors don't even know his name," chuckled a passing priest. "I respect your knowledge, stranger."

A templegoer the priest didn't recognize? That coupled with his odd speech made Laura ask, before she realized it could be offensive, "Are you not from here? Oh! Sorry, I mean—"

"It's fine." Theron waved it off. "It's true, I'm not from Amicae. I'm from the north. Navis area, practically Ruhaile. It's much warmer down here. Great place for winters."

"Are - - - a traveler?" said Okane.

"A courier."

Okane's head tilted. "- - - carry things? Don't trains do that?"

"I'm a special courier. I don't travel by rail. I'm not as fast, but I'm more reliable. Besides, not everything can travel by train."

"Like what?"

"Secrets." He put a finger to his lips. "Valuable things."

Laura didn't like the sound of it. "Valuable things" sounded like illegal, dangerous things to her. She glanced around for a distraction or even an escape, but Theron seemed satisfied to leave them at that.

"I'll have to be going now." He reached one hand into his robe and pulled out a coin embossed with the same cross he wore. This he set at the statue's feet. "Happy Underyear, and best wishes. I appreciate this meeting."

"It was nice meeting - - -."

Theron gave one last smile before pushing back into the crowd. They tracked his red robe until it became obscured. Okane leaned to the side, trying to get another glimpse of him.

"Have you met him before?" said Laura. "You were pretty talkative."

"I was, wasn't I?" Okane shook his head. "I don't understand it myself. I just felt as if I could trust him. Like he was familiar."

Laura looked back at the crowd, puzzling over how that could be possible, and came to an absurd conclusion.

"You don't think he was a Magi, do you? All the strange ways he was phrasing things, it would've been so much easier for him just to say 'you.' Unless he couldn't."

"He can't have been," said Okane. "Magi don't involve themselves with cities."

"Clae's grandmother did," said Laura.

"She was an exception."

"Maybe Theron is, too."

"No. No, if he was . . ." Okane pressed a hand to his chest. His vest crinkled, as if paper hid beneath it. The last time Laura had seen him store pages that way—

"Are you still carrying Clae's letter?" she whispered, aghast.

"It mentioned things," he said vaguely. "Laura, believe me, Magi *would not* come here. Maybe once, but not now. Maybe never again."

"I don't understand," said Laura.

"Trust me," he said, and he sounded pained. "If we see a Magi here, it's not a Magi. It's something bad. If we see Theron again, we go the opposite way."

If he was this urgent about it she wanted to know details, but Laura swallowed down her questions. Okane didn't keep secrets from her. Once he'd had space to breathe, space to feel safe, he'd tell her everything.

"I trust you," she said, and he relaxed immediately. "Tell you what, let's go to that church. This wasn't the peaceful stop I thought it would be."

It took some time to exit the temple, but from there they moved freely along the streets. Evening closed in, but every light on the street glowed; the only darkness visible hung high overhead, suspended from them by amulets and electric determination. More light shone from the houses on either side, windows open to the winter chill as parties raged inside and more candles guttered at the sills. Drums pounded on the next street, followed by hissing steam; the parades had begun.

"You'll know the church when you see it," said Laura. "Most churches these days are built simple, almost like houses. This one's old."

And it was. The curving road finally straightened, and a gap became visible in the buildings ahead. The Three Child Church rose from a gated compound, stone spires soaring to dwarf the neighborhood while the building rooted itself in a halo of grass. The black metal fence looked foreboding, but people went to great lengths to protect vegetation in the lower Quarters, and Laura didn't blame them. For the time being, Underyear banners flapped along the bars, and all the church's lights glimmered. The effect was almost as entrancing as Gustave's Moon in Puer. The only problem was—

"The gates are closed," said Okane.

"That can't be right," said Laura.

She hurried her pace. The gates had indeed been pulled shut. A man inside the compound threw chains around the close, pulling it tighter while locks lay waiting at his feet. A wispy white overcoat draped over his black clothes, marking him a priest, but he was also Ralurian and several inches shorter than Laura. He looked up at them, yellowish eyes extra stark against dark skin.

"We're closed," he said shortly.

"Why?" said Laura. "It's Underyear."

"Confidential," said the priest.

He looked ready to throw the locks at them if they tried coming closer, and that made Laura pause. Ralurian culture prided itself not only on terrible jokes (potato peels included), but also on daredevil attitudes. Maybe it was coincidence, maybe it was bias, but the priest's fear only compounded with Okane's unease in Laura's head. She snapped into business mode.

"What's wrong?" she asked.

"Confidential," he repeated. "Nothing for you to worry about. Return to the celebrations."

Laura dug in her coin purse and pulled out her ID. She flashed the multiple stars there and said, "My name's Laura Kramer, and I'm a Sweeper. My coworker and I work closely with the police department. Please tell us—" She glanced back at Okane to indicate his involvement, only to find that he'd stopped several feet behind her to stare at the church. "Tell us if there's anything we can help with, or if there's anything we need to get the police involved with."

The priest's hands stilled. "A Sweeper."

"Yes."

He stared at her ID a while longer before finally looking at her face. "Something's wrong in the church. I don't know what it is, I don't know where it came from or where it went, but I won't expose any more of my parishioners to danger."

"What makes you think something's wrong? Are there any—"

Laura broke off as Okane caught her arm. She turned to scold him, only to pause at his expression.

"It's an infestation," said Okane. "There's a massive infestation inside."

8

AN UNDERYEAR NIGHTMARE

Laura called in the infestation.

A conveniently located police box made the process easy, and within ten minutes the operator had assured her that police were on their way and that the MacDanels would immediately be notified. Laura privately doubted that "immediately" could be applied to anything during Underyear, but returned to the church and reported everything regardless. In short order, black uniforms appeared on the street.

"Are you all safe?" said Albright, striding at the front of her small group. "If you're standing still, I doubt it's on the move."

"I don't think it'll try running anytime soon," Laura assured her. "Not with all this light aimed at the building and Underyear everywhere else. There's nowhere safe for it to go."

"Do we have any casualties?" said Albright.

"Unconfirmed," said Laura.

"I didn't investigate," said the priest; during their wait, he'd introduced himself as Mateo. "My priestly group rotates our duties during the holiday. I came to relieve my senior, but as soon as I opened the doors, I knew something had gone terribly wrong. The church was dark, and empty. Silent."

"And it couldn't have been another cause?" said Albright. "Gas, electric malfunction? There was really no one?"

Mateo shook his head. "People would still be here if it were a power malfunction, if not in the church then here on the street. News would've spread. Besides that, the candles were out. The rule of Underyear, religious or otherwise, is that the light must never go out."

"Do we have any firm evidence that this is an infestation?"

"I have no evidence of anything, but I've read about infestations in the papers," said Mateo. "I believed it better to exercise all caution."

Albright seemed pleased to have someone treating monsters as a valid threat. She'd probably dealt with citizens treating them as overwhelming phantoms, or else trivial background noise; a logical person looking for the proper way to confront them was a breath of fresh air. She sent officers along the street to check the compound's perimeter, ensuring that lights caught every inch.

"The border is secure," an officer reported, dashing back from the patrol. "We've diverted a parade to keep them out of range, but otherwise we don't see an immediate threat to the neighborhood."

"Good," said Albright. "Any word on the other Sweepers?"

Before the officer could reply, Juliana came running onto the scene.

"Sorry for the delay," she panted. "It's murder getting through these crowds."

"I'm surprised we were even able to reach you," said Albright. "Not many people stay home and answer telephones today. Your brother's not here?"

"He's still recovering from the last job," said Juliana. "Besides, we had a last-minute guest. We couldn't leave him to fend for himself. Don't worry." She looked at Laura and Okane, and flashed the most genuine smile Laura had seen from her in a while. "We can handle this, just the three of us."

"I sincerely hope so," said Albright.

"Spinner guide you," said Mateo. He pulled the chains off of the gate and heaved it back open.

"Can we do this?" Laura whispered, glancing at Okane. "If it's as big as you say—"

"I don't think it's moving much," he replied. "Active and big, but I don't think it'll charge us when we walk in."

He startled when Juliana clapped a hand on his shoulder.

"Don't worry," she told them. "If all else fails, I've got a secret weapon."

She looked to make sure that Albright had turned away, busy talking with the other officer, before pulling something from her bag. It looked like an Amicae Egg, but instead of gold, its insides eddied dark, viscous red.

"Is that like a Sinker?" Laura guessed.

"Something like it," said Juliana. "But I've only got one, so it's a last resort."

Fine by Laura. She had a healthy wariness for Sinkers now, so she intended on bringing this monster down the old-fashioned way. She patted herself down, thanking her lucky stars she'd kept her utility belt on over her dress despite Morgan's despair over it. She had two old Eggs, Bijou, and flash pellets. She'd done well with worse.

The Sweepers crossed the compound. The church doors dwarfed them, but when Juliana took hold of the metal handles, they opened silently and easily. The entryway lay before them, its only light stemming from the street behind them. The room spanned the same amount of space as Laura's apartment, built in the same immaculate white stone as the exterior. Pillars supported a vaulted ceiling, its design indiscernible beyond the reflection off gold-leaf clouds. On either side of the room, large open doorways stood outlined by intricate carvings, ready to lead them to the main hall. Juliana eased further in, quiet as a cat.

"Clear," she murmured, and moved on to the hall.

Laura and Okane followed at a distance, and Juliana made no move to stop them. Laura felt antsy, not so afraid as before but still distinctly unsettled. She leaned in to whisper, "Do you feel it? It's not close?"

"Not quite," he replied, hushed. "It's a little ways away."

"Good. How far?"

"I'll tell - - -."

The main room opened before them. Tall windows stretched near the vaulted ceiling, admitting scant lighting. Their glow struck the great pillars, glinted off rows upon rows of carved benches. On the far side of the hall hung a massive golden star, highly burnished but hauntingly dim now. Laura knew there were side alcoves, hung with tapestries in different weaves and colors to represent righteous spirits, but they couldn't be seen now. The church's recesses might as well be entries to an abyss. Around them echoed the faintest strains of song, presumably from the parades outside.

"Prime location for an infestation," Juliana whispered. "Do either of you see any movement?"

"None," Laura replied, just as quietly.

"It's near the ground level," said Okane.

For some reason Juliana didn't question how he knew that. Instead she asked, "Distance?"

"Midway down the aisle."

Together they crept down the aisle. Laura held an Egg in one hand, ready to arm if she saw anything suspicious. Okane slowed as they went, as if any step might take them into the beast's range, and she held it tighter. At last they stopped. The song wove around them, but otherwise the silence pressed heavy.

"Here," said Okane, but it couldn't be.

Laura shook the Egg, and it began to glow. It revealed only a patch of worn carpet, identical to the rest of the aisle. Juliana stooped and ran a finger over it.

"No residue," she reported.

"It's here," Okane insisted. "Just . . . deeper."

"There's a basement," said Laura. "That's where Morgan had the catering job. They have buffets down there after special services."

"Then it'll be on the basement's ceiling."

Ready to burst through the floor if it got angry. Laura tried to step as quietly as possible as she led the others toward the far side.

Priests usually presided from the raised dais, and on the one occasion she'd been here before, it had been flanked by massive stands laden with burning candles and incense stuck in sand. So many candles burned on them, she'd barely seen the metal frames through all the melting stubs, and the Underyear votive pieces had dripped a rainbow of color onto the floor. As Mateo said now, all the candles had gone out, but that wasn't the worst of it. The stands had been thrown. One lay smashed across the dais steps, while the other had been tossed into the seats. It stuck up out of the ruined wood like a skeletal shipwreck.

The basement door stood to the dais's side. Laura gave it a sharp tug to make it open, and as soon as it did, the song became stronger. A single voice came particularly clear.

"Oh great Spirits, miraculous Spinner! On this glorious day we praise thee!"

Laura sucked in a harsh breath. "There are people down there!"

"The infestation must be concealing itself," said Juliana. "Let's get down there, but don't make any sudden movements. If they start panicking, it might react."

Laura nodded, and made her way down the staircase. The sound of voices grew louder as she went.

"As you have blessed us with your teachings, we strive to follow your creed! We ask you to look down on your devoted followers, to count our sins and deem us worthy to join you in the life everlasting!"

The basement floor came into view. Where the main church boasted lavish decoration, the basement, wide as the hall above and walled in brick, had none; no seats broke the room's expanse. Of the three large light fixtures, only two still worked; the middle had smashed, and the one closest to the stairs flickered. Festivalgoers in ragged regalia stood in a circle. They swayed to and fro, raising their hands and chanting as if in a trance. Their mechanical song continued in perfect unison.

"Spinner, Spinner, make us worthy, Spinner, Spinner, make us pure, Spinner, Spinner, you have woven us, Spinner, Spinner, lead us on."

"Everlasting!" The triumphant cry came from an old man. He didn't wear the white overcoat, instead a sash of patterned green; a priest's assistant. "Life everlasting! The life in this world is fleeting and flawed, but with death, the faithful are gifted eternal life and happiness! We, the faithful, the spun, we are the Spinner's chosen, and he welcomes us to his side. He yearns enough for our company to send us this gift!"

The man gestured at the center of the circle, at the very thing that made Laura's breath freeze in her throat. The infestation roiled in plain sight, twice as tall as a man and three times as wide, its surface frothing as thin tendrils looped drunkenly above and beside it. She'd seen something similar in an infestation before, and Clae's explanation leapt to mind.

They can get loopy at times, and less likely to move unless they're startled. That means it's content. Digesting after a big meal.

Digesting after a big meal.

"It ate them," she whispered. Her hands shook. "It ate *everyone in the church.*"

From the crowd of singers, two people stepped up to the dais. They watched the infestation with eyes full of weird, unfocused wonder. The old man cheered them on.

"Come forward, my children! Through this door we ascend to the kingdom of the Spinner! Embrace your fears and overcome them: this is pleasing to him. The Spinner will reward you for your bravery and piety!"

The infestation's tendrils curled lazily around the pair.

"Stop!" Laura cried, running into the room. "Get out of there, quick!"

The surrounding people didn't so much as look at her, though a few startled out of their trance. The old man jumped, blinked at her in surprise, and said, "Calm yourself, young lady. Your turn will come soon enough. The Spinner rewards patience."

Laura grabbed one of the people and pulled her away from the infestation's trailing feelers, clicking the Egg against her amulet and lobbing it at the infestation.

"Come on!" She tried to pull her farther away as Okane shouted, "Everybody get down! Get away from there!"

The woman stayed still despite Laura's tugging.

"Why are you trying to stop me?" she asked, her wide, mad eyes boring into Laura's. "I'm going to see the Spinner!"

"All you're going to do is get eaten by a monster!" Laura snapped, yanking harder. They had barely any time now before the Egg detonated; it flashed at the foot of the infestation, which reached down to poke at it in curiosity.

"Laura, get back!"

The Egg went off. Light flashed with a roar, glass shattered. The monster gave an almighty shriek and thick black smoke rose into the air. The force knocked Laura and the woman off their feet and caused everyone to stagger, the chant eclipsed by distorted sound. Heat seared the air and Laura scuttled farther away, finally dropping the woman's arm in favor of escaping burns. When she got far enough Okane heaved her to her feet. The gold kin curled like liquid flame, swirling dark around the black cloud of infestation with a rattling hiss. She'd never seen an Egg explosion so dark or so long-lasting. It sent a chill down her spine, and her mind reverted to the night Clae died, the wild kin. It felt the same. The kin was *angry*.

The two who'd nearly been killed scrambled from the light with shrill cries. The old man grasped at the air, unable to get close but reaching anyway, horrified.

"The gift!" he cried. "Our gateway! How could you? This is a treasure brought upon us by the Spinner, and you've ruined it!"

Juliana lurched forward, yelling, "Get out of the way! It's still alive!"

Up from the black cloud, tendrils lashed out and stuck to the ceiling, providing a handhold for the infestation to heave itself out of the Egg wreckage. Its black hulk looked slimier, scabbed and dry but shining even more reddish in the cracks. It squealed and opened its hideous red eye.

"Out!" Juliana yanked one spectator, then the next, off balance and shoved them toward the door. "Gateway nothing, that's a monster!"

"Monster" must have been a foreign word to this old man, for he straightened again, ecstatic. The infestation howled and lashed out. Tendrils went in all directions. Laura and Okane lurched apart to avoid one, and Laura had to make two more hopping sidesteps to avoid following attacks. Some spectators were bowled over or slammed into walls. An unlucky few found themselves wrapped in dark ooze. Instead of panicking they folded their hands and closed their eyes in semblance of prayer.

Dodging another flailing tendril, Laura pulled out her second Egg, cracked it against her amulet, and threw it. This time she wasn't so lucky. The infestation saw it coming and pulled aside. The Egg whizzed right past it. The weapon smashed on the far wall, releasing an explosion of light and heat, casting eerie shadows over them. The infestation gurgled mockingly and withdrew its feelers. Juliana cussed and threw an Egg of her own, but she was too late. The captured people vanished into the main mass of the infestation. The creature barely paused to absorb them before flinging out more feelers and swooping out of the way, leaving Juliana's Egg to smash, greenish and far more subdued, in the place it had been. The old man laughed and began preaching again, his words overcome by the sound of jubilant infestation.

With no more Eggs of her own, Laura began to copy Juliana's earlier actions, shoving people toward the door.

"Come on, stupid," she growled, hauling a man out of the way.

"The Spinner—"

"Laura!"

Okane's yelp prompted her to jump aside without even looking. Another tendril crashed down where she'd been, smashing the floor. She yanked at the man's arm, propelling him away from the blackness before turning back to the problem. The infestation swelled, writhing, feelers like tentacles grasping. On the other side of the room Okane attempted to usher people to the door, but Juliana shouted, "Leave them!"

He froze. "What?"

"It's not worth it! They don't want to leave. Try making them and you're just distracting yourself. Kill the *kaibutsu* first!"

"But they'll die!"

"Don't let them bring you down with them!"

The audience resumed their song. The man Laura had kicked out walked right back in, adding his voice to the din. Laura felt the urge to both punch something and run away. If she didn't know better she'd say they were all under a spell.

The infestation raised all its limbs and whipped them back down, faster than before. Laura threw herself out of the way. The gathered people barely flinched even when portions slammed into them, cutting off voices with sickening snaps of bone and sending cracks into the floor. Laura dug in her bag as she scurried toward Okane. No Eggs left, of course. She had some Bijou, but considering this infestation seemed to be an acrobat, they might do more damage to people than to the monster.

"Okay," she hissed as she grew level with him, "once we get out of this we make a pact. One of us has to learn how to use that gun properly."

Okane made a noise that might've been frightened mirth as he pulled out an Egg. "The other person gets to carry the briefcase. I've only got two of these."

Another of Juliana's Eggs smashed, completely missing the infestation as it swung away, swirling tendrils behind it.

Okane's eyes tracked its movement. "I can't get it if it keeps moving."

"We need to pin it down."

"How?"

"Grab its attention and trick it?"

As far as Laura could tell this infestation was accustomed to being fed by calm, welcoming people. It was fast and wary of Eggs now, but it had been coddled. It might have cut itself off from the hive mind as a result. Maybe it could be fooled?

"I'll be bait."

"- - - can't be—"

Laura ran forward before he could finish his sentence. The infestation was distracted, swinging back and forth as Juliana kept aiming at it. The Eggs missed by mere inches, making the creature hiss gleefully. Laura stumbled to a halt beneath it, raised her arms the way the other people did, and shouted, "Spinner! Spinner!"

She couldn't remember the rest, but her voice attracted attention anyway. The infestation stopped right over her, and its eye opened.

Shit. Laura shook, berating herself for thinking this was a good idea. Her legs trembled but otherwise refused to move. The eye narrowed laughingly, and the infestation sucked in all its tendrils. It plummeted.

Why couldn't she move? She had to move! Damn that eye! With its feelers gone the infestation's movement was limited, so it was suitably pinned down. She should run, but even her arms felt frozen.

A weird ripple went through the creature, but before it could change its mind, an Egg smacked into it from either side. The greenish Egg burst first, producing a hissing cloud even as the gold one erupted with far more power. The infestation shrieked, attempting to catch itself, but any of the feelers it formed burned away. Gold lines spread, crisscrossing the monster's surface, causing the blackness to dry out and flake as smoke spewed into the air. The eye snapped shut for protection, and new feeling flooded through Laura's legs. She tripped off the dais just in time as the infestation smashed down. Smoke whooshed outward and Laura choked on it as she rolled away. Once far enough she jumped to her feet, pulling her bandana over her mouth. She heard muffled cries of surprise but couldn't see anyone. The black cloud curled to fill all corners of the room with its reek. A smoke screen?

"Okane!" she called. "Okane, you okay?"

She got a distant response, but couldn't think on it long. Something rumbled, louder and louder and closer and warping until finally devolving into a horrible, piercing scream. The infestation bulled out of the smoke, hauling its fractured form on spindly legs. Laura dashed aside. She was closer to the wall than expected. The creature crashed into solid stone and flailed. Its shrieking boomed louder than any of the Underyear bands.

Laura reached for her bag; this close, Bijou would work perfectly. Hands grabbed her from behind. Probably Okane trying to haul her out of harm's way. She was about to give him a verbal lashing, but her arms were pinned roughly to her sides and a voice not Okane's rang close to her ear.

"Don't you take another step!"

The old man. She struggled, but he kept her restrained.

"Let go!"

"Oh no you don't!" He grabbed her hair and wrenched her head up, so she looked at the infestation again. "You, my dear, are going to repent! Calm yourself, and allow fate to guide you on this path. Ascend, and greet the Spinner—"

"Laura!" Okane cried again, closer but still distant.

The infestation twisted, still flaking. Its eye opened in its darkest portion. Laura froze again at the sight. The creature shuffled, regaining balance, and charged again. A magical *crack* came from the left and Okane bowled into them, grappling with the man's hold. The sharp movement jerked them around, the red eye slipped out of sight, and Laura could move again. She closed her own eyes to keep from being immobilized and wrestled herself free. She heard the infestation approaching, a rasping slide along the floor and swift sharp padding from its spindle legs.

Bijou, she could get the Bijou now. She yanked the marbles from her bag along with a wire. She squinted at them with one eye, determinedly not looking at the incoming monster as she flicked the wire. It sparked but the marble didn't catch. There was no glow, not so much as a shred of magic she could sense. She tried again, to no avail. Was it malfunctioning? The marble was greenish. Puer-made. Did they need to be armed differently than Amicae ones? Armed like the Eggs and Sinkers? Or would it blow up in her face as soon as it touched an amulet? Okane stumbled into her and looked around. She couldn't see his face but heard him wheeze in surprise.

"Damn it!" she hissed. The wire sparked slightly and she tried again, but still it refused to light.

A red flash caught her eye. Juliana's strange Egg arced out of the smoke. Its insides bubbled, flashing scarlet before landing on the creature's back. The resulting blast almost blinded her. The infestation screamed again, staggering under the strain as crimson light lanced through its body. It only managed a few more steps before exploding, sending ashy flakes and red sparks flying. From the resulting cloud flew a small object. It hit the ground with a crack and rolled to their feet. A small lantern bumped into the toe of Laura's shoe, its stony exterior fractured from the fall. This must be the amulet.

"Egg," she rasped, gesturing.

Okane dropped down and cracked his second Egg over the lantern. A sigh issued from it, and the infestation was truly dead.

"It's over," Okane sighed, setting hands on his knees and bowing his head. The old man crumpled behind them, wailing about his stupid dead monster. Laura wanted to kick him.

Juliana emerged from the smoke, her goggles large and insectlike above a gas mask that warped her voice. "Are you two all right?"

"We're in one piece," Laura replied.

"Good. Is that the amulet?"

"It is." She puzzled over it a moment. "It's not broken, beyond the fall. I thought Sinkers broke any amulet they touched."

"Sinkers do," said Juliana.

Then it wasn't a Sinker? But Puer's Eggs and Bijou were all green, and Laura had never seen kin weapons beyond the Sinkers in colors outside the yellow color range. She made to ask what *red* meant, but the smoke dissipated, and the words stuck in her throat.

The people around the room began to break formation, murmuring frantically, eyes wide with fright instead of awe. One of the women called for someone by name, with no response. As if they'd been under the control of a hypnotist—maybe the infestation's eye—and now set free, they milled about, the level of panic rising as they realized how many people were missing, the tarry stains on the walls, the splintered and bloody floor. So few remained. Fifteen out of however many people this church could hold on a holiday.

The Sweepers directed everyone out of the church. The police converged on the group and took people aside. Mateo hurried between them, holding hands, whispering urgently as he checked on each one's health.

"I'm glad at least one member of the priesthood is looking out for people," Laura grumbled. "Where'd that other one go? He should be in handcuffs by now."

"He hasn't left the building," said Okane. "I don't think he followed us up, but there's no way he can get away. The gate's the only entrance."

"In that sense, this job went well," said Juliana. She looked at Okane and said, "Good work out there."

He tilted his head, bemused. "I didn't do much. That was a—well, an interesting Egg - - - had there."

Juliana winked. Downright *winked*. "All thanks to *you*! I—Oh, there's our culprit. Let me get the chief. We're not letting him get away."

She hurried away.

"Thanks to me?" Okane scoffed. "What did I do?"

"I suppose you pinpointed the infestation?" said Laura.

Certainly nothing to do with the Egg. Still, she didn't feel comfortable. Today Juliana had focused entirely on Okane, as if Laura were an afterthought. Hadn't it been the other way around just yesterday?

At the church doors, the old man had finally appeared. He eyed the crowd warily, but tried to slink toward the gates regardless. He stopped short as Mateo blocked his path.

"A gateway to the Spinner?" Mateo spat. "Did you really believe that?"

The old man bristled. "Of course! The Spinner himself sent it! It spoke to me in the Spinner's voice, I cared for this gift so long, and now they've ruined it! The Spinner's will—"

Mateo fisted his hands. "You let people walk to their death! Did you even give them last rites?"

"Why should I? We were ascending to life everlasting!"

Laura didn't know much Spiritualist teaching, but even she knew that death rites were critical. They believed that loss of rites essentially condemned the dead to never enter the afterlife. Postmortem rites could be performed over a corpse, but with an infestation, with no bodies, all those people were lost. Mateo's composure shattered so completely, he slipped into the Ralurian verbal tic.

"You blasphemer, ra!" he raged. "Don't you dare claim to know the Spinner's will, ra! Murderer, ra! Forsaker, ra! You mar his weaving! A four-ra on you!"

The shouting caught the police officers' attention immediately. The old man panicked under their eyes and tried to shove Mateo aside. Despite his height the priest made a magnificent roadblock, and Okane jumped in to help him head the man off. A pair of officers ran toward them from the gate. The woman who'd been calling for someone started screaming.

"My daughter! Where's my daughter? Please, Spinner, no!"

"I saved them!" the old man cried, still struggling as handcuffs locked around his wrists. "They're beyond suffering! In the Spinner's hands!"

The officers heaved him away. The rest of the crowd watched, silent and grim. Laura caught a glimpse of red behind all of the black uniforms. Frowning, she craned her neck to get a better look.

Theron stood near the back, watching the proceedings with no hint of his earlier smile. He picked at his necklace, eyes narrowed, before he met her eyes. He inclined his head, then turned. As he did his eyes caught the light oddly. His pupils flashed blue, but only for a split second, and then he was gone as if he were never there.

(9)

WATCHER

Underyear ended with a bang, as promised by every year before. It was the last hurrah, the "true call to spring," and all the activity of the previous six days was amplified. It happened the same way every year, but Laura couldn't remember it feeling quite so desperate before.

"It's like they're afraid winter will last forever this time," she murmured as she stepped off the trolley.

"Maybe they are," said Morgan. Cheryl seemed far too interested in the crowds to care about the conversation, and maybe that was a good thing; Morgan looked morose. "Times seem dark and they're desperate for a change."

"Because of the monsters?"

Morgan nodded. "Nobody knows what to do without that sense of security."

"It wasn't security," said Laura. "An infestation still could've happened at Underyear and they'd have just pretended it was something else so no one could ever prepare for it or know the warning signs. We're safer this way."

"My head knows that, but my heart has some catching up to do."

"There they are!" Cheryl called.

They'd arrived at the tree. The trunk was still there with its scattered leaves, obscured by a wire-topped fence marked AUTHORIZED PER-SONNEL ONLY. Around the back, at the edge of the Quarter's wall, everyone from Acis Road had gathered. Mr. Brecht drank heavily from a hip flask and bemoaned the fact that his daughter hadn't come to the party; the Keedlers exchanged weary looks at this, Mr. Keedler shaking his head sadly while Mrs. Keedler asked if the girl had been invited at all; the pawnshop owner and two other natives sat aside, and while they hunched as if speaking of illegal deeds, they were really playing a game of "six levels to Barnaby Gilda" and seemed to be stuck on the link between the actor's latest film and one of the newest Litus imports.

"Butler," Laura whispered loudly as she passed them.

One of them clapped his hands, glasses sliding almost off his nose, and said, "That director worked on *Merriweather Skies,* where Gilda was the butler!"

"How did it take you that long, Ju-Min?" one of the others grumbled.

"He still got three levels to your five," said the pawnshop owner. "That means he wins the bet."

"Yes, *you* buy drinks for everyone," said Ju-Min.

"That doesn't count if he cheated."

"How, pray tell, did he cheat?"

"Someone just said it!"

"But they didn't mention any films, did they?"

Laura sped away from that discussion, Morgan snickering at her heels. Near the middle of the group, Okane was making small talk with Amelia, and both looked up at her approach.

"Glad to see you made it!" said Amelia, flashing a grin.

"Sorry it took so long," said Laura.

Amelia waved her off. "It's Underyear, of course the traffic's murder. Everyone's getting to their seats for the fireworks."

"Amelia said this was Clae's secret spot," said Okane.

"The Sinclair spot, more like," Amelia snickered. "They had an obsession with this tree. Rosemarie napped here and those twins climbed it like monkeys. Clae fell out of it once! After that Mr. Sin-clair invited other Sweepers with them so we could catch any fall-ing children. Underyear here was fantastic. I'd expected to see more ex-apprentices here again, but I suppose they're either dead or too ashamed to show their faces." The humor slid from her face, delving into melancholy. "It was Underyear when Anselm died. That might be part of it. There's only so much badness you can stand."

"You just have to remember the good times," said Morgan, sitting down on Amelia's other side. "No matter how much bad comes your way, it doesn't change the fact that good things happened too."

"I didn't know you were a philosopher," Laura teased.

"Is that your profession?" said Amelia, instantly intrigued.

"Oh, no," Morgan laughed. "I'm a cook."

That had Amelia even more interested. As she started grilling Morgan on ingredient replacements, Laura turned to Okane and said, "No sign of Juliana or Lester?"

"They haven't been to the shop since the start of Underyear," he replied. "Mrs. Keedler went out of her way to invite them, but Juliana said they're busy with business."

"Business?" Laura gave him a skeptical look. "I get Juliana's enthu-siasm, but who's open during Underyear, beyond the vendors? Unless she's badgering Albright, it can't be Sweeper-related."

"Apparently she mentioned a guest."

Laura's eyes narrowed, and she dropped her voice to a whisper. "You don't think it's the person who gave her that red Egg? It had to come from somewhere."

"Maybe it's an actual friend? She didn't mention any details."

"Hey," said the pawnshop owner, catching everyone's attention. "My friend Lin lost a bet and has to buy everyone drinks. Who wants what?"

Brecht raised his flask, but Mrs. Keedler caught his wrist and guided it firmly back down. The others rattled off their choices. The pawnshop owner nodded along, then said, "That's eleven drinks for six hands. Could someone help carry them?"

Laura became distinctly aware that she was the only other person standing, and said, "I'll help. It's bottles, right? I can carry lots of bottles."

She followed the little group back into the city streets. Stalls of food and drink were still there, but had followed the crowd toward the designated viewing areas. The streets were absolutely packed with people. Laura had to keep her eyes on the pawnshop owner's shell of sweaters to keep track of where she was going. Lin located a booth and ordered. In a matter of minutes Laura found herself with three bottles under her arm and a cup of mulled cider in the opposite hand. A whistle and crash sounded overhead, and she looked up in time to see green sparks in the distance.

"That's fast," said Lin. "When were fireworks supposed to start?"

"Ten minutes from now," said the pawnshop owner. "Let's hurry back."

They hastened down the street. The crowd had thickened, worse because a parade had reached them. Marching drummers and dancers led the way, followed by an enormous fabric dragon. Its lead handler leapt left and right, bearing aloft a pole so the head turned, rolled its eyes, and snapped its long black maw as if uncontrolled by human hands; the rest of its body was suspended feet above their heads to weave, serpentine, and men on the roofs hauled on lines to make thin wings spread like sails. Meant to represent the dark of winter they were chasing away, this was the only darkness allowed to stain Underyear. As a child Laura had watched versions of it pass, and imagined the Sweeper from her Coronae book fighting it; nothing else looked so much like the infestations Sweepers supposedly fought. Now, as a Sweeper herself, she had to admit the likeness was a little too close. Its red glass eyes were so accurate, she felt almost obligated to freeze under them. Creepy.

"Avoid the dragon," said the pawnshop owner, and cut straight through the dancers.

Laura tried to do the same, but went slower to keep from spilling. She got across as the dragon's head came past, and someone darted out to grab her. She squeaked, half surprise and half dismay as cider spilled over her fingers.

"How ungraceful," said the person.

"It wouldn't have happened at all if you hadn't grabbed me," Laura snapped. "Who even are you?" It took a moment for her to recognize the bowler hat, the sneer. It was a mobster, the Mad Dogs negotiator who'd been in front of the shop. Her eyes narrowed. "What do you want?"

"Just to make a proper introduction."

"'Proper' includes manhandling me?"

His grin became more sinister. "We can make this a lot less comfortable."

"What, like knocking me off a bridge?"

"As you'll recall, that was the work of another mob. The same mob who bombed our newspaper, so we're just as upset with her as you are. If you'll come with me somewhere quieter, I'd like to have a chat."

"No," she said stubbornly. "I'm staying right here."

With all the more witnesses if anything went wrong. The mobster seemed to think the same thing. He looked around before fixing his plastic smile.

"Then there's no time like the present. My name is Haru Yamanaka, and, as you already know, I work with the Mad Dogs. I've been asked by our boss to give you a proposition."

"That being?"

"Become one of our Sweepers."

Laura gaped. Her? A mob Sweeper? It was ridiculous! Haru seemed not to notice her shock, and continued, "With our current boss, we know how to treasure our Sweepers and how to help them best do their jobs. Materials, intel, techniques, the Mad Dogs can offer you all of this with a Sinclair twist. After all, Boss was one of you. He knows your quality, which is why he's so interested in hiring you."

"This is a joke, right?" said Laura. "You're only offering because you know that's what the Silver King was so upset about."

"Was she, now?" said Haru. "I'd say it's a valid concern. Joining us does seem to make the most sense right now."

She'd assumed this was a petty move in the mob war, to go alongside sabotaging the Silver Kings' Kin system back at Sundown Hills. He didn't sound mocking, though. He was serious, and that was scarier.

After a moment, she asked, "What is it that the Silver Kings want?"

"For you to remain neutral."

Laura raised a brow. "Neutral in mob politics?"

"Neutral in any, but that's not exactly an option anymore, is it? Being neutrally steered by the Council is what got poor Clae Sinclair killed, after all. Ooh. I touched a nerve."

"Shut up," said Laura. Her blood boiled and she wanted nothing more than to throw the rest of the cider on him. She took a deep breath, exhaled. *Channel Clae. Stay mean but keep your cool.* "The secret's out, so the Council can't hide behind lies anymore. We'll have all those materials, intel, and techniques without your help, thanks. We have Juliana MacDanel now."

"Is that what you think? That the Council has been wrestled to your side?" Haru laughed. "You're part of their shame. They want to bury you and close the door on any other memory of failure. It's the game of politics and skeletons in the closet. Why else do you think they appointed a foreigner over you?"

That last one threw her off. The jab at her lost title stung, but the rest was worse, foreboding.

She frowned. "They can't get rid of us. Not when there are so few—"

"It's you they want gone. With Sinclair dead, you're the poster child of his old regime and the citizens know it. They'll keep you on until a few more Sweepers are recruited, but after that? You may just vanish."

Laura felt cold. "They wouldn't."

"This is the same Council that approved the MARU. You remember the MARU, don't you?" His mouth thinned into a severe, cruel line. "I was fifteen and not even part of the mobs when a MARU agent beat me with a bat and hauled me to court under the claim that I was a mob spy. And that agent said *Oops, my poor captive slipped down the stairs on the way here.* That judge looked at me, at the child bleeding from the head with a broken arm and scared out of his goddamn mind, and said *Of course he slipped. How careless of him.* If the Council claims you're a mobster, you'll face worse even without proof. Or maybe they'll go for another angle. Maybe they'll threaten your family until you move to a satellite town. We know very well the lengths and cruelty the Council will stoop to. But the mobs?" He spread his arms. "Mad Dogs is family. We'll have your back through anything."

"Since when has family meant anything to you, Haru?"

The sharp tone made Laura jump. The pawnshop owner had returned. She held a soda bottle by the neck as if ready to use it as a club, and glared through her massive glasses. Haru looked just as unhappy to see her.

"Natsu," he ground out. "It's been a while."

"Not long enough," said Natsu. "Don't you have a brain? Interfere with Sweepers and the Silver Kings will be after your blood."

"It's not interference if she makes her own choices," he said breezily.

"So you'll respect her decision if she says no?" Natsu scoffed.

"For the moment, but she can always come crawling back to us." Haru stepped back, toward the street and the dragon's winding tail. "Just remember, Miss Kramer: the mobs have had your back through the entire upheaval and even the Falling Infestation. *We're* the reason the Council had to change. Consider your position if we were to withdraw that help. Furthermore, consider your position when the Silver Kings lose interest."

He tipped his hat and disappeared into the crowd. With him gone Natsu heaved a heavy sigh.

"Clae Sinclair didn't spend a year scaring off Mad Dogs agents just for you to accept their invitation the moment he kicked the bucket."

Laura gawked. "He—What? A year?"

"They tend to prey on Sinclair apprentices."

"Him specifically? Haru?"

Natsu's expression darkened. "Unfortunately. He's one of the Mad Dogs' favorites."

"He hasn't tried going after Okane, has he?"

Natsu lifted the bottle, gave it a threatening swish, and replied, "No. But we should get back to him. This Underyear's been tainted enough."

Natsu's friends waited on the next street. When they asked what took so long she waved them off with an excuse about the parade. They hurried back to the tree and passed out the drinks.

Okane accepted his bottle with a murmur of thanks, and Laura plunked herself down next to him.

"So," she said, "not to scare you or anything, but you haven't been approached by any mobsters recently, have you?"

He choked on his drink. "I—what—*no*," he coughed.

"Good, because they're apparently trying to recruit us." At his horrified look, she said, "Don't worry. I'll get Byron on the case. I'm sure he'll know how to solve this. Besides, if they make a move on us, Silver Kings will strike back. So long as a rival's interested and they don't want to start a fight, we're safe."

"Safe," he mumbled. "It doesn't feel that way."

"No, it doesn't." Laura cracked open her soda bottle. She rolled the cap between her fingers, pondering, before asking, "Do you think they've tried recruiting Juliana? She seemed so desperate to power up our magic with their Gin. If she couldn't cooperate with the police to get what she wants, maybe she decided to cooperate with the source instead? The Mad Dogs don't seem to like her, but what if that friend of hers is a Silver Kings negotiator? What if that's where she got the red Egg?"

"I don't think the mobs have that kind of technology," said Okane.

"You may have heard their business deals, but you didn't see them Sweeping. How would you know?" said Laura.

"I just . . . I know."

Trumpets echoed from all around, the emergency sirens converted to announce the start of the fireworks. All eyes turned upward. The first went off, a barely discernible line shooting upward before bursting into a cloud of fiery green. Following it came red, blue, a yellow far too close to kin-gold. As three pink-and-white salvos went off at once, something nudged the back of Laura's hand. It was an Egg. Okane seemed determined to sneak it over to her while everyone else was preoccupied, so she accepted it. It seemed the same as any other Egg, but then again it wasn't. Black paint had been dabbed onto the metal casing, and the kin inside was darker than normal. She puzzled at it before realizing she could feel something from it. Anger. An echo of the Falling Infestation.

"What is this?" she whispered.

"It's a one-of-a-kind Egg," he replied, just as quietly. "I made four, but I think - - - grabbed one by mistake earlier."

"Then what are they?" A pause. "Okane, you can't mean this is—"

"It has Clae's magic in it."

For a moment Laura could only stare. Anger rose hot inside her, but she kept her face smooth and said, "I thought we agreed not to put him into kin production."

He winced. "It was a stupid decision. A selfish one, too. I just . . . I wanted him to stay with us."

"You used him."

"We both used him before."

"Only because we had no choice."

"I don't want to use him anymore, just for this. Besides, I think it's good for him."

Laura scoffed. "Good for him? He's dead."

"He's not. - - - should be able to tell just by looking at the crystals."

"They're not much more than Gin at this point."

"But Gin is alive, too. It's sentient. Didn't - - - know? It's identified all of us already. That's one of the reasons it's so hard to steal, and why Sweepers create kin, instead of some allied company. It won't trust people it isn't acclimated to. It *recognizes* us. We've spent enough time in the shop, and Clae approved of us, so now the Gin and Anselm approve of us. If we hadn't been around, Albright probably wouldn't have been able to help carry them. They would've shocked her. It's not exactly smart, but it can think. If it can think, how can it be dead?"

Could something dead still feel anger? She rolled the Egg from one hand to the other, remembering the laughing sound of their old kin, the almost-words she'd exchanged with the Gin in the fountain, the flicker of movement she'd been sure was Clae. Was he still awake and aware inside a crystal shell?

"That makes it even worse," she murmured.

"Clae told - - - that the kin has a will, didn't he?" said Okane. "It takes on the will of the parent magic. That Egg has Clae's will in it. I might be stretching, but if kin can be spelled to report to amulets . . . couldn't this Egg report to Clae?"

She looked up at Okane again as blue light flashed over the scene, catching his eyes in an odd reflection. She couldn't really believe it, couldn't excuse it, but she wanted it to be true.

"So you don't actually want to use this," she checked. "Just carry it around. Like giving Clae some extra eyes."

"That wasn't even the original plan," said Okane. "I just thought of mementos. Like how some people have watch chains made of hair, or lockets with pictures inside? Like . . . a permanent candle. I'll admit, the logic's faulty."

"Very."

"I know. But it occurred to me, when I saw Clae's Egg and the red one used on the same infestation, that they're similar."

"The red one didn't feel angry," said Laura.

"No, it didn't have an emotion attached," said Okane. "But neither did the ones with only Anselm, right?"

Oh? *Oh.* Laura drew back. "You think that magic was pulled from someone like them?"

"There's a possibility. If so, if Juliana suddenly knows about what happens to Magi or even what we are, that would explain why she suddenly seemed interested in me, right?"

"And the mobs don't know about Magi. Do you think Theron might be involved? Magi-related, showed up on the same day . . ."

He looked back at the sky as another firework rattled from green to gold. "I sincerely hope not."

10

WARNING

Two days after Underyear's end, a letter arrived at the Sweeper shop.

Laura wondered at first if this could be another post-death letter from Clae, but the writing on the envelope was far too choppy. The return address showed it came from Basil Garner in Canis, addressed to "Sweeper Kramer." Thank goodness it wasn't another "Head Sweeper" one, but what did someone from Zyra want with her otherwise?

"Do you know Mr. Garner?" Juliana asked, lifting one of her papers to the light and squinting for a watermark.

"No, never heard of him. Do you know him?"

"He's a Sweeper-Ranger based in Canis, fairly high on the totem pole. Insufferable in person, though, and that's a real pity. Honestly we're all waiting for news about when he kicks the bucket."

"Is he old?"

"Just reckless."

Were Puer Sweepers all anticipating people's humiliation and death? How long had they waited for Clae to give up the ghost?

Laura shook her head and ripped the envelope open. The letter didn't start with a greeting, but a scrawled sentence: *Do not allow the head Sweeper to read this.*

What was that supposed to mean? Should she not be in contact with this person? Juliana hadn't seemed bothered. Unless that was an act? Laura bit the inside of her cheek and continued reading.

The letter was an apology. Basil seemed to be writing to say sorry for a long series of petty arguments he had with Clae, ranging from "Eggs of this color work better" to childish name-calling. The writing itself kept dipping into profanities before begging pardon. Laura lost interest fast, but every few sentences he'd written *please read the entirety of this letter,* and it wasn't terribly long.

"What's it about?" Juliana still looked nowhere but her paperwork.

"He's apologizing. I guess he didn't get along very well with Clae."

"He doesn't get along well with anyone. I suppose if you put two insufferable people together, you'll get a mess." Juliana relaxed as she spoke. Laura hadn't noticed her tense, but the woman appeared relieved. What had she expected Basil to write?

Halfway down the second page Laura stumbled on the problem, right in the middle of an apology for insulting Clae's mother.

> *Okay, so I've covered my ass enough. No one who opened this letter for a glance should figure out what I'm doing. I'm writing on behalf of Melody Dearborn. You sent her a message, but judging by what you said, it's pretty damn obvious you haven't gotten any of her or Blair's warnings. They'd come themselves to help you, but Amicae's Council forbade them from coming because, I don't know, they'd recruit your head Sweeper back? Which is not what they'd do, but you'd probably end up in chaos anyway.*
>
> *Melody's answer to your question: HELL NO. MacDanels were a problem in Puer and Blair never wished them on you. He wasn't even notified that they got the job until they left Puer, or he'd have objected. Long story short: crazy shit happens around the MacDanels. Equipment doesn't work. People go missing. Reports are inaccurate and no one can trace the source of confusion. Anyone who tries interfering with them gets in trouble. Usually "trouble" is unrelated, like an accident crossing the street or missing rent money, but you know what happened to the Sweep Blair actually wanted to send you? Lester locked*

her in a basement on a job and fucking left her there. Work-
ers found her days later and had to take her to the hospital for
severe dehydration and a head injury. There were maggots in
her head! Fucking maggots! Melody and Blair have been writ-
ing almost every day to try warning you about this sort of shit,
but you obviously didn't get the letters or telegrams, hence why
this is from Canis instead of anywhere with regular Puer ties.
MacDanels don't give a shit about Canis.

But Juliana's been sending back bogus little status reports,
with scary details. She said she'd cleared it with your Council
to move your sunk Pits and reallocate all the Gin at the base?
I distinctly remember Clae saying he had to purchase it, so it's
private property and the Council has no say. Not that it matters
what they think because that is a TREMENDOUSLY BAD
IDEA! No Sweeper anywhere would approve that. They're also
implying that they've got help from an unnamed source, and it's
not from any established Sweeper guilds, or we'd have stepped
in on the Pit matter. I'd guess it's illegal, dangerous shit going
down, and with someone who doesn't care much whether Ami-
cae's people live or die, so long as they get what they want.

I want to say boot the MacDanels out, but don't act immedi-
ately! The backlash will not be worth it! MacDanels are rotten,
but their new business partners might be even more so. Don't
confront them. Get your police involved, but do it quietly. Don't
let them know what you're up to. If you have to run, run. If
you have to get out of the city entirely, then know that Sweepers
are gossips and every city Melody's telegram routed through read
it. Everybody knows this is crazy. You've got offers to stay in
Puer, Terrae, and Canis. Vir's ready to officially request you as
"perimeter advisors" if you need clearance to leave through your
Council. Let us know if you need anything, but for the love of
god, be careful.

It then went right back to the apology for accusing Clae's mother of
being "a hogwash tripey bollard," as if the warning weren't there at all.

"Is something wrong?" Juliana looked up with a frown.

"Nothing," Laura lied. "He swears a lot is all."

"I didn't think you were bothered by such language," Juliana laughed.

"Speaking it is one thing, writing it is another."

Laura watched as she turned back to her work. Juliana hummed lightly, completely at ease. She looked like the newspapers made her out to be: friendly, trustworthy, dedicated. A little too dedicated, maybe. She hadn't been here even a full month, and already she'd been impatient enough to fall in with something dangerous. If she hadn't shared the who and why with the other Sweepers, she couldn't have mentioned it to the Council; even if she had, the Council clearly didn't know enough about Sweepers to judge their issues properly.

"Well, with all of his complaining, he jogged my memory," said Laura. "I need to run an errand before I go home today. It's not too busy, so do you mind if I leave early?"

Okane looked up at her from the other side of the counter, as if to say, *You traitor.*

"What sort of errand?" said Juliana.

"Ingredients for some dish Morgan wants to make. Apparently it was my mother's favorite, and Basil seems to have insulted Clae's mother a lot."

"Oh! That shouldn't be a problem," said Juliana. "I've only got paperwork, and it's something I can't share quite yet, so you're right. There's not much to do here otherwise."

"Thank you!" said Laura.

She slipped the letter into her vest and patted it so the paper crinkled. Hopefully this mimicked Okane's treatment of Clae's letter enough that he'd get the picture. Okane raised a brow, but otherwise made no comment on the letter's supposed importance.

Laura had no interest in groceries. No, if other cities were confirming her fears, she needed to act. The MacDanels themselves she couldn't judge, but the red Egg and their new business partner? A stranger steering the department—steering Amicae's safety—was the last thing they needed. She had to gain some control over the Sinclairs before it escaped her forever.

Elinor had given them permission to use Sweeper equipment as necessary. As far as Laura could tell, the safe-deposit box mentioned in Clae's letter would contain equipment. It was Sinclair property, but so was all the stored equipment in the armory. This couldn't be too big a leap.

The Central Security Bank was an institution in the Second Quarter, and looked as if it had been here since Amicae's birth. The inside reflected its upper-Quarter location, with carefully polished stone floors, carved tables supporting pamphlets of information, and shining yellow bars at each clerk's window. A few people conferred with the tellers, while others were led through doors to myriad offices farther in the building. Laura approached the closest open window, trying to ignore the echoes after every footstep. The whole place made her feel small.

The clerk looked up from a form, slid it aside, and smiled. "How may I help you today?"

"I'd like to pick up the contents of a deposit box."

"Wonderful. Do you have your key, number, and ID?"

"Yes, it's box six eighty-four," said Laura.

"Under Clae Sinclair?"

"That's right. It was left to me in the will." Laura rummaged through her purse before locating her ID and the little key. She set these down on the counter. "Is this all I need?"

The clerk studied her ID with a frown. "Normally we'd need a death certificate and documentation to allow you access, but he's rather famously dead, and you are listed as his beneficiary. Please sign this first."

He produced a card and slid this toward her. It seemed to be a record of anyone accessing the box, complete with signatures and dates. Clae's signature took up every line. Laura signed in the next available spot, and the clerk took back the card.

"Please bring your key. We'll access the box now."

He opened a small door and beckoned her inside. She followed him into the back half of the building. Away from the offices and main floor, these hallways seemed dark, but the lights clearly illuminated a wall full of small, numbered doors. They passed the hundreds, the three hundreds, the five hundreds, until finally reaching six. The clerk stooped to reach a particularly large door near the floor, labeled 684. He pulled a cord out from around his neck and put its key pendant into one of the two locks.

"Your key goes into the other. We'll turn at the same time."

Laura knelt and fit in the key, swallowing her nerves. A twist, and the lock clicked open. The door swung out, revealing the side of a drawer. The clerk hooked his fingers around its edge and heaved. The drawer rattled out. The box itself was metal, two feet across each way.

"It's heavy," said the clerk. "Did you want to carry it, or—"

"I'm stronger than I look," said Laura, offended. She reached in and tried to pick it up. Tried again. "Holy shit. What's in here, an anchor?"

"None of my business," said the clerk.

On the third try Laura finally got it balanced, and hauled it into her arms. The clerk shut the drawer and led her next into a small room with nothing inside but a table and a little statue.

"You can open the box here," he told her. "Once you've finished with it, touch the statue to signal someone to come back in. We'll replace the box, and help you with anything else you need."

The door closed, and Laura was alone. She dropped the box onto the table and glared at it.

"Now what in hell are you supposed to be?"

Safe-deposit boxes in films had always been shown as small, holding a few pieces of heirloom jewelry or else important documents. She'd expected paperwork, maybe a deed or more information on the sunk Pits. Not this. She flipped open the lid and peeked in, only to laugh.

The box held another box. A jewelry box. It nearly filled the safe-deposit box, and she had to maneuver it carefully to get it out.

Its dark wooden surface had been painstakingly painted with

blooming flowers that had faded over the years. The large lock and rounded handles were made of metal that might have been gold at one point but now looked dull, like a relic of better days. The box looked fit for a queen. As far as Laura was concerned, no one else could possibly have enough jewelry to fill it.

She ran her fingers slowly along its edge before pausing at the lock. It had the same keyhole as the armory. She pulled the key out and fit the swirl inside. Just like with the armory door, her fingers stuck. Tumblers rumbled inside the box before the lid popped open.

She wasn't sure whether to be disappointed that it was jewelry, specifically Sweeper rings.

Rings took up the majority of the space, nestled in slots in red velvet lining. Row upon row of slim gold bands winked "S.S.Am." Atop them rested a folded paper.

Laura—obviously you've gotten the key and the will is carried out. If this isn't Laura, and you have no clearance to see this, pray for your soul because I'll track you down and you will rue the day you were born. As you can see, this box contains Sweeper rings and amulets. I'm sure you can guess which kind.

Amulets? Now that she thought about it, the array of rings was shallow for such a big box. She pried up the edges and, as suspected, it proved to be a tray. Beneath it she found a hoard of circular gray objects carved with simplistic smiling faces. Gin amulets. No wonder it was so heavy; it held a fortune's worth, easily enough to pay for a whole pack of college tuitions.

These amulets have been passed down in Sinclair Sweepers for as long as we've existed. They were originally a gift from Thrax at the formation of Amicae, and as such have historical value on top of inherent. I won't bore you with the details—damn it, she wanted the details—but rest assured, these are extremely valuable. You're the one I'm planning on training to take my place. I don't want anyone but the head Sweeper in possession of them.

The rest of the page explained that the rings were tiny amulets too, how to get names engraved and removed. At the very end was a section scribbled, as if added last minute:

One ring isn't Gin, and it's obvious which one. Think of this one as a gift. It's Niveus, used for streamlining magic in combination projects—basically it regulates magic flow to calm and make output more even, but you already know that. You've had one of these before. Maybe you're not facing a test, but Sweeping gets stressful. Take your time and take care of yourself.

Laura pried the ring in question from its slot. Plain and white, it held no magic hollow and didn't give off the playful feel of Niveus amulets. She could remember back in school, the antics other students had gotten up to during exam time; she'd spent her allowance on a little white Niveus ring in high school, not unlike this one. At every difficult question on the test she'd turned it thrice on her finger. The boy who sold it to her claimed it would chase out all her stress and help her focus. The stress had certainly lifted, but she wondered if that had really helped. She'd fallen just short of the mark to get into Class One. She complained about this once to Clae, described how she'd been so upset she'd thrown the ring into the Sylph Canal. She didn't expect him to remember it. She swallowed a lump in her throat and slid it onto her finger.

"Well, if you were planning on me taking your spot, I don't see how anyone else has a right to complain about it," she murmured. "I can't have been worse than Juliana."

She cracked her knuckles, sucked in a breath, and laid her hands on the Gin amulets.

Hello, she thought.

One moment the box felt dead, and the next, magic stirred. The stones shifted, one rattling, another emitting a tiny magical pop, and golden fog ghosted between them.

Hello. Hello? Hello, wake. Long time. Friend? Where?

She didn't recall the larger Gin sounding quite as fragmented, but maybe that happened to smaller pieces. Or maybe they'd lain inactive so long, it took a while for them to be coherent.

"Hello," she said aloud. "I'm Laura. I'm Clae's friend. Do you remember Clae?"

Clae? Yes. Yes, friend.

To make amulets work, Laura implied things. *Faster,* she'd think, and the magic accessed all connotations of the word in her mind and linked it to the situation; it saw a dog running, a car speeding, and sometimes Laura even noticed, if briefly, the memory being accessed. For a moment now, it went in reverse. *Clae,* said the amulets, and she saw him. A fraction of a second, a fraction of memory and not even a clear visual, but for a distinct moment she was convinced he was there in the room with her. *Yes. Yes, friend.*

Well, Okane was right about Gin recognizing them, at least.

"Clae's not here anymore," she told them. A few amulets shuddered as if alive, and she hurried to console them. "He'd be here if he could. The only reason he's not is because he—he died."

But, an amulet insisted, *here? Clae here?*

It tugged on her mind, but this time she felt no memory accessed or shared. It probably meant insistence, the same way Okane had "shouted" before.

"He wanted to make sure you were safe," she continued. "He wanted to make sure you stayed with Sweepers, and I'm the person he wanted to take over, so technically he wanted you to stay with me. But I know you have a will, and you have a voice. You'd have to accept me taking you. Would you work with me in the future?"

Silence reigned. The gold fog thickened, curling around her fingers and billowing the soft scent of vanilla. When the Gin answered, it thrummed through each of the amulets at once.

Yes. Laura friend. Clae friend. Yes. See you.

Laura let out a shaky breath. "Thank you."

Sleep until wake. One by one the amulets stilled, and the fog began to fade. *See you. See you.*

The magic drained out of them, and in moments they seemed like nothing but mundane rocks. Laura slowly drew her hands away, watching for any further reactions even while knowing there wouldn't be any. She'd just managed a Gin transfer. Other Sweeper meetings needed multiple people introducing Gin to each other before the stone accepted its new ownership. She'd performed this alone, and with something like fifty individual pieces. They'd obviously collaborated somehow for this, but still. *Fifty amulets.* Nothing to sneeze at. Even better, holding complete ownership over the most valuable tools gave her power Juliana didn't have.

I could even restart the department, she thought as she replaced the tray and letter. As the box closed, the lock and mechanics clicked back into place. *If the Council doesn't listen, if it gets too dangerous to be run by the city, Okane and I could start a second, independent Sweeper guild. At the very least, it gives us some weight in an argument.*

Laura grabbed the handles of the jewelry box and heaved it up, ready to replace it back in the safe deposit. For now this would be the safest place for them.

The box wouldn't do much on its own, but if she had other people, other facts backing her up, it might just become a trump card.

For now, she decided, a visit to Byron Rhodes was well overdue.

11

BREAKING POINT

The office of Byron Rhodes was a niche place, a hole-in-the-wall building in the Fourth Quarter that Laura had trouble locating. It turned out to be nestled behind a theater rather than beside it; the only route to the door wound through a narrow alley reeking of paint and strewn with excess set design pieces. Laura mentally cursed whatever idiot thought it a good idea to dump such things in such a narrow path, before pushing open the door. Thankfully, she didn't put much force into it. The door smacked into something before it fully opened. A loud cuss issued from behind it and Laura jerked back immediately.

"I'm sorry!"

"Nothing! It's nothing!" came a voice, shrill with irritation. "The damn door just—"

A shuffling sound, and the door was pulled open again. The woman there stood a few inches taller than Laura, brown hair taut in an unraveling bun and lines stark in her face. She looked like she'd been working overtime on something tedious, eyes tired and back slouched, but assumed a horrendously fake smile and ushered Laura inside.

"I suppose you're here for Mr. Rhodes? He's on the phone at the moment, but it won't be long before he can see you."

The woman bared her teeth in another terse grin and closed the door before retreating behind her desk. The room was truly tiny. Laura felt like she'd been locked in a broom closet. Barely wide as she was tall, the area miraculously contained a heavy secretary desk and two uncomfortable chairs with faded red seats. Two more doors stood dark on the other walls. Laura settled on one of the chairs while the woman fussed over a large rock on her desk. It changed color at her touch. Presumably it worked the same as the little statue at the bank, alerting someone else that she needed assistance.

"This is kind of cramped for a detective office, isn't it?" said Laura.

"It's cramped for *anything*, but he keeps saying it's cheap, and he loves his hiding spots," the woman replied.

"It would drive me crazy working here."

"On breaks I escape to the filing room. Still cramped, but I have enough space to breathe. This whole place is more form than function. Rather like—"

"'Rather like Mr. Rhodes'?"

Laura jumped at the new voice. Byron leaned through one of the doorways, smiling. "Nice to know I'm appreciated, Miss Heightland."

"Nice to know you recognize your faults, Mr. Rhodes," she snapped.

Byron shook his head fondly. "Whatever you say. Ah, Miss Kramer. Sorry to keep you waiting."

He stood aside, allowing her to walk past. His office, while small, was still bigger than the first room. It allowed more homey touches—the painting on the far wall and statuettes on the desk among them—and ample legroom. The chair in front of the desk proved infinitely better than the one in the waiting room. Byron spoke to his secretary a moment more, then closed the door and circled to his own chair. He sighed as he sat.

"Miss Heightland is convinced I've got her living in a mousehole, but she's the one who insisted on having that clunky desk. I'd let her have this room, but my clients would never have privacy."

"I'm surprised your clients can even find this place," said Laura.

"True. I need to invest in a sign. Just nail it up on the theater. *For Rhodes, PI, take a hard left.*" He raised his hands, tracing the vague outline. "Yes, that'd do. But you went through the trouble of tracking this place down. I could've given you better directions over the phone."

"I didn't want an operator listening in and gossiping," Laura admitted.

"Not a lot of people think about that."

"A school friend became a telephone operator. She keeps quiet about personal things, but others aren't so considerate."

Byron nodded. "And what kind of personal things are you coming to me about?"

"You're supposed to be checking in on us."

"I am."

"And you haven't noticed anything weird?"

"Weird is relative," said Byron. "A Mad Dogs stakeout could be a move on the Sweepers, or it could be a wayward attempt at getting an interview for the *Dead Ringer*. A head Sweeper's sudden, extreme interest in the mobs could be a warning sign, or it could be healthy caution. That same head Sweeper having a surprise guest through Underyear and beyond could be innocent—"

"Or it could be cause for concern." Laura cracked a smile. "I didn't realize you picked up on that much. I haven't seen you around at all."

"I'm very good at my job," said Byron. "That said, I've only been able to operate on the periphery. I suspect that you, being inside the shop and up close to the action, have more valuable input."

"I might." Laura hesitated, then said, "I think Juliana's in league with the Silver Kings."

She launched into the story. She told him about the MacDanels' suspicions of a "secret weapon"; about the rumored oral history and Juliana's sudden interest in Okane at Underyear; about Lester inviting Haru as a distraction, Haru's proposal, and the Silver Kings' concern. She told him about the red Egg. She pulled out Clae and Basil's letters, setting them on the desk for him to read. Byron listened, nodding along. At the end Laura tapered into silence. She watched anxiously as he studied Basil's letter.

"Well?"

Byron slid the letter aside. "A red Egg, you said?"

"That's right," said Laura. "I've never seen anything like it before. Puer is green, our Eggs are yellow, our Sinkers are blue . . . it seems so starkly different. It doesn't fit. And if it's not made by a city's Sweeper department, if it's illegal like Basil says . . . surely it has to be one of the local mobs? I've never seen them in action."

"Ah, but you have," said Byron.

It took a moment for Laura to remember. "I suppose I did, back in the Falling Infestation. I didn't even realize they weren't with the Puer group. But those were Mad Dogs, and they already made it clear that they don't like Juliana. If the red Egg is from a mob, it has to be from Silver Kings."

"Silver Kings doesn't make red Eggs."

"How would you know? You're not part of them."

"I'm good at my job," Byron repeated, and his easy smile became rigid. "The mobs are a favorite subject of mine. You could say I specialize in them. It's why Heather chose me to look out for you, despite my being fired from the police force. I know how a negotiator's mind works."

Laura went quiet a moment. "You keep calling her by her first name."

"We're old friends," said Byron. "Or maybe she keeps me around as a relic. It comes in handy at times like this. I'll say it again: the Silver Kings don't make red kin, and neither do the Mad Dogs. Nobody in Amicae makes them."

"Then where did it come from?" said Laura, exasperated.

"Rangers sometimes deal in illegal trades," Byron said, but he didn't sound convinced. "They'll take things the trains don't. Maybe a rogue satellite town is supplying her with their own concoction in exchange for something. But if it's as powerful a mix as you say, they could copyright it instead. Sell it to any city they want, for an astronomical price. It doesn't make sense to treat it this way."

Not everything can travel by train. Secrets. Valuable things.

Laura sat straighter. "It could be carried by couriers?"

"Rangers take a lot of different job titles," said Byron. "Although, they don't tend to leave the bottommost Quarters when they visit cities. Have you had contact with someone suspicious?"

"At Underyear, there was a man at the temple. A man in—"

In red robes. Red beads in his hair. God, it was so obvious. How had she missed it?

"Did he identify himself as a Ranger?" said Byron.

"No, just as a courier. His name was Theron. He said he carried secrets. I don't know much beyond that, but I think Okane knew more. He wouldn't tell me why, but he was scared after we spoke."

"Okane Sinclair," Byron said slowly. "His record is shoddy at best. Do I understand correctly that the Sullivans once employed him?"

"What does that have to do with anything?" said Laura.

"You don't think there might be a link here to the Falling Infestation? An outside group, well-versed in Sweeping methods and therefore infestations, interested in steering our future? I've confirmed that Sullivan didn't orchestrate that, but whoever was behind that had to know how his company worked, down to intricate details. They were probably present at the Sullivan household or offices in the months before the infestation, possibly right under his nose. Also . . ." He tapped his finger three more times, mulling over his thoughts before finally saying, "I've found other allusions to Okane. Frightening ones."

"There's no way he's involved," said Laura, appalled. "He'd never—"

"I think he was another target."

"What?" She drew back, horrified.

"I cornered a drunk Mad Dog recently. I was hoping to get information on why their rivalry with Silver Kings turned into such a powder keg right now, but he was a fringe member and didn't know much about that. What he *did* know was that a certain individual came to the mobs looking to do business, and their boss laughed this man out of the building."

Laura frowned. "He knew his boss's opinions, but not where his group was headed?"

"Mad Dogs is a conundrum like that. They idolize their current boss, so anything involving him gets passed around and blown into tall tales," said Byron. "Something surrounding that story, though, was the man's demands. He wanted Okane. Not by name, but not many of Sullivan's house staff match his description. Mad Dogs took that to mean an arranged assassination. You don't demand a hit on someone for no reason, so Okane must have information they don't want to get out. He may be the key to the whole incident."

"But the Mad Dogs refused to help that man," Laura checked.

"They did," said Byron. "But they've left him to his own devices. If this man, this Theron, has allied with the MacDanels . . . that doesn't look good for Okane. They might follow through where the Mad Dogs refused. If this story about Lester is true, I'm worried."

Laura bit her lip, mulling over this new information. "But if Theron is hoping to get something out of Amicae, why would he have set up the Falling Infestation in the first place? Anything he'd gain would be gone."

"Deeper we travel down the rabbit hole." Something in Byron's eyes hardened, but he smiled anyway. "Perhaps it was meant to be contained after all?"

"And that's what he said," she finished with a shrug.

"I'm not surprised," said Okane. He didn't look at her, too busy trying to thread a needle; a torn shirt lay draped over his knee. "I told - - - Sullivan dealt with mobs. It stands to reason that he dealt with more rotten people."

He seemed completely content with the thought that someone wanted him dead, and for the life of her Laura couldn't understand why. Did he not care about dying if it wasn't by infestation? Had he always suspected this?

"But you don't remember anything that ties in?" she asked, plunking herself down in the old rocking chair. It creaked ominously and tipped, and she gripped the handles hard as it swung back upright. Okane snorted at her reaction, and she snapped, "Take this a little more seriously! Our new boss may have agreed to kill you!"

"Hush," he scolded. "They might hear - - -."

"As if," Laura scoffed.

She'd arrived late this morning, only to find Juliana and Lester cornered outside the shop by a strange woman in a long, dark coat. Neither noticed her slip inside, and the woman hadn't seemed ready to let them go anytime soon. In any case, it gave Laura ample opportunity to dash upstairs and relate the whole Byron incident.

"Juliana's been acting very familiar, for someone ready to kill me," said Okane. "She invited me to lunch today."

Laura shot up straight. "Did you accept?"

"No. I don't exactly feel comfortable around her. I said I already had plans with the Keedlers."

"Good. She might've been leading you to your assassination."

"I'm not important enough for an assassination, Laura."

"You are so stupid," she groaned.

"Noted," he hummed.

She watched him start stitching, brooding before finally asking, "You're not scared of this at all. Why?"

"If Theron's really behind this, and if he's really who I think he is, then he doesn't want me dead," said Okane.

"So you do know something," said Laura.

He pulled the thread extra slowly, studying the fabric. The single stitch took far longer than it should, as did the one that followed. Eventually he glanced up, as if checking whether she'd lost interest. She gave him an unimpressed look. He ducked his head again, defeated.

"He's something I don't want to acknowledge."

"So he is Magi?" said Laura.

"No," said Okane. "Yes."

"He can't be both," said Laura.

"He can, actually," said Okane.

Laura opened her mouth to ask how, but snapped it shut again at the sound of the door opening.

"Mr. Sinclair, are you still here?"

Lester? Frowning, Okane stood to meet him. Laura leapt up behind him and glowered at the intruder. Lester stood halfway through the doorway, partially cast in shadow. When he saw Laura, he stiffened.

"Ah. Miss Kramer. I didn't realize you were here this morning."

"That's me," said Laura. "Always here."

"Can I help - - -?" said Okane.

"I hoped so," said Lester. "Miss Kramer, Juliana's speaking with a client outside. Could you go out and help her?"

"No, I think I'll stay right here," said Laura.

Lester's eyes narrowed. "The matter is a private one."

"I tend to share everything with Laura, so not much is private," said Okane. "I thought - - - and Juliana liked transparency among Sweepers?"

"Does she know *everything* about you?" said Lester.

Okane tilted his head, wary. "That's a strange way to phrase it."

That response confirmed something. Lester moved, and somehow that shift changed him from mundane to dangerous.

"I think it's time we stopped pretending," he said. "Miss Kramer needs to be cut out of the deal before things get worse."

Okane raised an arm as if to shield Laura from sight. "I don't know what - - -'re talking about, but - - -'re not doing anything to her."

"Drop the act," said Lester.

He bore down on them. Laura didn't know what he was planning, but it wouldn't be good for either of them. She grabbed at Okane's belt and yanked the gun from its holster. The pictographs flared on its sides as she pulled the hammer back. Lester froze as he found himself looking down the barrel. For a moment they all stood still as statues, silent and tense.

"Well," said Laura, letting out a shaky breath. "I don't think Eliza had a gun. What's your move now?"

Lester's expression contorted. "What was that?"

"Eliza," Laura said louder. "You know, the friend Juliana talked about? Dead in an infestation? Once I heard what you did to Joan, it's not hard to connect the two. Is this what you do, Lester? Act all quiet and nice until someone trusts you, then club them over the head? Sabotage their equipment?"

"You do like to talk about things you don't understand," said Lester. "So you don't deny it."

"And how long are you going to stand there?" Lester glared at Okane.

"I don't know what - - -'re talking about, but I'm not on - - -r side," Okane retorted.

Lester snorted. "Still covering your own ass."

This at least gave them some information: if Lester assumed any Magi he saw was involved, Theron couldn't be working alone. Laura opened her mouth to demand answers, but another click sounded from the stairwell.

"Well, what have we here?" said Juliana. She stepped into view with her own kin gun, aiming it directly at Laura. "That's bad manners. Didn't we teach you basic gun safety already?"

"So much for Sweeper solidarity," Laura grumbled.

"She knows too much," said Lester.

"Well, we can't just shoot her. With the Mad Dogs ranting the way they are, she's high-profile." Juliana regarded them a moment before a smile slowly grew across her face. "Miss Cherry!" she called. "I think I have a solution for you!" Quieter, she ordered, "Put that away and follow our lead." When Laura didn't react at first, she rolled her eyes and turned to Okane. "You're the one who wants her alive, right? Get her to play along."

"Let's do what they say," Okane said quietly.

"What?" Laura hissed.

"We're at a disadvantage."

Laura didn't like dropping what felt like their only defense, but she wasn't eager to shoot a man in the face, and with the second gun she didn't like their chances much either. Scowling, she lowered her arm. Juliana stood away from the door and jerked her head toward the stairwell.

"Go downstairs, and be polite. Our guest won't appreciate any attitude."

The woman waiting in the shop was the same one who'd been talking to Juliana outside. She stood rigidly, arms crossed and expression severe. Now that Laura paid more attention she noticed her clothes looked utilitarian: riding boots, coat to keep out the elements, a wide-brimmed hat hanging down her back. A Ranger. Her eyes didn't flash like Theron's, but she shared their dark color, the black hair slicked back into a severe braid.

"Allow me to introduce you," Juliana said brightly; she'd brought the gun behind her back, but Laura had no doubt she'd pull it out again at the slightest provocation. "This is our newest client, Cherry. Cherry, these are two of Amicae's best Sweepers. I think they'll work wonderfully for your job."

Cherry looked them over, unimpressed. "You're not passing it up the line?"

"I'm confident in their abilities," said Juliana. "So long as you keep them in line, they'll be no trouble."

Cherry clicked her tongue. "If you say so. Nature of the job means we should leave immediately. How long will it take them to prepare?"

"No time at all." Juliana turned her too-wide smile on Laura. "Grab as much equipment as you need. You'll need some firepower out in the wilds."

12

THE WILD THINGS

Considering their only witness seemed in on the whole deal and obviously carried a gun of her own, Laura didn't argue. She bit her tongue and pulled out all the equipment she could carry. Juliana gave them another cheery farewell that they didn't bother answering as they left.

Cherry set a fast pace. She led them onto a trolley, then to the cable cars. Each time she took the seat directly opposite them and watched unblinkingly. It felt as if she were staring into their souls. Laura glared right back at her. They didn't speak at all until their cable car alighted at the Sixth Quarter station. Finally, Cherry cracked a new expression. As she stood, she flashed an awkward half smile.

"So. Your boss is a little weird, huh?"

"No kidding," Laura ground out.

"I didn't expect her to agree to my proposal so easily. I could've sworn there'd be more regulations to jump over. I don't blame your attitude, though. Last-minute trips to the wilds don't tend to end too well for city slickers."

Laura and Okane exchanged a perplexed look. As far as Laura knew, murderers didn't try striking up amiable conversations with their victims. Then again, if they were headed for an assassination,

Juliana wouldn't have let them go with so much valuable equipment. Were they being forcibly drawn into the MacDanels' deal?

"You don't have to worry," Cherry continued, swinging herself out of the cab. "I'm not the only one you'll be traveling with. We know how to handle the wilds. We'll keep you safe."

"Safe," Laura repeated slowly.

"Exactly."

Laura's previous trips down to this Quarter had been to an army barracks building and to the train depot. This cable car station had neither in sight, instead depositing them in the ramshackle Ranger district. Most of the structures here looked temporary, and the few true buildings were mismatched, as if portions had been added as needed. People walking the streets here looked totally out of place in the city, too rough, too earthy to be contained in its walls. Few paid attention to them, but one man stood ready and waiting, complete with a pack of saddled horses.

"Your other guide's name is Grim," Cherry announced as they drew near. "He's as much of an expert on the wilds as there can be."

Satisfied with the state of his horse and tack, Grim turned to face them. It was startling. His skin was porcelain white, the tousled hair poking out from under his hat stark to match. Only the slightest hint of color dusted his face; he had high cheekbones and a small pointed nose, and eyes of the palest gray Laura had ever seen on a person. He looked like a ghost wrapped in earthly clothing. Stranger still, Laura had the sudden and distinct feeling that she'd seen him before.

"He shouldn't be hard to spot." Okane sounded unnerved too.

"He's not much of a looker, is he?" Cherry snorted. "Don't worry. He's a big softie. Unless you refuse the candy. If he offers you something, just accept it. You can chuck the stuff when he looks the other way."

"I'll keep that in mind."

"Here." Cherry grabbed the reins of two unmanned horses and presented them to the Sweepers. "You can take these. Don't worry, they're good for beginners."

Laura looked from her to the horse, perplexed. Well, she supposed, if she was going to be forced into this, it was nice to have someone acting nicely about it. Best keep Cherry in a good mood.

"I've never ridden a horse before," Laura confessed. "How do I get on?"

Cherry boosted them onto the horses. Luckily the animals were patient and very used to this, so Laura settled easily. Okane looked ill in his own saddle. Cherry swung effortlessly onto her own black steed and trotted to the front.

"Everybody ready to go? Grim, did you go through the checklist?"

"Three times," he replied.

"Good. Let's head out."

The horses cantered one after another in unruly single file. Laura panicked at the idea of making her horse move, but to her relief it matched the others' pace without persuasion. They left the cable car station behind, setting a swift pace to the Sixth Quarter wall. Gaggles of soldiers watched as they passed, but only when they reached the door did someone interfere with their progress. The door loomed half as high as the Sweeper shop, made of wood with decorative iron reinforcement. A small building lurked to the left, and from here stepped a pair of soldiers.

"Halt!" one called, and the horses slowed.

"Good morning." Cherry tipped her hat and beamed at the soldier.

"Where are you off to?" the soldier asked, ignoring her greeting entirely.

"The wilds. We made arrangements for passage already. You should have the paperwork."

Wait. So this outing was city-approved? Either Juliana worked fast, or this was part of a much more sophisticated setup than Laura had expected.

The soldier held her arm out to the side, and her younger assistant scrambled to hand over a clipboard. She flipped through the pages and found what she was looking for.

"Four leaving, to return here within the month. Passports have been validated already."

"So, are we cleared?"

The soldier scowled at her tone but made another gesture. The door opened for them. Cherry's horse pawed the ground and lurched forward as if impatient to reach open air, and the rest followed more sedately. Laura craned her head to look around as they entered the doorway. She had always expected something big and interesting for the outer gates, but this proved plain, dark, and disappointing. Hoofbeats echoed along the walls for almost five minutes before they emerged outside of the city, which also disappointed.

For a long stretch around the city, Amicae tended agricultural fields. The buildings and crops retained the feel of the city, if greener, but far beyond Laura glimpsed the mountains dark blue on the horizon, and her spirits rose. Cherry set them on a route along a path worn by agriculture workers.

"Okay!" she called behind her. "We'll keep on until about two o'clock, and then we can break for food. Any breaks before then will be *fast*, understand? We don't have much time to get to our destination."

Laura sucked in enough determination to ask, "Where is our destination?"

"Not marked on any map, so you can't judge by it. A few days out," Cherry replied.

Fantastic. That gave her so much information.

The sun beat down heavily as they continued their trek. It wasn't the sweltering glare of summer, but close enough to it that Laura unbuttoned her coat as they left the shelter of agriculture. Here they entered the untamed flatland separating Amicae from the forests and hilly areas closer to the mountains, and wind rolled in from the ocean. The path became little more than a deer trail, the land sloped upward, and then they entered the trees. Most of the foliage had fallen, leaving twisted branches above their heads, but some of the plants retained their greenery and appeared lush as they would be in summer. A trail had been tramped down by travelers before, and they wound along it to ascend the hills.

As two o'clock rolled by they found a wide cleared space on their path, ringed by trees with a small circle of rocks encasing the blackened remains of a campfire. Wordlessly the Rangers dismounted.

Laura struggled to do the same, going through the motions slowly to make sure she got it right.

"Take a walk around and make whatever stop you need," said Cherry, digging through her saddlebags. "I've got some food for you afterward. It's not fancy city cuisine, but it's not too bad."

"You don't mind us going out of sight?" said Laura.

"I trust you not to try petting any wild animals." Cherry sent her a mock glare. "I don't need to tell you that, do I? City slickers know that much?"

"I might live in a city, but I do have common sense," said Laura.

Cherry laughed.

Laura wandered into the trees, perplexed. She walked until the camp was out of sight before deciding that was far enough. She reached for her belt, but paused. A hole yawned in the ground ahead, big enough that she could probably fit in if she wanted to. A ring of raised dirt surrounded the edge, dry and undisturbed. Baffled, she stepped closer. Was that some makeshift toilet to go along with the campsite?

"Cherry?" she called. "I—Uh, I have some common sense, but I don't really know anything about giant holes out here. Did a Ranger dig this?"

No response. Maybe the camp had fallen out of earshot, too. She squinted at the hole again, trying to guess its purpose. Far too big to be a toilet, and besides, it sloped into the ground. A hiding place? Shelter for the night? She made to take another step and found herself hesitating. She stooped instead, thinking to check how far it went. Darkness met her eyes. It had no far wall. A tunnel, then.

This isn't normal, she thought, unease rising.

"Don't get any closer."

The sudden, close voice made her jump. She clapped a hand over her chest and tried to get her heartbeat under control as Grim blinked at her.

"Oh, god. I didn't hear you at all."

"That's a knuckerhole," said Grim. "Don't go anywhere within ten feet of them."

Now that he'd delivered his warning, he had no further interest in being here. He turned and walked back toward the camp. Laura rushed after him, almost tripping over a tree root in the process.

"Hang on a second! A what? What's a knucker?"

"A dragon," said Grim.

"But dragons don't exist," said Laura. "Do they?"

"The professor seemed to think they did," said Grim. "We took him out here last year to study them."

Laura gave him a sidelong look. "I feel like proof of dragons would've been published by now."

"Knuckers are ugly things. They don't match the image most people have of dragons."

"Then what *are* they?"

"Rangers call them wyrms. Very large, very long reptiles with vestigal wings. They burrow in a wide and complicated network of tunnels, and hunt by surprising prey wandering too close to their knuckerholes."

Laura shuddered. "That sounds nasty. Are there a lot out here?"

"You never know," Grim mused. "There's no way to know how many holes a single one digs, or even if the digger is still alive. We avoid the holes as much as possible, or find some way to plug them up."

"Another thing to add to my list of nightmares," Laura grumbled. "Thanks for keeping me out of it."

He looked at her as if confused. "You asked for information. I provided the information."

Laura didn't know how to respond to that. She simply stared at his pale, pale face and thought, *How in hell do I know you?* Grim didn't linger, though. He walked on back to the camp. When Laura returned afterward, she found the Rangers in deep discussions, and Okane rubbing anxiously at his arms.

"A knucker?" he demanded when he saw her. "- - - saw a knucker?"

"Technically it was just a hole," Laura defended. "It was nice to know not to walk into it, though."

He sighed, exasperated. "We haven't even been here one day, and - - -'ve already had a near-death experience."

"On the bright side, we know they don't want us dead," said Laura. "Though to be honest, I'm not sure what they want from us. They're part of Theron's plan, right? If it's supposed to be so illegal and dangerous, why are they treating this like an everyday outing? They didn't care where I went just now."

"There's nowhere to run at this point," Okane pointed out. "They'd catch - - - before - - - got back to Amicae, and otherwise - - -'d get - - -rself killed by the wilds itself."

"Still." Laura leaned to the side to get a better look at the Rangers; Cherry was drawing a complicated symbol on one of the nearby trees. "This feels sort of off. Actually . . . Am I crazy, or have we met Grim before?"

Okane blinked at her in surprise. "- - - feel it too?"

"I mean, I feel like we'd have mentioned seeing him before. There were a lot of people at Clae's wake, right? Maybe we crossed paths there?" said Laura, but she doubted it. She'd have remembered someone that distinctive.

Okane shook his head. "I don't recognize his face. I'm more interested in how he feels."

"How he what?"

"Do - - - remember when I made - - - hear the word - - - were rejecting?"

Laura had to suppress a shudder at the memory. "I don't think I've ever heard another nonverbal shout."

"He feels like that. Like '- - -' personified. But also not." Okane looked perplexed. "It's almost muted, not directed at anyone, so maybe it's more accurate to compare it to an active amulet? But not really. It's more—"

"More what?" Laura encouraged.

Okane wrestled with his words. So quietly she could barely hear, he said, "He feels like an infestation. Inverted. Not a danger, but . . . like hearing a piano and violin play the same note."

Laura eyed him shrewdly. "You're not reacting, though. You don't even look tense."

"I'm not content," he said, "but there's an even bigger part of me that feels safe. For some reason. It says I've encountered this feeling in the past and it didn't hurt me, so why be anxious? But that goes completely against my other theories of why it's familiar." He gave her a hopeless look. "I'm very confused."

"You and me both," said Laura.

"Well, now that that's taken care of—" Cherry strode back to them and held out a hand with food. "Here, something to tide you over until supper. We'll have something bigger when we stop for the night. Eat up, and we'll get back on the road."

Laura found herself with a handful of biscuits and dried fruit. Cherry moved on to Okane, but Grim stepped up after her.

"Here."

He dropped something into Laura's palm before going back to his horse. The object was a piece of candy, the wrapper declaring it MARVELOUS MAGNUM'S DELUXE CARAMEL. Laura turned to give Okane a curious look. He gave an exaggerated shrug, but beside him Cherry mimed eating. Ah, she'd mentioned this before: accept the candy or toss it while Grim wasn't looking. Laura ended up eating it, and it had to be the oldest, stalest piece of caramel she'd ever tasted.

They stopped a few more times that day, so people could stretch their legs or run off into the bushes. Laura grew sore and uncomfortable. She wriggled in a vain attempt to find a better seat, but refused to ask for breaks herself. As the sun began to descend they rode into the smaller mountains, taking an elevated mountain trail. This gave a nice view of Mount Amicum, which loomed high and snowcapped, its crags much more easily viewed here than its shadow from Amicae. It got colder in the mountains, and still colder when the sun set, allowing darkness to fall around them.

With the dark came anxiety. Neither Ranger carried a lamp, so as the world grew dark Laura's vision suffered; so must the horses', she thought. Could their leader even see? They weren't about to walk off a cliff or slide off the path and down the mountainside, were they? Worry bubbled unspoken in her gut, but Cherry led them on at least half an hour after the sun had gone. The horses walked close enough together that when Grim's steed stopped, Laura's horse bumped into the back of it. The horses behind did the same, snorting and stamping.

"Are we there?" said Laura.

"Hang on a minute. I'll check it out," Cherry called back.

Laura could see indistinctly as the woman dug her heels into the horse's side and sped up the incline.

"What is she checking?" she wondered aloud.

"The rest house," Grim replied, his voice smooth and unperturbed. "There's no reservation policy in the wilds. It works on a first-come basis, but you can be driven out anyway."

"Driven out?" Okane turned to look at him, eyes flashing briefly in the moonlight.

"Outsiders like to think Rangers have an honor code, but that's fragmented at best. At times other Rangers are more dangerous than the animals."

"So she's looking for other Rangers up there."

"Yes."

"And what if she finds some?"

"We strike a deal, drive them out ourselves, or find somewhere else to stop tonight."

Laura fingered her horse's mane as she replayed various wilds-themed films in her head. Highway bandits, train robbers, murderous jailbirds; varying forms of Ranger villains paraded through her head.

"They don't make a habit of ambushing people, do they?" she asked.

"Usually they do. Not when I'm involved, though."

"Really?" Okane leaned the other way, trying to get a better look at him.

Grim looked back blankly. "It could be that they're unnerved by my appearance," he suggested, and Laura could believe it. The dark made Grim more unearthly, like a ghost come to haunt the party, and his pale horse didn't help the illusion.

After a while Cherry reappeared. She gestured at them to follow but said nothing. Everyone quieted and let her lead them to the top of the hill. There, nestled between large rocks and trees, Laura saw the shadow of a hulking building. Cherry opened the door, ushering them and the horses inside before barring the door. The room plunged into pitch-blackness. In comparison the outside had been a spotlight.

Laura stopped short, hand tightening on her horse's reins as she listened. Someone stumbled around the perimeter of the room, and lanterns were lit. Cherry carried one to the center while Grim lit another.

"Feel free to unpack," Cherry announced, hushed. "Horses by the door, people near the back."

The building was a single room, big enough to be a small church. Beams propped up the ceiling of wooden rafters, discolored by the years, and the chimney hung like a great brick vent over the circle on the ground, supported by brick pillars. The group tied the horses to wooden supports near the door. Laura and Okane helped Grim pull tack off, and a circle of saddles and supplies formed around the brick ring. Cherry started a fire, produced a pot from the supply packs, and concocted some soup. Despite all the movement the air was quiet and tense.

"Are we in trouble?" Laura whispered, and Okane nodded quickly.

"There's something nearby and it doesn't like us."

"You mean, like . . . ?" Like other so-called couriers? Had they arranged to meet with others here?

"Yes." He glanced uneasily at the windows. "It's not an animal. It's people."

"They may think we're competition," Grim grunted, setting another armful of tack on the floor beside them.

"One of the most lucrative, high-risk markets for a Ranger is what's called a head hunt," said Cherry, giving Grim a pat on the back as she passed. "We get a list of the most dangerous animals in the wilds and go out to hunt them down. We have to bring back a specific piece of proof from the downed animal to prove we deserve the pay, but that's one of the worst parts. Scavengers can ambush you, steal your evidence to steal the paycheck. They're not above killing other Rangers to do it."

"So, - - -'re saying these would be scavengers?" said Okane.

"Or maybe they think we're the scavengers."

They spoke as if they were the potential victims here, rather than the ones sneaking around. Laura gritted her teeth. She'd had more than enough of this. She dropped the saddle she'd been carrying, planted her hands on her hips, and snapped, "Let's cut the crap."

"Laura—" Okane began, but she plowed on.

"The people outside are your coworkers, aren't they?" She gestured angrily at the windows. "This isn't about headhunters or escorting professors. You're working with a man named Theron, aren't you? He's having you secretly transport equipment to Amicae, to be delivered to our head Sweeper. This destination you can't pin on a map, that's the manufacturing base, isn't it? I already know the secret. It's not worth trying to keep us in the dark, and you're doing a terrible job at acting like this is normal."

For a long moment, neither Ranger replied. They looked at her, blank-faced and gravely silent. Finally Grim turned to face Cherry and said, "Where did you say you got these two?"

"Don't look at me!" said Cherry. "Amicae's head Sweeper sent them with me."

"Do I know too much, now?" Laura raged, but mortification and fear crawled up her throat. What if she did know too much? What if they decided to shoot her and ditch her body out here in the wilds? "I'm obviously not equipped to fight you, but seriously. Let's all be honest here. This is tiring."

"I think you've got the wrong idea," said Cherry.

"Oh? So you're not moonlighting as couriers?"

Grim laid his forehead down on the brick ring and groaned, "They know about couriers."

"Shut up!" Cherry hissed. "You don't talk about couriers out here! That's like asking to get your throat slit in the night!"

"Then you're not involved?" said Laura, flabbergasted. "But—but you were glaring at us the whole time we were in the trolleys!"

"I was trying to pin you down!" Cherry protested, visibly flustered. "I didn't know who you were, I didn't know how you interact with other people! I don't know if you've got a bias against people like me!"

"You do take a little too long warming up to people," said Grim, still facedown on the brick.

Cherry swatted him. "I don't want to hear that from you!"

"But this doesn't make any sense," said Laura. "Why did you take us out here, if you're not leading us into a plot?"

"We needed Sweepers," said Cherry. "On our last headhunting job, Grim and I found a nasty infestation out here. The wilds is full of monsters, but this one was getting too close to travel routes. Amicae's the closest city, so we tried appealing to your ERA offices to get their rail Sweepers on the job. They told me they were on a tight schedule and it wasn't close enough to the tracks for them to care. I thought the city's head Sweeper would be able to point me in the right direction, maybe even arrange for Ranger-Sweeps from other cities to come help."

Laura cradled her head in her hands. "And you got Juliana instead."

"She said you were the Sweepers for the job!" said Cherry, exasperated. "I mean, you don't look like much, but you didn't even protest."

"She sort of had us at gunpoint," said Okane.

"She *what?*" said Cherry.

"Let's start over," Laura sighed. "I'm Laura, this is Okane, we're city Sweepers and I, for one, have never been outside Amicae beyond a train ride to Puer. We are . . . regretfully involved with some kind of departmental split, and it seems ready to rack up a body count. Juliana worked you into this so fast and easy, and I thought Rangers were involved. I'm sorry for jumping to conclusions."

"Don't worry about it." Cherry waved it off, but she hadn't entirely settled. "Getting thrown at a couple of strangers would be nerve-racking on the best of days, and it sounds like you've got good reason to suspect people. I thought you were just naturally cagey. I should've noticed something was up."

Grim finally raised his head. "Why would you be forced into the wilds? How does that factor into this split?"

"It's probably so Juliana can carry on with her plans," Laura grumbled. "She'd just discovered we knew about a plan. We don't know all the details, but just knowing was enough for her. She wanted us out of the way."

"Presumably she thinks we'll die out here in the wilds," said Okane.

Cherry recoiled in disgust. "What, she thought I couldn't protect you?"

"I think she just didn't believe we had enough skill," said Okane. "It doesn't matter how good our guide is, if our equipment is bad and we don't know how to handle such a strong infestation."

"Is your equipment bad?" said Cherry.

"No," said Laura. "It's a long story."

"Well, count your lucky stars that your boss didn't do her research." Cherry drew herself to full height and thumped a fist to her chest. "Grim and I are some of the best Rangers this side of Terual. Headhunting, reconnaissance, raids, we've done it all. There's no one better to serve as an escort. If anyone tries messing with you before you reach that infestation, we'll blow them to bits."

"Thank you." A giggle escaped Laura's throat, and she buried her face in her hands. "That's a load off my mind. I didn't realize how much that weighed on me until just now."

"I do have a question, before we change the subject," said Okane. "- - - mentioned that - - - knew about couriers."

"We're not discussing them," said Grim.

Cherry nodded. "It's like you said about your boss and that plan: just knowing about them is enough to get you killed. They don't like being seen. Don't like being known. If you stumble on one of their hideouts and they find out about it, they'll hunt you down. We've known other Rangers that died that way."

"They died painfully," Grim agreed. "Couriers want to know who you've talked to. They'll torture information out of you, then go and hunt down any other whisper of their existence."

"A small satellite town near Dea got completely wiped out by them," said Cherry. "The city blamed it on felin, but any Ranger knows the difference between a bite and a sword injury."

"But who are they?" said Laura. "Why are they so secretive?"

"Our current mission is keeping you alive," said Cherry. "Talking to you any more about them would be the opposite."

"Just one more point." Okane wove his fingers together tightly. "Just as confirmation. Couriers come from the south, don't they? They come from Zyra."

The Rangers looked at each other again. Their expressions clearly read *yes*, but Grim only said, "Who can tell?"

13

FLY FLEETLY

The next day they set out early. The horses trekked along a mountain path surrounded by thick copses of mixed trees and brush, a weaving route that took them deeper and deeper into the forest. Animals darted out of sight at their approach, but birdsong rang from the trees. A monkeyish creature with long blunt claws eyed their progress from its own tree limb before launching itself into the air, to glide along their path on flaps of skin like wings. The forest trek took the majority of the day before they reached the rockier slopes of the mountains. Their route hugged the slopes, becoming a thin uphill ridge. On this path they circled Mount Amicum and eventually broke away, descending once more toward the flatter lands separating the mountains from Terrae.

"We'll take the lowland route to reach our checkpoint," Cherry explained as the horses picked their way down, close to tumbling head over heels on the slope. "From here there aren't a lot of real paths. The road to Terrae goes out of our way. We're heading more towards Thrax and those roads are long out of use. We'll be more exposed, and there are a lot of dangerous animals out there. Felin don't do well in tight places and uneven ground. That's one of the reasons trains are so vulnerable to them—they're on the flattest part of the wilds, right where felin want to be. On the plus side, it's faster and physically less dangerous."

"So," Laura said, forcing bravado and turning to Okane, "looking forward to seeing some big ugly predators?"

He smiled, more a grimace than anything. "I admit, I do wonder what a felin looks like."

Laura shuddered. She'd run into one on the train to Puer, and had no desire to repeat that experience.

Come nightfall they remained in the foothills, scouting around for a place to camp for the night. Nocturnal animals stirred, blinking from the darkness with enormous eyes that reflected light the same way Theron's had. Chattering rose, branches creaked, and feet pattered, but even below this subdued din Laura thought she heard something else. Something that didn't belong. She told herself it was just the darkness making her jumpy and forced herself to stay calm.

"Are we staying in another rest house?" she asked.

"No," Cherry replied, curt and hushed, and Laura felt chided.

"Then what are we doing?" she tried again, barely audible over the creaking saddles.

"Rest houses are in the vicinity of cities and satellite towns," Grim explained. "We're beyond those now. There won't be a roof over our heads for a while."

Cherry stopped, raising a hand to catch everyone's attention. She gestured silently ahead and to the left, where Laura glimpsed light. A campfire?

Grim skirted the Sweepers, stopping by the flanks of Cherry's black horse. "What do you think?"

Cherry glanced back, taking stock of their caravan. "I'm going to investigate."

Grim's brow furrowed. "Alone?"

"No. We might need a show of force. Sweepers, you stay here with the packhorses. I don't want to risk you two being in the middle of a shoot-out. We'll circle back for you once we know what's going on."

Grim gathered the two packhorses and brought them to Laura.

"Stay off the path for now," he instructed. "Once we're clear, I'll come back for you."

The Rangers moved away. The horses left behind made as if to follow, and Laura jerked back on the reins to stop them. Her horse tossed its head angrily, but after two more attempts it gave up. She couldn't convince it to move off the path, though.

"Come on," she growled, pulling on the reins and tapping its sides with her heels.

"Let's just lead them," said Okane, swinging out of the saddle. After some hesitation Laura did the same, and they led the horses off the path. Once they were far enough away to deem themselves safe, they tied the reins to some lower branches and sat down to wait. They were downhill, so couldn't see the light anymore, but perched on a large rock and looked in that direction anyway.

"How long do - - - think they'll take?" Okane asked, resting his chin on his knees.

"Not long, I hope. I don't like being out here without them." A chilly breeze went by, and Laura shuddered. "The wilds are both mundane and scarier than I thought."

"Agreed." Okane looked around, as if checking for any eavesdroppers.

"Are you expecting a courier to come sneaking up behind us?" Laura said dryly.

"Honestly, I wouldn't be surprised."

Laura sighed. "You're going to tell me what all of this means, right? Sometime soon?"

"Yes, but the Rangers were right. This is their territory. It's better to explain in a safe place."

"And yet, you didn't do that before."

"I didn't think we'd be uprooted that easily."

"Well, there's no getting around it now. Whether you acknowledge them or not, they're part of this mess and we won't escape it anytime soon. Especially not if we don't know what's going on."

"I know," he whispered.

A sharp *crack* rent the air. A flock of birds took flight from a nearby tree, shrill and frightened, while the other sounds of nature came to a stuttering stop. The horses snorted and stamped, tugging at their tethers. More noise followed, pops and crashes and echoes that Laura registered immediately as gunfire.

"Oh, shit," she whispered.

Okane leapt up and grabbed the closest horse by the bridle, trying to calm it, but its eyes continued to roll. The guns kept going, and now that Laura listened she heard shouting too. She stood, shaking, as Okane's horse tossed its head and whinnied. A loud snap made her whirl around. A man had crept down from the path, a small object held in each hand. For a moment she thought Grim had come to take them out of the danger zone, but this man wasn't near pale enough. Worse, he brandished a pistol and a knife. Realizing his cover was blown, he raised the gun.

"Get down!" Laura yelled, launching herself at Okane. She knocked him out of the way, right before a bullet zipped past. It clipped the horse's harness and sent the animal into a frenzy. They scrambled away from its hooves and bumped into the next packhorse.

"Who's there?" Okane yelped.

"Get back out here where I can see you!" the man roared. "If you want to live, you'll do as I say! I've got a gang surrounding you!"

"That's a bluff," Okane hissed through his teeth, eyes flicking about. They rested on Laura for a moment, and she got the idea.

"Let's go," she agreed, and without any further ado, they bolted.

The man shouted in rage as they thundered away downhill.

Despite the amount of people dashing through forests in films, Laura found it difficult to keep a good pace. Undergrowth knocked into her legs, making her stumble and lose speed. She had to skirt trees and scramble over fallen trunks. Only patches of moonlight shone through the branches. She felt blind, but doggedly followed the crashing noises of Okane's flight. The man stampeded after them, but visibility wasn't much better for him. The few times his pistol fired, the shots veered far off course and smashed into trees or foliage. The hill grew steeper, then evened out into a valley. This made the going slightly easier, but Laura still breathed harsh, and she knew her clothes had ripped. She sighted Okane ahead of her, a flash of brown vaulting over a small ditch to the left, but otherwise relied on sound.

They bumped into each other what felt like an eternity later, as both swerved to avoid outcroppings of rock. They almost collided before realizing the other was there, and it took another horrified moment before they realized that no, they hadn't just run into their pursuer. They stumbled on, and barely ten paces after this they found another yawning hole in the ground with a circle of dirt around the edge.

"Hang on," Laura panted, grabbing Okane by the sleeve. "Careful here."

"What?"

"Circle around it and lie down in the bushes. I'll be right there."

Baffled, he darted past a few more trees and wriggled under one of the larger bushes. Laura approached the knuckerhole, heart hammering. Hoping desperately that there wasn't an animal down there, she kicked at the dirt circle and went so far as to slide her way in. She slipped onto her rear in the process and caught a glimpse of pitch-black tunnel before activating her amulets and getting the hell out. She could hear the man approaching and made a frantic bid for the underbrush. She dove into the vegetation much closer than Okane had, and not a moment too soon. The man blundered around the rock outcropping and paused. The moon shone just bright enough for him to see the disturbed rim of the knuckerhole.

Go for it, Laura thought, gritting her teeth. *Look at that, not at us.*

The man crept forward, weapons held in shaky hands as he approached the hole. He circled it, squinting down. To Laura's relief, his shaking subsided and he began to laugh.

"So that's where you went!" he guffawed. "You're a damn fool! Come here, you *hito*-loving scum! Can't hide down there forever!"

Laura let out a sigh of relief, pressing her head against the dirt. The ground was hard and cold, but her run had left her uncomfortably warm, so she welcomed the coolness as protection and luxury. Meanwhile the man had one foot on the edge of the hole. She turned her head to watch as he kept yelling.

"Boy, get out here with your hands up! No funny business if you know what's good for your little girlfriend. Don't worry about her, I'll take *good* care of—"

The words stopped abruptly. He barely had time to stiffen before something shot out of the hole. Laura saw rusty scales, bulbous wide eyes, and a heavily crested head on a serpentine neck, before teeth clamped down on the man's side and he was dragged into the knuckerhole. Only a lingering shriek and dropped knife remained. It happened in a split second, and suddenly Laura felt tense again, more frightened than she'd been before. The ground no longer seemed safe. Something tapped her hand, and she jumped. It was only Okane. He looked at her with wide eyes and moved his head, motioning for her to go. They shuffled along the ground for a few feet, and once out of the knuckerhole's range, leapt to their feet and fled.

They wandered through the woods for a long time. After every hill rose another, and they hadn't paid attention to landmarks so had no idea which direction they'd come from or where their guides were or if they were alive. The nightlife of the wilds returned to its earlier volume. While it sounded creepy, the smaller animals and herbivores making the noises wouldn't sing if there were predators around. Okane relaxed too, taking more time to observe their surroundings.

As they crossed a small clearing, Laura slowed and pulled out her pocket watch. She squinted to make out the numerals.

"It's past one in the morning," she groaned. "How long do you think we've been running?"

"Hours. I don't know, I didn't check."

"What do you think we should do now?" The idea of wandering more didn't appeal much. She was dead on her feet and cold. She rubbed at her arms, wishing for the horses and supplies.

Okane cast around. "We should find some kind of shelter for the night and sleep. We can keep going tomorrow."

"What kind of shelter? Grim said there wasn't anywhere with a roof for a long ways."

"Well," he grunted, hopping over a particularly large root as they left the moonlit clearing behind them, "Brecht's actually fascinated with the wilds. Back at Underyear, during the fireworks, he talked about some of the tamer animals and their habits. I think we just need to find a burrow we can fit in."

"Are we talking about abandoned knuckerholes? Because I'm pretty sure that man thought it was abandoned. Look where it got him."

Okane shuddered. "Not a knuckerhole. No way are we getting near one of those. Let's just keep our eyes open for something."

They kept walking. Twenty minutes later Okane ducked down, peered through the trees, then made a beeline for something.

"Did you find one?" Laura blinked furiously to keep her vision clear as she followed him to a dense thicket.

He appraised the outside, wandering first left, then right, before nodding. "I think this will do."

"It's not occupied, is it?"

"No."

"How do you know?"

"Smell. I don't remember what's supposed to be in this kind of den, but I remember it's supposed to be pretty pungent."

"You realize humans aren't renowned for our sense of smell."

Okane shrugged and knelt down. He inspected the thick grasses a moment more before flattening himself to the ground and crawling in. It turned out there was a small tunnel, not tall enough to fit in easily. Laura sat outside and watched Okane's boots vanish into the gloom. Abruptly there came a thump, and a wheeze of pain.

"Okane?" Laura peered into the tunnel, heart in her throat. "Okane, are you okay?"

"Fine," he grunted. "Hang on."

She heard shuffling. She couldn't see anything in the pitch-darkness of the tunnel but squinted anyway. Surely knuckers didn't live in thickets?

A twig cracked behind her and she whirled around. Okane stood there. He held up his hands and said quickly, "It's just me."

"You? But—" She looked between him and the tunnel entrance, baffled. "Where'd you come from? I didn't see you come out."

"This place isn't what I thought it was," said Okane. "I think - - -'ll appreciate it, though."

He gestured her to follow. They skirted the thicket, through more vegetation and into a small ravine. Okane pulled aside the branches of a sprawling tree, and there in the ravine's side was an open door. Laura brushed her hand over the weathered wood, and her fingers caught in the grooves of a carved cross.

"Could this be—"

"One of the couriers' hideouts," said Okane. "I'm sure of it."

Laura stared at him. "Weren't we supposed to be avoiding couriers? You were terrified of them earlier."

"As far as I can tell, it hasn't been used in a long time. It's covered in dust."

"And there's no sign of them outside?"

Okane couldn't possibly know how to track passersby, but he still said, "I'm sure. No other people are anywhere close to us. It sort of—" He gestured vaguely. "It feels empty here."

"If you're sure," she muttered, and walked in.

The short entryway opened up into a wide subterranean room. The rounded walls centered about a large chunk of glowing, yellowish crystal. The crystal stuck up out of the ground at an angle, weathered into a misshapen lump and ringed by stones as if it were a campfire. On either side of the door, patches of ground had been turned over, covered in leaves and boxed in by wooden frames; on the far side something similar had been done, but rather than leaves these smaller frames overflowed with pelts. Overhead the grasses and branches of the thicket twined sturdily together, forming a roof of their own and thick brambly walls. The tunnel could be spotted just above their heads, but it dead-ended into open air.

"I almost fell right through," Okane admitted. "Luckily some more thorns had been pulled over, so I had to slow down. Gave me time to realize what I'd crawled into."

"It's not quite as impressive as films led me to believe," said Laura, but relaxed all the same. It was shelter; she couldn't ask for anything more. "What's that crystal? It looks pretty important."

"Honestly, I'm not sure."

He knelt down to get a better look at it, and Laura did the same on the other side. The crystal was pale, pale yellow, fogged up like a winter window. Could it be an amulet running out of power? Frowning, she reached out a hand and pressed her palm against its side.

Brighten, she ordered.

Nothing happened. Was it just a rock after all? Okane copied her motion. She didn't know if he gave it an order, but as soon as he brushed it the crystal glowed. Laura felt a shift of magic, but it was wrong. Flat. She couldn't think how to describe it beyond—

"Dead!" Okane drew back, clutching the hand to his chest as if burned.

Laura blinked at him. "It's a rock."

"It's dead!"

"The magic, you mean?" She placed both hands now and concentrated. With the crystal going, she could feel its energy working. Where Gin thrummed loyal and steady, where Niveus danced excitedly, this crystal was empty. There but not there. Nothing, but it couldn't be, because magic still lingered but there wouldn't even be a hollow left when it was gone. She saw what he meant: it felt alive and dead all at once. A crystal coma.

A sudden, sick feeling jolted through her. Her eyes snapped open. *A crystal coma.*

"Is this like Clae?" she whispered. "Was this a person? A Magi?"

"It can't be," said Okane, horrified. "It looks nothing like a person!"

But Laura pictured Clae, imagined the same wintery fog crept across his crystal, and her mind drew far too many similarities. Could he be reduced to something like this? Would his magic drain over time to the point that anything left of him—magic, soul, otherwise—would cease to exist? Had they been stealing the last of Anselm's humanity all this time?

"It's not a Magi," Okane said firmly. "Magi turn when they're overwhelmed, and that emotion stays. Clae was angry when he died. I hate going near Anselm because he was so afraid when he died, he makes me scared now. If this isn't . . . If it's not *screaming,* there's no way it was alive."

"What else could it be?" said Laura.

That was harder to answer, but at last Okane settled on, "Recovered Gin."

"What?"

"Felin eat magic, right? Brecht said that there's a problem with packs of felin digging out Gin deposits and feeding until all the magic is gone and Gin is destroyed. Some Rangers pick up affected stones and carry them where felin can't reach, wait for magic to replenish, then sell the stone to cities."

The ground around them was hilly and forested enough that no felin could easily reach this place, so that at least made sense. Yes, this could be chipped and tired Gin recovering from an attack. Nothing nearly so grave as what her imagination came up with.

"Exactly," she said, forcing her brain to this conclusion. "I mean, if it was a person, there's no way anyone would keep it in their hideout like this."

But still the crystal glowed, and still she doubted.

∞

The next morning she woke to the musty smell of earth and furs, and an uncomfortable warmth at her side. This wasn't so strange— the crystal had readily produced heat all night—but in such a specific location? She blinked open her eyes and looked down. An animal was curled up there. It looked like a huge lanky dog, its thick coat fiery red save for the black bristled fur along its hackles, narrow muzzle, and abnormally long legs. Blotches of darker and lighter reds dotted its sides, but the brightest color of all was the yellow of its catlike eyes, which it fixed on Laura. It made no attempt to move.

"Okane?" she squeaked.

"Hm?" Okane sat up in his own box of furs. He was studying a page, and another beast lay flush against his leg.

"What's going on?"

He glanced at her, realized her discomfort, and said, "It's nothing to worry about. These are firedogs."

Laura was familiar with the term, if not the appearance. Firedogs lived in the wilds, named such because they gravitated toward heat. Ranger myths abounded with stories of men kept alive in winter by packs of firedogs. She'd seen the like in films, but the director obviously took some artistic liberties by using kingshounds instead. The shape was vaguely similar, but the colors could never be confused.

"This place is camouflaged as a firedog den," Okane continued, turning back to his paper. "The couriers must let them in frequently to keep up the disguise. They seemed happy to see us."

The animals seemed as tame as regular dogs. Laura rose gingerly, and her furry companion merely snuffled and rolled into the warm spot where she'd been. Three more firedogs had stacked up against the crystal itself. One of them kicked in its sleep, and Laura had to step over it to reach Okane.

"What have you got there? They didn't fetch you a telegram, did they?"

He held up the page. It was most definitely not a telegram. For one thing, it was many times larger than the usual note, and for another, it overflowed with complicated symbols. Laura was somewhat familiar with pictographs due to the usual labeling of Kuro no Oukoku, but these were three times more complicated. Looking at all the dense lines made her head hurt. She squinted, trying and failing to find a meaning.

"Is it . . . a letter?"

"It must be." Okane spread it over his lap again. "I know the language. It's Wasureigo."

"Wasu What?"

"The native people and Magi worked together a long time ago, and as far as I understand they still interact frequently. Natives call themselves Wasureijin, which means something like 'forgotten people.' 'Go' is 'language.' The forgotten language. My mother taught me to speak some dialects, but the actual writing?" He shook his head. "I know enough to tell it's describing landscapes, but I only learned individual letters. Grammar, syntax, everything in between . . . I can't tell - - - what it means. If it says anything about their plans with Amicae, I wouldn't know."

Laura sat beside him. "Do you think it says where the nearest paths are?"

"Presumably."

"Okay, let's see . . . which of these is one you understand?"

"'Forest.'" He pointed at one of the less-complicated ones. "See? It's a lot of letters in one. Two trees sheltered by a big tree. Forest."

"And are there any directions you recognize by it? Left or right? East or west?" His frown said no. She sighed. "I suppose they can't have left us a map. Too easy." She studied it some more before tilting her head. "What's that one?"

The symbol in question was easily the simplest one on the page, and came up multiple times: a cross potent.

"It looks like a number, but it's wrong," said Okane.

"Could it be a location?" said Laura. "There was a cross carved in the door here. Maybe it means 'safe place'? If we're traveling from one place to another, that needs safe roads, and it must overlap with Ranger routes at some point. We might be able to find someone on the way."

"What happens if it leads us into a group of couriers?" Okane said darkly.

"Then we'll approach with caution, and maybe get some answers to our current problems. If someone as obvious as Grim can sneak around them, so can we."

Okane gave her a long look, but he didn't seem to have any better ideas. "So if the cross is a location, and the words around it are descriptions . . ." He puzzled over it again, mouthing the words he knew. "So, I think it's talking about a continuing route. In one direction is the old . . . thing. Place. Settlement. But that's a bad place, so we head away from it. There are things in the middle . . . mountains are mentioned. . . . One big tree, then forest with the safe zone, then field, then rock, then river with safe zone. Big field and more bad after it."

"So if we can figure out where those are and go the opposite way—" Laura snapped her fingers. "Thrax. The old dangerous settlement, they must mean Thrax!"

"Could we see that from here?"

"In sunlight, maybe. We'd have to find a proper vantage point." Her mind raced. "Thrax is a stupid place to go in the first place, but the other bad areas might just mean spots in full view of other people. Couriers would want to avoid those. We should head for their so-called bad places."

"It's something to go on. Let's just make sure we leave this place intact. I don't want them figuring out we stayed here."

"Good call," said Laura.

They shuffled through the room, double-checking that nothing was out of place. With so little decoration to start with, the task proved easy. Okane folded up the paper and carefully stowed it under the furs, presumably where he'd found it.

"That's done. Shall we?"

The firedogs perked up as the pair made for the door. Once it was clear they were leaving, the firedogs leapt up and charged out of the hideout. They vanished by the time the Sweepers reached the ravine.

"They're weirdly well trained," said Laura.

"I wonder how the couriers did that," said Okane, pulling the door closed.

Laura was about to reply but paused. One of the firedogs stood at the mouth of the ravine, looking expectantly at them.

"He looks like he's waiting for us," she mused.

"Maybe it's part of the couriers' routine?" Okane guessed.

They watched it a while longer. The firedog gave an annoyed bark and trotted away. Laura and Okane glanced at each other. Word-lessly, they agreed to follow. The firedog led them over uneven terrain, glancing back every once in a while to check for their presence. The path it walked was narrow but well-trodden. A horse couldn't fit through here, but people certainly could. The firedog led them to a wide clearing on a hill. Its pack lounged among the patchy grass and tree stumps, soaking up the morning light. An enormous tree rose from the very middle of the clearing, dwarfing the surrounding foliage with its sprawling branches.

"Big tree," Laura whispered.

She hurried to its trunk and looked toward the mountains. On early mornings clouds tended to hang about the summits, but on this January day the clouds thinned. Ever so faintly, she saw the distant shape of a ruined city.

"There it is! Thrax! I saw it from the train the same way!" she laughed. "Not only is that map right, we must be close to train tracks! We can find help!"

"Then we follow the direct line," said Okane. "This way."

They went back into the forest, leaving the clearing and firedogs behind them. Sure enough, another little path wound here. It led them up and down a few more slopes, weaving between trees and bushes. After a particularly rocky decline, they reached a break in the trees and emerged into full sunlight. Before them the mountains soared into the sky, their jagged forms high above them but growing smaller and more indistinct as Laura followed them, until they became little more than a bluish haze on the horizon. The ground to their right remained rocky and difficult, but in the distance the landscape melted into the flatlands, gentle hills dotted with more copses of trees. Laura had seen a picture of almost the exact same view in a textbook before, and her spirits soared.

"I know where we are!" she cried. "We're on the edge of the Terulian Plains!"

Of course, location gave them little to go on at this point. They remained tired, hungry, and unsure where the map led. Laura had a general idea of the closest city: beyond Thrax, Terrae sat in the very middle of the plains. With so much vital farming area, Terrae grew more crops than it consumed; satellite towns would be scattered far and wide around it, and trains would constantly come through to pick up products to sell in other cities. Civilization couldn't be far out of reach. They only needed to track down a train or find a satellite citizen. If it were a train bound for the south or Amicae they could get back home, but even if their ride headed toward Terrae, they knew people there. Diana and the Terrae Sweepers had helped them only recently, and Clae had told them Terrae had old ties to the Sinclairs. It would work. They just needed to know which direction to focus their efforts in. They selected the highest and closest of the plains hills to serve as a vantage point and started navigating through the rest of the rocky foothills.

"What's that?" Okane asked, halfway down one of the slopes and gesturing to the side. "I haven't seen something like that before."

The grasses here grew shorter, pale green as opposed to the rich emerald they'd be in summer, but in multiple spots sprawled shapes made of rocks, raised earth, or brownish grass. Laura frowned as they passed a swirling design seven feet across.

"I don't know. I never saw pictures of them in the books I read. Then again, photographers would've taken a different path, wouldn't they?"

Okane looked around, taking in all the designs, and stopped short. "Hang on, I know what that one means. Water. I think it must mean the river with the safe zone."

The mention caught Laura's attention immediately. Her throat was parched: water would be very welcome. "Is it pointing somewhere?"

Okane heaved himself up the rocks nearest them. He squinted over the top, keeping himself low. After a while he descended again, confirming, "Yes, there's a river. No sign of anyone else, couriers or otherwise."

"Water" turned out to be a wide but short waterfall framed by colored rocks. At their dry points the rocks were regular gray, but closer to the waterline they changed into rusty reds, pale blues, and pinks with black crevices. The water came from somewhere in the mountains, cascading down into a wide pool so clear they could see the smooth rocks of the bottom, more blues and greens in heaps that had to be fifteen feet down. The water continued from that place in a stream, twisting away downhill but completely obscured from their previous position. Laura knelt and scooped up water with her hands. She took big gulps while Okane wandered closer to the falls.

"What are you looking for?"

"This was supposed to have a safe place, or another hideout. I guess I was—hang on."

Another symbol was carved into the rock by the waterfall, a cross potent in the middle of a circle. Okane ran his finger over the mark.

He furrowed his brows and dug in his nails. The rock scraped as he pulled the circle piece out. The symbol worked as a stopper, revealing a hollow area inside the rock. Okane reached in, and pulled out a square biscuit.

"It's a cache."

Laura's stomach growled, but she eyed the food uncertainly. "If we take it, they'll know someone came here."

"- - -'re right." His shoulders slumped; he must've been just as hungry. "Even if they don't find us, they'll take it out on passing Rangers, or even the satellite towns. It's not worth—"

A low *whoosh* of air from behind them interrupted him. Laura turned and felt the blood drain from her face. An enormous shaggy animal approached them, its doggy head crowned with curved bull horns. Its cloven hooves clicked against the stone by the pool while its mouth opened, revealing sharp teeth.

"What is that?" Okane squeaked.

"Canir!"

"It looks different from that taxidermy in the Sullivan house."

"Well no shit, it's alive!"

Laura clamped her mouth shut as the canir growled. Okane's free hand groped at his belt, as if he'd suddenly remembered he had a gun. She grabbed his arm to stop him. Maybe the gun would hurt a canir, maybe it wouldn't, but it would bring worse things down on them. The canir grew closer, to the point they could feel its breath on their faces. It turned its head to the side to look at them with one beady black eye. It gave a long, low snarl, but made no move to attack. A mechanical clack caught their attention, and they looked up. Grim stood atop the rocks, a rifle in hand.

"You messed with the cache, didn't you?" he said.

"Is that really important right now?" Okane stuttered, wincing as the canir let out another low breath.

The animal was completely unfazed by the new addition, and Grim didn't appear very concerned either.

"Put your hand on it," he ordered.

"And lose our fingers?" Laura scoffed.

"Not you, him. Just put your hand on it and keep it there. You'll be fine."

Okane gave him an incredulous look, but did as he was told. He reached out one shaky hand. The canir didn't react. Reassured, he pressed his hand harder against its thick coat. The canir's mouth closed, and after a short time it snorted and turned away, retreating back the way it came. Grim lowered his rifle.

"Replace what you took," he said, jumping down.

"How did you know that would work?" asked Laura.

"Things like that are rigged. They set it so canir act as guard dogs."

"The same way they have firedogs trained to cover their hideouts?"

Grim gave them a long look. "You two seem determined for trouble." He didn't linger on it long. "You went a long way off-track. What happened?"

"There was a man with a gun." Laura shrugged helplessly. "What happened to you? We heard more guns, but we couldn't see anything."

"Just a skirmish. Neither of us were hurt."

Grim shuffled under his coat and pulled out a flare gun. He loaded it, pointed at the sky, and pulled the trigger. It fired with a pop and rattling hiss, sending a green beacon arcing up over their heads.

"That should do it," he said to himself, putting the gun away. He clicked his tongue, and an echoing whinny came from the other side of the rocks. "I've got food with me. Put that back."

Wordlessly, they put the food back in the cache and replaced the stone stopper. Grim's pale horse ambled up to them, and he procured food from the saddlebags.

"Thanks," Laura murmured, accepting some jerky and beans.

He grunted in reply, doling out a share for Okane too. He dug through the pockets of his coat and gave them each a caramel in addition. He studied them until they began to eat, then nodded toward the cache.

"Don't touch anything with that symbol."

"We thought it meant 'safe place.' Were we wrong?" said Laura.

"Safe only for them," said Grim. "If they're paranoid about people finding them, it goes double for their supplies. Let them sneak around, and pretend you didn't find it."

"If couriers are so sneaky, how do - - - know about them?" said Okane. "They approached us first, but - - -—?"

Grim shrugged. "I'm sneakier than they are."

"Grim!" came a shout.

Grim lifted his rifle and waved it rather than call back. Within moments Cherry charged into view, the line of horses behind her. She pulled up and dismounted.

"Where have you two been?" she demanded, grabbing Laura and Okane by the shoulders. "We've been looking for you all night!"

"We got ambushed by someone with a gun, so we ran," said Laura.

"Why didn't you call for help? Just shoot back?"

"Shoot back and attract a felin? Even I know that's an idiot idea," said Laura.

Cherry rubbed at her head. "Right, all you have are Sweeper supplies. God, this is exactly why I wanted ERA Sweepers. Regular guns are part of their standard supplies."

"Well, you're stuck with us."

"I'm not complaining about your skill against infestations. I'm just concerned with keeping you safe on the way." Cherry coughed out a laugh. "Really, though. The day after I make a speech about how qualified we are, we manage to lose you. I'm glad you came out of that okay."

Grim patted her awkwardly on the back.

Laura cracked a smile. "You actually helped a lot for that. It was nice to know not to crawl into a knuckerhole."

"And not to disturb strange courier hideouts," Okane added.

"You're both insufferable," Cherry snickered.

"They resemble you," said Grim, and Cherry swatted him again.

"In any case, you have a great sense of direction," she said. "We're actually not far from the infestation we called you out for. If you're prepared to fight, we'll head for it now."

14

FELL BEAST

The horses crossed the flatlands with long strides, in more of a cluster than a line. Laura's and Okane's horses had been returned to them, and the packhorses galloped in the rear, with Cherry taking the lead once more.

"So what actually happened last night?" Laura asked as they clambered over a dry streambed. "Grim said that neither of you got hurt, but—"

"We made enough noise for them to realize we were coming, but they thought we were scavengers. They'd killed a felin and had the proof for payment, so they thought we were coming to steal it," said Cherry. "They hid until we came in, and as soon as they saw me, they lost it. Started yelling something about us being there to wipe out the rest of the goddamn island."

"What's that supposed to mean?"

"What, you can't tell?" Cherry turned in the saddle and pointed at her face, wearing a sneer more jaded than derisive. "My name's actually Sakura. I'm Wasureijin, one of the Forgotten People. Uninformed people would call us 'native,' but the label's so wrong it's laughable. My people created the monster you're supposed to deal with."

"Is that why that man was yelling about *hito*-lovers?" Okane piped up.

"He sounded pretty stupid, didn't he? '*Hito*' is a word for person. He called you people-lovers. Probably didn't realize it, though." Cherry straightened out again. "Anyway, we got into a scuffle. Poor Grim here didn't know what to do! He's so used to scaring people off he doesn't know what to do when actually confronted."

Grim's nose wrinkled minutely in embarrassment.

"I was able to take care of it myself. One of the other men might be dead. He got hit, but crawled off before we could so much as give him a bandage. The rest of them ran for it. And then we went back to find you, and all we found were the horses!"

"Sorry," said Okane, but she ignored him.

"We split right afterwards to try finding you. I thought we'd cover more ground that way, and reconvene later whether or not we had any luck. Not many people can say they survived a night in the wilds without help. You'll have some fantastic bragging rights when you get back to the city."

Grim lifted his head. Without any other sign his horse gained speed, galloping to the front of the group.

"It's close," he whispered.

"Is there anything special about this one?" Laura asked, grabbing the saddle horn as her own horse moved to keep up.

"The infestation is on the move, but considering its location, it's not that difficult to track down," said Cherry. "Wait a few minutes and you'll hear it too."

A howling rose in front of them, a low bellow that sounded nothing like the shrill sound she associated with infestations. Laura looked at Cherry, incredulous.

"What is that?"

"That would be your location."

They crested one of the hills and came to a halt. In the wide gully before them was a felin. The animal was big and thickly set, a lionlike abomination of gold and a myriad of brighter underlying colors, tossing its mightily spiked head and thrashing its long tail, burning eyes rolling in their sockets as it flailed. The deafening sound and the sight of the beast made the horses fidget, ears pressed back against their heads, and Laura had half a mind to run the other way. Strangely enough, it didn't seem to notice their presence at all. Grim's horse stepped in front of the others, the sole animal unaffected. Now that he had everyone's attention, Grim nodded toward the felin and said, "Look at its head."

The felin charged the opposite side of the gully, digging its claws into the grassy side as it collided and writhed, roaring again. With its head in plain sight, Laura spotted the problem. Wedged between the spikes there was a glint of metal. Whatever the object was, it was thin but larger than a human hand.

"Is that the amulet?"

"An artifact of the crusades, most likely," Grim replied.

"There's a lot of old amulets in the wilds," said Cherry. "During the high age of magic, people didn't think twice about leaving them behind. They had no reason not to, when there weren't monsters using them as shells. Sweeper excursions happened even before ERA started doing it officially, so a lot of those amulets have been picked up over the years, but the remaining ones are very dangerous. Some have become dormant in recent years and lose power that way, but you wake one up?" She snapped her fingers, as if this were all the explanation needed.

"But how'd this one get stuck on a felin of all things?" said Laura. "Felin eat magic, right? An infestation's the opposite of magic."

"It's possible that it simply tracked the magical hollow, without realizing what was inside." Grim kept his horse moving, calm as anything, and its own quietness seemed to infect the others. "Felin are magic creatures. The man who created them meant for them to combat infestations. They were built to be living rams, absorbing magic to wield against infestations in physical attacks. They didn't turn out as expected, but they retain that aspect of their construction. Your infestation has been fighting the influence of magic for over a week."

"Weaker or not, it's still stuck on another monster," Okane pointed out.

"True," said Laura, eyeing the beast reproachfully; even with Grim's steed in the way, her horse fidgeted badly. "Any tips on dealing with rampaging felin?"

"Look no further. Grim's one of the best headhunters in Terual," said Cherry.

His brow furrowed. "Felin are one thing. Infestations are another."

"And infestations are what we're here to take care of. Great how that works out," said Laura.

"What do you think, Grim, can you take her out from here?" said Cherry.

"I could."

"I don't think - - - should. Not yet, anyway," said Okane. "I mean, - - - said the felin is keeping pressure on the infestation with its magic, right? So long as it's alive, it'll keep doing that."

"But can you get close enough to do your job?" said Cherry.

"It's not like we're hitting it with sticks. We do need some distance. It's just . . . aiming." Laura gestured uselessly.

"That's a small target," said Grim.

"We can make it bigger though, right?" Okane glanced at Laura. "If we draw it out?"

"How do we do that? They usually come out looking for food, but this one's occupied."

"Would a decoy work?" Cherry suggested.

"If it's this preoccupied?"

As if to prove the point the felin rolled over completely, wheeling across the gully and hitting the wall so the ground shook beneath their feet.

"Maybe we can get the felin to drive it out," Laura suggested. "If they're supposed to combat it, just fire this thing up and we can help it out."

"You really want to piss off a felin?"

"Yeah?" Laura folded her arms, pressing down on her stomach to quash any nerves. "They can take each other out. If the infestation wins, we attack. If the felin wins—"

"Then Grim might get a good head hunt in." Cherry smirked. "So, if we want to bait it, we'll need amulets. Got any on you, Grim?"

He turned out his pockets, revealing only more caramels.

"If it's magic, I might be useful," said Okane.

Laura glared. "What's that supposed to mean?"

"I've been practicing."

"Do you have an amulet?" Cherry interrupted.

"No, I just have more magic than most people."

Cherry raised her eyebrows but didn't comment. "So we use you as the bait."

"As long as - - - make sure I don't die."

"You can stick with me," said Grim.

He gestured for Okane to climb over to his horse. After some hesitation Okane did, settling awkwardly on the saddle behind him.

"Hold on, but don't touch my skin," he ordered.

"Touch his skin and he breaks out in hives," Cherry snickered.

The gray horse trotted along the gully. Cherry followed.

"We ready, then?"

"I guess," said Okane. "Laura?"

She pulled out an Egg. An odd feeling shot up her arm, and she looked down. This wasn't the Egg with a painted lid, but somehow it still simmered with the angry feeling of Clae's magic. She reached back to her bag, tapped her knuckles against all the others in her inventory. Every single one echoed Clae. The painted Egg hadn't even been in the same section, tucked instead inside the smaller pack on her hip. How was this possible? Should she be worried? No. If Clae's will was somehow working through the kin, she could trust it. She swallowed her unease.

"Ready on your signal," she said.

Okane let out a shuddering breath and closed his eyes. Laura felt a light fluctuation in the air first, like an unsteady breeze or changing temperature, before she heard the distinct crackle of his magic. Grim jolted in the saddle. The felin's head lifted, eyes burning from yellowish to red. It snarled, and the infestation atop it fluctuated.

For a moment all was still; then the felin lunged. It couldn't scale the side but slammed into it, high enough for its head to breach the top and snap. The horses spooked and took off. Okane clung to Grim's back; with the new scare his magic wavered, giving off more popping, which only lent more speed to the horse's flight. The felin followed. Its spikes ripped chunks of earth from the gully slope as it thundered away. It kept throwing itself at the wall, claws scrabbling for purchase. Every little noise from Okane's direction drove it more insane. The infestation roiled, bubbling and sprouting tendrils, squalling a dreadful note of its own. Just as planned, the influx of power had driven more of it from the amulet; it had to grow and fight back if it didn't want to be extinguished.

Laura pulled out an Egg and dug her heels into the horse's sides. The animal didn't speed up; it kept level with Cherry and didn't budge. Grim hauled on his horse's reins, and it veered right. Cherry and Laura were almost upon them, and had to swerve to avoid it. The gully had grown shallow enough for the felin to barrel over the side. It charged past Laura as if she didn't exist, close enough to touch. In its wake came fatigue. She slumped, suddenly short of breath, and her fingers loosened. The Egg fell and smashed, unarmed and useless. Cherry wavered on her own horse but kept upright. Laura gritted her teeth and hauled herself straight again.

"I can't do anything like this!" Laura hissed.

"What, you want closer?"

Closer meant more drain; that wouldn't do. "Ahead? Out of its energy range."

The black horse sped up, and Laura's charged to catch it. Ahead the gray horse wove left and right. With every swerve the felin fell further behind. The beast with its heavy spikes couldn't master turning. Its momentum carried it several feet before its claws rent enough earth for it to change direction. On one turn it slid clean into a rock formation, and earth cascaded onto it. Cherry and Laura galloped past while it was stuck, and Laura lobbed another Egg. It burst on the felin's head. Kin roared, gold ripping out of its glass to claw at rock and spikes. The infestation was completely overshadowed. But the light didn't linger. The kin roar tapered, and the blast sucked itself right back in. The purple tints on the felin's sides grew darker. It bared its teeth with a stronger snarl, and the air grew heavy. Cherry's horse almost lost footing completely before escaping the danger zone.

"Damn beast," she snarled, gathering up the reins. "It'll absorb any attack you throw at it. Should've had Grim take care of it at the start."

But Laura was getting a nauseous, awful feeling that had nothing to do with the animal.

"Wait for it!" she called. "An infestation doesn't drop that easily!"

Whatever it was, Okane felt it too. He squeaked something unintelligible and beat his hand against Grim's shoulder. The felin took one step forward, then shuddered. Trembling, it arched its back, mouth gaping open before its torso dropped to the ground.

Blackness glinted in the crevices of the felin's armor, popping, shifting, sliding, seeping. The rock and dirt on top of the beast discolored and broke down from stone to dust. The infestation oozed across its back, tightening its grip, and the felin convulsed.

"Is it trying to use the felin like an amulet?" said Laura, horrified.

"Wasn't expecting that," said Cherry.

Such a thing should be impossible; infestations didn't inhabit corpses, let alone something still living. Then again, felin weren't natural creatures. Maybe the infestation found a loophole, or maybe it was just desperate enough to try.

The felin shrieked, and the infestation sprouted feelers. Some looped around the beast's crown while others slid up as if testing the sky. Smoke rose from the mass as the sun met it, but apart from some dryness, the light had no effect. The feelers reached several feet into the air and twined together, shifting, waiting.

Laura felt a jolt in her stomach. Instinct told her to *get the hell out of there,* but the pseudo-warning came too late. The tendrils separated and crashed down in every direction. Each gouged deep into the ground, rending earth and rock like butter. They halted, then heaved right, ripping up chunks of grass in a spin. One whistled overhead. Laura ducked, cursing.

Appealing as it was to sit on a horse, she couldn't so much as aim without the horse dancing out of control. She leapt off and stumbled before hurling the Egg. Halfway through its flight it smacked into a tendril and burst. Hissing kin spiraled up its length, reducing black ooze to barely more than grit. The infestation screeched. Tendrils coiled and writhed. The kin light snuffed out but smoke kept issuing, thicker and darker. Yellowish light glinted in the main mass.

The felin jerked one way, then the other, clawing at the ground and snarling before its midsection jerked up, producing a loud snap. The infestation gathered itself up into a single tower, spiraling skyward again before curling and expanding once more. Feelers soared over their heads before taking a sharp curve down. Cherry's horse leapt away from the incoming darkness, but she swore with the movement.

"It's pulling us in!" she shouted.

It took a moment for Laura to catch on. The feelers formed a cage, each one a thick black bar to seal them in. The bars began to rotate, gouging though the ground at their base as they swung clockwise. The motion grew steadily faster, and as it did the circling tendrils slid closer. The sun winked out of sight, eclipsed by a shroud of dripping tarlike ooze. Laura moved out of one bar's way, but her horse wasn't so lucky. Sludge splattered its hindquarters and immediately began to smoke. The horse shrieked. It leapt forward, bucking and twisting, but the sludge couldn't be dislodged so easily as a rider. It smoked all the more, producing an acrid smell as blood slid down the horse's leg. After a few more hops the beast crashed, writhing, to the ground. Cherry's own horse pranced beside it, eyes rolling.

Laura pulled out another Egg and rapped it against her amulet. Even without a shake, the kin flared bright in the gathering dark. The infestation shuddered. More tendrils shot down from the tarry ceiling. One plunged past Laura's side while another swooped overhead. She dodged the first, but lost her balance and dropped to the ground to escape the second. The Egg slipped from her hand and rolled downhill. She swore and made a grab for it. To her surprise, it came to a slow stop before wobbling back toward her. For a moment she wondered how messed up their kin had become, but then she noticed the ground. The infestation was lifting chunks of it, peeling up the earth to create a shield for itself and sending her own attack back at her. This was another of the things monsters knew from their link with the hive mind but rarely bothered with: the fact that Sweepers could be hurt with kin just as easily.

More tendrils heaved up slabs of earth and rock around her, sweeping in to make a cocoon, trapping her and the Egg together. She scrambled to right herself, make a bid for freedom, but the earth was already too close for her to squeeze through. Without warning, light flashed before her. The crack of a gun echoed outside, almost muffled. A kin bullet had landed barely an inch from the Egg. The resulting blast sent the Egg spinning into the air. Another crash from another gun, and the glass shattered. Kin seared outward. Laura dropped onto her rear to avoid it. The slabs collided just in time to block it out; the second shot had hit it just far enough away that only a wink of light remained in the makeshift cocoon. Outside, the infestation squealed. The walls shuddered under the blast. Laura kicked at the opposite side. The infestation might be hurt now, but it would lash out for revenge next, and she couldn't dodge it here. Dirt gushed in as another kick came from outside. A hand shoved its way in. Laura caught it and between the two of them she forced her way out. Cherry caught her as she staggered. Light danced over them, highlighting Cherry's face in stark flashes. Kin crackled and snapped, raining sparks and ash as it seared across the monster. Tendrils quaked under the force; entire portions snapped apart from the main mass to crash, splattering, against the ground.

"Come on," Cherry hissed, tugging her along.

Once Laura regained her feet they dashed through one of the new gaps. A tendril snapped after them, leaving smoke in its wake while gold spat in its flaking form. Another kin bullet landed with a bang to their left. The tendril flinched but didn't slow.

"Grim! For god's sake, will you just *aim*?" Cherry yelled.

In response, a flare whistled past her head. It smashed into the tendril, causing it to snap apart and sending the flare clattering away, spewing green smoke. The infestation attacked it, flailing graying tendrils to smother the smoke.

Laura scanned the area as they passed an outcropping of rock. Grim and Okane perched on a tall spire of stone patterned with a marred water symbol. Okane held the kin gun in shaky hands while Grim reloaded the flare gun, his rifle set nearby while he muttered shooting tips.

"Watch where you're shooting that thing!" Cherry snarled.

"- - - did say to aim," Okane pointed out.

"Not at my head!"

"I am a headhunter," Grim replied, swapping out the guns. "Okane, watch your grip."

"Right." He frowned at the infestation. "I don't remember kin lasting this long."

The *kaibutsu* had curled in on itself to create a crumpled black ball, hiding the felin completely. The remnants of fallen tendrils smoked and spat in the scarred landscape, curling black clouds tinted slightly green. Kin glinted in every piece, pulsing like embers in charred logs. Before their eyes it spread, cracking the black shell and spitting sparks through the gaps. The main mass smoked worse than a damp fire. The ball rose and fell, crackling, in motions like the breath of an animal.

Laura's stomach churned in nervousness and disgust. "Okane, toss me an Egg."

Cherry stepped up to the rocks, eyeing the infestation. "Grim, what do you think it'll do next?"

"I'm not experienced with infestations."

"Make an educated guess."

A pause. "The amount of magic there worries me. The felin might start moving again. On foot we can't outrun it."

"How could it run? It's been eaten," said Okane.

"It wasn't dead before. I doubt it's dead now that the infestation's targeting you."

The infestation shifted, heavier on the left and then heavier on the right. More feelers sprouted, but these collapsed under the strain of kin.

"I think one more hit should do it." Laura passed her new Egg (still hot, seething; Okane's supply had been tainted too) from hand to hand to hide her nervousness.

"It still looks pretty nasty," said Cherry.

"They're always nasty. I've got this."

She glanced up at Okane, who exhaled slowly and aimed the gun again. Her backup was ready.

She took a step forward. When the infestation failed to notice, she went faster, swinging her arm. How close did she need to be? After the scare and tumble earlier she felt bruised and sore; her heart hammered, and she could feel herself tremble with every step. Was her throwing arm still good?

While she worried, the infestation moved. It shuddered, working its way into a bubble with golden froth before flinging out more legs to heave itself forward like an enormous spider. Refuse flung from its limbs, more like watery ink than the tar of earlier. It bulled toward her.

Laura clacked the Egg against her amulet and squinted, gauging the distance. Thirty feet. Twenty feet. Ten. The Egg grew hot enough to burn through the glove when she threw it. Glass smashed against the monster, five feet away. Kin surged out, expanding to crash like a wave. It curled and coiled, severing limbs as it roared. The infestation wailed. Laura would've fled, but something appeared in the burning mass. The felin's head sprouted from the shower of light and swirling smoke. Its eyes flashed red, its jaws open in a snarl. Laura heard a distant shout before diving to the side. The felin's teeth plowed into the ground. It struggled to its feet and rounded on her, colors pulsing as magic crackled on its back. The crushing pressure returned. It hurt to breathe. Laura beat her fist against the amulet on her belt, arm shaking.

"Get me out of here!" she hissed. Her eyes started to blur. The amulet remained dormant, either uncomprehending or sapped as much as she was. What other orders could she try? *Run? Protect me?*

The amulet burned under her fist. The felin lunged again, but inches away it ground to a halt. Laura cringed as its breath puffed over her. It snapped its jaws, strained, but went no further. Kin sparked madly in its joints, intertwined with infestation. The more it moved, the brighter the light became. Every twitch produced a sound like a jackhammer, accompanied by showers of sparks. It grew louder, the light brighter, until it was almost white and the noise was like a train whistle. The felin's armor snapped under pressure. A foreleg popped from its socket. An ugly crevice opened on its snout. Purple and pink swirled discordant under its skin. The felin screeched. The infestation squalled. Kin trilled. All together the mass creaked, a container ready to burst.

Laura crawled out of its shadow just in time. A kin bullet glanced off the felin's crown, but a moment later another hit the crack in its face. The dam broke. Kin went off like a series of fireworks. The blast shook the ground. Sections of grass singed and caught fire as sparks skipped over them. Pieces of infestation flew to spatter among them, accompanied by billowing, noxious smoke. The felin collapsed. Its eyes flickered, red, yellowish, then faintly brown before fading entirely. Laura heaved a sigh and pressed her bandana over her face. The usual dark wave spread over her in a cloud. This smelled worse than any she'd smelled before, and didn't dissipate. If anything, it grew darker with every moment; the felin's shape faded to a hazy shadow.

"Get out of there! Laura, get out!"

She stumbled, tripping over rocks before breaking into a run. The smoke became thicker, almost viscous against her skin. She blinked furiously and tried not to vomit. It stank. It stung. It felt slimy.

After an eternity she blundered out, coughing hard and eyes streaming. Everything was too bright and blurry to make out, so she screeched when she was grabbed from behind.

"Stay still," Cherry's voice ordered from somewhere around her ear. "You've got some of that slop on you. It'll burn through you as fast as that horse."

Horrified, Laura froze. Hands wrenched her coat away; she heard it being flipped around as her head was forced back.

"Eyes open," Cherry commanded, and no sooner had Laura obeyed than water cascaded into her face. She gasped. "Clearing out your eyes. We don't want you going blind."

"You should've worn those goggles," said Grim, from the vicinity of the flapping coat. "Both of you, actually."

"I'll remember that next time," Laura croaked.

As she blinked, Cherry's face came into focus. Okane stood just behind her, looking over the Ranger's shoulder anxiously. Laura slapped on a watery grin and gave him a thumbs-up.

"Nice shot."

His lips twitched. "Sorry. I thought I'd be better at this decoy thing."

"You were fine. I just didn't expect that reaction at the end."

"City infestations are different from the wilds." Cherry scowled. "From what I hear, city ones stick to smarts and keep lower profiles, but out here, they *know* they're predators. They'll go after anything, and they'll go with a lot of power. This little disappearing act is a poison cloud. Even when they know about it, ERA Sweepers die in it all the time. You should see the death counts in Canis."

Laura shuddered but tried to pass it off as cold and good humor. "I'm glad to be in the cities, then! If they poisoned everyone, they wouldn't have much hunting."

"Their entire existence is a way to go down with teeth in the enemy's throat," said Cherry.

"Pleasant," said Okane.

"Wars aren't pleasant."

Grim held up the coat to inspect before shaking his head. "This isn't worth keeping. It's started dissolving already. Good quality, though. It slowed the eating process considerably."

"That's because it's saturated with magic," said Laura, giving it a sad look. She'd liked that coat. "Sweeper farc. I guess it does its job."

"We'll have to get Zavodsky to make - - - a new one," said Okane. He paused, then fumbled with the buttons of his own coat. Cherry swatted at his hands.

"Don't try to be a hero. I've got an extra jacket in my pack." She gave a sharp whistle.

Her horse galloped from the left, giving the cloud a wide berth. It slowed and stopped so Cherry could dig through the saddlebags. While she grumbled and sorted whatever items she'd stowed, the cloud began to fade. The breeze picked up, rolling the poison slowly westward. As it dispersed, the damage in its wake became more pronounced. The grass, already brittle, had shriveled and blackened. Where there had been patches of green, craters and cracked, bare earth remained. The felin sprawled in the middle of a great black stain. Its body was contorted, spine clearly broken and armor shattered. Not far beyond it lay Laura's horse. The tarlike substance had eaten its flesh right down to the bone. Spots and boils swelled on its still form; one of these burst with a hiss and released rancid smoke. The sight made Laura's stomach turn.

"Here." Grim walked over. He deposited a clutter of small items into her hands: hair ties, a bundle of folded papers, Bijou, a single Sinker. These had been stuffed in the pockets of her coat. "I suppose you need that amulet too?"

"If we leave it, it'll just host another infestation in the future. How long do we have to wait before it's safe to go down there?"

In reply, Grim strode into the war zone. Cherry threw the spare coat over Laura's shoulders and shook her head.

"Don't bother with him. He's like the anti-felin. Whatever effects are still there, he knows how to avoid it."

Grim approached the fallen creature, slow but confident. When he came within three feet, it shifted. Its eyes flickered. Kin sparks shot from the felin's rent back, lurid and jarring. Grim retreated quickly, but the light died out fast.

Okane shook his head slowly. "I don't know how our kin got so mean. It even attacks people now."

"It's got to be Clae's fault. That magnificent angry bastard," said Laura.

"But he was only in—" He paused, then pulled open his bag. He juggled three different Eggs in his hands, stared at them a moment before giving her a look of horrified realization.

After some circling, Grim crept close enough to seize the amulet. With that in hand, he grabbed one of the felin's headspikes, leaned his weight against it, and snapped it from the corpse. He carried these prizes back to the group.

"Good thinking," said Cherry, eyes fixed on the spike. "That's what, three thousand argents?"

Laura was more interested in the amulet. She'd only noticed that it was metallic, but now she could clearly see part of a sword. The blade only partially remained, a fractured piece sticking out of an intact hilt, its leather grip rotted but pommel and cross guard shining in the sunlight.

"That's an amulet?" Okane leaned closer to marvel at it.

"The Old Zyran crusaders used magic in their weapons and dumped empty amulets along the way when they ran out of power," said Laura. This was a high-magical piece. How old was it exactly? Five hundred years? Eight hundred years? "The magic must've been stored in the hilt. That's why it's in such good condition. I bet a museum would pay big money for it."

"You think?" said Cherry, genuinely interested.

"It's been contaminated," Grim pointed out. "Best leave it with these two. They know what to do with it."

"At least we're up one headhunting job." She turned back to her horse and gestured for them to follow. "Come on. The other horses are around here somewhere. If we shift the baggage, Laura can take the packhorse. Let's get going before any scavengers show up."

15

SELLOUT

A few days later, with the walls of Amicae towering ahead again, something white-hot seared through Laura's finger.

"Ow!"

Laura shook her hand with a snarl of pain. She felt as if she'd touched a hot stove. She had half a mind to pull off her ring, but already the feeling had died down to smarting.

"Anything wrong?" Cherry looked back while her horse continued its slow, steady pace.

"Nothing. Just this stupid ring." Laura twisted it ruefully. "Maybe it caught on something."

"I think that was magic," said Okane. He rubbed his own hand, as if he'd been zapped too. "The rings are amulets, right? All Sweeper amulets are rigged for something. Like the ones on our belts affect the ones in our shoes. I think something else affects these."

Few spells can actually be utilized. A flicker of memory: Clae striding through a train, carpetbag held fast. *I put one on the Eggs, sends an SOS to my amulets.*

"An SOS," she muttered.

Cherry frowned. "Is someone in trouble?"

"The armory. Okane, Amelia said the armory sends a signal to Sweeper rings."

Okane looked horrified, and he had every right to be. The armory had Clae and Anselm inside it.

"You're not going to that place, are you?" Cherry said suspiciously. "You told us you were going straight to your investigator, before any other bullshit comes up. If you're right about who's involved, you need help immediately. Don't make any stops."

"The armory has all of the Amicae Sweepers' magic equipment inside it," said Laura. "If something happens to it, we're not the only ones sunk. The entire city could be in danger."

Cherry crossed her arms in a huff. "In that case, we're going with you. Your boss can wave a gun around all she wants, but I'm faster on the draw. She'll have to think twice before threatening you."

"- - -'d do that?" said Okane, surprised.

"I'm taking this escort job seriously." Cherry sat straighter in the saddle, eyes narrowed. "Now what is that?"

It looked like the entirety of the Ranger district awaited them in the city's doorway. Rangers and horses milled around in an angry cloud. One of the closest Rangers sat on a scruffy pony, her face marred by burn scars. Cherry obviously knew this one; she trotted up beside her and asked, "What's going on?"

"I'm not coming back to Amicae anytime soon, that's what's happening," said the woman. "They're kicking us all out. No Rangers allowed for the foreseeable future."

"Can they do that?" Laura gasped.

"Sure can. We're technically only satellite citizens," said the woman.

"That's never been an issue before," said Cherry. "What's started this?"

"Rumor has it that the mobs are recruiting us," said the woman. "It's a load of crap, but this is the same place that bought the idea of walls being impervious to monsters. Common sense really isn't fashionable here."

"Well, I've got a job to finish," said Cherry. "We're getting in."

"Good luck," said the woman. She gave them a mocking wave as they passed.

The other Rangers didn't try stopping them. They grumbled and parted slowly, so before long the group had made its way to the front. The city side of the entryway was blocked off by a line of soldiers.

"Excuse me," Cherry called. "Who do I talk to, to get into the city?"

"Rangers are not permitted inside the walls at this time," snapped another man; this one wore the same uniform as the people who'd let them out five days ago. "Turn around and go somewhere else."

"I have business in Amicae," Cherry insisted. "I'm escorting your Sweepers back from an extermination, and I'm not leaving their side until I get them back to their head Sweeper."

"Sweepers?" the guard scoffed. "As if we'd send Sweepers into the wild. That's ERA's job."

"It should be, but here we are," Laura said loudly. "Do you need IDs? Because we can show you right now."

The guard spluttered. He doubled back to the soldiers and held a hushed conversation before returning.

"The Sweepers can enter once we confirm their identities. You, on the other hand, have no ID, have no clearance, and have no business here. You need to leave with the rest of the Rangers."

Cherry looked tempted to argue, but Laura broke in: "We can do that."

"I said I was going to get you there safe," said Cherry.

"You got us out into the wilds and back again," said Laura. "Thank you for all your help, but I think we'll be okay from here. Really, if you're not involved yet, I don't think you want to be, and I don't think you should."

"I feel like I'd be abandoning you otherwise," Cherry grumbled.

"Don't worry. We may not know the wilds, but we definitely know our way around Amicae."

That got Cherry to smile again, if only slightly. "If you're that confident, I won't argue with you. Just don't do anything stupid, all right?"

"Right," said Laura.

She and Okane dismounted. Grim gathered their horses' reins without a word. Laura didn't feel nearly as close to him as she did to Cherry now, but he'd been steadfast through the entire endeavor, and she still couldn't shake that feeling of familiarity. She paused beside him and said, "Really, thank you for all the help."

Grim made a motion that could've been a shrug or maybe just a shiver. "Good luck," he said, before backing the horses away from the lines.

Laura and Okane approached the guard. He made a big deal of looking over their IDs before allowing them entry. The soldiers watched them pass, silent and expressionless. With Amicae's stone underfoot, Laura turned and waved. Cherry waved back, and Grim lifted a hand too.

"I wonder if maybe we should've stayed with them," Okane murmured. "They could've taken us to one of the other cities. Didn't that Canis Sweeper say other cities were willing to shelter us?"

"I considered it," Laura admitted. Even now as the Rangers turned away, part of her wanted to run after them and beg for more help. A larger part of her said she was in the right place. "I'm honestly scared of what the MacDanels have managed to do in the little time they've been here. But if we run away, that means they keep going as they want. I'm not willing to let them do that, and I'm not willing to leave Clae here."

⸺◦◦◦⸺

No sooner had the Sweepers set foot on Fortore Street than an ambulance roared past. They had to scramble over the curb to avoid being flattened.

"Damn driver needs his eyes checked," Laura grumbled.

Okane seemed more concerned with the direction it had gone. "It's headed toward the armory."

"That doesn't mean anything."

"But if - - -'re sure the rings sent an SOS, and it came from the armory—"

"Maybe something happened nearby?"

"Enough to trigger a spell? Or maybe—what if something got Clae riled up? As a crystal, he's got no sense. No rationality. He's just angry. What if something woke him up and got him really mad?"

"You think an infestation picked here of all places to go crazy?"

Despite her scoffing, worry gnawed at Laura's stomach. It only got worse as they grew closer. They noticed the smoke first. It billowed, gray and foreboding, as the outskirts of a crowd came into view. A fire truck loomed amid a sea of black police uniforms. It seemed as if every single one of them was shouting something.

"Where's the fire?"

"Get that stretcher over here! We've got a man down!"

"Take your available men and spread out! If we shut down the cable cars we can trap them!"

Hovering by the edge of activity, Laura spotted a familiar bowler hat. She made toward it, calling, "Byron!"

Byron turned. It took a moment for him to spot them, but he waved them closer. "There you are. I stopped by the shop a few days ago and you were gone. Not even your aunt knew where you went. Where have you been?"

"On assignment in the wilds," Laura replied. "We just got back. What's going on?"

"There's been an attack on the Sweeper building." Byron nodded at the scene, chewing thoughtfully on his pipe. "I'd investigate further, but there's a city bigwig on-site."

"Bigwig like a head Sweeper?"

"Inspector. We've got some bad blood, so if he sees me all hell will break loose. I'll have to get the lowdown from Heather later. I haven't seen either of the MacDanels, but that doesn't mean they're not here."

A great whirring, clatter, and bang rose from the buildings ahead. A majority of the police ducked on instinct, but some, like Byron, gave only the smallest wince.

"The door's been making that racket ever since I got here. If you've got any idea how to fix it, I'm sure they'll thank you," he said.

The armory still stood, colored windows gleaming through the smoke issuing from the garage door. It looked as if someone had hacked the bottom corner enough for it to curl outward. The main entrance had been propped open with thick steel instruments. Strange gears and parts could be glimpsed on the back of the door; they ground to life, shaking and shrieking under the strain before the door jerked inward. The steel buckled slightly, accompanied by a hideous noise. Judging by the amount of damage to the crumpled metal, this had been going on awhile. A policeman flinched in his spot on the stairs before noticing them.

"What are you doing here?" he demanded. "This is a crime scene."

"He owns the building." Laura gestured at Okane.

The policeman paused. "We've already got—"

"Owner?" As the door shuddered, another familiar face peered out. Amelia hurried outside, flinging her arms wide.

"There you are! Where have you been? I've been worried sick!" She rested a hand on each of their shoulders, leaned close, and whispered, "The Gin is gone. I didn't get here in time."

Laura felt like she'd been doused in cold water.

"What?" Okane breathed.

"The Kin equipment upstairs has been scattered. All of the Gin's gone."

"Who did it?" said Laura. "Do you know?"

Amelia didn't get to reply. Juliana appeared from the armory now, too. Laura tensed at the sight, bracing herself for the worst. Would Juliana be angry that they weren't dead already? Would she try pulling the gun on them again?

"Oh, thank goodness!"

Juliana descended the stairs and threw her arms around Okane. He went rigid in her grip.

"I was so worried!" Juliana continued, and were those tears in her eyes? "You were gone so long, I thought they must've got you, too!"

"Who are you talking about?" said Laura.

Amelia pointed at the building. Something glinted on the siding: dark purple paint to match the door. With its similar color and all the people moving around it, Laura had totally missed the circle.

Mobs, she thought immediately, but paused. Every circle she'd seen used as a mobster target had been carefully, painstakingly applied. The MARU feared its perfect shape: unyielding, unending, harsh in the cleanliness of its single line. This circle looked hastily splashed, almost oblong. Besides, a circle was a threat. A target. Not a calling card.

This isn't right, Laura thought. *This is another shot at framing them.*

And who had already used the Mad Dogs as a distraction once before? Her gaze turned to Juliana. Juliana held Okane at arm's length now, looking at him like a mother inspecting a long-lost child.

"Are you hurt at all? The mobs didn't do anything to you, did they? Their infestation didn't catch you?"

"Please let go of me," said Okane.

When Juliana made no move to do so, Laura stepped in and swatted her hands down. "We haven't seen any infestations or mobsters today," she said firmly. "We just got back from a job *you* sent us on."

"I'd love to hear about it," said Juliana, "but I'm afraid we'll have to wait until this situation is resolved. If Amelia's right, then the city's Sweeper force is at a total standstill. If we don't get going again fast—"

"I'm sorry, could you move?" said the policeman. "The second stretcher is coming out."

The Sweepers stepped aside. EMTs ducked under the steel parts, bearing a stretcher between them. Laid out upon it was a young man. Laura had never seen him before, but his face seemed hauntingly familiar. He had silver eyes, the exact same shade as Okane's. Those eyes stared, glassy and empty at the sky, stark in a horribly pale face. A number tattoo had been inked onto his left cheekbone.

"Rex?" Okane watched his passing with a sickened expression.

"That's right," said Amelia. "I was first on the scene and found him. He'd been caught in one of the traps. It shouldn't have killed him, but he just kept bleeding. He spouted a bunch of Rexian propaganda at me before giving up the ghost, and threw a fit when Juliana tried to stop the bleeding."

"There's no sign of my brother in there, is there?" said Juliana.

"None."

Albright came alongside them now, brow furrowed and arms crossed.

"There was only the one body inside, and no additional blood," said Albright. "The intruders obviously struggled to escape afterward, but in the process of looting?" She shook her head. "This lockdown is so extensive I can't even see what's normally stored here, let alone whether it was disturbed."

"I wish Amicae's banks had this kind of security," the other policeman sighed.

"This isn't the time for jokes," said Albright. "Miss MacDanel, I'm sorry, but there's no evidence that your brother's been here at all. We'll continue to look for him. In the meantime we can assume that this was a direct attack on our Sweepers. I want you all to return to the shop and stay there for the time being. We'll have a large guard assigned to you."

"Of course," said Juliana. "Whatever the attackers were looking for, they didn't find it here. We won't let them attack our headquarters, too."

Albright nodded. "Baxter, bring them back. Take your unit along, too. Make sure no one so much as sets foot on Acis if you find them suspicious. Miss Huxley, please remain here for now. We'll need your help undoing the security."

Amelia gave her a blank look. "I'm on the Sweeper payroll. You ordered Sweepers to the shop."

"Regardless, we're in need of your expertise."

"I'd rather go with them."

Albright frowned. "It's not a request. We'll bring you to the shop after you help us."

"Or we could stay," Laura said quickly. She didn't want to go back to the Sweeper shop, to the exact place they'd been cornered last time. "I'm sure we could help."

"You are *targets*," Albright insisted. "We need you in a safe, easily defensible place. This isn't a good location. Follow Baxter."

Amelia scowled. She grabbed Laura's arm, leaned close, and whispered, "Whatever you do, make sure one of those officers is in the room with you at all times. I got a weird letter from Melody Dearborn, and Juliana wanted me to leave the scene as soon as I got here. Don't trust her."

"I already know," said Laura. "If you get the chance, there's an inspector here in the crowd. Byron Rhodes. Send him over as fast as possible. He knows the situation, too."

Amelia nodded and drew back. Albright watched this with a furrowed brow, but she didn't pursue that curiosity when Amelia joined her. Laura climbed into the back of Baxter's car, and the Sweepers left Fortore. Another police car took the lead, and still more followed behind.

"It's like a funeral procession," Laura murmured.

"Hopefully not," said Okane. "What was that earlier, about an infestation? And how long do - - - think Lester's been missing?"

Juliana spoke to Baxter in the front seat, grilling him about how, exactly, the Council would be alerted to the situation.

"The mobs can get away with anything now," she said. "Steps need to be taken to limit their influence. If the city can't even protect their Sweepers, that's a city doomed to fail. We need more protections. We need more people. We need more funding for those people."

Baxter nodded along but didn't answer. He couldn't possibly have any sway in the matter.

At long last they arrived at the Sweeper shop. Natsu sat on her front stoop and watched them pull in, suspicion written all over her features. When men started climbing out of cars and setting up stations, she slinked back into the pawnshop.

"Thank you for the ride," said Juliana. "We'll rest easy with you watching over us."

As the Sweepers crossed the street, Laura caught a snippet of the nearby officers' conversation:

"Hasn't Miss MacDanel's brother gone missing? I'm surprised she's acting so normally."

"It's called a level head. Goes to show she's a professional."

Or maybe she was calm because Lester hadn't gone missing at all. Maybe this simply painted Juliana as the triumphant victim, just in time for another newspaper highlight. But if so, how could they plant a Rexian? Why?

Laura's mind spun as they stepped into the shop. Okane sucked in a harsh breath. He strode around the counter and stopped by the stairwell door. Its handle and lock shone brighter than Laura had ever seen, but more than that, its shape was off. Close, but wrong. *Replaced*. Okane's hand trembled over it before clenching into a fist.

"It's nice to be away from prying eyes," said Juliana, as she pulled down the window blinds. She sounded downright casual, as if she hadn't broken into Okane's home, as if she hadn't held them at gunpoint and sent them into a death trap.

Laura seethed. She spun on her heel, ready to snap, but faltered as hands came up to cup her face.

"Why are you here, Laura?" said Juliana, but it came across more like teasing than accusing.

"I'm an Amicae Sweeper," Laura growled.

"And what would you do to keep Amicae safe?"

"Anything. Including going against you."

She expected backlash, but Juliana only laughed.

"See?" she said. "There's no trouble talking with her in the room. We're all willing to do whatever it takes to get the job done. So long as we're all on the same page, there's nothing to worry about." She sashayed away to settle on a stool, crossed her ankles, and smiled. "So, is Lester waiting to rendezvous with us?"

Silence. It took a moment for Laura to realize what was going on. Before they'd gone into the wilds, Lester acted as if Okane knew everything. Laura assumed they'd known otherwise when he insisted he knew nothing, but no. Juliana honestly still believed he was involved. Okane had obviously reached the same conclusion.

"I've been out in the wilds for the last five days," he said slowly. "Anything that's happened since has happened outside of my knowledge."

Juliana rolled her eyes. "I know you're not your boss, but you must have some idea of what's going on. Didn't you make a plan for everything?"

"Plans change easily," said Okane. "I might have a better idea if I know the circumstances. Could - - - explain to me the whole situation? Just for clarity. I'm sure that - - -r . . ." He gestured awkwardly at Laura. ". . . *new collaborator* will appreciate it, if she's involved now."

"There's just no getting around her involvement." Juliana shrugged dramatically. "She sticks her nose in too many things and doesn't let them go. I would've thought you'd try harder to divert her attention, but I suppose, you being what you are . . ." She gave him a mocking, piteous look. "You're not exactly built to keep a lady's attentions, are you? That said, if you were that determined to keep her in the dark, there must be a reason for it. You want her alive. She must fit into the plan somehow." Finally she turned to Laura. "You were right, we did have a secret. A *glorious* secret. Lester and I made a contract to power Amicae's abilities. I told you I'd ensure our success, didn't I?"

Laura felt cold. "So you approached the couriers?"

"The what? You don't really think I can appeal to newspaper boys for Sweeping."

"No," said Laura. "The wilds couriers. The people Rangers get scared of."

"Ha! Rangers." Juliana waved a hand dismissively. "I think you know what you're talking about, you just have the wrong name. Really, think about it. There's only one power in all of Orien that can properly take on infestations. We went to the best."

Okane set a hand on the counter, as if he'd suddenly lost his balance. "So - - - turned to Rex."

Rex? The idea floated disjoint in her head. How did Rex fit into this? She'd expected mobs. She'd expected Rangers. She expected couriers, whoever they were supposed to be. But then it clicked. Rex sent raiding parties into the wilds, Sweepers and otherwise. Rex would easily cut down satellite towns in their raids. Rex would happily kill off any Rangers they found, to keep alarms from spreading. With their frequent crusades, of course Rex would have powerful Eggs in their supplies. And of course, she knew where their contact had come from. Last year, before the Falling Infestation, before Laura had gone to Puer, three Rexian Sweepers had entered Amicae. Two had been captured, the third presumably to blame for the ruined bulwark and ensuing infestation. It had to be Theron. He'd lain low, looking for a chance to bring down a city for *glorious Rex*.

"What could you possibly get from Rex?" said Laura. "They're out raiding satellite towns and enslaving anyone they don't murder! They freely admit they want every other city dead, ourselves included! Why would you ever think they want to help us?"

"This is where your inexperience blinds you," said Juliana. "If Rex really wanted to destroy other cities, it could do that easily. You know what they did to Thrax."

"Oh, they *want* us all dead. The only problem is that all the cities are allied *against* them, so they won't take the risk," said Laura. "If you're trying to ally with them, you're just giving them an opening! You'll fracture Amicae from the alliance and open the door for Rexian interference!"

"It's so easy for Amicae's citizens to fall for propaganda," said Juliana. "I'll bet you believed that story about the walls keeping you safe, too, didn't you? Whatever. As wild as this sounds to you, the existence of other cities works as a boon for Rex. As other targets, we draw attention from infestations. Essentially, we cover Rex's back while they attempt to kill the hive mind. It's a mutually beneficial situation to begin with, but if we foster this relationship—"

"Mutually beneficial." Laura's hands curled into fists. "Is that what you think, when the raids get reported in the papers?"

"Anyone living in a satellite town has understood and embraced the danger of its existence," said Juliana. "It's not a happy story, but they could just as easily be taken out by infestations, wild animals, or even marauding Rangers. At least with Rex, we know the victims will be put to good use."

"You bitch," Laura hissed. "You absolute—"

"Now, now. Didn't you just say you'd do anything to preserve Amicae's safety?"

"You're actively throwing that away!"

"As a Sweeper, my ultimate goal is protecting my new city from infestations." Juliana stood again. She pulled aside the black drapes, reaching for something on the shelves. "With Amicae in the state it is, that's going to be a difficult task. The Council talks a big game, but they don't think the situation's changed. The wall is no longer something they can hide behind, but it never worked in the first place, and Sinclairs operated 'perfectly' even without proper attention. They think we should be *good little girls* and accept what we're told. Well, I'm not a demigod, and clearly neither are you. Whatever Clae Sinclair managed, it's not an option for us."

She found what she'd been searching for. Metal rasped as a broad, heavy knife emerged from its sheath. It looked like the dagger Juliana had wielded in the Sundown infestation, but its magical imprint wavered and its shape showed more violence than elegance. Juliana ran a finger lovingly over its flat edge.

"Remember when I told you how valuable that knife of mine was? Terulian versions are rare and hard to make, but Rex has magical weapons down to an art. Each of their Sweepers carries at least one of these. Good for clearing vegetation on campaigns to Kuro no Oukoku, and just as good for chopping infestations. This blade would otherwise cost us the same amount as purchasing this entire block of businesses. Our Rexian contact gave us the one he was carrying, but he promised us more. More blades, more Eggs, more assorted equipment. Even better, they'll be giving us their kin recipe."

Even friendly cities would never be so willingly helpful. Rex wanted something in return.

"In exchange for ours," Laura whispered, "you sold them our Gin. Our Kin. Everything stored in the armory."

"It's not as if that junk was helping us," said Juliana. "Puer prided itself on its advanced kin recipe, and here it barely did anything. Older Amicae equipment packed a punch, but you can't replicate those, can you? It's all useless. The only thing that can destroy infestations without question is Rexian technology, and they've proven it time and again. It won't matter who or how many we arm. With Rexian equipment, one person could take down an infestation singlehandedly. The Council will cheer about lower costs, and we'll have done our duty. That said"—she raised the blade so it glinted in the dim light—"I won't need a very big team, so I can be all the more selective about who's with me. Do you plan to stand with me, or against me, Laura? I'd love another woman on the team, but you'd have to stay in line."

Laura glared. "When is Rex supposed to be giving you all this? And what are you planning to do when they stick around and demand more?"

"We'll cross that bridge when we reach it," said Juliana. "Your answer?"

Laura puffed herself up. "You already know my answer, and it's *hell no*."

"What a pity," said Juliana. "We can't have loose ends. Hold still. This shouldn't hurt a bit."

She raised the knife.

"Wait!" Okane threw himself between them. "If - - - want my services, I require that Laura stays unharmed."

Juliana scoffed. "Could you make up your mind, already? So long as you can keep her quiet, fine. I'm not the one who has to explain it to your boss." She rested the blade on her shoulder. "Let's get down to business. We got your team into Amicae, into the armory, arranged your departure, and managed to set it all up to look like the mobs' doing. I assume your boss left Lester with the cache of our first payment. Where is that? We'll need to retrieve it."

Okane stayed silent.

"Well?"

"Why do - - - think Rex would send in a squad and dump all of their functional equipment before going back into the wilds?" said Okane. "It doesn't make sense."

"It doesn't have to make sense to me, so long as they make it work. Where's the cache?"

"They wouldn't do it," said Okane.

"*Where. Is. The. Cache.*"

But Okane had no answer, and didn't give one. Juliana kept glaring at him, but suddenly something occurred to her; her expression went blank.

"He said you were one of them. He said you were a sleeper agent, meant to make things run smoothly and keep Laura out of the way."

"I'm not," said Okane. "I'm sorry, Juliana, but they played - - -."

Her lips spread in a savage grin. "So that's it, then? Rex took everything and left me with nothing but a knife? Don't *pout* at me, you two. This is more valuable than all the trash in that armory. I haven't lost a damn thing." She brandished the knife again, and it hummed with energy. "I do not get *played*. I get *even*."

Both Laura and Okane took a wary step back. Okane's eyes were glued to the blade.

"We're not the ones who double-crossed - - -."

"Save your breath," said Juliana. "I can't have this kind of information getting out. It's all just business, and you're both unnecessary surplus!"

On that last word, she swung the blade. Laura and Okane lurched in opposite directions. The blade hit hard enough to dig deep into the countertop, and the glass pane below shattered.

"You think I'll let you run your mouth to the whole damn city?" Juliana wrenched the blade back out. "You think I'll let you walk out of here free?"

She turned after Okane, still swiping. He kept one step ahead of it, his magic crackling as the blade whooshed an inch from his stomach. Laura cast around for weapons. She still had an Egg in her bag, but she wasn't willing to use it now; not with so many other Eggs present that could catch under its energy, and not in such cramped quarters. Glass pieces from the old Kin setup still crowded the countertop, but what could a flask do against such a long knife? For lack of anything else, Laura snatched up one of the stools.

Okane tripped. He dropped backward with a yelp, catching at the counter for balance. Juliana aimed at his head, but Laura rushed her. She pinned Juliana to the counter's side with the stool legs.

"Go get the police!" she cried.

Juliana snarled and swiped. Pinned as she was, she couldn't gain much leverage, but the blade gouged the stool's seat; it missed Laura's face and hand by a hairsbreadth. She backpedaled on instinct, and only just managed to raise her defense again as Juliana followed. Every swing lopped off a piece of stool leg, and once she came close enough she chopped straight through the footrests. One of the legs fell off; another groaned at a weird angle. Juliana closed in. Something thudded against her back, and she stumbled. The object fell and broke on the floor, and only then did Laura realize it was a flask. Another glass container flew past them both and smashed against the wall.

"Keep - - -r eyes on me!" Okane barked.

Juliana turned for him again. Okane grabbed the largest of the glasswork and broke it on the counter; he brandished its splintered form by the neck.

Laura dropped the stool. She planted her foot on the underside of the seat and wrenched the longest remaining leg from its socket. She ran with it. Juliana had already slashed, Okane had already sidestepped. Juliana readied herself for another attack, but Laura wasn't about to let that happen. She brought the stool leg down on the flat top of the blade. Juliana's grip kept it from falling, but the angle made the wood slide straight down into her knuckles. Juliana screeched and dropped it. The blade clanged to the floor. Laura used the stool leg to hook and swat it away. The blade spun across the floor before coming to a slow stop just before the door.

Breathing hard, Laura aimed her improvised weapon at Juliana.

"You," she panted, "are a traitor to Amicae."

Juliana slumped against the counter, eyes wide and manic. "Who's the traitor here?" she spat. "I, who tried to improve this place, or you, clinging to rotted traditions?"

"- - - didn't even try to understand what those traditions are," said Okane.

"I knew enough! I saw enough!"

Laura sighed. Seeing Juliana like a cornered animal was both disheartening and infuriating. Hadn't she been so sharp? Hadn't she been such a good Sweeper? All of her talents and all of her posturing for the media, wasted.

Laura shouldn't have let her guard down.

Juliana smiled again, wide and cruel. "Don't think you've won just yet."

Her foot collided with Laura's shin. Laura lost her balance with a squawk of surprise. Okane immediately moved to catch her. Juliana scrambled past them both and rushed for the door.

"Stop!" Laura shouted.

Juliana snatched up the fallen blade, but she didn't face them. No, midstride, she cut open her own leg. Blood blossomed on her skirts as she caught the doorknob, and she threw the blade behind her. She burst outside, screaming, "Help! Help! They're trying to kill me!"

What?

Laura tore after her and halted in the doorway.

The blinds might have been down, but the shouts and breaking glass had caught attention. Juliana had tottered straight into a policeman's arms and now lay bleeding in the road, sobbing.

"It was them!" She pointed straight at Laura. "They're with the Mad Dogs after all! They were ordered to get rid of me!"

The two officers present looked up at Laura. The first one curled his arms more protectively over Juliana, while the second drew his gun and shouted, "Drop your weapon!"

Laura's mind crawled. Belatedly she realized she still held the stool leg; not a good first impression for this situation.

"It's not what it looks like!" she said, and realized, again belatedly, that no one innocent ever said that at a crime scene.

"I said drop it!" said the policeman.

He looked ready to shoot regardless.

If the Council claims you're a mobster, you'll face worse even without proof, Haru had said. *We know very well the lengths and cruelty the Council will stoop to.*

Laura's reputation had been tied to the Mad Dogs since the very first *Dead Ringer* article. It wasn't much of a leap to make the connection now; to most people this incident would prove their suspicions. In their loathing for the mobs, these policemen wouldn't question it or treat the Sweepers kindly. With this kind of leverage the Council could put Laura and Clae's legacy to rest permanently. It didn't matter that there was no proof. This would be the end.

Laura would not let it end.

"Eat shit, Juliana," she spat, and grabbed behind her. She caught Okane's wrist without a glance and towed him down the steps with her.

"Stop!" cried the policeman.

Laura dodged into the gap between Sweeper shop and pawnshop. The gun cracked behind her, and the bullet smashed pieces loose from the shop's siding.

"Faster!" said Okane, and she obliged.

Behind the shop rose the high wall separating Acis Road from the residential area behind it. Laura and Okane dashed along it. Laura glanced through the thin alleys at Acis proper and glimpsed more running policemen, heard whistles blown, shouting. At last the gate came into view. Another officer stood there, confused by the noise but not yet aware of the trouble.

"Wait!" he called as they charged past him. "No one's supposed to go in or—"

"You didn't see us!" said Laura.

"But I—What?"

Apartment buildings rose about them now, towering higher than the Cynder Block and stretching in every direction. They passed laundry lines, trash cans, groups of chatting residents, a game of street baseball. This section of Amicae was little better than a labyrinth, made still harder by the number of people and hiding places. Laura never doubted that mobsters lurked here, and it disgusted her to think she was here to hide the same way they did. She only paused in the shadow of an apartment's main doors. For a while she and Okane simply stood there, catching their breath.

"Where are we going?" said Okane.

"Away from there," said Laura. "God, that Juliana makes me want to—Ooh, I should've hit her with that stick."

"That would've made the situation worse," said Okane.

"Would it? Because I think we're at the brink of failure right now."

Laura sagged against the wall and closed her eyes, trying to shut out her frustration, but it didn't work. Anger bubbled in her chest. "I can think of a few ideas, but for a plan . . . Byron will get facts, but no one will pay attention to facts if mobs are supposed to be involved."

Okane studied the cracked pavement underfoot. "Should we approach the Mad Dogs for protection?"

"And prove her right? I don't think so," said Laura. "If we're not playing into one person's hands, we're playing into another's."

Okane relaxed somewhat. "I hoped - - -'d say that. Regardless, I don't think we have any support at this point, or anywhere to— Laura? What are - - - thinking?"

Laura clenched her hands so tight, her nails dug into her skin. "I know what I'm going to do, but you don't have to come along."

"And that is?"

"I'm going to Rex. If they really escaped with the MacDanels' help, they can't be far in front of us. Clae and Anselm aren't totally out of our reach, and I'll be damned if I let Rex do whatever they want with them. Clae's letter talked about his fears if Anselm was discovered, and I don't want any of those options to happen to either of them. I'll get them back safe, and once I do that I can focus on fixing Amicae."

Okane stayed quiet. Laura's eyes remained fixed to the ground, but she heard his sigh and noticed when he started checking through his bag.

"We don't have a lot of equipment left over from that wilds infestation. I've got a few Bijou, flash pellets—"

Laura looked up. "What? I just said, you don't have to—"

"Clae was the closest thing I had to family and safety since my mother died. I'm not about to let someone desecrate his body. Besides." He pulled his gun from its holster and popped it open, surveying the ammo inside with forced nonchalance. "I can't let - - - invade a hostile city on - - -r own. That would make me a terrible friend."

Laura cracked a smile. "Bringing you along probably makes me a terrible friend."

"Truly, we're irreversible mini-Claes," said Okane.

"I can't deny that." She paused, then said, "Thank you."

"For what?"

"Being you. I just remembered old school friends like Charlie, and let me tell you, they wouldn't be ready to charge into Rex with me."

"Losing our minds seems like a prerequisite for the job," said Okane, but he seemed pleased. "The only weapon I have with much power is this gun, and it's only got three bullets left."

"I thought you brought some spring-loaders," said Laura.

"I used most of them. The only one I have left is the round of Puer bullets, but I'm not about to try that."

"You mentioned that before. Why was that, again?"

"They sort of rasp when they go in," said Okane. "It's not too unlike the Amicae variety, but they feel just a little too big. I keep getting scared that they'll stick in the barrel instead of firing correctly."

"That doesn't sound like a terribly good idea."

"No, it really doesn't."

"Then we'll have to conserve those bullets," said Laura. "I'm in the same state as you, just one Egg left. It's probably for the best. Trains don't welcome their customers carrying weapons; they think a robbery might happen."

"Oh?" Okane perked up. "We're taking the train?"

"I don't see any other option for getting there," said Laura. "You've heard of hobos, right?"

16

CATCH HIM ON THE RUN

Sweepers had free transport on any of the city's various lines and even on trains across Orien, but that required inspection of Sweeper status symbols, and the movements of Sweepers were under constant surveillance. Laura never had a problem with this before, but now she dreaded being arrested or locked up on the train, to be returned to Amicae without even a shot at Rex. Even registering as a normal person and paying (unaffordable) would end up with them in the logbooks and easily located. Hobos usually passed unnoticed, so that was the best way to get out of Amicae undetected.

Unfortunately, Laura had none of a hobo's wiles.

"Is this it?" she hissed to Okane, as they skirted a humming train engine.

Okane shuffled through a copy of the train schedule filched from the station's doors and stumbled on the loose rock of the train bed.

"No," he answered, flipping the paper over to scan the back. "That's 477. It's taking a detour to Avis."

"Then where's our train?"

Laura stood on tiptoe to squint around. This did absolutely no good, as she didn't reach even a third of the engine's height and therefore had no good view of the train yard they were walking through.

She'd be better off looking through the gap below the trains, but the idea of getting so close to the wheels repelled her. Other tracks nearby were crowded with cars, all supply carriers as the passenger trains lingered in the station. Their sought-after train, number 221, was scheduled to leave for a supply trip to Litus at six fifteen. This would go right past Rex or even through it, but when Litus was involved trains were amazingly punctual, even early. They had nine minutes to find this train and no clue where it was. Okane's hands shook as he looked around again. Laura liked to think she was faring better, but she could feel panic closing in too.

"Just our luck, we'll probably run into the rail yard police," she grumbled.

"They won't give us much trouble though, right? I mean, we work with the police."

"Wrong type of police. They'd throw us in a cell as soon as look at us. But that's only if we're lucky. We might end up with some broken bones first."

Okane shuddered. Laura cast around again, checking for any workers, and spotted movement. She ducked to peer between a pair of cars. A train moved on the far tracks, slow but gaining speed. White numbers labeled each car, designating the contents, but there, near the bottom left, was the number 221.

"That's it! That's our train!"

"What?" Okane leaned in beside her. "Can we still get on?"

"We can damn well try! Come on!"

Laura dashed away, following the train's movement. She tracked their target in the short glimpses between cars. Numbers, numbers, slate-gray cars, startled worker.

"Hey!"

Laura cursed and sped up. The worker jumped out of his freight car and waved his arms, shouting, "We've got trespassers in the yard!"

Finally they reached the smoking engine. They leapt over the rails in front of the pilot and made for the other line. Another worker made a halfhearted grab at them but missed. A clattering rose to the right, a chorus of voices demanding directions to the trespassers.

The first rail yard policeman appeared around another still car, baton raised.

"Where do you think you're going?" he demanded.

He didn't wait for a reply, but swung the club at Laura. She side-stepped it easily, but had to jump away from another whistling truncheon as a second man came to join the first. She wrenched on her goggles and slung a flash bomb at the ground. It burst with a solitary crack and blaze of white light, instantly blinding the men. They stumbled back and tripped over themselves, swearing profusely. Laura's eyes watered behind the goggles, but her vision was clear enough. She had to get away before that commotion brought more of them.

Another train blocked them from the 221, this one moving in the opposite direction. With a loud pop, Okane jumped and vanished between the running cars. Laura gritted her teeth and slapped at her amulet. With its influence she grew faster. She tracked the cars, the timing, and leapt. Unfortunately, the amulets didn't carry her all the way through. Two-thirds across the gap, she lost momentum and grabbed wildly at the balcony rail. It crashed into her ribs fast enough to knock some of the wind out of her, and she slumped. Her feet dropped, and, horrified, she cried, "Up!" The amulets reacted with a searing heat and slight hiccuping sound, jerking her legs back up with force enough to almost dislodge her. She gathered her legs under her and jumped again, this time clearing the cars entirely before hitting the ground. She scrambled up, shaking to dislodge the gravel and wincing at the sting in her hands.

Shouting from more rail yard police registered in her ringing ears. She struggled up, and halfway through the motion a set of hands caught and steadied her. She looked up sharply, but met silver eyes and forced herself to relax.

"We're almost there," Okane told her.

They kept on, crossing two more sets of tracks. In front of them, Train 221 picked up speed on its amulet-enhanced wheels. Once it reached full acceleration they'd have no chance to board. But there, to Laura's astonishment, she saw their opening. One of the boxcars hadn't been properly latched. Two in the oncoming line had their sliding doors thrown wide open, showing off the crates and luggage inside. If this was some kind of trap, Laura didn't know and didn't care.

"There!" She pointed, catching Okane's attention. "Aim for the first car."

They sprinted. Laura activated her amulets again, this time with clear instruction, and to her relief they made no unusual reaction. Again Okane made the jump first, but she followed close and matched his flight. They fell through the open doorway, landing hard on the floor of the car before scrambling about. Laura leaned her head out of the door and spotted a pack of rail yard police behind them. The men had come in after the other train's passing, and now looked around wildly in search of their targets. She pulled another flash bomb from her bag and tossed it as their car passed another stretch of still trains. The bomb hit a coupling and bounced, flashing in the air. Laura pulled back out of sight as the police whirled around.

"That should distract them until we're out of the yard."

Together they heaved the door shut and locked it. The sounds of shouting men fell behind, and soon the only noise was that of the train and the wind rushing faster and faster against its sides. The noise warped, and all lights went out. Okane made a startled noise, but she found his shoulder and patted it reassuringly.

"Don't worry. We're going out the gates."

Before long the darkness lifted, and sunlight peeked in again. The train gave a shrill whistle, and it was off into the wilds.

They settled against the opposite side of the boxcar, in the shadow of two crates and a mailbag. Laura rested one elbow on the rough beige fabric, likely crushing a decent amount of envelopes with the motion. The floor rattled beneath them, light flickering in the gaps between boards in the sides. Cool air ran in, stunted, to chill the space. Laura shivered and drew up her legs to salvage as much warmth as possible.

"We made it," Okane sighed, slumping against the wall as his eyes slipped closed. "For a moment there, I thought we wouldn't."

"Yeah. That was a scare."

The entire day had been one scare after another. It all crashed down on her, now that her body had stopped moving. She rubbed at her left temple, trying to ease the sudden ache there. Something brushed her free hand, and she realized what it was a second before she looked down to see Okane entwining their fingers. He didn't look at her, just stared straight ahead. She tightened her grip and kept massaging her head. After a while, Okane heaved a sigh and tilted his head so it rested against hers.

Over time, they settled into a lull. Laura might have drifted off entirely, but the rattle of the train remained constant. How much time passed she had no idea, but night had descended by the time Laura heard the noise. Over the clatter of the cars came a lower thunk, the ring of approaching footsteps. Laura straightened immediately, dislodging Okane as she did. He jerked back into awareness.

"Laura? What's wrong?"

"Do you hear that? I think people are coming in here."

They paused. A muffled noise reached their ears, and Laura recognized it as the opening of train doors. Cursing, she pulled mailbags down over them for better cover.

"Don't let them see you!" she hissed. "They throw hobos off the train while it's moving!"

There was no more time to speak before the door to their car opened. Voices rose above the din, loud enough to be heard but not loud enough to be understood. Laura tensed as they approached.

"—don't get it," one of the people was saying. "I mean, if we just—"

"The powers that be have decided it's a bad idea," the second person sighed.

"But isn't that where we need to concentrate our powers most?"

"You'd think, but we're not welcome there anymore."

A heeled boot came to a stop in front of the mailbags. Laura could see it through their faulty shelter, and her eyes slowly trailed up, taking in the owner. The woman before them was very tall, skin dark and slick black hair tied back in a bun so tight it must've hurt. She wore a dark blue uniform and matching frock coat lined in black with thin silver piping; a few badges caught the dim light on her chest, but the thick belt she wore, covered in bags and pockets and, closest to

them, a holster with a revolver, had Laura preoccupied. If train workers weren't averse to throwing people off of speeding trains, would
they be willing to shoot stowaways on top of that?

"Not welcome?" echoed the other person, a younger boy with blond
hair and the same uniform, as he picked his way through the car.

"Rex seems to think they've got it covered. Litus isn't pleased, but
there's nothing we can do when the entirety of that army is standing
in the way and ripping up tracks. This will probably be the last trip to
Litus for a long time," the woman replied.

"How long? I mean, the city can support itself for a while, but if
it's really cut off from the rest, couldn't that make it another Thrax?"

The woman hummed, leaning against the stack of crates. Okane
leaned away from her, and Laura dug her nails into his hand to remind
him not to move. They didn't know if these *were* train workers. What if
they were vigilante types roaming the train in search of entertainment?

"I don't think Rex is after them right now. They're pumped up
about something, sure enough, but would they really make it so obvious if they're trying to bring down another city? Even they know
they'd get enormous backlash if anyone gets wind of it. They'd lie low,
not boast. They only have the right to boast if they see their scheme
through to the end. Isn't that right, you cheat?"

The woman's voice changed to a harsh snap at the end, and she
yanked Okane up by the collar. Laura sprang up after him, whipping
an Egg out of her bag. The woman yanked her gun from the holster
while her cohort fumbled at his belt; luckily whatever gun he might've
had was missing. For a moment, everyone froze.

"Let go of him," Laura hissed.

"Put that down," said the woman.

"Not until you let him go."

The woman's eyes narrowed, flicking from Laura's face to the Egg
in her hand. "Who are you?"

"We're Sweepers," Laura spat. "So you hurt a hair on his head and
you'll be in deep shit."

"Sweepers?" the woman scoffed. "If you were Sweepers, you'd be in
the passenger cars, not skulking in the baggage."

"Says who? It's none of your business what we're here for!"

"It is, actually."

"Who are you supposed to be, Sweeper police?"

"ERA Sweeper, so yes," the woman replied tersely. "Give me your names and tell me exactly what you're doing here."

Laura kept her mouth shut. ERA Sweeper? That explained the uniform, but from what she could remember, Eastern Rail Alliance Sweepers operated on a different authority than city Sweepers did; their interactions were few and far between, with no head Sweepers on the train lines, only railway officials to call the shots. She didn't feel comfortable sharing any information with these people.

"Um," Okane piped up. "Is it just that - - - need IDs? Because we do have those." To emphasize this he held up his right hand to show off his ring.

"What's that supposed to be?"

"It's our Sweeper ID. Amicae uses rings."

"Amicae? Are you Sinclair Sweepers?"

In the background, the boy perked up. "Sinclair? Like Clae Sinclair?"

"What's it to you?" Laura demanded.

The woman let go of Okane, and he took a step back toward Laura. She held up her gun in a surrendering motion, and made a big deal of putting it away.

"Sorry about that," she said. "We've had problems with hobos claiming Sweeper status in the past. Can I see that a little more closely?"

Scowling, Laura pushed past Okane and held out her own hand. The woman leaned closer and smiled at the little inscription on the ring.

"Sinclair Sweepers of Amicae, right?" She drew back. "Clae had one of those, too. Easy enough to recognize."

"- - - knew Clae?"

"Kind of." The woman smiled ruefully. "I met him a long time ago. Did he ever tell you about the time he got called out into the wilds and roughed up a pack of Rexians? I was there."

"And you're . . . ?"

"Keya Mallick. This is my assistant. I suppose you'd call him an apprentice? Felix Ayers."

Felix gave them a choppy, nervous wave. Still suspicious, Laura returned the Egg to her bag. Keya seemed heartened by the motion.

"I heard about Clae taking apprentices. What's your name, then?"

"Laura Kramer." She stated her name flat and proud. If Keya knew anything about Clae and his apprentices, she probably knew their names already. There was no point lying.

"I'm Okane Sinclair," Okane added, not so forcefully.

Felix bobbed twice in excitement before realizing his actions and forcing himself to stop. Keya laughed.

"So there's still a Sinclair left?"

Okane gave a halfhearted shrug. In any case the name seemed to have won the others' trust, as Keya beckoned them to follow her.

"Let's get somewhere more comfortable. Can't leave such esteemed guests shivering in the baggage car, can we? Come on. We can get you something to drink while we're at it."

Laura and Okane shared a glance. Laura didn't trust these strangers as far as she could throw them, but what choice did they have?

Keya led them back the way she'd come, forward through the train. Two cars up, the dim light illuminated a car painted much darker than its neighbors. The door was labeled ERA: SWEEP DIV.

"This is our car," Keya called as they crossed over the gap. "ERA cars are spaced along the train. There's an armed guard up with the passengers, but we're back in transport. It's not exactly luxurious, but you can stay with us until we get to Litus."

"Thanks," Laura mumbled.

Keya either didn't sense her lack of enthusiasm or ignored it, opening the door to allow them in. The inside of this car was mostly open, though cases and shelves jutted out of the walls to break up space. The open shelves bore Sweeper weapons, mostly bullets and Eggs, while four cots were on the walls, two on each side like bunk beds. In the middle of the room sat what looked like a small iron stove on stubby feet, flames flickering behind its grille. A wrinkled woman in uniform squatted near it. She looked up at their arrival to smile, showing off a wide gap in her teeth.

"Hey, Darcy," Keya greeted. "Guests, this is Darcy. She's a Sweeper too. No last name. Darcy, these two are from Sinclair Sweepers."

"As in Clae Sinclair," Felix added helpfully.

Darcy said nothing, just spread her lips wider.

"Darcy hasn't spoken a word in all the time we've known her," Keya whispered, before motioning them toward the cots.

Laura and Okane sat on the lowest bed on the right. Laura barely registered the rough blanket, too busy observing the people and trying to predict what they'd do, how to get away. In her mind she was simply being held prisoner. Politely, but still. At some point she and Okane needed to get off the train to reach Rex and take back their own. Keya pulled off her coat, hanging it and her belt inside one of the closets. That done, she sat on the cot opposite them.

"Laura and Okane are on their way to Litus in an unorthodox way," she laughed, patting Darcy on the back.

"We didn't have much of a choice," said Okane.

Keya leaned back, crossing her legs. "Once we get to Litus I'll help you sneak out. Sweepers aren't out to undermine anything. You're probably the least likely to be terrorists or spies, since you know the current order keeps us all alive. Only Rex is stupid enough to ignore that. I'll trust whatever mission you're on."

Okane bowed his head. "Thank - - -."

Laura played with her fingers for a moment before asking, "What did you mean, when you were talking about Rex earlier?"

"What, that they're delusional?"

"No, that they're . . . bragging."

"I guess Amicae hasn't heard. We visit cities that keep close eyes on Rex's movements, and Amicae's too far north to hear anything but the biggest news. See, most of Rex's troops outside the city are like infestations: stupid until they've been trained and controlled by a hive mind. When the troops hear something from their commanders, they mirror the news. Bad news? They're surly. Good news? They swagger.

They're swaggering something fierce. That begs the question, what kind of good news could that be?"

"Attacking another city?" Laura guessed.

"If you were listening, you'd know that's a bad idea. Besides, they're upping their isolationist policies to the point they're cutting off the path to Litus. I think they're setting up another crusade. A big one."

"How is that any different from usual?"

"Cities in Zyra have Sweepers doubling as Rangers that stay in the wilds for weeks on end. The Rexian ones pulled back. That means problems for us, since they spanned vast territory and someone has to pick up the slack. But they're not going back into the city proper. Spies from Canis say Sweepers circled to the southwest. They do that on a smaller scale when they're preparing for a crusade."

"And how big, exactly, would this be?"

"Biggest crusade to date. We've never seen these numbers congregating." Keya's eyes narrowed. "Even small crusades get the hive mind angry. A crusade on this scale could mean backlash enough for every satellite town to go under. Proper cities could go under."

"Why are they doing this?" said Okane. "Why now?"

"Who knows? Same reason that they're boasting, I'd guess."

Laura suspected she knew why. She had no doubt Rex had gotten news of the Falling Infestation, and its accompanying "wrath of god." As far as she knew there had never been such a large and destructive use of kin before. Newspapers bragged and even Rangers had reported seeing strange light from far out in the wilds, so there was no way it could be covered up. Besides, Clae had said it himself: whatever secret the Sinclairs kept, Rex wanted to use it for their crusades. They would use him to attack the hive mind. But how would they do it? Would they just make kin, or would they try to break him apart, for Gin amulets? The thought made her shudder, and she dug her nails into her palm to distract herself from the thought.

"Whatever it is, it'll be disastrous for the rest of us." Keya nodded, taking Laura's motion to be a different kind of trepidation. "Especially Amicae. How many people are in your Sweeper program?"

"A pitiful amount." Laura scowled, twisting and wringing her fingers. "The ones left behind are barely capable."

"Must be an important mission if you have to leave your city vulnerable."

What Sweepers were left to take care of Amicae? Juliana was incapacitated at the very least, and Lester missing. Amelia had retired over a decade ago. The only functioning Sweepers left were mobsters; hopefully they'd cooperate enough to keep the city safe, rather than pitch in with their rivalries. Without her realizing it, Laura's fidgeting grew worse, and Okane leaned in so their shoulders bumped, startling her out of her thoughts.

"We didn't have much choice when we left," he repeated.

"If this 'mission' goes well, we won't have trouble fighting off infestations," Laura added.

"Are you getting more people?"

"Retrieving them, I suppose."

"Grand! If there's any Sweeper guild I don't want to die out, it's the Sinclairs."

Eventually Keya noticed the time and announced she had to do her rounds of the train. She bid them take two of the beds, donned her coat, and left. Felix lost some of his confidence when she went, so while he still looked excited by their presence he didn't start a conversation. Darcy beamed and gestured for them to sleep. It was late enough that Laura didn't mind, so she clambered onto the top cot and settled in. Darcy moved to the iron contraption and ran her hand over the top. It must've been amulet-based, as she remained unharmed and the light dimmed to near darkness, only enough to make out shapes. Laura pressed her face into the lumpy pillow and waited for sleep, but wasn't tired enough and was still paranoid. A while after the others had climbed into bed she heard rustling from below and imagined Okane rolling over.

"So," he said quietly, "Keya knew Clae?"

Was he talking to Laura? She was about to reply "How should I know," but someone else answered first.

"She met him a long time ago, but he was still pretty amazing, even then." Felix didn't sound the least bit sleepy.

More rustling. Were they sitting up to talk?

"- - - seem to think highly of him."

"Of course. Some Sweepers become legends after a while, but he was a legend while living!" His giddy tone left no room for lies, and Laura felt a twinge of something bittersweet. "I mean, how many other Sweepers do you hear about that can defend an entire city single-handed? Wasn't he fifteen when he started, too?"

"He wasn't entirely alone," Okane pointed out.

"Mostly, though. Nobody's ever been able to do as much as he could. He was like a force of nature! He was famous! Anybody who called themselves a Sweeper would want to meet him."

"He was a workaholic and the bane of the city Council," said Laura, peering over the edge of the bed. "I think you're the first people I've ever met who seemed excited about him."

Felix laughed. "Nobody ever said he was supposed to be nice. People always said he was really mean! Keya told us he was rude, too. Doesn't change the fact he was amazing at his job. He was so good he even intimidated Rexians!"

"I'm not sure 'intimidated' is the right word," Laura sniggered. "Healthy caution, more like. He shot one of them in the knees when they tried to break into our shop. He was kind of trigger-happy now that I think about it."

"It took - - - this long to realize?" said Okane.

Laura let out a breathy laugh and rolled over to face the ceiling. Her last Egg, the painted one, hummed from inside her bag. What would Clae think about this gossiping, if he could hear it? He'd never seemed very concerned with rumors until they zeroed in on family matters.

"How were you related to him?" Felix asked. "Were you his brother? Cousin?"

"I guess - - - could say I was adopted into the family."

"Really? That must've been so great!"

Okane mumbled something incoherent, but was interrupted as the fourth person in the room made herself known. Darcy rapped her knuckles against the side of her cot. Felix made a guilty sound.

"We can talk in the morning. Sorry, Darcy!"

17

DITCH TIME

The next morning, Keya announced that they were rounding one of the larger mountains and fast approaching Vir. As far as Laura could remember, that meant they were halfway to Rex.

Keya ushered her guests two carriages forward and into the dining car. This car was decorated lavishly with paneled walls and ceiling, expensive multipaneled windows, and some of the fanciest tables and chairs she'd ever seen. Laura sat in a padded chair before a table covered in immaculate white cloth. Okane observed the space with less appreciation and made a point to take up as little space as possible. Darcy and Felix sat across from them, and Keya pulled up another chair.

"We've got special permission to bring you here, since you're guests," she said, gesturing at their plush surroundings and the other people all dressed to the nines. "Usually ERA workers get slop back in our own car. Hope you don't mind if we take advantage of you."

"Doesn't make a difference to me," said Laura.

"Good! I've been craving something with actual flavor for a while."

A waiter approached them, pausing by the table to give Keya's position a disdainful look before facing them properly. "Good morning, esteemed guests. May I bring you a drink? Is there a particular dish you desire?"

"Get me an omelet," said Keya.

"Would you like a drink to accompany that, ma'am?"

"Coffee."

"May I have the same?" said Felix, raising his hand as if in a classroom.

Once everyone had ordered, the waiter left. Laura wasn't concerned with the contents of her breakfast, but Keya talked of nothing else until the meal arrived. As they dug in, she moved on to a new subject.

"To reach Litus, we'll have to go close to Rex. That's one of the reasons they're so adamant about stopping the trains."

"Really?" Laura's head jerked up. On maps the train route went close to Rex, but there was no way to tell how close it would be in reality. "How close to Rex is it?"

"You can see it from the tracks." Keya grimaced. "We only set it up that way because the other option would be going through the mountains themselves. The railroads may end up having to go through with that anyway. I hope we don't have to turn around."

"You think they've ripped up the tracks already?" asked Felix.

"There's no way to be sure right now, but we'll know in sixteen hours. That's when we'll reach the next gatehouse."

"Gatehouse?" Laura echoed. "What do you mean? They have gates on railroads?"

"Kind of." Keya laughed. "There are mini stations set along rail lines. Satellite towns and Rangers send news or mail to them, and these span the rails. They're little castles that the rail companies use as checkpoints. Crews at every gatehouse set up communications and boarding of supplies. Trains rarely stop at them, though. Any news we need to know gets tucked into a special bag that we pick up on the way through. Gatehouses link to telegraph lines, so they should know the situation with Rex and pass word along. If all goes well, we'll pick up speed and steam past without trouble."

"And if Rex has ripped up the rails?"

"We may have to retreat back to the gatehouse and sort ourselves."

Laura had little concern for whether Rex had gone through with their attack on the rails. Either way the train would get close enough to Rex for her to see it, and then she and Okane could jump ship right on the enemy's doorstep. It would probably be better if the train did stop. Then it would have to slow down, and they could climb off with the excuse that their mission was important enough that they'd have to continue to Litus on foot.

"Will ERA take action? I've heard rail companies don't take well to vandalism," said Okane, pushing a piece of pancake around his plate and refusing to look at anyone.

"Not with Rex. That's their territory, after all. We'd have better luck taking down a felin with pebbles."

"That kind of undermines the rail company's authority, doesn't it?" said Laura.

"Yes, until you offer complainers the opportunity to do better."

"Pardon the intrusion." Another waiter had arrived, this one older than the last, with a holier-than-thou air about him. "I've been asked to inform Miss Mallick that she needs to report to the forward ERA carriage."

"Great," Keya groaned, tossing her napkin down on the table. "They're probably jealous that I got to eat here while they were stuck with slop. I'll be right there."

As she disappeared through the door, Laura leaned forward to ask, "Who's in the forward ERA carriage? Regular troops?"

"Sweepers and bodyguards don't get along too well," said Felix. "For some reason we're always in competition, sort of like police and military inside cities."

Everyone at the table was more or less done with their food, so they stood and went back toward their own car, Laura asking questions the whole way. She asked about various jobs for ERA members on the trains, how often they came across infestations or animals they had to fight off, what was it like living on the road, what got Felix into Sweeping? Felix was happy enough to answer, while Darcy and Okane followed in silence. Darcy had a good-natured expression on her face, and Okane perked up now that they were out of the dining car. He paid still more attention at Laura's next question.

Felix had just finished explaining a family history of railroad involvement when she asked, "Have you ever seen hobos?"

"Sure I have! My grandpa was a bull, after all."

"A what?"

"Railroad policeman. He'd track down hobos and throw them out, maybe drag them off to jail. He was always mean about it, so I feel guilty whenever I see one myself. Most times I just let them be. Pretend I didn't see them." He twiddled his thumbs, embarrassed.

"I've always been curious," said Laura. "How do hobos get on and off the trains? They make it look easy in films, but it can't be."

"They don't all make it." Felix shuddered. "That's one of the reasons my grandpa said he was so angry about hobos in the first place. Most of the hobos you see doing it these days are pretty old, since inexperienced ones die young."

Judging by that reaction, Felix had witnessed a few of these young deaths. Laura felt bad to keep pushing a sensitive subject, but it was vital information. She waited a moment, then, "So there's a trick to it?"

"They tend to work the same ways. I've never seen one get on. They're really secretive on the way in, but I think they look for open doors."

Just like we did, Laura thought.

"Getting off is tricky too. Most hobos hop off just inside the walls of the city and run before they reach the rail yard and the bulls. By that time the train has slowed a little, but not by a lot. They've got to wait until it slows, then they get on the outside of one of the cars and hang on to the ladder." He mimed clinging to the rungs. "Then they drop down and start running on the ground. When they get the hang of it, they let go, and they're out safe. I've seen a few literally jump, though! Wait till the train slows, pick a soft-looking spot, and jump out and try to roll when they hit the ground. They rip themselves up most of the time, though. I saw one die that way before, too. Keya said he broke his neck. Jumpers usually break bones."

Laura grimaced. "Remind me never to jump off a train."

"Can't see why you'd need to. Sweepers get special privileges, after all. You're not going to get tossed in the slammer by a bull."

Laura and Okane lingered in the Sweeper car for the rest of the day. Keya returned, complaining. Apparently they'd scolded her for invading the dining car (the invitation had only been for actual guests), and made the demand that the Sinclair Sweepers be kept out of the way. She and Felix were assigned extra rounds, so they slouched off; Darcy remained, smiling blithely and tapping out a tune with one foot as she knitted something lumpy and green. Laura spent her day bored and restless, trying to sleep; she hoped that maybe, if she napped enough, she'd store away enough energy to go a few days without it when they reached Rex. Okane stretched out on his own bed, but it was impossible to tell if he was sleeping.

Keya and Felix passed through the car occasionally, but it was only during the night that they gave more than a tired greeting. The lights had dimmed down by this time, Darcy snoring away, when the door swung open. Light flooded in from the lamps outside, silhouetting Felix's small frame.

"Hey!" he whispered loudly. "You've got to come see!"

Laura squinted at him, leaning over the side of her bunk, and he looked up at her, the dim light illuminating his excitement as he hissed, "We're coming up on the gatehouse! It's hard to see at night, but it's still amazing! Most passengers never pay enough attention to notice."

Curiosity lured Laura out of bed. She and Okane followed him out to crowd the platform. The train was turning to avoid the foothills of the mountains. The peaks couldn't be seen from here, but Laura remembered the map—why else would they be turning on the flatland? Few landmarks could be seen in the light of the train, but midnight darkness couldn't disguise the building before them. The rails were built atop a ridge in the landscape, the flatlands rolling down and out to the sides, but in the gloom ahead was a structure of stacked rock, rising along the ridge and forming a wall beyond. More walls rose in the same fashion, staggered in different heights along the slope, the foundations of a monstrous building. Jutting up to span the tracks was a building not made of stone but seemingly wood, big and dark though light shone through intricate latticed designs on the upper floor. The roof was gabled, wide with four points curving down, out, and up at the tips. A hole ran through the middle, enough for a large train to pass through. While it was difficult to discern any detail, the shape itself was beautiful.

"That's the gatehouse?" Laura breathed.

"I've never seen anything like it," said Okane, leaning to get a better look.

"It was built on the ruins of one of the big native castles," Felix told them.

"Was it one of the castles they tore down in the wars?" Laura asked, and he nodded.

"I think it burned down, so only the foundation's left. The rail company likes to use old fortresses as gatehouses if they can, but they rebuild on old sites too. You'd think they'd go with the regular mainland designs, but there are two or three they made like this. They're all in Zyra, though. It's nice to look at, isn't it?"

They continued to watch in amazement as the train approached, and Felix tugged at their clothing, pulling them back into the train's shelter as they arrived. The train slowed no further but sped through the opening, briefly flooded with light as stone walls flashed past, and then they were out, back into the dark and surrounded by the ruins of the old castle.

"How were we supposed to get any messages like that? That was too fast to hand something over," said Laura.

"They set up a bag of mail on a wire. We've got a hook to grab it on the way through. Whatever messages they wanted us to get, we definitely got it."

⚬⚬⚬

Laura woke the next morning to the sound of someone tripping over the little oven. Felix looked up sheepishly to apologize. Keya was already gone, talking with the other ERA workers about information they'd gotten from the gatehouse. Judging by the fact that the train didn't slow, the attack on the rails must not have come to fruition. Felix went off to do his job, and Laura climbed down to the floor.

"Hey." She tapped the side of Okane's mattress. "You up? We should get breakfast."

The blanket shifted and he peeked out from under his pillow, eyes clear. He'd been awake for a while.

"I don't want to go there again," he announced, before pulling the pillow down again.

"What? Why not? You didn't like the food?"

"I didn't like the atmosphere."

Laura knelt down a little further and whispered, "Too Sullivan for you?"

The brief movement of bedding wasn't exactly clear but she got the message. She turned to face the last of the other Sweepers; Darcy reorganized something in the closet.

"Excuse me, Miss Darcy? Keya said you usually have breakfast in here. Can we do the same?"

"- - - can go to the dining car without me," Okane mumbled, but she didn't dignify that with a response.

"The dining car is pretty high-class, and it was nice being there yesterday, but I'd feel more comfortable here."

Darcy hummed. From a closet she procured two cans, which she opened and set on top of the little oven. She tapped its side and the flames roared with more vigor. She held up one hand with the fingers spread: five minutes. The little oven warmed the food, and Darcy handed them large spoons. Okane crawled out of his blanket cocoon and they sat on the edge of the mattress to eat out of the cans.

"Thanks," said Laura, scooping some of the food into her mouth. The unidentifiable contents tasted bland and had a weird texture, but she wasn't about to complain. "I don't want to ask for too much, but could we leave this car, too? I'd like to walk around. Can we go a few cars down and back?"

Darcy smiled again and shrugged. Clearly she didn't care.

Shortly after finishing, they slinked outside.

"Are - - - looking into something?" Okane asked, as they crossed over to the next carriage.

"We've got to get off soon, whether the train stops or not."

"That's why - - - asked about the hobos?"

"Exactly. We just need to find somewhere safe to get off."

"Is there even a place where the train gets slow enough?"

"They've got to go slow around Rex, right? Even if they haven't ripped up the tracks there yet, they still could before we get there. Nobody wants a train to go full-speed into damaged tracks, especially if that means putting passengers at risk of getting captured."

"Captured?" Okane echoed as they stepped through the narrow aisle. "I thought they already had all the slaves they need from attacking satellite towns."

"They work people hard enough to kill them. There's never a safe time to interact with Rex."

If they were captured, there would be no rescue. Rex's forces could fight off any attempt. Satellite citizens sometimes committed suicide over facing Rex at all.

Okane lapsed into silence. Hopefully he wasn't worrying himself sick over what they'd be running into. Laura herself refused to think about it. Instead she focused entirely on finding the optimal escape route for the next phase of their ramshackle plan. They had to double back all the way to the car they'd hid in earlier before spotting one of the side doors unblocked.

"I guess this will be our exit, too," Laura sighed, rapping the door with her knuckles. "There was a ladder next to it. We can use that like the hobos do."

"How will we know when to do it?"

"We can ask how long it'll be until we pass Rex. They've got enough on their plates, so they shouldn't be suspicious. Let's ask them now."

They trekked back the way they'd come, and ran into Keya on the way. She stood on the back of the Sweeper car, her expression severe. The door behind her was open and Felix peered around her, curious but reluctant to come all the way out. Laura paused in the other doorway. Why did she have a bad feeling?

"Something wrong?" she called over the sound of the train.

"Yeah. Yeah, there is." Keya's eyes were narrowed, angry. "How about you come back with us?"

"Come where, exactly?" Laura clenched her hands.

"Back up the train. The others would love to discuss a little . . . *issue* that came up in a message from the gatehouse."

"What kind of message?" Laura snapped, but she had a good idea what it was.

"You know very well," Keya snarled. "Two Sweepers collaborated with mobs and let them steal all the Gin? Attacking your head is some backstabbing bullshit, but Gin? You've abandoned an entire city!"

"That's wrong!" Laura argued. "We didn't steal any—"

"What did the mobs promise you for that?" Keya spat. "Money and a comfy place in Litus? Or maybe you're just running out of shame?" She pulled out her gun and gestured sharply. "Get over here! I've got no intention of playing nice with traitors!"

Laura took a quick glance at Okane, who jerked his head back toward their presumed escape.

"Sorry, no," she said quickly, slamming the door shut. She heard a muffled curse, but was already dashing away after Okane. They fled to their selected car. While Okane moved to open the side door, Laura yanked on the stacked cargo. She dislodged some of the larger crates, and sidestepped quickly as they came crashing down in front of the door. Hopefully that would buy them time. The side door opened with a pop, a rumbling, and a crash. Cold air whipped into the car, and the flatlands beyond became visible. There, silhouetted against the pale blue sky, was a five-tiered city with distinctive spiked towers: Rex.

"Ladies first!" Okane shouted.

Laura scowled but hurried over anyway. She stuck her head out and squinted. Despite the wind it seemed the train had slowed. She reached out for the ladder, caught hold with one hand before sliding one leg out to join it. After a moment she heard a muttered "Here," and Okane took her by the other arm, trying to support her.

"Don't fall," he pleaded.

Steeling herself, Laura swung fully onto the ladder. She felt some resistance, but she made it and clung there a moment to collect herself. Inside the car, Keya hammered away at the door. Fast. She had to be fast. Laura slid farther down on the ladder and took her feet off. The ground flashed by fast enough that it took some time before she did more than skip over it, but she managed to start running, enough to somewhat match the speed. She looked up, elated, but felt the blood drain from her face. Keya might have been pounding on the door, but Felix had leaned out to look down the side of the train. He pointed his own gun at her, but he'd frozen. He winced, possibly at some command Laura couldn't hear over the train, and pulled the trigger. The bullet hit the ground feet away from her, and with a squeak of surprise and fear, Laura lost her grip on the rungs. She stumbled and threw herself away from the train, afraid of getting caught under the wheels, and crashed to the ground. She remained there, dazed, before her mind caught up and she scrambled to her feet. While slower than usual, the train had still traveled far beyond her. She ran, ignoring the sting from her fall.

"Okane!" she yelled.

Had he been caught? She felt a brief stab of horror before someone leapt from the train. Okane hit the ground and rolled head over heels before coming to a flailing stop. No one came after them.

"Are you okay?" Laura panted, coming to a stop beside him.

Pops and snaps issued from his prone form, and that coupled with the fact that his clothes now looked little better than rags made her worry even more. To her relief, he stirred and pushed himself over, lying on his back instead to blink, stupefied, at the sky. After a moment he wheezed, "*Ow.*"

"Ow is right! Didn't you hear Felix talking earlier? People die jumping! What were you thinking?"

"I was thinking I'd get shot otherwise."

Laura made a strangled sound, but she wasn't as much irritated as concerned. The popping lessened but continued nonetheless. What was his magic working so hard on?

"You sure you're okay?"

"Passable," he grunted, sitting up. He looked mournfully after the train as it shrank into the distance. "Now what do we do?"

"I suppose we go to Rex." Laura gestured at the city, and he grimaced at the sight.

"- - - think they'll just let us march right in?"

"If we can jump off a train, we can walk into a city," said Laura.

Okane blinked at her, then groaned and flopped right back over.

"We stay out here and we're prey for felin or Rexian troops. We try to go back to some friendly city and we'll either die on the way or get arrested as soon as we get through the doors. Have you got any better ideas?"

He pursed his lips, looking tempted to say something nasty in retort, but he held it in and heaved himself up once more, faster this time. "Fine. But I hope - - - know I can't be sneaky like this." He tugged at loose scraps of his shirt.

"We'll figure something out."

He said nothing, but the look on his face conveyed more than enough doubt.

They hobbled in the direction of the city. Each had a collection of scrapes and bruises, though while Okane had far more, Laura knew hers would remain longer; he always healed abnormally fast. He leaned on her in the beginning, one of his ankles unable to bear his weight properly, but as time went on the crackling sounds dissipated and he switched to limping independently.

Truth be told, Laura had no idea how to get into an enemy city. She'd spoken with bravado, all the while thinking desperately how they could sneak in. The old film played in the back of her mind, ten identical women and the whole of Rex looking like a single brood. The more she looked at Okane the more he looked distressingly not-Zyran, even beyond the clothes, and she was hardly better. They'd stand out like sore thumbs. Perhaps they could pose as Rangers? No, Rex wouldn't tolerate outsiders of any kind, and their Sweepers served every Ranger purpose for them. Slaves, then, from the fields outside? She racked her brain for stories or excuses and found nothing. She came to the unsurprising conclusion that she was a terrible schemer.

Every step brought them closer, and she grew more nervous. They reached the surrounding farmland around noon, and Laura chose to walk on the main road. If they at least acted as if they belonged, people would be less suspicious. It wasn't as if everyone kept their clothes in good shape in the agricultural areas, even in cities that cared about their well-being; her mother being a prime example. Okane had misgivings, but it turned out to be a good idea. Forty minutes after they started on the gravelly road, a large truck trundled up beside them. The driver asked who they were and what they were up to. Laura made up a story about them being farmworkers who'd missed an earlier car and were desperate to get into the city ("No, really, my friend here just took a nasty spill off some equipment!"). For what? Well, the Carmen film had mentioned a weekly check-in with food vendors inside the walls. This was apparently a reality, because the driver fell for it hook, line, and sinker. They clambered in and settled themselves among bags of supplies, and the truck drove on. The driver chatted to them about one thing or another, mostly farm-related. Laura replied with what little she knew from her mother's experiences tending fields, but to her relief the man was more inclined to talk their ears off than get meaningful input. As they approached the walls and the towers soared above their heads, Laura's confidence faltered.

"Um," she piped up, "sorry, sir, but I think we forgot our papers. They might not let us in."

"No worries there!" The driver laughed. "Usually you'd be in trouble, but the past few days they haven't cared. Not so many soldiers at checkpoints, not so strict. They're all going south. They don't care about a couple of farmers."

"Do you know what they're gathering south for?" Laura asked.

"Some kind of attack, I imagine. I'm looking forward to it! When our boys go out to battle, they bring back laborers. The more riffraff like you they catch, the better off we are. Just imagine, a whole new platoon of workers! We could use them for the uzel harvest. I've never liked those thorns, and I doubt you will either."

True to the driver's words, only one soldier stood at the entrance. The soldier checked the vehicle registration and cast a suspicious look at the two passengers, but after assurance that they were faithful Rexian servants, he let them through without complaint. The driver let them off in a market in the lowest Quarter, where stalls lined a street overflowing with produce and shoppers.

"Good luck finding your group," he'd called after them, and Laura thanked him. Okane didn't say a word until they'd passed a large display of rice bags.

"We really will be slaves if they figure out what we are," he said.

"So we don't get caught."

Easier said than done. Besides, if they were caught trying to steal something as valuable as Gin, there might be something worse than farm labor in store.

The streets of Rex were familiar and yet not. Just as in the film, every road and building was in pristine condition or left to affectionate but well-tended weathering, as if it were the Second Quarter instead of the Fifth. People bustled along sidewalks, many headed for the market but others moving away and deeper into the city while automobiles—darker and boxier, leaning toward a military look—cruised by in the streets, as many as would be expected on the Tiber Circuit. Every building united in common architectural styles, and every road bore a clear marker. It was a sort of quaintly unified thing, the kind that screamed that no one had dared to make it their own; false like a film-set façade with nothing inside. A few buildings had paint scrawled on the sides and in alleys, which might've been graffiti, but all were strategically placed with slogans emblazoned across patriotic imagery.

HAIL, CITY OF KINGS! one declared, red lettering above a dramatically rendered kingshound. ONWARD TO THE FOUR CORNERS, RAISE PURE BLOOD! Others echoed it: praise to the city, support the destined advance, the chosen people meant to overcome the rest and become the pinnacle of human potential. One that caught Laura's attention in particular was a splash of paint following the ramp up to the next Quarter: a horde of men in uniform and shaved heads, with identical features save for numbers on their faces. All seemed posed but lifeless, and Laura felt distinctly uncomfortable at the sight.

"At least we'll know a Sweeper when we see them," said Okane, eyes lingering on the propaganda. "Think we can just follow one back to their headquarters?"

"Maybe. I don't think we should do anything for today, though. We're not in the best shape."

"Where should we go, then?" He looked miserably at the sky as if it might give him answers. "Do - - - have money for a hotel on hand? Money for food?"

"Didn't really think of that," she admitted.

"We didn't think anything out," he agreed.

"Let's focus on the job for now. Find out where the Sweeper offices are and scope things out, then back off and find somewhere to crash. I have a little bit of money, so maybe we can beg help from a cheaper hotel?"

A haphazard plan was better than none at all, so Okane nodded.

They couldn't find any Sweepers whatsoever.

Laura thought that with the breeding program they'd run into one at every turn, but the Sweepers must've gathered outside after all. Despite the clear street signs they found no maps, forcing them to ask for directions. While not identical, the people here had a very distinct look. Every single one was white, light-haired, high-cheek-boned, and without so much as a blemish. But despite the flush of life in their faces, they looked even less human than Grim. These people turned up their noses at the sight of them (Okane in particular), and gave little help. Some ignored them entirely, looking the opposite way and hurrying past as Laura called out, while others made snide comments on their state of dress and general position in life. Three persons in total spoke to them like actual people, and all three answered along the same lines.

"Sweepers? Oh, you don't go to them. You call and they have an officer come by. It's not proper to be in the company of a Sweeper. They're violent and stupid. Bad bloodlines, you know. They're only good for one thing and it's not conversation. No one really knows where their offices are, but if you go to the police they'll take care of you. Shall I point you to the nearest station?"

By the time they reached a bookshop in the Third Quarter, Laura frothed with rage.

"Forget their Sweepers, the civilians here are hell to deal with," she growled, eyeing the few pedestrians on this street. "And the graffiti rattles me!"

"It's not all going to be easy," said Okane.

"But getting any information is like pulling teeth."

"Maybe if - - - tried smiling a little more?" He pointed at his own face. "Maybe they're getting scared at this point."

"I'm that bad?"

"A little."

She took a deep breath in, held it, and exhaled, trying to force her features back into calm. She held this attempted serenity for a minute before glancing at him for approval. Okane's shoulders gave a little bounce and he shook his head in weary exasperation. Good enough. Laura turned to scope out the area, selecting a new target. A lone young woman ambled along the opposite side of the road, possibly a target for information. Better still, she wasn't blond. No, if anything that darker skin and curled brown hair marked her as Kalu, not Zyran at all. Finally, a non-purist. Laura made a beeline for her.

"Excuse me?" she called, sweetly as she could manage.

The woman turned to look over her shoulder. Laura could only see half of her face, but that visible eye was strikingly brown. The intensity of the color made her stop short. *Marvelous Magnum's Deluxe Caramel,* she thought dazedly, before realizing how ridiculous that sounded. The woman blinked, and her lips turned up in a very fake smile.

"Hello. Something wrong?"

Startled back to her senses, Laura shook her head quickly. "Oh, no! It's just—would you happen to know where I can find the Rex Sweeper offices?"

"Sweepers? Why would a young lady be looking for the Sweepers?"

"Personal business." Laura flashed a false smile of her own. "We just need some directions. Are you familiar with them?"

"Depends on who's asking."

"As I said, it's personal."

"Oh, that *really* explains things. I'm *so* inclined to help."

Laura felt ready to snap. Okane tugged lightly at the sleeve of her coat and whispered, "We can just ask someone else."

The woman sneered. "Sounds like a giver-upper."

Of course, not even a non-purist here could be dependable. Laura sighed, yielding to Okane's pleading. As they walked around her the woman pivoted to watch them, a mean smile on her face. "Two giver-uppers, then."

"Yes, we are," said Laura, already searching for someone who looked less offensive.

"Giver-upper. Coward. Yellowbelly. Chicken." The woman followed them, calling out taunts. What a child.

Much to Laura's displeasure, no one seemed at all interested in helping them. The passersby glanced over, but otherwise gave no indication that they'd noticed anything. Okane walked closer, almost brushing shoulders.

"Do - - - think we should ask at an official office after all?" he whispered.

"I was trying to avoid that. We'd have to make up a story, or—"

Before Laura could finish her sentence a hand descended on her, thumbnail digging into her spine while fingers curled about her neck. Judging by the squeak from Okane, the same thing happened to him. The Kalu woman steered them close together, her head between theirs. Laura twisted her head around to rebuke her, but froze immediately. Thin numbers stretched on the woman's cheek: 1100100. *Shit*.

"You're a Sweeper," Laura whispered.

"Well. Not really." The woman slid her way between them, pulling them flush against her and moving so her arms draped over their shoulders, in a less dangerous position but still enough to make Laura feel trapped.

"If you're not a Sweeper, what are you?" asked Laura.

"Why don't we talk this over with some drinks, hm? There's a café just up the road. My treat."

"Why don't I trust you?"

"Honey, don't trust anyone in this town. That goes especially for dream boy." She tilted her head against Okane, peering up at him. He leaned away, but her arm kept him from getting too far.

"And yet you want us to have drinks." Laura reclaimed the woman's attention, and when those brown eyes turned on her again, they sparkled with something more like excitement than scorn.

"It's easier to talk there than on the street."

The café's small room held a cast of thin chairs and tables, the metal of them twisted in plain but decorative shapes that dug uncomfortably into Laura's back when she sat down. Laura couldn't make out any of the individual conversations around them, but the loud babble filled the room and carried over the heads of the customers and the coffee bar. Laura, Okane, and the woman claimed the empty table by the large window. As soon as she released him, Okane took the chair next to Laura and scooted it as close as humanly possible. The woman occupied the third chair, back to the window. She was a small person, but sat in a way that took up the entirety of the chair and beyond, like a king sprawling on a throne. She observed them the way a king would inspect peasants, too.

"Why so interested in Rex Sweepers? Seems to me like this is the *last* place to go on holiday."

"We're not 'on holiday,' we're here on business," Laura replied.

"Ooh, business. Elaborate." The woman's eyebrows rose and her eyes sparked a mocking curiosity.

"Private business. If you aren't a Sweeper, you've got no right to the information."

"Oh. Oh, baby." The woman leaned over the table and rested her elbows on it. In films this might have been a move for the actress to show off her breasts, but her coat hid what little bust she had, making the gesture useless. "Sweepers here don't have much information at all. They're like dogs. Their handlers direct them."

Laura let this information sink in. Did that mean this woman was a handler? Did handlers get tattooed as well?

"Who exactly are you?" she asked.

"The name's Zelda. No last name. Haven't picked one yet."

"I'm sorry?"

"Well, they didn't give us names to begin with, and once somebody gets a name, it sticks throughout life, doesn't it? Need to find one that fits right."

She stood up, reaching to pluck the tray from a waiter. She set it down in the middle of their table while the man kept walking, arms propped up as if he were still carrying the tray.

Laura looked between her and the waiter, flabbergasted. "You can't just take that! We're trying to keep a low profile!"

"And - - -'re doing such a remarkable job of it," Zelda said dryly. "Sit back down, he doesn't notice and he doesn't care."

Sure enough, the man kept walking as if this were an everyday occurrence.

Zelda handed out the cups she'd stolen. Laura found herself with a tall soda glass of peach-colored substance with chocolate sprinkles on a whipped topping. Okane received a shorter ceramic mug with something dark like coffee under a cream pattern; he looked at it like he'd been offered poison. Zelda claimed a pale pink drink in a teacup. A lone tea remained between them.

"Okay, Zelda, I still don't know who you are."

"My face should make me obvious, right? These numbers mean I'm part of Rex's Sweeper breeding program."

"But you said you weren't a Sweeper. And I thought the Sweepers didn't have names, just numbers."

"That's why I had to find my own." Zelda sipped loudly from her cup and smacked her lips. "I was in the breeding program until I was five, and then I gave them the slip. They haven't found me since. Wonderful thing, this magic."

"Magic?"

Zelda gestured at Okane. "Of course. What, did the info not get out? We're bred from people like him."

Laura's mouth clicked shut again. Okane's hands tightened on his mug, but while he avoided eye contact he didn't look surprised.

"Rex rounded up a bunch of those magicky people during the witch hunts, turned them into breeding stock. With magic in our blood we repel monsters, so we make great Sweepers. Perfect little soldiers.

Of course all the inbreeding results in some, shall we say, *undesirable* conditions. And then our little magic Sweepers need to be kept very close so they don't go making their own decisions and getting out of control. Part of why we don't have names. That's why I got out as soon as I could."

"How did - - - know about me? Was it the eyes? The speech?" Okane whispered.

"I feel it. The speech was the real tip-off, though. Don't use that word if - - - can help it here."

She did the "you" thing too. Laura leaned back against the metal of her chair and looked at Okane. "You knew about this?"

"I did," he confessed. "It's one of the reasons we're never supposed to trust anyone from Rex. Honestly, it's more dangerous for me here than it is for you."

Zelda smiled. "Glad to see - - - understand. Don't get caught. Rex always wants new stock."

18

TREASURE IN THE LABYRINTH

Rex's evening traffic trundled slow along the roads, headlights trailing over the pavement and briefly illuminating sidewalks and windows before fading again. As one of the passing automobiles lit the sign of a clothing store, the letters on the window cast an eerie reflection.

"Is this really a good idea?" Okane peered around for witnesses.

"Of course it is!" Zelda snorted, sashaying to the door.

"But he looks like a tramp," said Laura. "Nobody in their right mind would let a hobo into his shop, especially in this Quarter, right?"

"Nobody's going to see a tramp. Magic, remember?"

True, they'd stayed in that café for an hour as Zelda snatched food and drinks from unsuspecting waiters and they'd left without anyone giving them a bill, but Laura remained skeptical.

"How exactly does your magic work?"

"Same way all magic shit does," said Zelda, twisting the doorknob and swinging it open. "It's self-preservation instinct going on overdrive."

Laura and Okane followed her into the shop. An old man with a graying mustache sat behind the counter to their right, eyes fixed on his newspaper as if he'd heard no customers at all. Shelves lined the other walls, while racks and displays of the latest styles cluttered the middle. The stock mostly catered toward men, but some women's coats and gloves could be glimpsed on the far wall. Zelda took a quick look at Okane's rags and beckoned them further inside.

"Think about all the times magic gets used. Go on, list them."

Laura glanced at her companion. "I suppose it helps him land on his feet? He heals fast. Runs fast."

"Sometimes I'm stronger. I'm lucky, too," he added.

"Luck has nothing to do with it, only reflexes," said Zelda. "What magic usually does is pump up a person's attributes. Temporarily multiplies whatever one of us has. That's type number one. Type number two—"

She paused, picked up a shirt from the nearest display, and motioned for Okane to try it on right then and there.

"Type number two is the same as our little speech impediment: works on other people. Problem is, when a person has number two, they're lacking in number one. I have number two, but I can't bump up my speed when I'm running from something and I can't let off a flare if an infestation tries to get me. Sweepers might think that's useless, but it serves me well. Other kids in the breeding program? Not so lucky. They don't display the right attributes, and they either go into hard labor or they get culled. I escape notice. When my magic is going, no one realizes I'm here. I'm like that thing in the mirror: in the corner of the eye but gone before it's clearly seen. Unless they're specifically looking for me, they don't notice at all."

"That's amazing," Laura whispered, awed despite herself.

Zelda preened, lips curling into a smile that looked more malicious than pleased, before faltering.

"Didn't I say to try that on?"

Okane held the shirt closer to his chest. "I don't know where the dressing room is."

"Just do it here." Okane looked away and blushed slightly. "What, embarrassed to change in front of ladies?"

"Don't make fun of him," said Laura.

"I'm really not comfortable," he said.

"Well, a changing room is out of the question. Get too far from me and - - - don't get the benefits of my magic. The geezer will hear every move." Zelda jerked her thumb at the shopkeeper.

"You work on noise, too?"

"Little things. Can't disguise a foghorn, but a squeaky door, sure. I just muffle it is all."

"You can't just stand outside the dressing room?"

"And let that geezer breathe on me?" She shuddered. "No."

"Nice to know your compassion goes so far," Laura drawled.

Okane fidgeted. "Could I at least go on the other side of the rack?"

Zelda rolled her eyes. "Fine."

He hustled away immediately. Laura heard him shuffling around, and turned to check on the shopkeeper. The old man picked his nose, newspaper up so no one outside could see it.

"So what's this business with our Sweepers?" asked Zelda. "They're mindless, but most of them are brutes anyway. The inbreeding really didn't help tempers."

"It's still a private thing," said Laura.

"'Private' isn't in my dictionary. Secrets don't mean shit to someone who's uncatchable."

"It's—Well." Laura squirmed, trying to figure out exactly how much to tell this woman. She turned around to ask Okane's opinion, and halfway through the motion realized her mistake. She didn't see much before snapping her head back around, but she saw enough. A mess of symbols scarred his shoulders and back. Her stomach lurched.

"What are those?" Zelda's voice rang low and flat next to her ear; she'd peeked at the same time as Laura, and her face froze in shock.

"Shh!" Laura hissed, trying to gesture that this was not an acceptable topic.

Zelda snarled and caught her by the arm, dragging her in close to growl, "*What happened to him?*"

Laura squeaked in surprise at the motion and gathered her thoughts before answering, "Not everyone understands magic, do they? I'm sure you're not a stranger to that. Some people react worse than others. Just don't say anything about it, okay? He doesn't like it."

It wasn't much of an explanation, but Zelda took it. She stared at

Laura's face a while more. "But we don't scar easily." Her nails dug painfully into Laura's arm before drawing back again.

"I think this shirt is a little big," said Okane, thankfully ignorant of their conversation. "Is there a smaller one?"

"Sure thing, dream boy!" Zelda chirped, and she tossed another over the rack. Her voice had returned to its normal tone, but it took a while for the steeliness in her eyes to fade.

They rotated around the store, swapping Okane's torn clothes for new Rexian styles, but after he collected a new outfit they gravitated toward the overcoats.

"These do nicely for camouflage," Zelda declared, pulling one of the coats out by the sleeve. "Latest fashion. All the respectable people wear them. Get too far away from me and some kind of disguise is necessary." She raked Laura's clothes with a scathing glance. "No wonder nobody wanted to answer any questions. They'd sooner step in dog shit than answer such an unfashionable girl!"

True, Laura still wore Cherry's spare coat, but underneath it she still had the expensive kin-infused gear.

"People back home think I look great," she grumbled, pulling the coat tighter around herself.

"Must be a Terulian thing." Zelda smirked at the surprise on Laura's face. "What? I'm not stupid, that accent's not Zyran. I'm still waiting on an explanation of this Sweeper business too, of course."

"What do you think?" Laura peered over at Okane.

He mulled over it for a moment, tugging at the cuffs of his new shirt. "It would be nice if we could have - - -r help. As - - - can see, we don't have much to go on at this point. Without a guide, we're probably sunk."

"True." Zelda tossed an overcoat at Laura, and snickered as she scrambled to catch it. "But I'm not helping anyone until I know what's going on."

Odd words from someone who'd already helped them find a meal and warm clothing. Nevertheless, Laura told her. Not in excruciating detail, but enough to give Zelda the general idea. She didn't mention Clae or Anselm, just the Gin stones.

"Sweepers, then," Zelda mused, trying on a new set of gloves and dumping her old ones on the shelf where they'd been. "Here on a retrieval mission."

"That's the deal," said Laura, buttoning up her new overcoat. It seemed more showy than functional this far south.

"But here's what gets me. Sure, cities would come running to recover their Gin, but Sweepers? Really? More than that, why would Rex specifically target - - -? What's so special about that city?"

"Have you heard of Clae Sinclair?" Judging by Felix's reactions on the train, Clae's name had power beyond Amicae that Laura had never realized. Sure enough, the name brought an immediate reaction.

"Wait, - - -'re *Amicae* Sweepers? When I think Amicae, I expect a little more . . ." Zelda flipped her hand at them, grimacing. "Intimidating? Bigger?"

"Are Rexian Sweepers that much more imposing?" said Okane.

"In their own way," said Zelda.

"Did you hear about the commotion around Amicae in November?" said Laura. Judging by Zelda's widening eyes, she had. "Rex has always been after some sort of Sinclair secret. When they heard about the incident and knew Clae would be out of the way, they came in to raid our armory."

"Did they get the secret?"

"There wasn't a secret. But they did steal a journal that had vital points of the city structure. Pit locations, weaker defense points, Sweeper-wise, anyway. We need to get it back."

A total lie, but Okane made no move to correct her.

"They've probably been through that book and learned every secret. Not much point to getting it back," said Zelda.

"If we get it back we can reinforce everything, right? Besides, maybe Sweeper handlers are stupid too and haven't gotten around to it yet."

Zelda pouted as she perused the hat section, looking bored again. Helper or not, she was still Rexian. She might be willing to look out for people like her, but that didn't mean she wouldn't follow Rex's teachings, or that she cared about the fate of other cities.

"How's this," Zelda said at last. "We visit the headquarters, we chat some people up, we snoop a little, and I go home. Then, sometime in the future, I get a big fat reward."

"What kind of reward?" Laura asked, suspicious.

"Depends on my mood. Depends how much trouble we get in. Maybe I'll want a candy bar, maybe I'll want a million argents. We'll see."

"Candy we can do, but money's not something we're rolling in," said Laura.

Zelda let out a harsh bark of laughter. "Deal."

Night fell completely over the city, but the neighborhoods Zelda walked through remained bright and boisterous. Deeper into the city, businesses became less formal, and soon they passed signs for more lecherous attractions, which pointed down alleyways and mazes of streets. Laura would've believed it was a red-light district if Zelda hadn't laughed and told them it was located in the Second Quarter. Other walkers jeered at one another, but the trio went unnoticed all the way to the inner wall of the Third Quarter. The inside walls of Rex were structured like those of a castle, bearing the tall towers that had been visible from the train, dotted with windows but otherwise bleak if not marred by propaganda posters. Zelda clapped them on the shoulders as they drew closer.

"Welcome to Sweeper headquarters!" she announced. "Sure, there are other facilities, but this is where all the action happens."

"Here?" Laura squinted up at the closest soaring tower.

"The entire ring around the Second Quarter: the wall itself and a good chunk of the interior," said Zelda.

Okane looked faint. "We have to search the entire thing?"

"Not necessarily. I've got a friend in there who might help us."

"A friend who can see - - -—?"

"Of course. Come on!"

She led them through the front door, which stood completely open with no one to guard it.

The inside of Sweeper headquarters looked as bleak as the outside. No one made any attempt to liven up the stone walls or the scuffed floor, and the halls felt narrow due to the sheer amount of people moving inside. Light shone from intermittent bulbs in the ceiling, dull and yellowish. Windows let out more light than they took in, little more than a break from the monotony. Halls had low ceilings, and went in a myriad of different directions, up or down or left or right, with no signs or hint of a landmark to orient oneself, until it became a labyrinth. Laura was completely lost after they turned the second corner.

Zelda had seemed short to Laura at first, but she quickly came to the conclusion that she wasn't an exception. Sweeper after Sweeper marched by, numbers on their faces, heads shaved and identical uniforms pristine, almost all of them several inches shorter than her. She felt almost glad for it; she found it easier to look at the buzz cuts than their narrowed eyes, the otherwise blank faces. She tracked similarities, though, in the shape of the faces and individual features. They also had one unusual trait.

"Their eyes are so bright," Okane whispered, hitting the nail on the head as a particularly short woman with brilliant green eyes stalked past.

"That's one of our traits," Zelda replied quietly. "Magi's, I mean. I heard somewhere that we used to be called 'jewel-eyes.' Don't make eye contact."

"Why not?"

"They can see through my magic easier. Their magic cancels it out or something. Make eye contact and they'll latch on. Some of them don't even need that to see me, though." She trailed off as a noise came from ahead.

The sudden commotion proved to be a group of Sweepers wearing a heavier uniform, laden with darker clothing and an abundance of weapons and ammunition. Wherever they were going, they looked ready to do damage. Sheaths, guns, ammunition boxes, and more equipment out of sight clanked and jangled as they marched in time, led by a wiry man with small glasses who gestured madly with one hand as he read off of a slip of paper in the other. Maybe a pep talk, Laura supposed, but the man spat his words so it sounded more like an insult or a rant; none of his followers showed any emotion. Zelda slowed to a stop as the line traipsed by, and the other two halted close to her.

"Where is your friend?" Laura spoke as quietly as she could manage, suddenly paranoid that these people could hear her.

"He should be nearby. We're cutting it close, but he's more attentive than the rest of these degenerates. He might know something. Aha!" She raised one hand, flashing her teeth and singing, "Hey there, Ivo!"

A strange movement started in the second line from the back. A Sweeper there paused. While not as tall as Okane, he rose head and shoulders above his fellows, his features a stark difference to the other Rexians despite the number tattoo. He looked more Wasureijin than Cherry had. Whatever the case, his dark eyes fixed on them and Laura knew at once that Zelda's disappearing act had no effect on him. He glanced at the head of the line before stepping out and walking over to them.

"What are - - - doing here?" he asked, his voice deep and almost deadpan.

"We came to visit!" Zelda smiled. "These are my new friends. Say hi to Ivo!"

Ivo looked severely unimpressed. "I don't answer to that. - - - know my number. Use it."

"Hello, Mr.—" Okane squinted at the other's face. "1100106."

Ivo (Laura would never remember the number, so she ignored it completely) stared at Okane as if puzzled by his presence, but Zelda butted in before he could ask any questions.

"Look, Ivo"—"*Number*," he muttered again—"we've got an itsy-bitsy problem. A group of Sweepers went and stole their stuff not too long ago, and they really need to get it back. Where would someone put stolen Gin in this place?"

"Gin?" His brow furrowed. "Does that make these people Sweepers themselves? From another city?"

Laura wanted to jump in and deny it, but no, Zelda nodded before she could get the words out.

"These two are here courtesy of one Clae Sinclair, and they're willing to do anything they need to do to recover what's theirs."

"Isn't Clae Sinclair dead?" Ivo scoffed.

"Regardless."

Ivo's shoulders sagged, and Laura came to the conclusion that he wasn't naturally deadpan, just tired and not happy to be dealing with them. He looked at Okane, then at Laura, resignation drawing on his features, before sighing, "This Gin is the reason for the new offensive, isn't it?"

"That depends. What's the new offensive?"

"We're crusading again." He tilted his head at the ongoing line of Sweepers. "My squad is being sent out in one of the early stages, and others will follow in waves. The handlers say this will easily crush any resistance and ensure our victory this time, but—"

He stopped. Clearly he wanted to say more, but he was reluctant to speak. Zelda frowned.

"This is my little circle." She gestured around them. "Nobody outside can hear if Mr. Sweeper has some autonomy. Go ahead and talk."

"I'd rather not fall into the habit."

Laura could draw her own conclusions. *The crusaders come back when they're sufficiently mauled,* Clae had told her, but this sounded more like an all-out offensive. If Rex threw wave after wave of Sweepers into it, that meant a lot of people would die, but weren't they supposed to be valuable breeding stock? Laura herself had no faith in the crusade idea, so she could only see terrible consequences ahead. How angry would the hive mind become? The backlash could mean hell for the rest of the cities, maybe even complete destruction.

"Our Gin is held at the western point," said Ivo, jolting her from her thoughts. "If stolen objects get incorporated into our kin production, it would be there. However, they had to remove something from there yesterday due to 'an incident.'"

"What kind?" Laura asked quickly.

"I didn't see much, but I believe it was some kind of magic gone haywire. Whatever the culprit, it caused considerable damage to the western structure and burned many of its carriers. Three of the carriers are in the medical wing, and a fourth proved flawed."

"Flawed?" Okane echoed.

"Genetic deficiencies," Zelda explained. "Some people don't stop bleeding."

The dead Rexian from the armory came back to mind, bled to death when he shouldn't have. So that's what happened, a ticking time bomb he might not have even known about until the end?

"The object is still active in the northern point," Ivo reminded them.

"Doesn't sound like our target," said Zelda. "How—"

"Actually, it does," Laura interrupted. "Part of the Gin exchange is meant to introduce it properly to the new owner, right? Otherwise it doesn't work right and hurts you?" She looked at Okane as she spoke, and understanding dawned over his face.

"Angry kin," he whispered. "That's exactly what we're looking for."

"*Angry*?" Zelda looked skeptical.

"Do whatever, but do it fast. If they realize their trump card has gone missing, they might call us back." Ivo gave a dismissive wave of the hand and trailed off after the line. As his eyes caught the light, his pupils flashed blue.

"Don't get killed!" Zelda cheered, waving after him.

He grunted in acknowledgment, and the Sweeper in front of him turned to give him a strange look.

"Northern point, then," said Zelda, breaking into a fast walk. "Positive this is the Gin?"

"Completely."

The trio moved faster now through the winding corridors. Luckily they'd been northward to begin with, so the northern point came into view quickly.

As Laura understood it, the "points" were parts of the wall that jutted out like spurs, one for each direction, with four of the five towers rising from them. The entrance to the northern point was marked by a compass rose with a capital "N" set above a doorway. Inside, the halls were wider and branched off into large rooms. They passed a canteen filled with Sweepers as Zelda made a beeline for a stairway, then descended two floors, peeking out at every landing.

"Not this one either," said Zelda, shutting the door before the others could see a thing.

"What's in there?" Laura asked. She heard noises she couldn't identify.

Zelda's expression matched the one she'd worn after seeing Okane's scars. "Elite training. It's not pretty."

"What kind of training does that involve?" said Laura. "Graduating to other weapons, or—"

"Nothing that kind." Zelda sighed, apparently resigned to her curiosity. "Weaponry training is ongoing with all levels. Elite training has to do with transporting infestations."

"With *what*?"

"Are - - - really that surprised?" said Zelda.

"I—Well, I knew it was possible," Laura muttered. "If the mobs plant infestations, they need to carry them somehow. I just figured they went for hibernating amulets. You make it sound a little more specialized. And besides, Rex isn't fighting rival mobs. The only rivals they'd have would be . . ."

"Other cities," Okane finished grimly.

"Are they targeting a city?" said Laura.

"Honestly? Yes. They've got their sights set on Fatum. Nothing's been put into motion yet, though."

Without realizing it, they slowed to a stop, giving Zelda ample opportunity to lean against the railing as she continued, "Sometimes on crusades, handlers find things. Old cities, records, things like that. A few years ago, they convinced themselves that they'd found the secret to safely handling infestations."

"But that's impossible," said Okane. "Everyone knows that they ate their original masters. If they knew how to handle them—"

Zelda shrugged. "This is just what I've observed. The way they see it, they need a hollow for the infestation to take root in, but then it needs to be covered in this . . . paint. I don't know how to describe it. The stuff they've got looks like a giant pile of bird shit, I'm not going to lie. But they paint it on an amulet, and it forces hibernation. They've been developing a water-resistant variety for the assault on Fatum, and developing ways to convince little infestations to grow in glass floats."

"Oh." Laura pressed a hand to her mouth. "That is such an under-handed move."

"I don't follow," said Okane. "They want to make infestation Eggs instead of kin?"

"No, they're going to float them out," said Laura. "Glass floats hold up fishing nets. Infestations don't cross water on their own, and no one would be suspicious about a fishing net. Fatum would reel it in, and once the paint flakes off . . ."

"Good-bye, Fatum," Zelda said dryly.

"That's sick," said Okane.

"That's Rex."

Without warning the ground jolted beneath them and the lights flickered. Laura wobbled and grabbed the railing as dust shook loose from the ceiling. A growling, scraping sound echoed from below, and the tremor stopped just as suddenly as it had come.

"Was that an earthquake?" said Laura.

Zelda didn't answer, but took off down the stairs. Luckily the few people they passed were too bewildered to notice their noise. Zelda stumbled to a stop in front of a metal door and groped for the handle.

"What's this place?" Laura demanded.

"Testing room," Zelda grunted. "Did they lock this stupid—aha!"

The door swung open. The testing room stretched a long way, di-vided into sections by chain curtains that didn't quite obscure the goings-on. The trio emerged on the second level of the room, a railed-in observation deck. A man and woman stood there, far too tall and wearing different uniforms than the Sweepers. They turned at the sound of the door, though their eyes skipped over the newcomers.

The man scowled. "Hasn't that door been fixed yet?"

The woman made a noise that might've been irritation or acknowl-edgment as she walked over to shut the door. The man turned his attention back to the floor below, and Laura crept to the edge to see what had him so interested. In the closest section of the training ground a cluster of Sweepers circled around something that glowed bright yellow. A shimmering cloud hung in the air, obscuring any details.

"What did they call this phenomenon in the newspapers?" the man mused. "The heavenly something?"

"The Wrath of God," said the woman.

The man laughed. "The angry god of Amicae, then? No wonder that city stayed afloat so long. It certainly wasn't due to other talents."

"By all means, it should've collapsed on itself a decade ago," the woman agreed, pushing her glasses farther up on her nose. "We won't have to worry about them anymore, of course. We have no further plans with their head Sweeper, correct?"

The man sneered. "None. She should've known we had no interest in her, but the weak don't pay attention to common sense. She grov-eled at our feet, begged for our strength, not that it would've done her any good. Her blood was subpar. A tool doesn't change that. The weak don't need much to undo them." He looked back at the Sweep-ers below, and the satisfaction slipped from his face. "Come on, you wretches! You were supposed to put a lid on it yesterday!"

One of the Sweepers looked up at them, expressionless. "There ap-pears to be no way to safely subdue it."

"I didn't ask for safety!"

"If those are - - -r orders."

The Sweeper gestured to the others. Each of them held a long metal stick, but at the top rested a large chunk of white rock—Niveus?—so they looked more like absurd mallets than true tools. The Sweepers crept closer to the source of light, slow and cautious at first and then lunging, jabbing with the sticks like spears. Another noise rang out, a bizarre mix between a snarl and a shriek, and the gold light surged outward with force enough to knock the attackers off their feet. The ground shook again, harder this time. The chain curtains clattered and the balcony itself groaned. The Niveus pieces shattered before they hit the ground, what looked like lightning snaking between them as their wielders screamed. With the cloud cleared, Clae could be seen on the floor, crystal crackling with energy.

"It's proving quite troublesome," said the woman. "Has a backup plan been cleared yet?"

"Can't you make kin out of it anyway with all this magic flying around?"

"With all this heat, water keeps evaporating. There's no chance to distill it into something usable."

The man snorted, folding his arms as the Sweepers below made another attempt to get closer. "There's no other way to calm it?"

"The former handler doesn't appear to know of any."

Laura's breath caught. A former handler was here? Hadn't Lester gone missing?

Meanwhile, the man looked less than pleased. "Could he be withholding information?"

"Doubtful," said the woman, expressionless as the Sweepers below writhed in pain. "We've exposed him to the crystal multiple times, but the energy rebounded on him just as easily as our stock. Lester MacDanel has been severely injured as a result. He has no interest in suicide, and no semblance of loyalty to his previous cities. He's made no attempt at negotiations. I don't believe he has any knowledge of how it works."

"Well, bring him in again!" the man snapped.

"Further exposure could result in his death," said the woman. "Unlike our Sweepers, MacDanel isn't expendable. He's the only Amicae handler we have. It would be wise to move cautiously in regard to him."

"Then maybe we should go back and get the other MacDanel. See if that bitch has a better idea."

Only then did the woman smile, and only slightly. "Didn't you just say that the weak cling to power? If she'd known this existed she'd never have let it go."

A third tremor caused them all to wobble precariously, and one of the Sweepers screamed as a bolt of energy hit his arm. The woman gave a disinterested hum.

"Perhaps if we let it sit unprovoked for a while it might calm."

"We don't have 'a while.' The offensive starts in three days and we need magic pumped out of this rock as soon as possible."

"Agitating it may be taking more time than it would otherwise. This avenue has proved fruitless. I propose we guard the area and otherwise let it be. We'll check in on a regular basis but not approach. Is this acceptable?"

"That is not Gin!" Zelda snapped, rounding on Laura. "That's a crystal man! What kind of—"

Laura winced. "You know how you said Clae Sinclair was dead? Well, he's actually not. He just . . . had an accident."

"An accident? An *accident*? That's a giant yellow rock that's been killing and injuring anyone in a five-foot radius! A man doesn't just accidentally turn into a rock!"

"People like us can, actually," said Okane.

Zelda gaped, pointing down at Clae as she exclaimed, "I could end up like *that*?"

"There's a distinct possibility, yes."

"Oh, this has to be a joke."

19

BAD ROAD

"How long did you know it was Rex?"

Laura lay on her back, looking up at the worn springs of a barracks bunk. A dust bunny stuck to her elbow and her position under the bed was hardly dignified, but she tried to keep some gravity in her tone anyway as she continued, "Because you did know, didn't you?"

Silence. Okane hid under the bed opposite hers, presumably cramped the same way. Their current position kept them hidden from any passersby who might open the barracks door. They'd been on top of the beds to sleep last night, but Zelda left after they woke, intending to scout around. She'd insisted that they'd slow her down, and that no one would look in here anyway. Laura and Okane hadn't been so certain. Hence, hiding.

"I know you can hear me," she said. "We're not that far away, and you can't keep hiding this forever."

"I know," said Okane.

Laura tilted her head. Sure enough, he mirrored her pose, looking sullenly up at the underside of the mattress.

"Well?"

"I knew it as soon as - - - mentioned Theron might be Magi." His tone came flat, as if he were distant from the words. "Back when Clae asked me about Anselm, we realized that both of us knew so little about Magi, and we agreed to share what we'd learned. I only had frivolous things to tell him. Fairy tales. When to wear certain jewelry pieces. As a child, I didn't take in much beyond that. Clae was the opposite. By the time he started learning from Rosemarie, he was completely focused on magical function, to keep himself alive. She died before she could relate much. So in that sense . . . if we were to look at Magi like a knife, Clae knew how to stab someone with it; I knew that it looked pretty, and it was meant to go with this sort of ensemble. I felt guilty for that." He closed his eyes, breathed in deep to steady himself. "Everything he taught me had a purpose, had a meaning. Nothing I shared could help him stay safe, or have any impact. But he said that didn't matter. He said something about . . . how function doesn't mean anything if it isn't grounded. He said it needed a heart. He said the stories were the purpose. The heart. Meaning."

"That's weirdly nice of him," Laura murmured.

"He was like that, if - - - talked about anything beyond Sweeping," Okane chuckled. "Rare occasions, since he was a workaholic."

He went quiet for a while. Laura felt almost guilty when she prompted, "He told you about Rex?"

"The breeding program was necessary information," said Okane. "He wanted me to know not to trust them, if they ever showed up. Rex doesn't go out to other cities often, but Sweepers do take trains; it wouldn't be absurd to think our paths would cross eventually. Like Zelda said, they're always looking for more blood to reduce inbreeding. The Sullivans wanted to exploit me, but Rexians would do so on a much deeper level. If they catch me, they'll strip away everything I am: my choices, my personality, any kind of individuality. One of the reasons Magi never come out of hiding is because they know Rex would catch them. Magi caught by Rex never escape."

The thought chilled her. Distantly, she remembered one of their earlier conversations: *Why do you keep your hair so long? It's the one thing Sullivan never got interested in. The only thing I had full control over.* The Rexian Sweepers here, children of captured Magi, all had shaved heads—one piece of the puzzle denying their personhood. Just like in the film, it was small details that made Rex horrifying.

"But if you knew that already," she said, "what was so important about Clae's letter?"

Okane's hand went to his chest, as if to check the letter, but these weren't even his clothes. The envelope must be back in Amicae.

"An additional detail," he said hoarsely. "Do - - - remember when I told - - - my old home fell to infestations?"

"That's when you and your mother came to Amicae."

He nodded. "In his letter, Clae pointed out that there must've been other survivors. They had to go somewhere. There's a good chance that Rex caught some on their raids. I don't remember any faces from that time, but I'm terrified that I'm going to look at one of these Sweepers and I'm going to recognize one."

The door swung open without so much as a knock. Laura drew back without thinking, and a flicker of movement showed that Okane had done the same. The door swung shut, accompanied by peals of laughter.

"Wow, they don't teach Amicae Sweepers how to hide worth a damn, do they?"

Zelda's voice mocked them, and from what Laura could see she was alone. Relief and annoyance crashed over her.

"We're more accustomed to running and throwing things," she grumbled, dragging herself out from under the bed.

"I suppose the Sweepers here aren't that different." Zelda shrugged, her motion awkward due to the box balanced on one hip. She set this on the floor between them and opened it, revealing tins of food.

"Is this Sweeper fare?" Laura picked one up and squinted, searching for a label.

"General military fare. I took these from the expedition supplies. Enough Sweepers will die that they won't need all the stores they've got."

"- - - make it sound like an everyday thing," said Okane. He sounded normal, but his eyes held none of their usual light. After that little revelation, Laura couldn't blame him at all.

"It is," said Zelda, pulling out tins. "Rex treats Sweepers here about as good as working dogs. It's a bother when they die off, but the handlers and officers don't care beyond that."

"Sounds like a great place."

"That's why I want no part in it." Zelda smiled. "Eat up! Most of the Sweepers and support details have left the city, so we've got fewer people to look for us and doors wide open."

"So in theory this might be easy," Laura mused, popping open one of the tins. She frowned at the pale orange slop inside. "Ick. What is this?"

"Very nutritional. Not sure beyond that. Care for a spoon?"

"What is the plan, exactly?" Okane peeled the lid off another tin and stirred the contents with a stolen fork. "We can't just go in, grab them, and leave. It doesn't matter whether or not we can be seen in the act. If Clae and the Gin go missing, they won't overlook that. They'll come after us quickly. Besides, what happens when we escape? There's a huge distance between us and home, and we can't just walk across the wilds."

"Is there any way to get on a train back north?" asked Laura.

Zelda hummed, leaning her chin on her hand. "I suppose there's a satellite town. Kind of a port city, to trade with Fatum. The roads to it should be clear. Someone could hop on the train there."

"So we steal a military car, get the Gin in there, then slip out with the Sweepers," said Laura. "We'll swing around and drive to this port city, and catch the train back to Amicae."

"Can - - - even drive a car? I've only seen - - - on a bike," said Okane.

Laura scowled. "It can't be that hard."

"Oh, honey," Zelda said pityingly, but she looked ready to laugh.

"This all assumes that everything goes well, which I doubt it will," said Okane.

Laura frowned down at the food. Of course that was wishful thinking, but what else could she do? She wasn't a grand schemer, so the straightforward was all she could come up with. It wasn't like he'd suggested anything better.

"I took a look around," Zelda butted in, "and I found that regular

Gin, too. Stored in one of the war rooms a floor below, packed up. Apparently they're not taking the transfer nicely, though they haven't been zapping people like—" She paused and gave them a nauseous look. "Right. *Sinclair.*"

"Is there a way to get them all out? The crystals are lighter than they look, but we'd still need multiple trips. I don't think we've got any helpers for it, especially if that Ivo person is already outside the city," said Laura.

"Not to mention I couldn't cover for any helpers normally, and magic interference from the Gin could throw it off badly," Zelda sighed.

"So we have to be extra careful?"

"Stay extra close, and no loud noises."

They later walked the hallways in silence, clustered tight together. Laura wasn't sure what "extra close" meant, but she wasn't taking any chances. She practically breathed down Zelda's neck as they turned corner after corner. As they walked down a passage with numbered doors, Zelda made a soft happy noise and motioned them left. A pair of men stood there, one puffing on a cigarette while the other laughed at a joke; neither were Sweepers. A large dolly was parked beside them, laden with boxes stamped AMMUNITION. Zelda crept closer, leaned down, and grabbed one end of the dolly. She watched carefully, tugging lightly so the wheels moved ever so slowly. The men paid no attention, but Laura got the idea. She leaned down to grab the corner of the dolly, and after a moment Okane did the same on the other side. Between the three of them they inched the heavy cart away. Once they judged it a safe distance Zelda took the handles, straightening it out and wheeling it away easily.

"With this, we don't need multiple trips."

"You can cover it with your magic?" Laura's eyes flicked around, taking in the Sweepers walking past. No one seemed bothered.

"For now."

While the cart was cumbersome to steer, they didn't run into anyone, and soon enough Zelda pulled up by another door.

"Gin is stored here with one of the on-site Kins," she explained. "Get the door for me."

Laura hurried to do so. There was indeed a Kin inside, a glassy setup far larger and more complicated than the one in Amicae, featuring odd shapes she couldn't understand the use for. The kin inside it ran red as blood. Laura hadn't had doubts about the Rex-MacDanel link, but such obvious confirmation of it still fell on her like an invisible weight. She couldn't think on it long, though: at least three Sweepers walked through the steam. She froze, fearing that any moment one would look around at the sound of the door. The edge of the dolly nudged against her calves, and Okane hissed, "Inside, fast! There's a group coming this way!"

She moved aside and the dolly rattled in, bumping lightly at the side of the Kin's table. The glass clattered and the nearest Sweeper swiveled, peering for the source. Her bright eyes paused on the door. She strode over to close it, and Laura gave a shaky sigh.

"Where's the Gin?" Okane asked.

"See the right wall? They're shelves. Amicae Gin is at the far end, mellowing."

"What does mellowing mean?" Laura whispered as they maneuvered the cart down the narrow aisle.

"They have to let it sit and reset before it lets them handle it properly. Sweepers call it mellowing. Of course, that's usually used when things don't go as well as they should during official transfers," said Zelda.

"I suppose Gin stealing isn't exactly common," Okane grumbled.

Near the back corner, away from any of the other contents of the shelves, two large boxes sat at waist height. Laura didn't have to open them to know immediately that it was their Gin. It felt as if an invisible, familiar cloud surrounded the area, heating her ring and easing the strain from her shoulders. It recognized them. She pried the lid off the closest box and found, nestled in hay, the Gin they'd gotten from Puer back in November. She rested her hand on it, and while the surface seemed much warmer than usual, it didn't hurt.

Hello again, she thought.

Hello, the Gin echoed in her mind. *See you, Laura. See you.* The words were accompanied by flashes of the armory, the Rexian thieves, the distinct feeling of being separated, and where did the other ones go? No matter. *Friends here now. Friends find them.*

We're here to take you all home, she thought, and concentrated on thoughts of Amicae.

Home, the Gin replied, and felt pleased.

"Don't get burned!" Zelda whispered, alarmed.

"Don't worry, we're good. It knows us."

Okane glanced around, then heaved one of the ammunition crates open. "Put them in here," he said. "That way, if the magic fails—"

They'd be less noticeable. Laura shot him a grin before setting to work. They swapped the Gin and ammunition, tossing bullets into the shelved boxes and shoving hay and heaving rocks into the crates. It wasn't exactly quiet, but the Kin machine covered their noise well enough.

"That'll do it." Laura clapped her hands, observing their work. Unless someone opened those boxes very soon, they wouldn't be missed. "Now we just have to—"

The door opened again. The Sweeper there stood as tall as his five-foot-four frame would allow, a rifle slung under one shoulder.

"The southern point requires more Gin," he announced. "Bring two units immediately."

"Yes, sir," one of the Sweepers replied. She gestured at one of the others to follow, and they made their way toward the back corner.

"Shit," Laura muttered, shrinking back as the pair approached. "Are they headed for us?"

"Of course they are!" Zelda spat, heaving on the dolly. It creaked but didn't travel far, corralled between table and shelves. "If they don't slow down, they'll run into our damn cart!"

Laura looked around for something to keep them busy. She couldn't see clearly with the smoke. The only plausible thing to move was the Kin. At first she balked at the idea of damaging something so crucial, but hadn't they just mentioned another Kin in another point? Even better, breaking this would mean diverting other resources from the crusades.

Laura balled up a fist in her overcoat sleeve and swung at the Kin.

She caught a circular container, toppling it from its wire holder to drag tubing and glass cases to the floor. The entire glass section on this table smashed against the ground. The cacophony halted the Sweepers immediately, scattering sharp fragments everywhere and spilling red liquid. A great pinkish cloud obscured the area. Laura had already turned, vaulting over the dolly toward the door. The Sweeper there had run forward, shouting at the din, so she slipped past easily. Okane and Zelda propelled the dolly through, and as soon as they cleared the door Laura slammed it, shutting out the hissing and spitting of scalding kin.

"We've got to get Clae," Okane panted as they ran, eyes wide with panic. "We've got to get him fast!"

The dolly clamored and bumped, almost tipping as it sped over loose brick and warping in the floor. One of the people ahead started at the noise and Laura's heart sank. Zelda or not, their rush drew too much attention. She shoved at the person's back as she passed, making him stumble before he turned and yelled at the one beside him, accusing the other of pushing him.

Luckily the battered flooring smoothed out as they left the western point, and the few remaining personnel presented little obstacle on their dash northward. Zelda navigated the maze with little more than huffed curses at tight corners, and soon they rolled to a stop. One more corner, and they'd reach the door to the testing room's lower level. A guard had been posted on either side of the door, Sweepers with grim expressions and large guns in their hands. Laura squinted from around the corner, trying to devise a plan to pass them.

"Any ideas on distractions? I'm not too keen on bashing them over the head," she joked. She still shook with nerves from breaking the Kin, but hopefully the others didn't notice.

"Do we even need one?" Zelda growled.

"Considering the door is probably locked, *yes*," said Okane.

"Do you think they could tell if we stole their keys?"

"Their handlers have the keys," Zelda snorted.

"No key, locked door, angry Sweepers. What are we supposed to do?" Laura moaned.

"Break in from the top?" Zelda suggested.

Okane sent her a dark look. "And somehow carry two crystal people up again? Fat chance."

"Dream boy's a killjoy."

"I'm being *practical*."

"You're both getting on my nerves," Laura groused.

Okane gave an angry huff of his own and pulled one of the ammo boxes open, sifting through it for something useful. He pulled out a box of bullets, pulled a single one out, and held it up.

"Let's jam this in the lock and light it up."

"Oh my god," Laura whispered, rubbing her temples. "I thought you were supposed to be the voice of reason."

He flushed in embarrassment, but stubbornly continued, "It would break the lock."

"And get a lot of attention!"

"Can - - - think of any better—"

"Sir!" The guards snapped to attention.

A man strode down from the other end of the hallway. It was the same man who'd been in the testing room yesterday. For a companion he brought a prisoner, rather than the woman from before. The prisoner shuffled, chains clanking from the shackles on his hands and feet, and a hood had been thrown over his head; he couldn't see for himself, and simply stumbled where the man pushed him.

"Can't say I recognize that one," Zelda murmured. "It can't be new blood. They never let Magi leave the cells."

Laura's eyes narrowed. "That's got to be Lester."

Lester stopped when the man jerked him back by the new prison clothing; he slouched, quivering, as the man eyed the Sweepers there with contempt.

"Move aside."

The Sweepers sprang back to their posts. The man pulled a key ring from his pocket and selected one of the pieces to unlock the door. As he did, he spoke: "You will remain at your posts unless specifically ordered to move. You will not speak of my being here to anyone, let alone Commander Deringer. Do not enter this room under any circumstances. If the prisoner escapes this room . . ." He shot Lester a disgusted look. "Shoot him on sight."

"Yes, sir."

The door opened with an audible click. The man stepped inside, shoving Lester before him before closing it. No other sound followed.

Zelda let out a breathy, disbelieving laugh. "He left it open. My god, dream boy really is lucky."

They stood there a moment more before it really sank in, then lurched forward. When they were halfway to the door, the ground shook, hard enough that Laura staggered into the wall, and the boxes vibrated on the dolly. A grinding snarl reached them. Yellow light flickered under the door. The guards wobbled but didn't move to investigate. That only made it easier for Laura to walk between them and open the door. Luckily Zelda was close enough that the movement didn't catch their attention—their eyes remained fixed on the opposite wall. Okane and Zelda angled the dolly to fit the doorway, and they were in.

The warm air in the testing room carried the heavy scent of burnt vanilla. The man sprawled on the ground several feet from Clae, his uniform singed badly and ugly blisters forming on what skin wasn't bloody.

"Ugh," said Zelda. "Don't go near him. He's electrified jerky at this point."

Laura hadn't planned on it. She scanned the room and spotted Lester quickly. He'd escaped the magical wave by clinging to the right side wall, and now curled there in a shuddering heap. Her mouth thinned into a severe line, and she walked toward him.

"Laura, what are - - - doing?" said Okane. "- - -'re going to leave Zelda's influence."

"I'm getting answers."

She knelt down in front of Lester, grabbed the hood, and yanked it off. At the sight of his face, she recoiled.

Lester had been burned, horribly. His skin was bloody and peeling, shimmering in the depths; this had been done with kin. He'd escaped this last dose of magic, but just as the handlers had said, he'd been injured badly in the last few encounters. As he looked up at her, his scabs pulled loose with a hideous creaking sound.

"Don't move," Laura said quickly; she raised her hands, to placate or keep him away, she didn't know. "Just—Oh my god, what happened?"

"He took a crystal to the face," said Zelda. "What else could possibly have caused that?"

Lester made a weird sighing sound. Beyond the shaking of his body she could sense the echo of the burn, the continued essence of Clae's magic. It had become hate with a target now. It still burned, but its tinder wouldn't last long.

"Laura Kramer?" he rasped. "Of course. I should've known you'd go this far. You seemed the type."

"Stubborn to a fault," she said dryly. She wanted to rage at him for taking part in this fiasco, but seeing someone this badly hurt made the anger sputter and die before reaching the surface. She felt more tired then vengeful as she asked, "Was it worth making this deal with Rex?"

"Quite obviously, no."

"Tell me what they wanted. What all the details were. It's too late for you to survive, but I'm going to make sure Amicae does."

Lester gave a rueful smile that looked more like a grimace. "So even you can tell that." He was quiet awhile before asking, "Miss Kramer, do you know the rites of Spiritualists?"

Last rites, he meant. After the Underyear incident, she'd reflected on that. Technically, Mateo had reassured the survivors, salvation could still be achieved for the dead lost to infestations. Spiritualists believed that to reach the Spinner's paradise one had to be free of any guilty weights. One needed to confess one's sins. If someone lived honestly and confessed regularly, they'd have no trouble finding their way after death. Laura suspected Lester had kept most things to himself. Listening to a confession was the last thing she wanted to do, but the Rexian deal must be included.

"I'll listen," she said.

He was quiet for a long while, but at last he said, "I killed my fellow Sweeper, Eliza. I meant to shoot the infestation, but I hadn't practiced enough. My aim was off. I hit her. I killed her."

So Laura had been right.

"I wanted to tell Joseph Blair immediately, but I was afraid. Juliana found us and said she'd take care of it. She . . . she disposed of Eliza, and I didn't object. She took credit for everything Eliza had done when she hadn't even been there, and was hailed as a hero. The praise didn't belong to her, but I didn't say anything. I believe in my heart that this first time she genuinely wanted to help me, but that praise was addictive. She wanted glory. She started telling me to do things, threatened to tell the other Sweepers what I'd done if I didn't follow her orders. I was weak. I was afraid. I didn't want to face what I'd done, so I followed. I sabotaged other Sweepers' equipment so she could shine. I delayed them, sometimes forcibly, so she could take credit. She was clever and covered her tracks, but Melody knew something was wrong. She asked me what was going on. She said she'd support me, said she'd protect me, but I was still too ashamed to speak. When Juliana found out, she panicked. She wanted to leave, but she couldn't stand the idea of being anonymous. She wanted everything. She wanted the top. She wanted to lead the Sweeper city. She told me to delay Joan, so she could steal the interview spot. The only way I could stop Joan was to injure her. Badly. I was afraid I'd killed her too, but I was still too afraid for my own skin. I didn't call for help. I abandoned her and locked the door behind me. I was so relieved to hear she lived, but it didn't excuse what I did. Nothing could excuse that."

He took a long, shuddering breath.

"My following sins were against you and your city. I trespassed. I harassed you. I didn't question Juliana's paranoia when she found you were 'better,' and never raised a complaint when she tried to be rid of you. I'd resigned myself to the destruction of individuals, but then it grew worse. We began collaborating with a Rexian Sweeper. He approached us for shelter and offered us Rexian ties in exchange. He'd originally wanted help from the mobs, but they framed him for the Falling Infestation."

Wait. What?

"What do you mean, framed?" Laura said sharply.

She remembered the day well: the bulwark tree cut down, a kingshound painted stark among its leaves. It had unmistakably been Rex's calling card. And hadn't the rumor been that the Mad Dogs' leader refused to work with him?

"The one Sweeper would serve as their distraction," said Lester. "I don't know more than that. I don't know which mob it was, or what their goal could be. But Rexians are strong enough to enter Kuro no Oukoku. Their equipment must be the best. Juliana wanted it. He promised to deliver their kin recipe in exchange for whatever Clae Sinclair left behind. So I broke into the other building. The armory. I never expected people to be there. I never thought that maybe your kin didn't work because it didn't want to. I knew I'd made a mistake, but it was too late. They took everything. By letting them in, I doomed Amicae. People I'd carried, but the weight of an entire city . . . And I began to think, what is a city but a mess of individuals? I would care about a faceless crowd of Elizas, but not the one who'd taught me how to win at Underyear games? A number frightened me more than loss of humanity. I'd closed my heart to other people. I regret. I repent. I didn't deserve to know Eliza. She didn't deserve to die. Every time I hid from my actions, not only did I lose myself, but I dishonored her memory. She was strong, and she was proud. For now, at least, I can be like her. I can be like Eliza."

He met Laura's eyes and said, "Don't trust Juliana. She may not be the hands that hurt people, but it was all her intentions. She won't stop here. She'll ruin you. Call Puer and tell their intelligence . . . tell them to go to 6649 West Kallas, in the Third Quarter. Eliza is under the concrete. It's a body that shouldn't exist. It'll be proof enough to raise an investigation. They'll demand that Juliana come back for questioning. She gets flustered when confronted. She'll fall apart. It's just a matter of reaching that stage."

"Are you sure you can't make that call?" said Laura. "If we can get you out of here—"

"Don't throw away what chance you have," said Lester. "Just leave me a gun. Next time a Rexian pokes his nose in, I'll give him a surprise. They'll think thieves are still in here. It might buy you some time."

Laura wasn't sure she trusted him with a weapon while they were lifting Clae. Before she could protest or ask the others for advice, Okane opened one of the crates. He dug up a single pistol and pack of bullets. He pressed these into Lester's hand and said, "I was part of the deal, wasn't I? That Sweeper wanted to take me back to Rex."

"He told us you were one of his agents, keeping a low profile," said Lester. "He said you'd leave with him at the end."

Zelda sneered. "Clever! So he'd have all the more reason to kidnap his 'partner,' and if anything went wrong, he had someone left to take the fall."

Lester felt at the gun, popped it open and loaded it without so much as a glance down. "Thank you for hearing my confession. You should leave before you need one, too."

They backed away. As they went, Laura leaned close and whispered, "Why'd you give him a gun so easily? He's the one who betrayed Amicae in the first place."

"This way they can't catch him again," said Okane. "I'm sure other Magi wish they had the same option."

"How do we do this?" said Zelda, ignoring their whispering. She kept the cart firmly parked between her and Clae. "Big angry crystal man probably won't let us pick him up any easier than he did anyone else."

"As far as we could tell, he works the same way as Gin," Laura replied.

After some hesitation, she approached him. She took measured steps, still wary despite her confidence. The air closer to Clae shimmered with heat. She stooped, reached out. She had a moment of hesitation—what if he really didn't recognize her?—but she shook that away immediately. So what if his kin was so violent? This was the same Clae who'd had faith in her. She'd never doubted him before, and wasn't about to now. She set her hand on his shoulder. Magic thrummed under the crystal's surface, warm and alive but so much more potent than the Gin had been. Despite the clear presence of energy, she couldn't feel any type of connection like the ones Gin so easily made; no tugging at memory, no implied words. On the other hand, there was no magical backlash. Slowly the crystal dimmed, and the hostile feeling tapered away. Clae had calmed. Laura sighed in relief.

"Okane, come here and help me get him on the cart."

They each took one end, lifting Clae off the ground and onto the boxes. It took a few tries. While not actively attacking them, Clae remained extremely hot. Eventually they had him balanced on top of the boxes, and after only a short time looking, they spotted Anselm in another section of the training room. He proved cooler, easier to carry and wedge between boxes and handlebars. Lester didn't move or speak as they left.

The guards remained ignorant of the open door as they squeezed back through and rolled off. They moved slowly now so the crystals wouldn't fall, and Zelda insisted on walking still slower than that.

"Too much magic," she whispered, observing passersby. "Could be interfering with mine. Besides, people pick up on things moving fast pretty easily."

Laura would've loved to sprint down the halls. Forcing herself to dawdle alongside angry-looking Rexians frayed her nerves. She kept one shaky hand on Clae's arm to keep him from falling and tried to draw strength from that as they plodded on.

Zelda located an elevator. Thankfully the dolley fit. They leaned against the ammo boxes, trying to take up as little space as possible as the elevator stuttered down its shaft. Trouble met them at the ground floor.

"We get out, we make a break for the garages. They're outside the building. With any luck, we'll find a covered car ready to go." No sooner had Zelda said this than the elevator door opened, revealing a pair of men with a dolly of their own blocking the way.

"We need these uniforms on the third floor," the first man said, scribbling something on a clipboard. "You'll run into the quartermaster's men up there, but the main office—"

"Shit," Laura whispered. "They think this is an empty elevator, don't they?"

"Get them out of the way!" Zelda hissed, clambering back over to the handles.

Okane set a foot on the opposing dolly and shoved it away, catching the men in the shins and making them stagger. Another kick, and the cart rolled easily to clear the way. Zelda wrenched the dolly around and Laura hurried to steady it as they tore out as fast as they could. The men behind them started shouting, one about intruders and the other about a ghost.

"Great," Zelda growled, "now they'll be looking for us."

"- - -r magic works on everyone unless they're specifically looking for - - -?" Okane checked.

"If they're focusing right, yes," Zelda seethed. "Glancing around on guard duty is one thing, but actively seeking out a thief is another!"

Several openings yawned in the side of this long room, like open garage doors. They slipped through the nearest exit with no trouble, emerging into open air. Laura had no idea what Quarter this was, but the paved road they ran on was wide and pristine black. More walls jutted up in the distance, peeking over buildings and blocking their view of anything beyond the closest structure. A carport had been erected opposite them, stretching a mile long and sheltering a collection of military vehicles and equipment. A few of the boxy automobiles had their lights on, engines running as supplies were loaded into or unloaded from their covered backs. Laura skimmed over the nearest cars, picking out the one with the least amount of people and pointing.

"That one! No one's there!"

Neither of the others answered, simply adjusted their course. They skirted dangerously close to another unloading party and had to heave back against the dolly to stop its momentum by the car. Laura clambered up, throwing the canvas flaps aside to peer into the dark trunk. More boxes, no people.

"Clear!"

"Then get them in!" Zelda gestured wildly.

A faint, shrill noise reached them, echoing from the open doors and windows of the Sweeper headquarters. Laura faltered. "What's that?"

"Alarm! Get moving!"

They scrambled to pick up the crystals. Zelda danced anxiously around them as Laura and Okane hauled first Clae, then Anselm into the truck bed. On the first Gin box, Laura lost her footing on the truck and had to flail to catch herself; Okane hurried to correct the movement and Zelda gasped.

"Don't drop it! They're looking, they're looking!"

Sure enough, the people in the carport had heard the alarm and seemed to have some idea what it was for. They checked around their workstations for anything amiss, faces drawn and eyes flicking back and forth across the wider area. Laura only caught a glimpse of this at first, but at the sound of a loud creak, she paid more attention. Was someone coming toward them from another direction? Again the creaking groan, louder, closer, and she realized the noise came from the box in her arms. She barely had time to exchange a panicked look with Okane before the bottom of the ammunition box broke altogether, and the Gin plummeted to the ground. The impact came as an earsplitting *crack*. The pavement fractured, but the Gin remained whole and unharmed. Laura stared at it a moment before looking up. The workers looked right at them. Zelda's magic had been broken. For a full five seconds no one moved, just stared, dumbfounded, and then a man two stations down took off toward the main building, shouting, "They're here!"

Okane tossed the broken box aside and snatched up the Gin, lobbing it into the trunk.

"Can either of - - - drive?"

"No," Laura squeaked.

"I can!" said Zelda.

"Start driving!" Crackling noises accompanied the movement as he lifted the second Gin box on his own and shoved it inside.

Zelda dashed to the cab and climbed in. She must've tested the gas, because the truck pitched forward a few feet before slamming to a halt again. Laura reeled back into the truck bed at the stop and clambered back up, reaching out to help Okane in.

"No seats, but it'll do, right?" she laughed breathlessly.

Sweepers poured out of the building, directed by three men in different uniforms who shouted above them. They closed in rapidly, scattering the workers and raising varying weapons. Okane looked at them, then at Laura, eyes wide.

"I can be a distraction," he rasped.

"What?"

"I can distract them. They want Magi."

"Are you crazy? We don't need a distraction! Get your ass in here!"

"If I can get their attention, they'll be too busy to shoot," he whispered, and Laura could see he was beginning to really believe it. "I've got this. Don't worry, I'm fast."

He ran around the truck toward the Sweeper lines, and she leaned out to shout, "So are they! Idiot!"

Okane gestured at the truck cab, and she heard Zelda say something. Cursing, Laura made to climb out. She had one leg over the back door when the truck growled into movement, reversing fast enough to send her tumbling again before hitting the brakes once more. Shouting came from ahead. She heard Okane yelling something, but before she could make another bid for freedom, Zelda hit the gas.

20

VALENS

With a military vehicle going top speed, Laura had no chance of jumping out. She had enough trouble avoiding cargo in the truck bed. Clae, Anselm, and the Gin slid at every turn, scraping across the floor and smacking into what boxes were tied down. She tried to steady them at first, but after a few near misses clung to a stack of boxes and gripped the rope, lifting her feet out of the way whenever a loose piece skidded over. As far as she could see the crystals were nigh indestructible: they didn't gain so much as a scratch during the bumpy ride.

She could see nothing outside during their escape, only a few glimpses of fading daylight through the flapping canvas in the back, but she could tell when the shouting quieted, when the car began to slow. A few bullet holes let in light, but Okane had been enough of a distraction. The Sweepers' gunfire had been delayed while Zelda drove through the carport. They'd escaped unharmed. Whether Okane had slipped away, she had no idea. The more Laura wondered the worse she felt.

"If he gets caught, this is all your fault," she growled, kicking half-heartedly at Clae as he slid past.

The crystals rattled to a stop as the truck's engine cut out. Silence pressed in, bizarre after so long. After a moment's hesitation, Laura picked her way to the back and pulled the canvas aside. Zelda had parked the truck in an alleyway, cast in shadow by tall buildings on either side. The sound of shoes on pavement grew closer and Zelda walked into sight. She paused, stared at her. Laura looked right back.

"Why did you leave him behind?"

Zelda's lip curled. "He took the attention, why else? Made it harder to relocate us when my magic kicked back in."

"That's the only reason? He could be a prisoner right now, but it won't matter because it was a little harder to notice a racing truck?"

Zelda folded her arms, eyes narrowing. "Don't act all high-and-mighty. We all could've gotten caught back there."

"And we all could've made it out!"

"There's no way of knowing that."

Laura knew that. Escaping at all in the middle of Rex was a wonder; everything had gone remarkably well up to this point. Even losing someone now counted as lucky: one instead of two or three lost, escaping with everything they'd come for. Logically, they'd succeeded. It didn't feel like a victory.

Laura pressed hands against her eyes. "I told him I wouldn't let anything like the Sullivans happen to him again. I can't—I didn't—"

Zelda didn't reply immediately, and when she did, her tone softened. "I told him to meet us at the clothes store we were at earlier. That shop is right around the corner. If he's still free, he'll come find us."

Doubtful, as far as Laura could tell.

Zelda returned to the cab; the seat there must be more comfortable. Laura dragged Clae closer to the canvas flap and sat next to him, holding one of his crystal wrists in one hand. She hoped this would ground her, give her a sense of purpose. It worked well enough, she supposed, and here she could keep an eye on the end of the alley while Zelda presumably watched the other side.

What now? Is there any way we can help him? she thought, trying to prompt something from Clae the way she had with the Gin. If he had passed on his will to Eggs, and picked and chose who could touch him, surely he could reply like that? But he didn't. No ghost of words, no implication or shared mental image. Magic hummed under her fingers like a mock pulse, but it was muddled. Incomprehensible. She might as well be looking for meaning in a patch of mud. She hung her head with a flat laugh.

"I miss you."

The gold flickered some, but there was no other response.

One thought hung over her with awful clarity. *What if Okane never comes back? What if that's the last time I'll ever see him?*

It hadn't been so bad with Clae—his death had been so sudden, so lost in other events, there hadn't been time to agonize over possibilities. This was awful. She gripped Clae's hand, trying to draw some kind of comfort. Magic shivered under her fingers. She inhaled deep, remembering Gustave's Moon. Clae, so present and alive it seemed he could never be erased.

Still going back for other people.

Her eyes snapped open again.

Thank you, Laura Kramer.

Was this communication with Clae? Gin made its own words and plucked at multiple memories on the rare occasion it had a point to make. This had been one solid impression, less a conversation than a recollection. Did she imagine support because she wanted it? The more she looked at Clae, the more she realized it didn't matter. She couldn't just sit there and wait if Okane was in danger. She jumped out of the truck and circled to the cab. Zelda sulked in the driver's seat, and raised a brow at the sight of her.

"Did - - - see something?"

"I need you to watch Clae and the Gin," said Laura.

"To watch—Wait, where do - - - think - - -'re going?"

"To find Okane."

"Oh, no," Zelda snarled, kicking open the door. "I didn't risk my life smuggling a set of idiots through high security and get shot at just so some ingrate can skip back into danger!"

"Okane's already in danger."

"Forget him! He knows where to find us—"

"He knows the store name. That's like finding a needle in a haystack," said Laura. "How many people and stores are in this city? And how many people are actively looking for him? There aren't any maps, and it's not like he can ask for directions."

"Just trust him to find his way!" said Zelda.

"It's not about trust! This is about being there to help, because he shouldn't have to do this alone!"

"Well, I've stuck my neck out far enough," said Zelda. "If - - - want to go running off into Rex, it'll be alone."

"You don't have go with me," said Laura.

Zelda faltered. "What?"

"I can't go back to Amicae without Okane, but I can't risk having Clae or the Gin falling back into their hands. If I don't come back, I want you to get them out of here."

Zelda blinked at her. Her lips tipped up, her head ducked, and she laughed. It wasn't a kind sound. Her head stayed down even after she'd finished.

"I kept thinking I'd escaped them, but I'm not that different from a Rexian Sweeper after all, am I?" she murmured. "I didn't think twice about letting him go. When it comes down to it, I thought he was expendable, too." Laura didn't know how to respond to that, so stayed quiet until Zelda finally looked up at her. "What are we planning here, exactly?"

"I'm going to try finding Okane."

"- - -'ve mentioned."

"The city's huge, and even if I knew where I was going, Okane didn't. I can't plan on where to find him. I want to have enough time to properly look and try getting back here, but we can't wait forever. How long would you give us, before it's too late to escape?"

"They're not about to stop unloading Sweepers," said Zelda, drumming her fingers on the car door. "They might close down a few exits, but it'll be easy enough to find the operating one. If only one's operating, the line will be longer and it'll stay open longer. If they just bump up security on all gates, it'll be over fast and we'll miss our window of opportunity. I'd give us five hours at most."

"Honestly, I expected less," Laura chuckled. "Okay, if I'm not back before five hours are up, leave the city and bring these back to Amicae."

"What if Okane returns and - - - don't?" said Zelda. "He'll try to pull this exact same maneuver."

"Remind him that Rex doesn't have any incentive to keep me alive," said Laura.

What little mirth Zelda had drained from her face. "- - - realize that's a valid argument, right? If they figure out who - - - are, they'll kill - - -."

"I knew that when I left Amicae."

Zelda shook her head but didn't argue. "And what am I supposed to do when I reach Amicae? They won't let a Rexian through the gate, let alone let me bring these to wherever I need to. They might just shoot me there."

"See if you can send word ahead," said Laura. "Directly to the police chief, but even better, if you can reach Byron Rhodes, they'll hear you out. Byron's been following the Sweeper situation ever since the Falling Infestation, and he knew something weird was going on with our new boss. I told him everything I knew before we got chased out of Amicae. If you share your side of the story, and if you bring back what Juliana sold, he'll support you."

"He'll support me," Zelda murmured. "That makes it sound as if I'd be there a while."

"Isn't that what you want?" said Laura. "You'd be out of Rex's reach."

"Ha! Maybe. I've got to say, that wasn't the reward I was expecting." Zelda swung her leg, tapping Laura with her toe. "Fine, I'll go with that. - - -'ve got five hours. Best get going while - - - can."

"Thank you," said Laura.

Zelda simply waved her off. Laura took the hint and ran.

The identical streets of Rex flashed by as she tore through with amulet-enhanced speed. Left, right, left, up the ramp to the Quarter they'd left, and she kept on into the maze with no clue whether she was even going the right way. The street names meant nothing if she didn't know where they led. Few people walked the streets to ask (nightly curfew, she remembered from the Carmen film), not that she would've. If she asked too many suspicious questions, she could bring the Black Guard down on her head. Of course, the sight of a strange girl running around after curfew might bring them down on her anyway.

She paused at a corner, the streetlight glowing overhead as she tried to calm herself down. Panic would just give her tunnel vision. Calm. *Calm, Laura, for the love of god.* Would there be any clues to Okane's location? None came to mind. She couldn't listen in on any chatter from whoever currently chased him. She didn't know how to find them any easier, and she doubted they'd allow anyone to follow them, citizen or not. She wished she had something like the statue in the Amicae banks: a single touch, to signal *I'm here* to someone else. But something else gave a similar signal, didn't it? The armory had sent a signal to their rings. If all the Sinclair rings were rigged in a single system for the armory, surely there must be a connection from ring to ring?

She pulled off her glove, pressed the ring to her lips, and tried to focus. She thought of Okane, of his ring, of the way those Gin amulets had remembered Clae.

Take me to him.

For the longest time there was nothing. And then, miraculously, she felt pressure at her heels. The amulets pushed her. She choked out a startled, wondrous laugh, and followed.

As she ran, the amulets plucked out implications in the back of her mind. They came more vaguely than usual, not words but the distinct sense of being closer, closer—*STOP!*

On a stab of instinct Laura changed course, darting down an alley and stopping short. The amulets' push had stopped. Wary, she looked around the corner.

She'd reached the outer edge of the Quarter. It wasn't unlike Amicae's terrace: a wide space beyond the line of buildings, the edge a sheer drop over stone sides. If Rex had Underyear fireworks, this little plaza would've made a good viewing platform; even in the evening gloom she could make out the shadow of mountains unsettlingly dark along the horizon. Five people occupied the open plaza. A tall, striking man in a black overcoat, with the medals on his chest and the gun

at his belt, had to be a member of the Black Guard. Three Sweepers flanked him. They all looked at a man crouched on the ground,
dressed in the ragged garb of the slaves she'd passed in the fields.
His wide-spread arms shielded the last person from view, and Laura
realized with a jolt that this last person was Okane. He lay on his side
as if he'd fallen; he'd drawn the Amicae gun at one point, but it now
rested a foot away from him. He wasn't moving. She couldn't see his
face. Fear rose in her throat, so overwhelming she hardly heard them
speak at first.

"Stay back!" cried the man in rags. "Leave this man alone! He's not
a Sweeper!"

The guard laughed, icier than the January air. "Do you think you
can order me around? And here I thought they'd already declawed
you." He stepped forward, slow and steady like a beast sure of its kill.
"I'll have to reiterate your earlier lesson, with a bit more *insistence*. So
long as we preserve the most vital parts, the program won't care if
there's damage. You two, pin him down."

The Sweepers circled in obediently, drawing their blades. The man
shook.

"No Rexian hand will touch him," he hissed. "Not while I draw
breath!"

That was their only warning.

The man tackled a Sweeper to the ground before they could react.
They rolled, snarling, the Sweeper's magic popping. The man grabbed
blindly at the Sweeper's belt and snatched up a red Egg, held it overhead like a rock.

"Get him immobilized," the guard snapped, pulling out his gun.

The second Sweeper swung her blade but the man saw it coming.
He rolled himself and his victim so the blade missed and wrought
sparks from the pavement. Even before the sparks died, he'd smashed
the Egg into his victim's face. The Sweeper screamed.

Laura wouldn't get a better distraction.

She ran out from under cover, rolled Okane onto his back, put her
fingers down his collar, and felt a pulse. He wasn't dead yet, thank
god. A shout made her look up. While all Sweepers had gathered

by the man in rags, the guard had spotted her. He stepped toward them, face twisted in rage. Laura lunged for the dropped gun. She had no idea if it held any bullets, but the gun still hummed gold when she pulled back the hammer; probably a good sign. The guard was at nearly point-blank range. She pulled the trigger. The pictographs flared as the hammer pitched forward, but there was no flash of kin. The gun simply clacked and wheezed. She barely had time to feel betrayed before the guard descended on her. He yanked the gun from her grip, but rather than threaten her with it, he tackled her. The breath whooshed out of her lungs and her head knocked against the pavement so hard she saw stars. The guard pinned her there.

"Stop right there!" he bellowed at the Sweepers. "Paragon, if you dare—"

The man in rags rose on his feet, eyes flicking for an escape route. His victim floundered up. With the Egg inactive it hadn't torn very deep into his skin, but glass shards and the metal casing had left their mark, and he blinked madly to try washing crimson kin from his eyes. He wrenched a gun from its holster.

"Stop!" the guard barked, but it was too late.

The gun fired, but it didn't hit its mark. Maybe the partial blindness ruined his aim, maybe it was because the man ducked, but a red flash exploded from one of the other Sweepers. She doubled over with a horrible wheeze, and the other two froze.

"I told all of you to stop," the guard snapped. "Paragon, if you want this woman alive, you won't resist."

The man in rags looked at her. He stilled, and she could see the numbers sloping, red and distorted, on his left cheekbone. His gray eyes flicked again, from her to Okane, and slowly he raised his hands. The uninjured Sweeper moved in, wrenching his arms behind his back. Now that all seemed under control, the guard smiled again. He shoved Laura's head harder against the pavement and stood, the Amicae gun gripped tight in one hand.

"That's a good pet. All of you, such good pets."

The wounded Sweeper straightened. The bullet had scorched clothing even now staining red, but she looked at them with an impassive, if pale, expression. "It is our honor to serve Rex."

"On to the four corners," the other two chorused. "Raise pure blood."

"Only the purest, and only the most loyal." The guard gestured the gun at the Sweeper who'd been blinded. "Is loyalty the act of ruining our tools?"

"No, sir," said the Sweeper. "I will carry out the punishment to redeem my failure."

"See that you do."

With that, the Sweeper raised the gun and pressed its barrel against his head. Laura closed her eyes as soon as she realized what was happening, but she couldn't close her ears to the gunshot, the spatter, the thud. When she dared open them, the angle only gave her a look at his boots. She was glad she couldn't see more. The Sweepers looked on this as commonplace, and the man in rags had his mouth pressed into a thin, morbid line.

"So many tools defective these days," the guard sighed. "We only want the optimal pieces in our machine. Anything that threatens Rex's advance must be eradicated. Remember that lesson, paragon. Escape your cage again and you won't be considered necessary."

Laura sucked in a harsh breath. The guard had turned on her, and she found herself looking down the barrel of Clae's old gun. Something Puer-green glimmered in its depths as the man in rags began to struggle.

"- - - said - - -'d keep her alive!"

"And let her help you a second time? I think not," said the guard. "That's a weakness of yours, paragon. Rex would never breed such gullibility."

"Only Rex would breed such perfidy," the man spat.

"Words," said the guard, and pulled back the hammer.

The sides of the gun glowed still brighter, and with it the insides. No. The insides weren't supposed to be that luster, and certainly not green. A bullet sparkled in the barrel, stuck from her earlier misfire.

Regular gun failures could be disastrous. She didn't want to think what would happen with extra firepower. She glanced at Okane.

Away, she thought, and her amulets hummed in anticipation. *On my mark, away.*

"You can't escape so easily," said the guard, guessing her intentions. "You run, I follow. There's nowhere to hide." He looked at the man in rags again, bared his teeth savagely. "Maybe this will be lesson enough for you, paragon. You err, and others suffer."

His finger tightened. Laura's amulets squalled. She skidded across the ground as if flung, and only barely managed to bring Okane with her. As they tumbled toward the Quarter's edge, the gun exploded. Shrapnel shrieked out with a shower of blinding green and gold. The initial explosion was bad, but the heat and magic caught the other bullets and the din quadrupled. Sparks shot thirty feet in the air and skidded along the ground, hot enough to scorch pavement in its wake. In the midst of it all, the guard screamed. The man in rags bucked. His captor scrambled to subdue him, snapping, "Rectify this!"

The other Sweeper lunged. Laura rolled out of the way just in time. The machete clanged down where she'd been. She sprang to her feet and slammed her shoulder into the Sweeper. She caught the Sweeper in the midsection, pinning the other's arm between them. The impact jarred her enough to drop the blade, made her stagger, but she didn't back down. Her eyes flashed vivid, verdant green as she shoved back. They grappled, stumbling and clawing at each other. If Laura saw such a scene in a film she'd scoff at such childish behavior, but now she was scared out of her wits. Her hands were already slick with her opponent's blood but the Sweeper kept on undaunted. Was it a Magi trait? Rexian training?

The Sweeper pulled her off balance, tried to twist her arm for painful leverage. Laura lashed out desperately with her free hand. She caught the injury with full force, and this time the Sweeper balked. Laura bared her teeth and kept punching. The Sweeper's composure cracked fast. Laura could see a switch even without words: the Sweeper's eyes narrowed, from panicked pain to something resolute and beyond it. She pushed Laura further off balance and kept pushing, stumbling faster and faster. They headed toward the Quarter's edge. Neither could survive the fall, but the Sweeper knew that. She'd kill herself as easily as her teammate had.

Laura kicked out and tripped them both. They came down hard, barely inches from the edge. But the Sweeper hadn't given up. She pushed all the harder. Laura tore the skin of her hand as she scrabbled for a handhold. She grabbed at the Sweeper for lack of anything else, and her stomach dropped as her body tipped. Halfway over already, and vertigo hit her. The Sweeper bared her teeth in macabre victory, shoved an arm under Laura's back, and sent them both reeling over the Quarter's edge.

The spires and rooftops of the outer wall whirled, wrenching up and then sharply down in her vision before something snagged at her coat. She spun the right way up with a violent jerk, whatever hook sliding from her shoulder to sleeve before finally catching her cuff. The jolt made her screech in surprise. Whatever had caught her didn't catch the Sweeper. Too late the Sweeper tried to adjust her spin to double her grip and haul Laura with her. The last Laura saw, the Sweeper plummeted, eyes like acid and face more monstrous than an infestation. For a moment Laura felt separate from the earth entirely, buffeted by the wind and suspended by one stinging arm hundreds of feet above the closest building.

"Are - - - all right?"

Reality rushed back in. Her head jerked back up. The man in rags looked back at her. His eyes were as gray as the Sweeper's had been green, and the telltale crackling of magic echoed from him. He swung another arm down and grabbed her just above the elbow.

"Let's get - - - back on solid ground."

Laura's voice didn't seem to work, so she simply nodded and grabbed on to him. In her awkward ascent, she had to twist around, and even with magic on his side the man needed to lie on his stomach to keep from being pulled down himself. She rose inch by torturous inch, finally coming close enough to swing a leg up and over the edge. She rolled onto the pavement with a shuddering sigh of relief.

"Thank you," she wheezed.

"It's lucky I got to - - - in time," said the man.

How had he—Laura raised her head to look at the plaza, and quickly decided that, no, she didn't want to know. The last Rexian Sweeper must've been put out of commission somehow. Hopefully less violently than his fellows, but considering their determination that was unlikely. Wait. Determination. Rex knew full well that thieves and Magi had escaped into the city, and with all that noise this location couldn't stay secret long; they wouldn't stop chasing until they caught or killed him. She had no time to lie here. She had to get Okane out of here now. She pushed herself up.

"I'm really thankful for the help, but I have to leave," she said, crawling for Okane. "If they find us again I don't think I can fight them off."

Okane hadn't moved. She shook him lightly, but his eyelids didn't so much as flicker.

"He'll recover in time," the man in rags said grimly.

"Do you know what happened?" she asked.

"Rex employs a special brand of crowd control," said the man. "Think of it like a felin's influence. One grenade drains the energy of twenty people."

"No wonder he's out cold." Laura pulled Okane's arm over her shoulders and tried to lift him. Maybe it was her own jitters or maybe he was just heavy, but she had to drop back to her knees. "Um, any idea when he'll wake up?"

"It depends on the victim." The man in rags helped lift Okane. He looked at her again, eyes like quicksilver, and Laura's stomach dropped. "But he will recover. Let's move him before anyone else shows up."

Laura started walking, and quickly realized that she had no idea how to get back to the truck. She'd tracked Okane through the Sweeper ring, but as far as she knew, the larger Gin pieces hadn't been incorporated into the armory network; how could they, when at least one of them rotated away from Amicae every year? Perhaps she could try linking to Clae's ring, but hadn't that crystallized beyond all hope?

"Are you a Sweeper?" she asked.

The man didn't answer but gave her a supremely dark look and she decided that no, he was not.

"I know you're not like those people, that's obvious! I'm just trying to figure out whether you're familiar with the city or only the fields."

His brow rose. "- - - believe I am a farmer?"

"You're dressed like the people outside. I mean . . ." She looked pointedly at his clothes.

"Rex doesn't care about presenting me to anyone," said the man. "What is - - -r escape route? How many others are here for infiltration? Is this Eos's work?"

"Eos?" Laura repeated, baffled.

The man looked crestfallen. He looked ahead rather than at her.

"How many?" he said again.

Laura's first instinct was to say nothing, but this man had already thrown himself into danger for them. Who would he rat them out to, the very people he'd attacked?

"Just the two of us. The only other person we've been working with we found in the city."

"And where is she?"

"In the getaway truck." For the life of her Laura didn't know where to find it, but elaborated, "In the alley by Gregory's Garments. I don't suppose you know where that is?"

"I do," he said, and towed them away.

It took forever to reach the shop. The man walked with purpose, but he kept leading her down alleys and side streets. She learned the reason after a trash can behind them overturned and a Rexian handler ranted at his Sweepers for his own clumsiness. The Sweepers looked at him with vacant, lifeless expressions that made Laura shudder. She'd almost met her death at that kind of face. To make matters worse, it began to rain. Cold, wet, and tired, Laura refused to complain; she at least had a coat to warm her, and the man had nothing. She was so turned around, she almost didn't recognize it when the truck came into view, the windows of Gregory's Garments shining dully beyond it.

"Zelda!" she called.

A figure moved at the truck's side, and Zelda cried, "What the hell? How did - - - get out?"

"It doesn't matter," said the man.

He and Laura heaved Okane into the vehicle. Laura climbed in to lay him down beside Clae. As far as she could see he had no injuries, so she turned back to the man—652, according to that scrawled tattoo—who watched with a hopeless expression.

"Hell yes it matters!" Zelda snapped, coming alongside them. "If one of the paragons gets out and snaps a Sweeper's neck, they're going to take serious action!"

"They had already taken serious action," the man defended.

"But why?" Zelda hissed. "The most well-behaved of all the paragons? Why break out now?"

"*Because.*" He clenched his fists, looked back at the truck. Zelda frowned at Laura a moment before understanding dawned.

"No."

652 ignored this. "Get out of Rex, quickly. Staying so long already means their forces have spread out, so be careful not to be seen."

"We can do it," Zelda said quietly. She paused, then said, "Don't get in too much trouble."

"Of course not." The man in rags turned away, heading toward the alley's mouth again.

"Wait," said Laura, "aren't you coming too?"

The man paused but didn't turn around, as if by looking at them he'd seal his fate and come along despite his best wishes. "It's best that I don't."

"Rex doesn't treat traitors well," said Zelda. "Traitors die."

"Everyone dies, Zelda." He tipped his head back, closed his eyes against the rain. "I doubt Rex will see fit to execute me. They have no proof, after all, whether or not I killed any Sweepers. The witnesses are dead."

"They'll find out," Zelda hissed.

"They'll find out too late to convince the organization of anything. No. I will simply be a paragon who escaped his cage and yearned for freedom. Any rumor of a renegade Magi man will be tied to me. I will be the focus, so - - - can escape."

"That's the same kind of bullshit he spouted before he ran off." Laura flung an arm in Okane's direction. "We can escape this way. We have a truck, we have Zelda's magic—"

"Rex doesn't let their prizes go easily. If - - - want to escape, - - - must first beguile them. Don't worry, foreigner. I've lived many years here. I will live many more. Take care of him. Please."

He ran from the alley before Laura could protest any more.

"Don't bother chasing him," said Zelda, watching his disappearance with grim features. "He knows the consequences far more than Okane did. He's strong. If he says he'll survive, he will."

"But—"

"But nothing. If we want to get out of Rex, we have to do it now. Five hours was a generous estimate, and we've already used most of it."

Laura glanced from Okane to the alleyway, still torn, but she wasn't about to risk it now. Zelda got the idea and doubled back to the front of the truck.

The vehicle moved much slower now, blending into traffic instead of racing, so Laura sat on the floor without trouble. She pulled off her coat and tucked it under Okane's head, hoping it would work for a pillow. He stirred at the movement.

"Okane?" Laura leaned closer. "Hey, can you hear me?"

His eyes flickered open. He blinked blearily at her before groaning and reaching up to his face. He rubbed at his head, face screwed up in pain before something occurred to him and he tried to sit up. Between the movement of the car and his own instability, he didn't make it. He flopped back down, and she reached out to steady him.

"Don't worry, you're okay. You're with me and Zelda. We're going to escape. You're okay now."

"Laura," he rasped, "where's that man?"

"The one with the red numbers?"

"Yes! He was just . . . Where did he go?"

"He helped carry you here and went back into the city. Why, did something happen?"

His eyes were wide, maybe panicked or maybe just disoriented.

"He called me Valens," he breathed.

"What does Valens mean?"

"That's my name. I haven't told—No one should know that name!" He covered his face in his hands and whispered, "My name, my name," with increasing horror.

The truck rolled on through the streets of Rex, darkened shops and packs of Sweepers and soldiers. Laura caught glimpses of them out the back, but no one stopped the truck as it ambled its way into a line of other military vehicles. As soon as they joined the procession, people stopped looking at them entirely. They might as well have been invisible, all the way down to the outermost wall.

A group of soldiers stood at the main gate, making a show of inspecting everything going through. The line must've gone for hours when finally a pair of guards moved toward them. They barely took in any detail of this particular truck's appearance (the bullet holes should've been a giveaway) before declaring it acceptable and waving it through. Laura almost laughed as they drove through the gateway and out of the city entirely.

Enormous lamps fixed atop metal fences lit the surrounding farmland as bright as daytime. It took what seemed like an eternity to leave its halo, and the line of trucks began to drift, leaving more and more space between the vehicles. This was cover enough. While passing through a darker section, Zelda broke away to follow one of the farm roads. She went without headlights for a long while. The glow of the agricultural lamps grew small behind them and the road uneven beneath them before the truck came to a stop. There came a rapping sound against the back of the cab. Zelda was calling her up.

"I'll be right back," she told Okane. He only groaned.

She climbed out and circled to the front, where Zelda leaned out the window.

"This is as far as I'm going," she announced.

"Only here?"

"I only said I'd get the happy couple in and out, right? Good luck from here on."

It took a minute for this to really sink in. Laura had to swallow a lump in her throat. "Are you sure? I meant it, when I said you could go to Amicae. With us in tow, it'll be even easier to get you in safely."

"Tempting, but no. Not now, anyway," said Zelda. She looked to the distance, where the other trucks had gone. "I've got unfinished business here. I've had plans in the works for a while, but - - - two made me consider them seriously."

Laura didn't understand, but she nodded anyway. "Will you leave us the truck?"

"I'm not that heartless! Go on and take it."

"I don't suppose you could tell me how it works?"

Zelda sighed and leaned back, gesturing at the equipment. "It's just a less comfortable version of the usual car. Steering wheel, ignition, brake. Simple. It's got a big gas tank, so just keep driving down this road here and it'll get you to the satellite town, no problem. Just don't push too hard on the gas or brake and it'll be smooth sailing."

Laura doubted this, but didn't argue. She stood aside as Zelda clambered out of the cab, sighed, and stretched.

"So what do you want from us? The payment?"

Zelda hummed, swinging her arms. "I went through a lot of trouble for a pair of idiots. Betrayal of my own city, the horror! I need a big reward to make up for it."

"Unless you're accepting whatever supplies they were hauling, I don't have anything to pay you with."

"I'll come up with something eventually. Keep an eye out, all right? This isn't the last - - -'ve seen of me."

"Thank you for all the help."

Laura held out a hand. Zelda eyed it before breaking into a grin and shaking it in a tight grip. "Ugh, stop being so sentimental. Save it for the invalid."

Speaking of which . . . "Could I ask one more question before you go?" Laura asked.

"Oh? What's that?"

"What's a paragon?"

The smile slipped off Zelda's face. "'Paragon' is what they call the purebloods, real Magi like dream boy. Hot commodity."

She turned and walked away, following the edge of the road. "See - - - later, dream team. Try not to get caught without me!"

Laura pushed aside the canvas on the back of the truck, heaving herself up to see Okane and tell him what was going on. He remained sprawled on the floor, shaky and mostly unintelligible.

"He knew my name, who here could know? Who—?"

Okane had been afraid of recognizing someone in Rex, but he'd obviously never considered being recognized himself. When the man in rags had helped lift Okane, when he'd looked at her with his face so close to Okane's, the resemblance had been painfully obvious. No one could look that similar without being related by blood.

Laura went back to the cab, settled herself in the driver's seat, gripped the wheel, and looked out into the night, black as an infestation, no stars or moon to light her path. Laura felt, for a moment, adrift from the world again. Suspended. Unreal. Lost.

"I've done worse," she told herself, flexing her grip. "I've been out in the wilds at night without even a car, and I did just fine there. It's not like there's a knuckerhole in the middle of the road. I can do this. I can totally do this."

Only somewhat reassured, she started the engine and flipped on the headlights.

The road out of Rex led due east, toward the Malamare. It took a while for Laura to get used to the car, the steering and the pedals, but eventually she settled into a constant speed. The terrain was moderately hilly and undergrowth crept in on the roadside, at some points stretching out onto the pavement. The shape of Rex in the side mirror preoccupied her more. She didn't think she'd relax until it was well out of sight. As she made a turn and dipped downhill, the city's light vanished and she let out a long sigh. Finally. She pulled over to the side of the road, hitting the brake pedal and pulling back on the lever to her right. The truck shuddered and jolted, but eventually slowed to a stop. With the engine off, she closed her eyes and took her hands off the wheel. She'd been gripping it so hard her hands ached. She flexed them, hissing at the feeling.

"That satellite better not be much further," she mumbled.

She jumped at the sound of a door opening. Dozens of terrible possibilities ran through her mind—wilds monster, Rexian follower, infestation—but the culprit was none of them. The door creaked on its hinges as Okane climbed up, settled himself, and pulled it shut behind him.

"Hi," he said.

"Hello. Uh, nice to see you. It's been—" She did a quick calculation. "—an hour now?"

"Sorry I didn't come up earlier. By the time I pulled myself together, - - - were already driving."

"Don't worry about it. Are you doing okay?"

"Fine."

She kept looking at him, and after a moment he averted his gaze.

"I think that was the least-fine reaction I've ever seen from you," she said.

"I was a little confused," he defended. "I mean, I wasn't expecting that."

"You're the one who told me other survivors may have been caught," she reminded him gently. "I mean, maybe he didn't say it directly, but Clae hinted at this possibility, didn't he?"

"Yes, but I never—" He stopped, bit his lip. "My father traveled outside the haven before it fell, so he couldn't be with the survivors. Mama always thought he was still out there somewhere, but for me . . . I never expected to see him again. Especially not after she died. I don't even know if that man was him. Maybe I made a mistake, heard wrong."

Laura wanted to butt in, *His eyes are just like yours,* but convincing him that his father was alive might not be a good idea. Would he wallow in guilt over leaving the man behind? Would he want to go back for him?

"What was your father's name?" she asked instead.

"I don't remember. I only called him Papa at that point."

"How about your mother?"

"Marina," he sighed, his sadness almost palpable.

"Marina and Valens, huh?" she mused. He nodded mutely and she repeated the names, committing them to memory. "Should I be calling you Valens now?"

"No," he said immediately. "I don't want that name anymore."

"But you said it yourself, it's your name."

"I'm Okane now."

"Why? I mean, I'm sorry, but you're always offended when people like . . . say your eyes look like money or associate you with it. 'Okane' means money, and it's something Sullivan slapped on you, isn't it? Why would you want to keep that instead?"

"Being Valens is what got me into trouble in the first place."

"I don't think I follow."

"Neither did Clae," Okane muttered. "I just—I haven't been Valens in a long time. I want to be called Okane now."

Laura leaned back in the seat, still confused but yielding. "If you ever want to switch, just let me know. Valens isn't that bad a name, but I'll call you Okane if that's what you want."

"I'd appreciate that."

⚬⚬⚬

The real bump in the road faced them as dawn spread dim across the horizon.

Trains ran along well-maintained tracks that had been cut into the landscape, altering the earth to ensure a level surface, but regular routes had no such care. Roads in the wilds went up and down hills with the roll of the land, helped along by the odd bridge at some points, though those weren't nearly as well maintained as the train variety.

Or, who knew, maybe this one had been.

The road to the satellite town crossed a river, not a huge one but certainly wider than canals in Amicae. A bridge had once spanned the distance. The ends still sat on either bank, rising for a foot before dead-ending in thin air, the bridge's rubble strewn in the riverbed and much of it washed away entirely.

"What do you think, Rex or someone else?" said Laura. "Somebody definitely tore that down."

"Maybe the town? The train routes are one thing, but I don't see what Rex could gain from this," said Okane.

"This is the main port with Fatum, isn't it? Cut supplies to them, and depending on how much Gin they have to help grow crops, they could end up starving. Easy pickings once Rex gets moving and attacking cities."

"Surely they have enough food, though? It's on an island."

"A lot of cities specialize in certain things and trade for others. At least one of the islands focuses on clothes, so they don't have much in the way of food production. That's not our problem right now, though. We can worry about them once we're back in Amicae."

"How are we supposed to do that when the bridge is out?"

"Maybe there's another one nearby?" Laura suggested. "If the satellite town knows about this, they might set up temporary crossings. Or maybe there's a shallower spot. A shorter crossing."

"I suppose it's worth checking," said Okane.

Laura drove off the road, trundling onto the grass and bumping over brush; the vehicle handled well on rough terrain, she decided, as she parked it in the shadow of nearby trees. Even Cherry and Grim hadn't gotten up this early, so Laura didn't expect anyone to come across the truck, but better safe than sorry. She and Okane split up, she going one way along the river, he the other. It didn't look promising. As she walked, the ground rose and became uneven, the banks getting steeper and steeper, the surrounding vegetation thicker. By the time she finally stopped and considered that maybe this wouldn't work, she'd reached a point fifteen feet above the water's surface, and the opposite bank towered just as high. Even if she found a better crossing, the sheer number of trees blocked any path the truck could take. She doubled back, and found Okane waiting for her.

"Did you find anything?" she called.

He shook his head, hopeless. "It only gets wider. Another tributary runs into it from the other side, and then it hits a cliff. The drop goes as far as I can see in both directions, and I'm not keen on challenging a waterfall. But I found something worse."

"Rexians?" Laura guessed.

"Tracks," said Okane. "Enormous ones. I think there are felin on this side."

With the amount of Sweepers and corresponding magic outside Rex's walls, Laura wouldn't be surprised if felin were closing in from every side; they might see the crusades as a buffet. But felin acted on any opportunity. If any caught wind of their truck, they'd be in trouble fast.

"Can you tell how recent they are?" said Laura, hurrying back to the truck.

"The ground was wet. I'm guessing it's fresh." Okane hopped into the passenger seat and heaved the door shut behind him. "I don't suppose - - - had more luck on - - -r end?"

"None," said Laura. She gripped the wheel, stared down the river before them. "Not unless you want to drive off a slightly smaller cliff."

Doubling back and trying to find a different route was madness; they'd land themselves in the middle of pursuing Rexians or attract felin. Besides, there might not be another road to Fatum at all. They had no guide this time. They'd be lost in the wilds all over again.

Okane came to the same conclusion. He frowned at the water and said, "Do - - - think we could make it over in the truck?"

"This is a military vehicle, isn't it? It's built for these occasions." Laura wrenched the wheel around. She didn't have much confidence in the idea, but as far as she could see it was her best bet. She kept talking, trying to bolster her own confidence again as they approached. "Charlie was over the moon about the ones in Amicae. Interchangeable parts, can drive right over train tracks . . . The Amicae versions can go through water deeper than the tires. Ours are tough, so we can cross any terrain in any weather when going to defend a satellite town. If Rex is taking these all the way to Kuro no Oukoku, they must be pretty damn special."

"So it's actually meant for this sort of situation," Okane checked.

"Exactly. We're already at the shallowest part of the river, so it should be easy. Hang on."

The tires met the bank, churning mud and bending reeds beneath them. The bridge remnants stuck out farther than the rest of the riverside, tiny spits of land that proved ridiculously soft but still stayed above water. Laura kept on it, so close to the bridge that the truck's side scraped against it. The opposite bank matched this one; if she could make it to that spit, their time in the water would be halved. In the meantime, the truck fared well. Water reached only halfway up its wheels, and they kept a steady pace. They might actually make it. The truck had reached just over the midway point when the tires slipped. The rocks made it hard to steer properly to begin with, but Laura found herself out of control. She stomped on the gas pedal, but the engine only sputtered before cutting out entirely. She kept stomping it to no avail. She hauled on the wheel, but while the tires moved, it wasn't by much and the only momentum they had now was the current.

"Rexian piece of crap!" she snarled, smacking the wheel and causing the horn to wail one sharp note.

The truck lost traction entirely, skidding downriver until it bumped into a sandbar laden with bridge debris. For a moment Laura sat frozen, convinced they'd be swept away again. When the truck remained still, she started to scramble up.

"Let's get out of here."

"What about Clae and the Gin?" said Okane.

"We climb back there and carry them out!"

Laura forced her door open. Water gushed in, flooding the floor as she climbed out. The loose canvas allowed her to find and grab the metal frame, using this and a small ledge on the side to shuffle above the water level. She pulled her pocketknife from her bag and jabbed at the canvas, starting with a bullet hole and ripping it open from there. With a suitable entrance made, she scrambled in. She grabbed Clae first, heaved him off the floor and back to the ripped portion, where Okane waited. He eyed the crystal, then the water below, grimaced, and dropped off the side of the truck. He sucked air as the water splashed up past his knees and plastered himself to the truck.

"You okay down there?" Laura called.

"It's c-c-cold!"

He shucked off his coat, tossing it aside in the river and shaking all the more. Laura felt bad, but better to be cold than too heavy and dragged under.

"I'm pushing him out now, okay? You ready?"

"Yes!"

Laura gritted her teeth and pulled Clae higher, tipping him so he scraped his way out of the truck. Okane caught him and sloshed backward, giving her room to jump out. She cursed as the water soaked into her clothes, and in no time she shivered as much as her companion. Between the two of them they balanced Clae and waded toward shore. She hadn't noticed the current before, but she could feel it tugging at her, hard and cold and threatening. If it could take a truck down, surely she wasn't safe either. She smacked her amulet on one staggering step, and felt some warmth in her shoes as the two there activated as well. *Keep me rooted as I walk,* she ordered them, and immediately it became easier to keep steady. Okane didn't think to use his amulets, but judging by the crackling sounds, his magic had kicked in to serve the same purpose. Still, it was slow going. It felt like forever before they made it to the opposite bank. After trudging up the slope and depositing Clae in the tall grass there, they doubled back. The truck tottered, but settled somewhat as Laura climbed in again. She passed one of the boxes of Gin out.

"Give me another one," said Okane, shifting the box for a better grip.

"I don't think that's a good idea," said Laura. "What if you're too heavy? What if—"

"I don't think the truck's going to be here long, so the faster the better. I can use my amulets."

"I don't—"

"I'm lucky, remember? Just hand it over!"

"Ugh, fine!"

She pulled the second Gin out and dropped it onto the box. The wood splintered and Okane staggered, but he kept his balance and, amid a chorus of cracks and pops, made for the bank again. With him gone Laura reached for Anselm. As she set hands on the crystal, the floor lurched beneath her. The bridge debris had dislodged, and now the truck washed downstream. The floor tipped—surely it wasn't about to roll—and Laura flew into a panic. The magic in her amulets steadied her but also slowed her movement. She dismissed her previous order, grabbed Anselm, and rolled out the back of the truck as fast as she could. She fell feet-first, but hit hard enough for the water to splash up into her face. Her feet scrabbled for a hold on the riverbed, but here the water hit her at hip height, and the undertow tugged hard enough that she slipped entirely. Water closed over her head. She fought her way to the surface, coughing violently, but Anselm's crystal weight bore her underwater, farther downriver, and her waterlogged clothes became far too heavy. She barely choked out a yelp before she went under again. She kept struggling, but her strength failed quickly. It was a godsend when she bumped into another pile of debris. She dragged herself up so she could breathe and clung to the rock and crystal, trying to figure out how to heave herself out without losing Anselm.

"A little help, here?" she panted, hoping she was loud enough to be heard over the roaring water.

She couldn't see Okane but heard frantic splashing coming toward her. But it wasn't Okane who stumbled through the water from her left. Grim's boots dislodged rocks, impeding his progress. His hat, coat, and gloves were missing, his mouth set in a grimace.

"You people," he hissed, grabbing Laura by the shirt and hauling her higher on the rock pile. Laura scrambled to keep her grip on Anselm.

"Watch it!" she squeaked.

"Drop that!"

"I can't!"

"It'll drag you under again. It's not worth it."

"We can't lose him!"

She didn't care if Grim saw Clae or Anselm at this point; they couldn't be lost, no matter what. He tried to pull her up again, but when she kept clinging to her burden, he realized it was a lost cause. He switched position, plunging one arm under to hook the crystal, the other hand lifting her. His skinny frame held more power than she expected. One good yank brought her to better ground, and between the two of them they bore Anselm toward shore.

They were closer to dry land than Laura thought, and relief flooded through her as she saw Okane running down the bank toward them. Grim shifted his grip, from bearing Anselm's weight on his forearm to taking the crystal in hand. A startled grunt was the only warning before Laura was dragged down by even more weight than before. She scrambled to keep upright, swinging the crystal into her side in an attempt to balance out. Grim's grip had gone lax, and he plunged into the water.

"Grim!" Laura screeched.

"I've got him!"

Okane plowed into the river and lunged after the other man. Laura hesitated; only after he caught Grim did she slog to shore. She stumbled through the mud, teeth chattering like a windup toy. She dumped Anselm unceremoniously amid the grass and turned back to help as Okane waded through the shallows and onto land. He hooked his arms under Grim's to pull the man out, and the Ranger's boots dragged troughs in the mud. He dropped to his knees, depositing his load with a little more grace before checking for a pulse. Grim had been limp this whole time, his skin now paler than ever against the grass. Okane sat back on his heels, hands up and eyes wide.

"He's not breathing! Laura, what do we do?"

Laura felt her own face pale and she dropped to the mud across from him.

"Grim? Hey!" She slapped his cheek lightly, but he didn't respond. His eyelids didn't even flicker. "Come on, come on, wake up! You can't just—" Clearly he wasn't waking, so she looked hopelessly up at Okane. "Do you know how to do rescue breathing?"

"I don't even know what that is!"

Laura scooted closer, trying desperately to remember the films she'd seen. She angled her hands over Grim's chest, but was that the right position?

"What are - - - doing?"

"Chest compressions!"

"What?"

"You have to—"

"Hey!" Laura's head jerked up. A familiar horse crested the hill, carrying Cherry toward them at a trot. "You two? What are you doing here?"

"Do you know rescue breathing?" Laura shouted.

Cherry drew close enough for confusion to be visible on her face, rapidly draining to horror as she saw what they knelt over. She kicked her horse faster, cantering swiftly to them, swinging wide so she could jump off. She stumbled while the horse wheeled back.

"What happened?" she demanded, checking Grim's pulse and tilting his head back.

"He pulled me out of the river," said Laura, fidgeting as Cherry started with chest compressions. "He was fine, but halfway out he fainted! I don't know why or how, it just happened!"

Cherry's response came delayed, she being too busy breathing air into Grim's lungs. She switched back to chest compressions. "How long?"

"Maybe a minute?" said Okane. "I only just pulled him out."

Cherry growled something in anger and worry, then pinched Grim's nose and went back to breathing. Laura settled back, watching with a growing sense of dread as Grim still failed to move.

—∞—

This gatehouse wasn't the piece of art the last one had been. This was one of the surviving crusade pieces, made of stone with no latticework, no curved roof, no wood to speak of in its interior. It sat across the tracks like an ugly toad, its gate door gone and lower walls converted to allow trains through. The castle keep was only habitable from the second floor up, ground completely abandoned for walkways that stretched from keep to walls, metallic additions the original owners might've pondered at. Three people manned the gatehouse: a telegram operator and two beefy guards, who received no guests for months at a time and had no idea how to react when the motley group crawled in. The keep was equipped for far more than three, though, so Laura found herself in a barracks room on the third floor, sitting on a bunk and staring into space as she listened to Cherry's voice on the other side of the door.

The woman's voice sounded hollow, scratchy at points, as she explained their situation. Grim lay cold and motionless on a bed in a different room. Every time Cherry so much as mentioned his name her scratchy tone worsened. It was awful to hear, but Laura listened anyway. Her stomach flip-flopped, and she wondered, *Did I sound like that when Clae died?* Okane hovered by the door, cringing at her tone, but too restless and too afraid to sit still. The nonliving inhabitants of the room were on the cots farthest from the door, Clae on a mattress all his own while Anselm and the Gin were piled onto the one opposite. Cherry and her extra horses had been able to transport them here safely, with one very obvious change.

During her scramble out of the river she hadn't paid much attention to Anselm beyond keeping hold of him, but as soon as she went to retrieve him afterward she noticed an immediate difference. Anselm's body usually curled into itself, covering a face twisted in fear, but he'd shifted so he looked more like he was peacefully sleeping. The crystal's surface had smoothed out, his arms folded by his chest instead. Even the color of the stone had mellowed out into something brighter yellow. How this had happened she had no idea, and the sight was creepy. Laura watched him, almost ready for him to sit up and say hello, while Cherry continued talking. She said something about transporting the corpse.

Grim's dead too. How could that *have possibly happened?*

One minute strong enough to pull two people out of a river, the next, stone dead? He might have had white hair but otherwise seemed far from old. Some inherited condition, perhaps, linked to his strange coloring? But then, how did Anselm change? Had Anselm taken Grim's life?

". . . to Amicae. We want to make sure he has a proper burial," said Cherry. "Amicae's been forbidding Rangers entry to the city, but this should be an exception. The only family he had lives in Amicae."

"I don't understand," Okane murmured. "If Grim was a citizen, couldn't he have gotten through the lines, when they brought us back?"

There was a knock on the door and he leapt back as if scalded.

"Excuse me?" came a reedy voice, much closer than Cherry's. "May I come in?"

Okane looked back at Laura. She gave a halfhearted shrug. He eyed her a while longer, then opened the door a crack. There was movement beyond, and the sound came clearer.

"Oh, hello! I'm Clarence, the communications operator. I wondered if I could talk to you for a moment."

The obvious use of "you" put Okane at ease, for some of the tension left his shoulders. A young man, with glasses so thick they blurred his features, shuffled into the room dressed in pseudo-regulation clothing: uniform pants and shoes, and an ugly mustard-yellow sweater and striped tie. He offered a bashful smile and a quick, self-conscious wave.

"I'm sorry, but Miss Cherry said you were Laura Kramer and Okane Sinclair? Is this correct?"

Laura tightened her hold on the blanket. He was a telegram operator. Of course he'd heard of them. They were probably going to be arrested and sent back to Amicae.

"We are," she said anyway.

"Good! Er, well, not good in this case." He glanced over his shoulder at the discussion outside, before sitting on one of the beds. "But I've got a message for you from Amicae."

"From Juliana?" Laura growled.

"From a Mr. Byron Rhodes."

Laura looked up in confusion while Clarence dug through his pockets. He pulled out a scrap of paper with a message on it. "We got this two days ago and we've been passing it on to the ERA Sweepers as they go through. Ahem! 'Regarding Kramer and Sinclair of Amicae Sweepers: No charges filed. Sweepers fired but wanted home. Return alive and unharmed. Framed.'"

Laura stared at him, uncomprehending. Wanted home. Fired. Framed?

"I don't understand."

"The first telegram that went out for your arrest was unauthorized," said Clarence. "As far as we can tell, anyway. Your head Sweeper ordered it, but a message like that should go through the police department first, so it goes to the right destinations. This Sweeper lady just sent it out everywhere she could. It must've cost her a fortune! According to this one, sent via your police, the order for your arrest is withdrawn. They want to make sure you don't get hurt on the way back. Cities really value their Sweepers, and maybe you're not employed as such anymore, but you did them a great service. They're not about to forget that."

"But why would they withdraw our arrest?" Laura pressed.

"It says here you were framed, right? So they figured it out and dropped the charges."

But Juliana had been dead set on them taking the fall. Lester said she wouldn't give up, and Laura couldn't picture her doing so either. Had Byron revealed what he knew? Had someone else come forward? Could this be a trap of some kind?

Okane looked just as confused as she felt. "Seriously?"

"You two are free to go home now. In fact, we're obligated to get you on the next train."

"With Cherry?"

"Oh, yes, I suppose so. If you're not comfortable with it, you can ride in a separate car. I think that might even be better. I'm not sure if it's the grief, or—" He chuckled uneasily. "She keeps acting as if that dead Ranger will sit up and join the conversation."

Clarence babbled something about denial. He talked to them a while longer, a brief, clipped kind of conversation, but Laura was thinking.

Most of her security and support network had been ruined in the past few weeks. She had no job to return to, an actively hostile reception waiting for her, and an ex-boss determined to shut her and Okane up for good. But she refused to give up now. She'd infiltrated and escaped Rex, she had all the Gin and the Sinclairs in tow, and she knew where all the pieces connected now. She just needed to contact Byron and Albright, and get the truth out. If she could kick Juliana out of Amicae, then she could finally count this a victory.

21

HOMECOMING

The train arrived at exactly 2:06 in the morning. Clarence woke them all shortly beforehand and ushered them onto the walkways outside. Laura shivered in her borrowed coat and watched as a train came in from the west, its lights shining bright enough to be seen miles away. It moved much slower than the trains she was used to, but then again it was coming for them.

"This is the last scheduled train from Litus," said Clarence, rubbing at his eyes under the glasses. "From here on, the railways are trying to cut off whatever trade Rex could steal."

"What happens to Litus, then?" she asked.

"Canis will trade with them by boat. It's not exactly convenient, but there's no chance of raids that way."

"Is this the same train that was going to Litus the day before yesterday?" asked Okane.

"I think that one's at the port for Cor right now."

Okane let out a shaky sigh, and Laura felt tempted to do the same. Facing Keya and Felix after their fiasco of a departure was the last thing she wanted to do.

The train came to a stop halfway through the gatehouse. With a rattle the roof of a cargo car came apart, each half rising like a drawbridge to reveal the inside. Three baggage handlers stood amid a mess of luggage, peering up at them.

"Hello there!" cried one, presumably the man in charge.

"Good morning!" Clarence called back. "I hope you don't mind if we lower everything down?"

"That's what we're here for, sir!"

The two guards edged over, carrying a roughly hewn coffin between them—kept on hand in case the very people carrying it fell in the line of duty—and inside it lay Grim. Clae rested in a similar box, Anselm and the Gin in another. A crane machine jutted from the walkway, over the car. Clarence grabbed its cord, which ended in an odd harness, and they fitted the coffin into this. After a few test tugs they reeled it up so the box swung out into open air, then lowered it into the car. The baggage handlers caught and unhooked it before carrying it aside and coming back for the next. Soon all three coffins had been lowered this way, and the cord reeled back up. Clarence adjusted the harness, unclipping something here and reattaching it there, before presenting it to his audience.

"This isn't foolproof, but it's a harness for you. Who wants to go first?"

"I will," said Laura.

Clarence guided her in, tightening a strap at her chest and directing her feet into the thicker loop at the bottom. Once it was secure, they swung her out; she clutched at the cord above the harness and tried not to think of falling. Soon enough hands caught her sides, steadying her and pulling her in. One of the baggage handlers helped her toward the door.

Okane and Cherry descended behind her, and the harness reeled up for the last time. The three waited in silence as the handlers shuffled around. The door to the forward car opened, and a woman in an ERA Sweeper uniform walked in. A beagle tugged at the leash in her hands.

"Welcome aboard," said the Sweeper. "We'll be taking you to a specially prepared car shortly, but before that there's a procedure we need to run through. It's just a formality, so please don't think badly of us."

"What kind of procedure?" said Cherry. While her eyes still looked red, her tone had gone from the rasp to her usual authority.

"This dog is trained to sniff out any infestations and empty amulets. We need her to check you for any threats."

"That shouldn't be a problem," Laura forced out.

Neither of the others objected, so the Sweeper loosened her grip on the leash. The dog bounded up and started sniffing. Laura jumped as its wet nose brushed her hand, but it didn't stay interested in her for long. It moved on to the others, snuffling about before returning to its owner.

"I'll also have to check the departed," she said. "If they have any such amulets on them, they'll need to be monitored or purified. Don't worry, we won't confiscate them indefinitely."

She led the dog over to the coffins. Laura held her breath—would it be trained to recognize Gin too, or, working with Sweepers, would it be too used to kin-related energy? It let the first two coffins alone, but on the last it became interested. The dog sniffed more, scratched the wood, and started whimpering. The Sweeper drew closer, frowning.

"Open it up," she ordered.

The baggage handlers looked reluctant but didn't argue. They pried the lid off, and the dog launched itself up to smell inside. Despite the dog's enthusiasm the men turned away, looking ill; it was Grim's coffin. The dog sniffed his face and hands.

"Your dog isn't trained as well as it should be," said Cherry. She reached into Grim's pocket and tossed a handful of stale caramels onto the floor. "I'll give him credit for being able to smell those through a coffin, though."

The Sweeper colored in shame, reeling the dog in. "I'm so, so sorry," she whispered.

"Don't worry about it. I'd rather have the infestation check now than have one manifest in the middle of a train ride." She glanced up at the baggage handlers and smiled sympathetically. "Let's put that back on, shall we?"

The men rushed to replace the lid.

The Sweeper led them to a car near the back, a so-called mourning car. Compartments held coffins in place, while the rest of the car mimicked a dim parlor. A curtain could be pulled around specific sections for privacy. The baggage handlers transported the coffins safely into their slots before leaving. The Sweeper stayed a minute more.

"We hope you'll be comfortable in here. For the most part you'll be undisturbed, though an ERA officer may come through during patrols. If you need anything at all, please approach the attendant in the cars ahead. Do you have any questions?"

"None," said Cherry. "Thanks for picking us up."

The Sweeper gave another short, embarrassed bow, and led her dog away. Once the door closed, Cherry heaved a long sigh and turned to the others.

"Well, this has been a pretty shitty reunion, but I'm glad to see you two are doing okay!"

"I—yes, yes, it's been shitty." Laura coughed out a laugh. "Sorry, but you're acting a lot more upbeat than I expected."

"I thought I'd never find you!" Cherry leaned back against Grim's coffin and rapped her knuckles against its side. "Hear that? You were right. They went straight to Zyra."

She keeps acting as if that dead Ranger will sit up and join the conversation. Laura had thought Clarence exaggerated that, but no, it proved uncomfortably true.

"Were you looking for us?" she asked.

"Of course." Cherry crossed her arms. "After we got rejected at the gates, I looked for ways to get in. I wasn't about to let you go alone against your boss if I could help it. But then we got word that something else had gone down, and that you'd left Amicae all over again. While I'd been trying to get inside, Grim gathered information from other Rangers, and he made the connection between your red Egg and Rex. I figure the girl who'd confront and scold a would-be captor would be just as eager to take on the enemy, so we caught the next train to Zyra. You must've caught your thieves before they even reached Rex!"

"We actually went into the city," said Okane.

"You what?" Cherry stared at him. "No offense, but how in hell did you escape in one piece?"

"Sheer dumb luck," said Okane.

Laura elbowed him. "We had help from a Rexian. She got us in and out safely. Of course, as soon as we got out of her sight, we went and got ourselves stuck in a river."

Cherry nodded. "And then we heard a city slicker honking their horn. And when Grim—" Her smile faltered. After a moment she murmured, "I really should've known. Rescue breaths. As if that would've worked on him."

"Did he have some sort of condition?" Laura asked hesitantly. "You mentioned he got hives before, but—"

Cherry shook her head with a rueful smile. "Something like that. Something not like that. He's always been a mystery. It's strange, though. Whenever I considered him dying, I pictured him . . . falling apart, or just gone with the morning. This was very anticlimactic. Very human. I'm still not convinced it's real."

"Did I hear - - - say he had family in Amicae?" said Okane.

"That was a lie," she replied. "As Rangers, we're considered satellite citizens, so if cities go on lockdown we have no legal right to get inside. If, on the other hand, there's a family tie inside the city, who are they to stop them from reuniting with the body and his poor, grieving widow?" She dabbed theatrically at her eyes. "I've seen bodies arrive by train before. A group of professional mourners carries the coffin wherever it needs to go, and let me tell you, no one interferes with professional mourners. If we leave Grim and your Gin with them, it'll all be safe. With that confirmed, I'm free to escort you wherever you need to go."

"Are you sure that's a good idea?" Laura fretted.

"Positive."

"But Grim—"

Cherry's expression grew serious. "Grim's entire home got flattened by a Rexian attack. He was the only survivor. He never liked to show much, but I knew him long enough to learn that Rex was the only thing he ever hated. If there's potential for Rex to take down a city, he'd do anything to prevent it. He'd be in on this plan."

Laura and Okane glanced at each other. He tipped his head in meaning, and she agreed; to Cherry she said, "We'd love to have your help."

———

It took two full days to reach Amicae. The train sped through flatlands, crossed a bridge over a mighty river ten times bigger than the one they'd gotten stuck in, rounded the mountains, and steamed on toward the eastern coast. Few distractions reached the mourning car, and they could only go over their stories so many times before Laura went crazy. She spent most of her time sleeping on the second day, and had to be woken when they finally arrived.

"Laura? Laura, we're here. - - -'ve got to wake up. Please?"

Laura grumbled and blinked her eyes open. "What?"

Okane looked relieved. "We've reached Amicae. We've actually been here a while, but - - - slept pretty deeply."

"It's only a matter of time until they unload us," said Cherry, checking through her bag. "All the other passengers have already disembarked."

Laura straightened to peer out the window. All she saw was a brick wall.

"Are we in the depot?"

"Makes it easier for priests to reach us," said Cherry.

The compartment door opened, and Laura leapt to her feet.

"Your transportation is ready," said an attendant. "Are you prepared to disembark?"

"We are," said Cherry.

The attendant nodded and drew back. In came several men dressed in black. They gravitated to the coffins.

"Are these two together?" asked the man who had to be the lead mourner. It took a moment for Laura to take in the white overcoat, and another to recognize the man.

"Mateo?"

Mateo gave a short, surprised laugh. "I didn't expect you to remember me. Yes, I'm Weaver Mateo, from the Three Child Church. Thank you for your service to our parish. I haven't forgotten how you helped us." He finished this off by bowing.

"It's no problem!" Laura said quickly. "I'm just glad they're okay."

Mateo straightened. He gave the coffins a sad look. "I don't want to weigh you further at this time, but . . . I've been following your story since Underyear, and read all of the recent news articles. Is one of these meant to represent Lester MacDanel?"

"No," said Laura. "These are—"

"Brave Rangers who died to return Amicae's magic," Cherry butted in.

"Then the Sweepers' magic really was stolen?" said Mateo. "But—Ra. Please forgive me. My attitude is very unprofessional and insensitive—"

"You're fine," said Laura.

"I'd actually be interested in hearing what's gone on while we were gone," Okane said carefully. "- - - said - - -'ve been keeping up with the papers?"

"Yes?" said Mateo.

"What exactly did they say about Lester MacDanel?"

Mateo glanced between the two of them, uncertain, but said, "A Sweeper building was attacked last week. It was reportedly an act of the mobs, and they left an infestation on-site that Juliana MacDanel destroyed before law enforcement arrived. The story is that you were bitter over the loss of your title, and collaborated with the Mad Dogs to give them the magic and to be rid of the head Sweeper, with the infestation meant to cover your trail. Lester MacDanel was reported killed by this infestation. The Mad Dogs have, of course, denied involvement. They've tried to defame MacDanel's testimony. They seem to think she sold you to Rex for some reason."

"*For some reason,*" Okane muttered darkly.

"They're rather vehement about the subject," said Mateo. "It's been the *Dead Ringer*'s headline for days."

The Mad Dogs must've remembered the Rexian Sweeper's demands and finally put two and two together. If only they'd stopped Theron before all of this happened . . .

"They're not completely right, but they're on the right track," said Laura. "We're not the ones who stole the magic. We're the ones who brought it back."

She spoke with all the authority she could muster, and it worked. Mateo showed no signs of doubting her. Instead, he said, "I'll accompany you."

Laura's bravado deflated. "I'm sorry, what?"

"It's dangerous for you out there, if anyone recognizes you," said Mateo. "I may not be able to do much, but the presence of a priest tends to make people think twice before making a scene. There are other priests here to help mourn. Let me speak with them first."

He hurried away.

"We're building an entourage," Okane muttered.

"It's a good thing," said Cherry, patting their shoulders. "Remember what I said? No one messes with a professional mourner. Not Rangers, not mobsters, not anyone."

Speaking with the priests took very little time, and soon Mateo returned to their side. Multiple teams of mourners took up the coffins and carried them out, and the Sweepers followed. The depot was crowded, but a hush fell over those nearby as the coffins passed. Soon the mourners had vanished through the depot's side doors. Laura took a deep breath of depot air: steam, grease, cigarettes, and spice from the food carts. It was by no means pristine or orderly, nothing like Rex. It smelled like honest chaos. It smelled safe. It smelled like home.

"What are we doing from here?" said Okane.

"Taking back Amicae," said Laura. "Let's get Juliana out of here."

She strode into the crowd. Okane and the others followed close behind.

"How?" he asked.

"Get the police involved. I don't know if I want the regular po-lice, since she's already got them to accept her side of the story, but Byron—"

Someone stepped in front of her so fast, she almost ran straight into him. She stopped and scowled.

"Who—Oh! Byron!"

It was indeed Byron. He raised a brow, severely unimpressed. "What was that about me, Miss Kramer?"

"You're exactly who I wanted to see," said Laura.

"Of course." His gaze flicked up to their companions—Cherry glowered, a hand under her coat and presumably on a weapon, while Mateo seemed glued to Okane's left elbow. "And who are these people?"

"Escorts," Cherry said shortly. "To make sure nothing happens to them."

"Don't worry, this is the investigator I told you about," said Laura. "I trust him." Cherry didn't back down, but she didn't make any move to intimidate him, either. Laura turned back to Byron and said seri-ously, "We need your help with Juliana MacDanel."

"Yes, the woman you supposedly attacked. Just because her suit hasn't come to court doesn't mean—"

"She's a danger to Amicae."

For a long time Byron didn't say anything. He sighed, stepped out of their path, and flopped onto the nearest bench.

"Byron?" Laura ventured. "You saw the letters, didn't you? You know she and Lester—"

"Juliana MacDanel has appeared in almost every newspaper, look-ing like the lost maiden of a satellite raid. At this point she's won more pity than a kicked dog and more hearts than Barnaby Gilda, and at every turn she's saying it's because these ungrateful Sweepers wanted to retake their title," said Byron.

"We aren't even the ones that hurt her," said Okane. "She attacked us and we retaliated, yes, but that cut on her leg was self-inflicted."

Byron rubbed at his eyes. "I figured as much, but we've got some very biased witnesses involved. You've got to understand, *fleeing the scene* is a very clear sign of guilt to most people. Without solid leads beyond Juliana's story and the *Dead Ringer* screaming your support, the public had a very clear side. Almost everyone I know has aligned with Juliana." He shot them an annoyed look. "Where did you even go? The last information I received said you were headed to Avis, but—"

"Rex," said Laura.

"Please be serious."

"I am being serious."

He glared at them longer, but when neither of them spoke and their companions remained straight-faced, he paled. He turned to look after the coffins, whipped back to face them. "Then that—"

"Sinclairs and Gin," said Laura. "Incidentally, all of them sold to Rex by Juliana."

"I can serve as a witness to that," said Cherry. "I found them as they were escaping that city."

Byron lurched to his feet. "We need to get you all out of here. I'm getting you straight to the chief to figure this out, and there's no way in hell I'm letting MacDanel's supporters get you first."

"Mr. Rhodes!"

Laura looked up at the shout. Annabelle wove through the crowd toward them, notepad held so tight it started to crumple. She stumbled to a stop.

"I—Mr. Rhodes, you have to get them—"

"What's wrong?" said Byron.

Annabelle had to gasp for air before saying, "They know! Kramer and Sinclair's return was leaked!"

"What? To whom?"

"All the papers! Boss said I had to run fast if I wanted to catch them! *Dead Ringer* had the news, too! Said if I didn't run, the Mad Dogs would have them!"

Byron swore. "Did you see anyone else?"

"Sir, it's a miracle they're not already breathing down our necks," said Annabelle. "Some were already outside, waiting for you to come out. I came in to warn you, but they'll think I'm stealing the scoop and come in after me. If nothing else, my photographer—"

Another shout caught Laura's attention. The usual crowd stalled around the main doors as a wave of people entered. The newcomers held notepads and recording devices, cameras borne aloft with flash-bulbs gleaming. They looked ready to descend on a film star.

"It makes me wish Sweepers never became newsworthy," said Annabelle.

"If they're coming from the front, the side exits are our best bet. We'll follow the mourners," said Byron. "We'll avoid the crowd, and avoid pictures from most—"

"No," said Laura. "If *fleeing the scene* makes me automatically guilty, I'm staying right here."

"Can you hear yourself?" Byron snapped.

"It's not a good idea," said Annabelle. "Even if you say everything right, opinions have already been made. You won't win anyone over unless you uproot the problem entirely."

"Agreed." Cherry looked increasingly uneasy as the report-ers closed in. "I'm all for taking stands, but this one seems pretty pointless."

"Isn't this the best way to uproot the problem?" said Laura. "I said I'd get the truth out, and this seems like the easiest way to go about it. This way no one can interrupt me, and they'll have to read through my side of the story."

"And what happens when the *Dead Ringer* gets here?" said Byron. "If the Mad Dogs make a scene—"

"Then I'll tell them they can stay behind me, but I need to make a point that Amicae won't believe if they're the ones who print it."

"And if the Silver Kings show up too?"

"As far as I can tell, I'm the closest thing to balance there is right now."

"You know that, but they don't," said Byron. "These people shoot first and ask later. Worse, if they pick out Mad Dogs in the middle of this mess—"

"I'm staying," Laura said firmly. "You and Cherry take Okane somewhere safe."

"If - - -'re staying, I'm staying," said Okane.

"You're both ridiculous," said Byron, but didn't protest further; the reporters were upon them.

Mateo sped to the front of their group, but he couldn't block the three consecutive camera flashes. Laura winced and squinted at the pressing crowd, the deafening shouts. Now that she faced these people, all she wanted to do was crawl in a hole. She forced her shoulders back, head up, and concentrated. She tried to channel Clae's old coolness, but not just that; Clae had presence but Juliana had poise. She'd emulate them both.

"Please calm yourselves," said Mateo, his arms spread. "These people have been through much tribulation recently, and should have peace. I—Please stop taking pictures, ra!"

"Excuse me," Laura called, hopefully both loud and polite. "Could you all back up a step or two? I'll be happy to answer your questions, but I'll need some breathing room to do so."

Mateo looked back at her, uncertain. "Is this wise?"

"Probably not," she murmured. "I want to give it a try anyway."

He stepped aside. The reporters shuffled. They only gave her an additional inch and a half, but it was something. Laura turned to Annabelle.

"You were the first one in here. You're with the *Sun*, right? What questions did you have?"

Annabelle looked like she'd swallowed a lemon. Laura felt bad for putting her on the spot when they'd switched gears so suddenly—conspirator to journalist—but if she was going to bolster anyone's career with a big scoop, she'd rather it be her. Luckily Annabelle recovered fast.

"Is it true that you attacked Juliana MacDanel on January seventh?"

Ouch. Before Laura could answer, others jumped in.

"Where did you go afterward?"

"Did you intend to kill her?"

"Were the mobs involved, as implied by the resurgence of circles?"

"For what reason did you attack Miss MacDanel?"

"It doesn't matter," said another voice. At once Laura froze and the cameras switched targets. "What's done is done."

Juliana. Byron hadn't exaggerated. She looked like a poor woman in the aftermath of a Rexian raid: pale and sad, a crutch under one arm, and clothes carefully disordered. She was perfectly presented, all the way down to the wearily hopeful expression. A policeman flanked her on either side, but behind them were more people that Laura dreaded. To Juliana's left came the Silver King who'd chased Laura off a bridge. On her right walked Haru and the Mad Dog from the shooting range. The mobsters were aware of each other, but their expressions showed only snide amusement and they held cameras of their own. Willing to stay under cover, then. Hopefully they'd stay that way.

Where Laura focused on the mobsters, no one else did. The reporters clamored at Juliana now. She raised a hand; the talk stopped, and reporters listened intently. Juliana looked at Laura with sickening sadness and said, "I forgive you for what you've done to me."

From the corner of her eye Laura saw Okane's hackles rise. She held out a hand to stall him.

"Thank you," she said, smoothly as she could manage. "But I don't think I'm the one who needs to apologize."

Juliana shook her head. "You never did accept me taking your title. I tried being kind to you two, but if that doesn't change your loyalty, I don't know what could."

Laura first instinct was to rage over *how much* kindness there was in holding people at gunpoint, but reeled that in. She wouldn't be tempted into destroying her image so easily with all these people around.

"But while I can forgive you for myself," said Juliana, "I can't ignore what you could do to any future Sweepers. I'm sorry, Laura, but we can't allow you to remain unchecked. Officers, please arrest her."

The officers didn't look particularly happy about this, but they must've believed the story. They moved toward her. The mobsters moved too. The Mad Dog stepped forward, grinning, hand slipping inside his coat. Haru dropped back, but the Silver King beelined to intercept.

"It's strange," Laura said quickly. "You haven't asked us anything about your brother."

For a moment Juliana's face went blank.

"Lester," she murmured. "Please, insult me all you want, but leave his memory in peace."

"I suppose you've told everyone that he was eaten by an infestation?" said Laura.

Annabelle chimed in: "The story is that you planted it as a distraction, so you could steal the Sweeper magic supply."

Laura scoffed. "And I suppose the Mad Dogs are supposed to have given it to me?"

"Are you implying that the Mad Dogs acted independently?" said another reporter.

"I'm implying that there wasn't an infestation to begin with," said Laura. "Lester didn't die in Amicae and you know it."

Juliana turned to one of the officers and loudly whispered, "I'm so sorry. I knew she spun stories, but I never thought—"

"Why should we damage a building we had all access to?" Okane snapped. "What would even be the point of a distraction?"

"So you're saying you didn't steal the magic," said Annabelle.

"No, but we sure as hell got it back," said Laura. "Which is incidentally where we met Lester."

"So you accuse Lester MacDanel of the theft," said Annabelle.

Juliana covered her face with her hands. "Lester," she moaned. "What kind of terrible situation did he get into? I knew I should've called for help when the Mad Dogs approached him! They backed off then, but with their claws already in one Sweeper—"

"Oh, please," said Laura. "The Mad Dogs didn't order Lester to attack Joan. You all recognize the name, don't you?" Laura looked around at them all. "The woman hand-selected by Puer's head Sweeper for us? The woman who should be where Juliana is now?"

The name indeed struck a bell. Even the mobsters faltered. The Silver King's brow furrowed, and Laura could swear the Mad Dog mouthed, *Told you so,* at his rival.

"Joan had a terrible accident," said Juliana. "For you to trivialize her pain—"

"Oh, no, I think it's very serious." Laura raised her hands, wrists pressed together. "You can arrest me if you'd like. I'd be thrilled to speak with Chief Albright. I can fill her in on both Joan *and* Eliza."

Juliana's fingers twitched. When they drew down, her eyes burned with hate but her tone stayed in the same whimper.

"You can talk to her as long as you want. Joan would tell you, I had nothing to do with her accident, and Eliza . . . My poor friend Eliza's been dead for two years now."

"An infestation ate her, didn't it?" said Laura.

Juliana nodded and dabbed at her eyes, apparently overcome with grief.

"What a handy excuse," Laura seethed. "So, no body to examine? No way to prove foul play in Puer?"

Juliana gasped. "You don't mean to say Lester had a hand in that? I can't believe that. I won't."

"- - - witnessed it!" said Okane.

"I did no such—"

"You wrote the report," said Laura. She had no idea if that was true, but the Juliana of today thrived on paperwork; if only she and Lester had been present at the end of that infestation, and if Lester was anywhere near as torn up then as he was at his confession, the only other witness had to complete it. A perfect opportunity to embellish her accomplishments. "You were there during the infestation. You saw everything. You were the only one who knew Lester shot her. You—"

"Shut up!" Juliana shrieked.

She shook, breath hissing through her teeth. Her calm was shattered, but she could still play it as being distraught. Laura knew better. She'd shown the same jitters right before attacking Okane. The mask was breaking.

"Maybe my brother did wrong, but he's just died! Please let me at least process that before making accusations!"

"That was your first big job, wasn't it?" Laura pressed. "You were so impressive and everyone thought you were so brave, but you didn't do anything. Eliza did all of the work, and you stole credit for it! You couldn't even leave her that!"

"*I* finished off that monster!" said Juliana. "She was long dead by then!"

"So - - - did see her die," said Okane.

"Stay out of this, Rexian!" she spat.

Okane bristled, but he wasn't the one to reply.

"Oh?" the Mad Dog drawled. "That's not a Rexian. His looks and personality are all wrong. Look, he hasn't even got numbers on his face."

"Confirmed," said the Silver King. "He doesn't match any of the Rexians we've seen in the past few years."

Only now did the officers and reporters notice them; the discomfort surrounding this shouting match descended straight into anxiety, but no one dared leave.

"Juliana would know a Rexian when she saw one," said Okane, glaring at her. "She's the one who made deals with them to sell all our magic."

"That's a lie," said Juliana.

"Then the number-faced man staying at your apartment since Underyear, he was just a coincidence?" said the Mad Dog.

Juliana rounded on him. "You're from that trashy *Dead Ringer,* aren't you? All you publish are lies and bias!"

The Mad Dog laughed in her face.

"Miss MacDanel," one of the police offers said urgently. "If you could please—"

She shrugged off his hand and leaned closer to the Mad Dog, snarling, "I'm not afraid of you or your mobs! All you exist to do is scare people for your own benefit, and I'm not afraid of you!"

"God, is she trying to get shot?" Byron grumbled, still eyeing the side doors.

"You're not even a good Sweeper!" said Laura. Luckily this redirected Juliana's wrath; more bloodshed hopefully averted. "All those times you came out on top, you had Lester sabotage everyone else! You've never actually done any of this yourself!"

"You have no idea what you're talking about," said Juliana. "How long have you been a Sweeper? A year?"

"And I'm still better than you," said Laura. "You're not interested in real leadership or improving your work. You just want your name in the headlines, and you won't let anyone take your glory. If a yearling Sweeper like me can upstage you, what happens to any apprentices of yours? Will you keep them weak so they fall to infestations?"

"My apprentices will thrive, because they won't be egomaniacal copies of Clae Sinclair!" Juliana retorted.

"When will it end, Juliana? How many Sweepers have to die to feed your ego? Lester, Eliza—"

"*Eliza, Eliza,*" Juliana spat. "You never knew her! You don't even know anything about who she was, let alone how she died. What makes you think you have any right to argue with her name?"

Because Laura's name could easily have been part of Lester's confession. It could've been Laura. It could've been Okane. Eliza was only the beginning.

Laura sucked in a steadying breath and said, "You didn't kill Eliza, but you covered it up. I can't trust someone like you with Amicae's future. This city is everything to me, and I won't let you destroy it for nothing but your own ego."

For a moment there was silence; then Juliana threw her head back. Her laughter echoed around them, magnified by the lack of everything else. Even outside their uncomfortable reporter bubble, the depot workers and travelers stopped moving, stopped talking, to observe the uproar. Travelers and reporters exchanged wary looks.

"I'm sorry," Juliana giggled at last, wiping tears from her eyes. The mask had returned, impeccable. "I shouldn't have laughed so hard. It's all been getting to me, what with the stress and the injury. I started thinking about this seriously, when it shouldn't be taken as such."

"Excuse me?" said Laura.

"Let's think of this in terms of fact, rather than hearsay," said Juliana. "What can be observed and proven is this: Amicae's Council was pleased with my interview and offered me the position of head Sweeper. I brought my brother with me as a Sweeper. I tried to lead you in Puer's training, but you didn't believe in it, and you resented being fired from the position I took. On the same day Amicae's magic was stolen, you left me bleeding in the road and ran instead of obeying the officers present. You left Amicae with no explanation. Lester disappeared even before you did. You've returned with an elaborate story, but there's no proof to back any of it up. How are we to know if you really spoke to Lester? How are we to know if anything he supposedly said is true? I'll give you credit for your acting, but that's the only thing we can weigh. The rest is hot air."

Cherry's face went red; she could serve as a witness, but all she really had to go on was Laura's word, and if Amicae discounted Laura's story, Cherry's perspective wouldn't hold water. Laura needed to target Juliana herself. She had to uproot the problem at its source.

Laura closed her eyes. "So, Eliza was eaten by an infestation?"

"Yes," said Juliana.

"And Lester was eaten?"

"He must've been."

Laura sighed and opened her eyes. "I can't give you Lester's body, but I can tell you where Eliza's is."

Juliana remained unfazed. "Laura, don't you remember? What's eaten by infestations can never be recovered."

"Precisely."

A pause, and realization flooded over Juliana's face: white fear, red anger, expression twisting as she hit the tipping point.

"Puer," Laura said loudly. "6649 West Kallas—"

"Shut your mouth!" Juliana screeched.

"Third Quarter—"

"You little—"

Juliana lunged. The nearest police officer wasn't prepared, so she yanked his gun from its holster easily. For one heart-stopping moment

Laura looked down the barrel, Juliana snarling at the other end, flash-bulbs popping on either side. Then, miraculously, it changed course. The gun went up. A bullet hit one of the hanging clocks, shattering its glass face. The Silver King had slid in and knocked her arm up. Another sharp movement and the gun clattered to the tile. The Silver King hooked one leg under Juliana's, twisted the arm still in her grip, and sent her crashing down. She knelt over Juliana, flicking out her knife and raising it.

"Stop." Haru caught the Silver King's arm.

She glared at him. "I'd have thought the Mad Dogs wanted this ending."

"Balance can't be kept if we don't understand what affects it," said Haru.

The Silver King studied him before saying, "True enough." She tucked the blade away and sent the officer a dirty look. "Take care of this woman, or we'll do it for you."

She left. The crowd parted for her immediately.

"Mobster filth," said Juliana, still trembling on the ground.

"I really don't think I'm qualified for any of this," said the still-armed policeman, while his coworker gingerly picked up the fallen gun. "We're just here to check vendor licenses, not this."

"Well, it's your problem now," said Haru. "Considering there are, say, fifty witnesses to an attempted shooting here, I'd say an arrest is in order."

When the officers still hesitated, Byron prompted, "Rights of the accused."

This startled them into action. One knelt down, pulling out hand-cuffs and reciting the rights. Juliana didn't take this well. She clawed at him, eyes wild.

"I didn't kill her! Lester killed her! Lester did all of it!"

"Please hold still, miss!" said the second officer, moving in to help. "This behavior isn't very dignified!"

Juliana didn't give a rat's ass about dignity now. She lunged again. The officers hurried to cover their belts, but she'd aimed at Laura.

Cherry and Mateo threw themselves in front of Laura, but a hasty grab at cuffed hands stopped her from reaching them.

"You think you've got the best of me?" Juliana raged; Laura felt flecks of spit land on her face and recoiled. "You're the one who's finished! I'll run you out of this city, you and your whiny sidekick! This isn't over!"

"Please take her away before she makes things worse for herself," said Byron.

The officers each fit an arm under one of Juliana's.

"This is treason!" Juliana howled as they turned her toward the nearest police box. "You can't arrest your head Sweeper!"

In the wake of this, no one seemed to know what to do. Juliana's breakdown was probably newsworthy, but it meant destroying the media darling they'd built up. The reporters came to see Laura's ruin; some were obviously upset by the twist, and Laura couldn't blame them.

Byron stepped forward, catching everyone's attention with a commanding tone. "My clients will decline any further questions. This has already been a rough morning, and we'd prefer that the chief of police be the first to hear a full report. Thank you for your understanding."

Laura forced herself to relax. Only now did she realize Okane's tight grip on her shoulder.

"Are you okay?" she asked.

"I should be asking - - - that," he said. "I . . . That scared me a little. I'm glad that woman acted in time."

"I suppose it helped that Juliana didn't have a knife this time," said Laura. "I don't mean that as a joke. That scared me too. Tremendously."

"Do - - - think that's enough to get her out of Amicae?" said Okane. "Do we need to take it up with the Council, too?"

"I think a telegram to the Puer Sweepers will do the trick," said Laura. "They can invoke Terulian Law, maybe even get Coronae involved. They'll take her away. In the meantime, if she's in jail, she can't come after us."

Honestly, no. On paper Juliana was the only remaining Sweeper in Amicae, and Clae had always implied that head Sweepers were beyond the usual law enforcement. Then again, Clae hadn't attempted to shoot someone in the middle of the depot. Besides, if the Council put so much effort into her image they might insist on keeping her. She could be released in a matter of hours, could easily return to the shop and Okane's home. Even if he managed to figure out the new lock, he wouldn't be safe there.

"You should stay with me for the time being," said Laura. "I can only offer you a couch, but it's a step up from hiding in Rexian barracks."

From his rueful smile, she knew his thoughts had followed the same line. "I'd appreciate that."

"I assume you don't have a place to stay, either," said Mateo, looking at Cherry. "The Ranger district seems to be emptied. I can provide lodging at the church. The dead will be brought there anyway."

"That doesn't sound like a bad idea," said Cherry. "But damn, you two, I realized your boss was crazy, but I didn't understand to what extent! She looked ready to rip out your throat!"

"Hopefully we won't have to deal with her for long," said Laura.

"Not if the chief has her way in this case," said Byron.

They made their slow way out of the depot and toward the cable cars. Cherry and Mateo drew Okane into a conversation, but Laura stood closer to Byron as they waited for the cab to arrive. Ever since talking to Lester in Rex, she'd been considering an idea. It came together on the train ride back, but she wanted to go over it with someone first. Byron had picked up on everything she had, when it came to the MacDanels and Sweepers. Maybe he had insight on this, too.

"You have a suspect in the Falling Infestation, don't you?" she said. "Not Sullivan, of course, but it's not Rex, either."

Byron grinned. "It sounds like you have a suspect, too."

"The kingshound gave it away," said Laura. "It may be associated with Rex, but more than that, it's a *mad dog.* Just another version of the MARU circle."

"Perceptive," said Byron.

"What I don't understand is why," said Laura. "They took down their own infestation? Is that what it is? If their boss is an ex-Sinclair, he'd know too well what kind of danger that brings."

"As much as it galls me to say it, there may be a good reason why the Silver Kings are on a rampage," said Byron.

"The balance," Laura said flatly.

"They do go on about that." Byron breathed out a cloud of smoke. "They're ruthless about anything they deem a threat to survival, usually to themselves but also for the city at large. You know what sparked unification and backlash at the MARU? The Council had an idiot plan to steamroll the native districts in the Fifth and Fourth Quarters. A 'relocation' plan. Anyone with a brain knew it was a bullshit story meant to cover a fucking genocide. It didn't reach the papers, but it sure as hell reached the mobs. I cheered when Silver Kings assassinated the councilman responsible, but I can't forgive what they did to me and to bystanders."

"So they think Mad Dogs are a threat in the same way?" said Laura.

"Maybe. Maybe it's all egos. I've been on the edge of the game so long, I can't say."

"You said you were an expert," said Laura. "Were you in the mobs at some point?"

"MARU."

"Oh." She looked out over the tracks again. "Have you got any tips on staying out of this mess?"

"If they want to involve you, it's hard to stay out. Keep insisting on neutrality. Silver Kings at least will respect that, and they'll be determined to keep you that way."

"They haven't helped me much at this point," she grumbled.

Byron chuckled. "Maybe today turns a new page. They might have new faith in you now."

Laura shook her head. "But you can't think of a reason for the Mad Dogs to set up that infestation? Not any hint from your MARU days?"

"That's the problem. The leadership's changed," said Byron. He breathed out again and studied the smoke as if it were the most interesting thing in the world. "Mad Dogs has always been an oddity, but when the new boss came in, he gave them focus. They're easily the most Sweeper-oriented mob here, so they know very well what they were doing and how to defend against it. They weren't acting on a whim, and there's no way something so elaborate could be a mistake."

"You said before that maybe they meant to contain it," Laura recalled.

"I think that's the case," he agreed. "Why? Who can tell? But it must've been clear to them."

22

APPROACHING DARKNESS

"Okay." Morgan shuffled around the kitchen, sifting through items on the counter and purse swinging with the motion. "I'll be gone until at least four. I'll pick up Cheryl from school, so you don't have to worry about that."

"Because I was so worried," Laura grumbled, pouring herself another cup of tea. Okane smiled warily, unsure if this was a joke, while Morgan ignored her.

"Without office hours you have a whole day ahead of you. Heaven forbid, I wonder if you're planning to do me *favors*."

She'd taken Laura's return surprisingly well, considering she'd been gone a week and a half with no warning. It helped that Laura arrived with a full escort: priest, Ranger, investigator, and multiple policemen. The police and Byron assured her that she'd talked with Albright and the police planned immediate action in regard to Juliana; Cherry shared that Laura had been under her wing most of this time and therefore safe in the wilds; and Mateo offered the softer reassurance of *everything will be just fine*. Cheryl had gained bragging rights, because none of her classmates had Rangers over for dinner, did they? Morgan still remembered Okane as "that nice boy who doesn't know how to celebrate Underyear," so it didn't take much convincing to let him stay the night. He'd spent the morning following her around the kitchen and handing her ingredients; Morgan had jokingly asked if he wanted a job at the catering office.

"There's not much to do here otherwise," Morgan said now, plucking up a notebook to stow in her bag. "I think Charlie will be back from school around noon, though, so I'd suggest going out. That boy's become such a gossip! He was talking about those articles from the papers and implying things about you to all the neighbors. Well! I caught him in the act and gave him a piece of my mind."

Laura sucked in a horrified, excited breath. "Oh, no. You didn't!"

"I did!" Morgan brandished her keys like a weapon. "And he won't forget it anytime soon. He's out of my good books permanently. I'll miss having someone to clean out the plumbing, but apparently there wasn't much else to lose. Although, one of those policemen yesterday was young and handsome. Maybe today you should drop by and see if he's available?"

Laura forced a grimace. "*Morgan.*"

"I had to try! Oh, and Okane, you'll be with us for dinner again tonight, right? How do you feel about chicken à la king?"

"Chick—What?"

"It's good," Laura chuckled.

"Then I'm sure I'd like it."

"Wonderful! I'll make that, then. Maybe I can convince my boss to let me host another tasting party," said Morgan, rubbing her hands together. "That's twice in three months, but I'd love your input. We're always working on next season's cookbooks. I'll let you know about it later!"

Once she'd left, Okane leaned forward. "I like - - -r aunt."

"So do I," said Laura, unable to quash her smile anymore. "I was worried for a while that she'd never stop pushing Charlie on me, but she keeps surprising me. We really should leave before he comes back, though. I'd rather jump off the First Quarter wall than talk to him."

"Well, I do have an idea of where to go."

Laura's eyes narrowed. "You say that as if it's something to hide."

"Maybe? I'm not entirely sure it's legal." He laced his fingers together and took a deep breath. "I want to check the sunk Pits."

It took a moment for Laura to remember what he meant. When she did, she leaned back in her chair, already tired. "Juliana was really interested in them. She wanted to reallocate the Gin there into our kin production, didn't she?"

"Exactly. Doing that would leave the Pit itself vulnerable to infestations." He frowned. "Not just vulnerable, but perfect. It could become a breeding ground the likes of which we've never seen."

No one would agree to help her with that, Laura wanted to argue, but she couldn't know for sure. Basil's letter had implied the Council approved many things they hadn't understood.

"We could ask the Council for a list of approved items," she said, tapping her fingers on the tabletop. "No, that wouldn't work. Even if they agreed to get it to us, it would take forever to issue the list; it would be too late to do anything by then. I don't think they'd agree to give us anything in the first place. We're not on their payroll anymore. Technically we have no right to the information."

"The sunk Pits are my property," said Okane. "I have every right to that information. I'll bring the estate administrator into this if I have to."

"It would still take a ridiculously long time to get the information. Do you know where to find those Pits?"

"They're located in spurs along the outer Quarter walls," he replied. "They'll be very distinctive locations, and I'm told those areas of the mines have good signage. If we can get down there, it'll be easy to track them down."

"We can get down there," said Laura, standing. "We may not be official anymore, but the Council hasn't revoked our IDs yet. We have enough stars on those to get anywhere we need to go in Amicae."

"So long as the person checking IDs doesn't know about our situation," said Okane, but he stood too.

"Stars are stars," said Laura. "Let's do this."

—∞—

The door to the interior yawned wide open, ready to admit any workers. They slipped in with no trouble. The usual din of the interior had dimmed somewhat. In the wake of the Falling Infestation many of the machines and factories had been trashed. While some were fixed up quickly, others remained ruined. Some damaged equipment had been removed entirely—one of the elevator shafts was conspicuously blocked off—and scaffolds for repairmen had been erected along walls and walkways. Nevertheless, spirits remained undaunted and production went on, evident by the smoke, lights, and noise. They made a beeline for one of the elevators and waited by a crowd of miners.

"Excuse me." Laura approached one and waved for his attention. "Which level are you going to?"

"Fifth," the man replied.

Laura glanced back at Okane. "Where's our destination?"

"Seventh level," he replied.

The man frowned at one, then the other. "Seventh? That's—Hang on, have I seen you before? Aren't you Sweepers? Don't you usually go up?"

"We have reason to believe that some of our equipment down there could be damaged," said Laura. "I'd like to check its status, and arrange for repairs if necessary."

"Are you even allowed to go down?" said the man, suspicious.

"We can't waste time when it comes to infestations," said Laura. "We have the credentials if you need them. Want to see our IDs?"

"No, no, that's fine. Just let me talk to the operator."

The man hurried away, clearly happy to escape them. They followed him to the operator. Laura didn't catch most of the conversation, but the operator squinted up at her.

"Don't worry," he said. "I'll make sure you get down there. Just get on the lift with the rest of them."

As the elevator clattered up and open, the crowd moved forward and the pair moved with them. They stood close to the grilles as it rattled closed again.

"Going to the fifth level," announced the operator, dull and tired.

"Wait! Stop that elevator!"

The operator jolted to full awareness and looked around. The miners stood on tiptoe to squint at the disturbance. Okane made a choking noise.

"Is that Cherry?"

Cherry ran across one of the walkways, with Mateo dashing behind her.

"Hold it! You're not getting away without giving me a goddamn answer, you absolute idiot! Stop that elevator!"

"This one?" the operator called, gesturing at the elevator.

"No, the other one! You with the bandana, stop the—Augh!"

She gestured violently at the next mine shaft, where the elevator had already begun its descent.

The operator shook his head, obviously not willing to question it. He hit the button and the floor jerked beneath Laura's feet. She pressed harder against the grille.

"Cherry?" she called. "Cherry, what's going on?"

Mateo turned to her first, abnormally pale and holding some kind of shroud. "Risen!" he yelped. "Ra—risen! He's walking! It's impossible, but he's walking!"

"Be careful!" Cherry shouted. "Something's down there! I don't know what the hell it is, but it's not good!"

"What do you mean?" said Laura.

"I said, it's not—"

A nearby pipe shot out a burst of hissing steam. The sound covered up Cherry's voice. The Ranger cupped hands around her mouth and shouted, but Laura couldn't make out any words over the noise.

"Not good? What kind of 'not good' are they talking about? Infestations?" she whispered.

"Cherry can't sense them," said Okane. "I don't know what else she could mean, though."

Cherry couldn't sense infestations, but she could spot people. Bad people in the mines? The Rexian Sweepers had fled the city without looking back, and Juliana had no ready sidekicks. That only left the mobs. If the Mad Dogs had planted the Falling Infestation for some convoluted reason, would they set up a secondary infestation to push this hidden agenda? Without knowing their goal Laura couldn't predict their moves, but she knew one thing for sure: if they did plan another catastrophe, she'd stop it before it grew. She'd keep it from eating anyone.

"Keep an eye out in the tunnels," she said. "This smells like dog."

The elevator took them down into the dark. They went for long stretches of blackness, only kept from blindness by a single bulb in the elevator ceiling and the glimpses of light as they passed level after lit level. When they reached the fifth, the grilles opened to expel the passengers. Laura and Okane stood aside as miners flooded out. Once the last man left, the grilles closed and they rattled down again. The farther they went, the sharper the chill in the air.

The grilles opened again to the seventh level and they stepped out. Laura wasn't sure what she'd expected to see in a mine, but a completely wood-paneled space hadn't occurred to her at all. Thick wooden beams supported both the roof and a wooden ceiling, and it seemed the builders had been determined to block out any hint of rocky wall with the same wood slats. Electrical cords looped overhead, traveling out of sight in most cases while a thicker cable connected lights in a line along the ceiling. The floor was so dark it looked black, but the shine of metal tracks glinted through the grime. These tracks forked off, a set for each of the four branching paths.

Directly in front of them, a map hung nailed to the wall. The circle patterns could easily be interpreted as the city's walls, but the map sprawled far beyond these, and Laura couldn't make out what all the color-coding meant. Okane seemed to understand it perfectly, because he stepped up to it and ran a finger over the Third Quarter line.

"As I understand, no one actually mines in the seventh level anymore," he said. His quiet voice echoed ever so slightly. "The real valuable stuff is deeper down or out, and they didn't want to disturb the Gin."

"Miners have gotten superstitious about Silverstones," said Laura. "They're scared of getting close to begin with."

"The closest one is . . ." His finger followed the line, from the red dot of their location to a black "X" chamber. "Here. We'll reach it if we go left."

They took the left path, walking in the middle of the tracks. Laura hoped no coal car would come to mow them down, but the farther they went, the less she feared. Despite the lights, there was no movement, no sound apart from their own. The only muffled noise she could detect came from below. They were alone in the cold.

"What are we looking for, exactly?" she asked after a while.

"The Pits are in alcoves along the main circuit, following the walls."

"Did I see more of those marks on other Quarter lines? We might have to go deeper to reach some."

"There were more circuits originally. The outermost Pits were in the Third Quarter, so we should be on track."

"We must've had a hell of a lot of Pits."

"This was the Sweeper city, wasn't it?"

"Point taken."

"There were originally fifteen Pits in Amicae," Okane explained. "The three in the First Quarter haven't been touched, but others were sunk in smaller sets over the years. There were three more in the Second Quarter, and nine in the Third. I'm glad they're not all active. We'd need a huge amount of Sweepers to maintain them."

"At one point we had them. I wonder what those first Sinclairs would think if they could see the state of the Sweepers now: only one Sweeper, and she's a murderous backstabber."

"I think they might cry."

"It makes *me* want to cry."

"I guess that man in Rex was right," Okane sighed. "The weakest don't need much to undo them."

Laura snorted. "We aren't weak. Big operations like Puer couldn't handle what we managed with just two or three of us, even Joseph Blair admitted it. If we had the people, we'd be amazing."

"A moot point when there's no people."

"Maybe we should make that our job. Recruiting more people. Maybe even start up a separate, independent Sweeper business!

You have all the equipment, so it's not too far-fetched. The Council wouldn't have any say if we're a business apart from them. But then we'd have to renegotiate all the old agreements without their help. That would take some figuring out. We'd have to recruit anyway."

"If Clae couldn't recruit, what makes you think we can?"

"Clae didn't have our flexibility," she pointed out. "No one's going to join a department they don't believe exists, and with the wall policy gone, we don't have that issue. We have notoriety. We can attract all the daredevils in the city if we play our cards right."

Okane smiled at first, but the mirth slid quickly from his face. He stopped short of the corner, his eyes down, pondering. Laura stood next to him, suddenly concerned.

"Hey, we don't have to take the daredevils. We can vet people as they come in. I'm sure we'll find someone we'll get along with."

"Can - - -, um—" He raised one finger, brow furrowing.

Laura went quiet. The mine's silence weighed heavily on her, but Okane tilted his head just slightly, as if straining to hear something. She stepped closer and whispered, "What are you hearing?"

"I don't think we're alone down here."

Laura frowned, fighting the urge to peer around the corner. "Is it a miner?"

"No. Whoever it is, they're broadcasting their intentions. They feel malevolent. They feel like—" He sucked in a breath and gave her a horrified look. "This is bad. It's an enemy."

If he was that certain, Laura wouldn't question it.

They slinked close to the wall and ducked down. Okane pulled a spare kin gun from his belt, and Laura unearthed one of her few Eggs. She held her breath, straining her ears. Footsteps came from the next tunnel, slow and quiet. If she hadn't been waiting for it she never would've noticed even in the silence of the mine. Whoever it was moved at a snail's pace. Surely a miner would stride through as if he owned the place? As the quiet stretched out, this person gained speed, closer and closer. *Does he think we're gone?* Laura wondered. Soon the slight crunch of dirt came from barely two feet away, and then stopped entirely. Laura gritted her teeth, grip tightening.

A face appeared. The stranger barely had time to peer around the corner before Laura lunged. She smashed the butt of her hand into the other's nose, causing him to reel backward. Her hand stung but she ignored it, launching forward to overbalance him entirely; he hit the floor with a thud. Okane leapt out after her, kicking the stranger's hand and causing the gun there to skitter out of his grip. The stranger thrashed, trying to regain his feet, but they pinned him, and Okane jabbed the gun into his temple.

"Stop moving!" he ordered.

The stranger stilled. He glared up at them with bright blue eyes, blood streaming from his nose. Despite the grime on his face, the number tattoo remained bold and legible. He bared his teeth in a grin. The blood bubbled as he gave a snort of laughter.

"Hello, *paragon*."

23

JUGGERNAUT

The blood drained from Okane's face.

"Were - - - looking for me?" he whispered.

"Don't flatter - - -rself," the Sweeper sneered. "Filth won't be needed when Rex finishes its march. We're already on the brink of victory."

"This is what you call victory, huh? Crawling around underground like a worm?" Laura gripped his arm tighter and twisted, just enough for his expression to twitch in pain. "Rex was marching south. What are you doing here?"

"Nothing a weak mind could comprehend."

"So you don't even know what you're doing?"

"A pawn doesn't need to question the king."

"Where are your handlers?" Laura demanded. *In my experience they move in odd numbers, typically multiples of three.* Two more Sweepers had to be lurking somewhere nearby.

"The voices are with the body."

"Where's the 'body' then? How many Sweepers did you bring?"

The Sweeper laughed again. "Weaklings have no room in Rex's glorious future. Amicae will burn."

That wasn't a number, but it gave a good idea: enough Sweepers to attack the city and expect victory. Had the entire march turned around?

"Keep hold of him," she hissed, jumping up.

"Where are - - - going?"

"There are telephones by the elevators. We have to warn someone."

"Ha! It won't make a difference."

Laura scoffed as she looked around, judging the fastest route to take. "Oh yeah? Why's that?"

"Because they're already here."

Okane barely had time to look up and dive out of the way. A bullet hit the ground where he'd been, sending up a puff of dirt. The shot echoed around the barricaded walls, followed by a rain of bullets. Laura and Okane tumbled around the corner again.

"Shit! Were those more Sweepers?" Laura winced as a chunk of wood blasted free of the wall.

"A whole pack of them, from one of the other passages. This one must've been a scout," Okane wheezed, pulling back the safety on the gun.

Said scout hauled himself up, but before he could get far a bullet smashed into his skull. Laura jolted back at the spatter of blood.

"Whatever information you got out of him, it'll do you no good," someone called. The "you" remained prominent in his speech. It must be a handler. "Come out where we can see you. Give up and we won't hurt you."

After they willingly killed one of their own?

"Not a chance in hell!" Laura yelled.

The handler obviously hadn't expected otherwise, but he sounded amused as he replied, "If you insist on impeding us, I'm afraid there will be consequences."

"Bring it on, ugly!"

"Laura!" Okane hissed. "We have one kin gun, an Egg, and maybe three Bijou. We are *not* equipped to deal with this!"

"All we have to do is make a big enough commotion," said Laura.

"In a mine? Who'll hear us?"

"Miners, obviously!"

Okane swore and raised the gun. During their bickering a Sweeper had snuck up on them. He rounded the corner with a glowing blade. Laura jumped aside while Okane reeled back. The blade collided with the wall and stuck deep in the wood as two more Sweepers rounded the bend. The kin gun fired, lodging two rounds in the first man's abdomen before the bullets burst with a sizzling yellow light and the smell of burning flesh. More blood splattered; the Sweeper staggered back with a yowl, bowling into more reinforcements. A woman sidestepped him, swiping with her own blade. A hazy reddish afterglow arced in its path. Okane jerked away, tried to aim the gun again, but she moved too fast, closing in and forcing him to retreat.

Laura tried to get in under her swing, but hadn't so much as twitched before the next Sweeper charged. This one carried no blade, but her left arm was encased in a bulky gauntlet, not unlike the ones Laura had glimpsed in the armory. That alone made her retreat. The Sweeper roared loud enough to make her hair stand on end. Light flared up the gauntlet's sides and knuckles, twisting pictographs of blazing red that blurred as it hit the ground. Her fist dug into the earth up to her wrist. Shots of light branched into the surrounding ground before dirt erupted into the air with a bang.

Laura stepped back from the resulting cloud, narrowing her eyes against the grit. A blur of red was her only warning before the Sweeper bulled out of the dust, swinging her arm again. Laura ducked. The gauntlet whistled overhead. Laura could feel heat radiating from it, felt the resulting breeze tug at her hair. Gritting her teeth, she lunged and tackled the other woman at the stomach. The Sweeper was sturdier than Laura expected. She staggered only two steps before snarling and swatting. It wasn't even a good hit, but Laura screeched in pain. The smell of burning was almost overwhelming. She let go before a heavier blow could come. The Sweeper followed her movement, one strong step and another swing of the glove creating another crater in the floor. Laura rolled out of reach and back to her feet.

Debris bounced off her coat as she dug into her bag. The Sweeper was incoming again. She grabbed the first thing her fingers touched and brought it up as she moved to block. *Basic,* Clae had told her once, walking her through the motions as if it was obvious that someone would one day go after her in a fistfight. *Step to the outside. Deflect. Once they're off balance and open, strike.* Hand one knocked the punch aside so the crackling fingers missed her entirely, driven still farther with a strike of her right forearm. But as she blocked, she jammed the item—Bijou, she realized belatedly—into one of the glowing grooves by the elbow. This was a bad idea. She knew it the moment she saw the Bijou changing color, from gold to something bronzy.

"Oh, hell," she muttered, and fled.

The Sweeper moved to follow, but the Bijou activated and she went no farther. The bead went off with such a shrill noise the entire tunnel shook. Sparks burst into existence, shooting out at high speed to scorch anything close. One caught the Sweeper full in the face while others blackened the walls and snapped at incoming reinforcements. The grooves of the gauntlet went white hot, metal shuddering about it before the whole thing exploded. The tunnel lit up like a firework. The blast shook everything, snapping and burning wood, scorching dirt, a blinding cacophony that drowned out any sight or sound of the Rexians.

Laura retreated further toward the elevators, looking around wildly. Okane hugged the wall to her left; the flashing light illuminated his torn coat. He took another Bijou from his bag and threw it into the blaze before them. Another crack and this activated too, lending the haze a yellowish luster and spewing sparks to such an extent the light cables on the ceiling snapped. The bulbs closest to the fray went out, while the others rattled so hard some swung loose from their holders. The temperature fluctuated with the sudden rush of heat, carrying with it dirt, splinters, and debris.

"Somebody had to have heard that," said Laura, muffled now as she pulled her bandana up. "Let's start retreating."

"How far?" Okane walked sideways, keeping his back to the wall and watchful eyes on the clearing smoke.

"Far enough for help to reach us. Not far enough that these goons can get to the elevators."

"Something tells me that's a very fine line."

Even before the cloud settled, Rexians came running out. The residual energy caught a few, who collapsed as kin zapped by their legs, but they made no sound of distress and ten more trampled over them with no remorse.

The closest Sweeper jerked back as if wrenched by the shoulder. *Ka-clack*, came a sound from up the tunnel. Had another Rexian circled from behind? Laura whipped around. Another figure advanced toward them, rifle in his hands. His pale eyes narrowed and he pulled the trigger again; this time the crack of the bullet echoed loudly, and the Sweeper fell entirely. Laura's heart beat in her throat. Holy shit. That couldn't be—

"Grim?" she spluttered.

"Laura!"

At Okane's shout she ducked. Good thing too, because the Rexians hadn't reacted at all to the new addition beyond spreading their attack. A blade clanged into the wall where she'd been. She pulled an Egg from her bag, clacked it, and swung. It rolled into the Rexians' midst before blowing. Few had bothered getting out of the way—Rex's Eggs mustn't burn half as harsh, but this one sizzled angrily. The blast engulfed three Sweepers and seared any close to it, crackling up toward the ceiling. Screams echoed off the walls. A few fell flailing, skin wrecked and peeling off the bone. Laura fought to keep down her breakfast, hands shaking as she felt for another Egg.

Better them than me, she thought desperately, willing it to be true. *Them before me!*

A Sweeper lifted a gun at her, only for a rifle blast to catch him in the side; his bullet hit the lightbulb instead. The bulb died at once, as did all the others branching down their tunnel. Wires sparked, casting them all in sharp relief. Grim was almost upon them now. Another gun surfaced among the Rexians. Two sharp cracks and he staggered, but he didn't fall. The bullets hit with a screech, more like metal on metal than any flesh sound. Grim kept on as if uninjured, raised the rifle again. One, two more Sweepers went down. At last the Rexians paused. They milled, some hesitating while others charged into their backs. The handler swore loudly over the din.

"Around the bend," Grim barked.

Laura and Okane ducked around the next corner and he backed in after them.

"What are you doing down here?" he asked.

"Us? What are we—" Laura sputtered. "You died! You fell in the river and—I saw you in a coffin! You were dead! Oh my god, no wonder Cherry and Mateo were—That was a fucking burial shroud! How are you even down here?"

Grim pulled back on the rifle's bolt so the spent shell popped out, and twisted the lever back down. He patted at his coat, found nothing, and frowned. "That's not important right now."

"Of course it's important! Did you fake being dead this whole time?"

"No, and that's not relevant to this situation."

They didn't have any further time to argue. He gripped the gun tight and swung it like a bat. It collided with a Rexian's nose as she rounded the corner. The victim dropped her blade and fell but more pressed in, streaming around their fallen comrade. Okane shot two more but they barely slowed before Grim swiped at them with the bent rifle. The lights flickered before cutting out here too. All that could be seen clearly was the glow of kin weapons, the flash of eyes reflecting it like a cat's. Laura groped at the walls, narrowly avoiding the chaos. The dropped blade still gave off a faint glow, easy to pinpoint and easy to grab. It felt awkward in her hand, but this weapon wouldn't run out the same way her Eggs did. Even if she couldn't fight with any skill, it could at least force them to keep a distance.

A scream echoed off the walls and her hair stood on end.

"Okane?" she yelled.

The only answer was another cry and a thud, metal clanking hard against the track. Three gunshots went off in succession, the kin light just barely illuminating a Rexian on the ground with Okane under her. The Rexian's lip curled, her arm lifting in another glowing gauntlet as the gun clattered uselessly, bullets spent.

"Get off of him!" Laura snarled.

She planted a foot on the Sweeper's side and shoved. The Sweeper twisted, bloodied gauntlet flashing, but Laura swiped with the blade this time and forced her off balance. This was enough for Okane to get his legs up and kick her away. He rolled out, scrambled up behind Laura. She could hear him cursing, weirdly high-pitched, and the clatter of dropped equipment.

"Are you okay?" she demanded, stepping back and forcing him with her; his shoulder bumped into her back, giving away the tremors racking his body.

"Bloody," he replied, high-pitched. "Can't see out one eye but I think it's just blood. I'll—I'll be okay."

Laura bared her teeth, put all her strength into deflecting another blade. Really, that was a lucky swing—the Sweeper stumbled with the momentum.

"Bijou! Do you have any handy?"

"Dropped 'em."

She rapped her amulet. Warmth flared in her boots and she brought a foot down on the nearest Bijou. She caught it just enough to light the Bijou and send it screaming up the tunnel. It hit another on the way, squalling and spouting sparks to light the walls again. Grim hurried out of the way, but the Rexians packed the tunnels too tightly. Another wail started up. Laura turned, looking for more Bijou, and caught sight of Okane's face again. The right side was mottled, scratched and burned and slick with blood—only one eye remained visible, narrowed against the pain. He dug through his bag, blinking through more blood as he unearthed a wire. He glanced up at Laura before giving a jolt. The wire crackled in his hands and he threw it past her, right into the face of another Rexian. The man cried out. The wire fell. Laura wasted no time in kicking it toward the rest of the fallen items, then grabbed Okane by the sleeve and ran as it began to spark.

She didn't know how many Bijou he'd dropped. Light seared through the tunnel in a rattle of liquid flame. Wooden panels snapped and flew; they had to dodge down another passage to keep from being hit by one. Grim flung himself after them and pressed against the wall, eyes wide. *Maybe three Bijou* was a definite understatement.

"Did you have to light that so close to us?"

"I didn't have much choice," Laura snapped.

Something else glinted in the main tunnel, coming from the opposite side from the Rexians.

"Oh, great, we've got company. I swear, if that's another group of Rexians . . ." Laura dug through her pockets, but nothing there seemed like a viable solution. "Do you think we can break the elevator? Keep them from getting into the city proper." This group had many times the number of that tiny invasion force of last year, and the one man had both evaded police and gained a foothold through a corrupt citizen. If a Sweeper could be tempted by Rex, she had no doubt others could be, too. If all the Rexians in this tunnel made it into Amicae, the consequences could be dire. "The miners must have radioed in by now, so that could buy enough time for help to come."

"Time where intruders could destroy your very foundations," said Grim. "It doesn't matter so much now. That's the first wave."

"The first wave of what?"

Laura could finally see that the glinting came from more guns. The people running toward them weren't Rexians, but they wore no uniforms. They looked like—

"Rangers?" Laura gasped.

Cherry ran near the front; she gestured angrily for Laura's group to back into a side passage, and once that was done, she screamed, "Give them hell!"

The Rangers aimed, and the crack of gunfire echoed all around them.

Cherry ducked into the side passage to look them over. "What's your status?"

"Injured," said Laura, gesturing at Okane. "You have no idea how happy we are to see you, but—How did you even get down here? I thought Rangers weren't allowed in the city."

"We got in the same way as your uninvited guests," said Cherry. "There are vents to the mines further out in the agricultural grounds.

The Rangers were all hanging out there to see if Amicae would let up on the ban, and radioed in when they saw suspicious activity. Since I'd been in contact with them yesterday, they went straight to me. And when I talked about Rex invaders in front of the coffin, *someone* finally got interested enough to wake up." She punched Grim's shoulder. "You owe me, you asshole."

"I owe you for not dying?" he said dryly.

"Yes," she spat. She turned back to Laura. "As far as I can tell, the Rexians are pissed because you took the reason for their big crusade. Most of their forces are moving south anyway, but this is a renegade unit sent for recovery."

"- - -'d think they'd know they can't handle Clae in the first place," Okane grumbled.

"Information on the crystal's tendencies probably wasn't relayed," said Grim. "Besides, Rexians seem to think they can force anything to bow to them."

Laura coughed out a laugh. "They think they can force their way in and out with a massive set of rocks and crystals?"

"Or it could be a mission of vengeance," said Grim. "As you can see, they're sore losers."

Sore enough to get their Sweepers killed? The whole experience in Rex showed their Sweepers as disposable assets, but wasting so many of them on the eve of their greatest crusade had to be stupidity. There had to be a good reason for their return here; a significant trade-off.

Meanwhile, the two forces clashed in the still-sparking tunnel. Maybe some people would realize their plan had gone awry and pull back, or at least change tactics, but the handler kept calling for advance. The Rexians didn't even flinch, just kept coming. They came without fear, with full knowledge they would be mowed down, but they pressed on with no hesitation. They charged over their comrades' corpses, kept running even while riddled with bullets, and flung themselves at the defenders. Each wave came fast on the other's heels, and while the Rangers had firepower, they didn't have that kind of determination. The first line fell to half-dead Sweepers, knocked down and crushed as the second line rushed to reload their weapons, and by the time they did it was too late. No space remained between their sides now; the tunnel became a mess of bullets and twisting bodies. Soon the chaos moved to this tunnel's entrance. Cherry pulled a knife of her own and jumped out into the fray. Grim pulled Okane farther from the conflict, and Laura stood between them, brandishing her stolen blade for lack of anything else; any Bijou or Eggs would hurt their defenders as easily as the enemy.

Three Rexian Sweepers dodged into the tunnel. Cherry yanked one back and Laura swung at the second, but the third circled around her. She had a moment of horror, completely convinced that she'd be stabbed in the back, but the Sweeper passed her by entirely. He'd definitely seen her—the lingering eyes proved that—but he had another target. He ran past Okane and Grim to duck into the next tunnel, heading west. That tunnel entrance bore an arrow and a bold black "X." He was after the Pits.

Laura swore. Still more people flooded into the tunnel but she couldn't just let him get away.

"Take care of Okane!" she shouted at Grim, and took off.

The clamor echoed but ahead the Sweeper was alone. The din covered her footfalls for a long stretch, but it didn't last forever. The Sweeper whirled around and shot. The bullet hit the wall near her head and she stumbled. Two more shots landed just off the mark and she dove behind a mining cart. Bullets ricocheted off its metal side with a warped noise.

"Give up!" Laura shouted, even as she cringed. "You can't run forever!"

"Rex does not run," said the Sweeper.

"You're at a disadvantage," said Laura. Ivo and Zelda had seemed logical. Maybe this Rexian would listen, too. "You've already run into the first wave of resistance, and that's not even Amicae's real forces. You think they'll stop here? Soon you'll be entirely surrounded. They'll trap you, maybe kill you. The only way out for you is to escape now."

The gun remained silent. Had she struck a nerve? Slowly she leaned to peer around the corner. A bullet ricocheted just below her chin. The heat seared her skin and she fell back with a screech.

"It doesn't matter if we're trapped," said the Sweeper. "All that matters is victory. Amicae will be eradicated."

"Not if I get you first," she snarled, and threw her weight against the cart.

Despite being made of metal it held no cargo; after a few seconds of straining it moved, and once it got going it coasted fast on momentum. She ran with it in front of her like a battering ram. This served as a shield well enough, hopefully serving as a good bluff in the same way. She gripped the blade in one hand, ready to pounce as soon as the Sweeper came in sight. But nothing appeared. No bullets bounced off the cart. No sound reached her beyond that of the wheels. She stopped short and straightened, letting the cart rattle on without her. The hall was empty. He'd left while she'd been distracted.

"Of course he did," she grumbled, tapping her amulet and ordering speed. She had to get there first. No matter what, she had to keep the Pit safe.

Right. Right. Left. She tore around "X"-marked corners without any heed for the Sweeper ahead and his gun. She could hear an awful noise ahead: straining amulets. He had to be running full out. So long as the noise didn't stop, he hadn't found it. She had a chance. Exactly as she thought this, the screeching hit a higher pitch. A dull *boom* echoed through the mine, making the floor tremble. Lights swung merrily and the boarded walls creaked. Laura rounded the corner. This passage ended in a door, a reinforced piece of metal that had bent under massive strain, lock and hinges warped and useless.

Her father once told her that miners left pillars in their carved-out rooms, thick and strong to preserve the structure and prevent cave-ins. In the middle of this room stood a pillar, but it wasn't stone. It stood out stark against the rock, as if a black metal chimney had been painstakingly unearthed from the ground itself. At its base, enormous Gin stones piled up about it like tinder for a fire. Their subtle sparkle had leached into patches of the ground; for five feet around its base the earth had gone eerily pale. A few colorful amulets lay against the Gin, mismatched and charging.

The Rexian Sweeper staggered for it. He wrenched a ruined gauntlet off, ripping flesh with it before throwing it at the Pit. It glanced off the black metal, leaving an ugly gouge. The Gin glowed brighter, flaring with a rattle and hiss like boiling water. The fallen gauntlet leapt and snapped as its circuitry overloaded.

Silence descended for a moment; then the Gin's glow spiked. A surging wave of heat swept out in an ugly haze. Laura futilely threw her hands in front of her face. Her ring smarted and her last Egg burned in her hip holster. The air went dry. The Sweeper cried out and she squinted through her fingers at him. His skin burned, red and peeling as if from horrible sunburn. Why wasn't she affected?

The Sweeper ring glowed like Gin itself. Slowly, it dawned on her: the rings linked into the same magic system governing the jewelry box, the armory, all meant to signify their own link into the system and protect the wearer from magical backlash. Where the Gin of their magic production remained on rotation, the Pit's base stayed forever—a permanent addition to the system, able to send and receive alerts if anything went wrong. This magic must've recognized her through the ring and diverted itself.

The Gin wave dissipated, but before its haze could fade she heard the rasp of a blade.

"Give me that ring," said the Sweeper.

Laura took a step back. "Not a chance."

"Then I'll cut it off - - -r corpse."

He lunged. For all the power behind the attack, he was very predictable. Laura backed up fast, so his attack missed entirely. She gritted her teeth and swung, but the Sweeper recovered fast and blocked easily before retaliating. Laura ducked and scrambled for the Pit. If she could get close enough to the Gin, the energy would shield her, keep him from getting close. Then she could attack. He followed. She could hear Gin groaning behind her, feel the tingle of magic in the air, but he paid it no mind. *Clang, crash, shriek!* He caught her blade and she stumbled. The edge snagged her sleeve and cut through to the skin from biceps to elbow. She hissed in pain. If she didn't throw him off now she'd never have a chance. She kicked a rock on the floor, and it clanged into the Pit's side. The magic there rattled and pulsed, readying another wave. A clatter from behind alerted her just in time to whirl about. The Sweeper caught her with one hand this time, squeezing her injured arm. The pain caught her off guard. She gasped; her knees buckled. The Sweeper kept leaning, pressing closer, eyes gleaming.

With a breathy, garbled sound, the golden wave surged again. Laura felt a jolt of elation, but it died fast. Sure enough, the ring glowed, but the protective current around her had extended. The Rexian got caught halfway into the protective radius; it wasn't pushing him away now. He bared his teeth and lurched forward. Laura reeled. As she threw him off, regaining her balance, he grabbed at her belt. An Egg scraped past her amulet, flashing red as he threw it. He didn't have to aim. They were already close enough. She never should've backed up in the first place. She squeezed her eyes shut.

The Egg detonated, throwing both of them back. Metal screeched, accompanied by crackling and short bursts of blinding white light. Laura couldn't see details amid the too-bright flashes. Tiny amulets tumbled past her, their magic wavering with nonsentient confusion.

Whatever remained of the Pit wasn't metal. The chimney had split and warped, but beyond the Gin's golden haze Laura couldn't make out any details. Rock and debris clattered down past the tangled shape and piled on the floor with the Gin. For a long while, they both lay stunned. Debris kept shifting, but Laura couldn't hear it. Her ears rang. Eventually, the Sweeper propped himself up: slowly, on arms, on knees, and finally, shakily, to his feet. He looked at the Pit's wreckage with a savage expression.

"So much work," he spat, "for one weak city."

Laura forced herself up off the ground. She wavered, but gritted her teeth and spoke as strongly as she could. "Is that all you wanted to do? Fantastic. Get lost."

The Sweeper didn't bother to look at her. He pulled something from his belt, round and white. He peeled away the outer layer. Chip after chip fell, revealing something glassy and red.

"The handlers should've ordered this in the first place," he said. "But no, they wanted an 'easy' route. They wanted the satisfaction of

Amicae handing over its lifeblood freely. The handlers are the ones who teach us not to be greedy. They should learn the lessons themselves."

He seemed to be talking to himself. Laura's eyes stayed fixed on the item in his hands. Rexian red. Not an Egg, not kin, but something terrible. Maybe she hadn't seen it, but she'd heard of it. What had Zelda said, before?

"What are you doing?" she said sharply.

"The clearest and most secure method of attaining Amicae's power source is by destroying all of its defenders. Plant an infestation inside an unreachable place, a place where no one would suspect. A place with access into the interior." He looked at her now, sneered. "I don't know who planted - - -r 'Falling Infestation,' but they had a good plan. Ours, on the other hand, is perfect."

The last of the white casing fell away, revealing a glass float. Something darker swam inside it, not bloodred or any kin variety. It was black as night, black as an abyss. An infestation, stirring after forced hibernation.

"Once this enters the Pit, it will be invulnerable," said the Sweeper. "- - - cannot stop it. It will consume us both for fuel, and it will consume everyone in the mine before rising to the surface. Amicae will die, and Rex will take - - -r magic from its ashes."

"Wait a second," she gasped. "You can't be serious! You'll die here, too!"

"I'm aware," he replied, and walked for the Pit.

Laura pushed herself up and stumbled into his path. She had to stop this. He kept walking, unconcerned. She held up her blade and he batted it hard enough to knock it to the ground. Laura stumbled, half momentum and half trying to keep a distance. She bumped into the Pit. She groped at the pillar, trying to find a new weapon. Her boot clinked against a slab of Gin. A chance. She stomped, giving the same order she had on the train back in November.

"Wake up!"

The magic didn't come from below. Her hand against the pillar burned. Light flared at her back, bigger and brighter than the explosion before. The Sweeper paused. Laura barely had time to take in his confusion before she gasped. Searing pain arched up her arm and shoulder. It branched into her chest, hot and prickling, all the way down to her guts. Her lungs seized up. Her eyes stung.

Is this how I die? she wondered. Was this the pain of an old, infected amulet? She bared her teeth. If it ate her, she sure as hell wasn't going alone. She made a grab for the Sweeper's arm.

At once the burn in her chest redirected. The pain formed a solid bridge across both arms, up the one and straight out the fingertips of the other. The Sweeper's hand convulsed. He tottered, dropped the grenade. Was he screaming or was that the blood boiling in her ears? No. His mouth was open. Definitely screaming. He fell back, landed on his knees, and groped at his chest and throat. He gurgled, blood pouring out his nose and ears as eyes turned red. His chest gave stunted heaves. Laura struggled to turn away, to stop looking. She forced herself away from the Pit. The pain stopped as soon as she parted with it, and all the strength left her. She fell to her hands and knees. Her vision swam. The Sweeper wheezed. He fell with a thud. She couldn't read his number but she saw his still eyes, his bloodied teeth. He didn't speak or move again.

The room listed left and right, but maybe that was just her. Her arms screamed agony, shaking to hold her weight. Vanilla scent clogged her throat. She could hardly breathe. She wheezed, distantly aware of tears filling up her goggles.

I don't want to die. I don't want to die.

More red wobbled past her fingers. Blood? Was she—? No. Glass. What killed the Sweeper had left the infestation unscathed. It headed for the Pit. If it infected the other amulets, Amicae was dead. Okane would die. Morgan, Cheryl, the Keedlers, Brecht. All gone, just like Clae.

Damn it.

Damn it.

Damn it.

She hardly realized she spoke aloud, curses falling from her lips as she forced her limbs to move.

"Not this time. Not them too."

All she had to do was break the amulet. Destruction of the amulet meant destruction of the inhabitant. Clae had done it with the mask. She'd done it at Sundown Hills. She could do it now. If she was dying, she could do this much.

She grabbed for it, planning to smash it against the ground. As she reached, a spark started at her other hand. It zipped like a light up a fuse, up, over, and down that arm again. Light streaked from her fingers, crackling about the glass. The infestation writhed and screamed, the sound tinny through its prison before the glass shattered. The creature shuddered and dissolved into smoke, eaten up by more crackling energy. The world spun faster, colors sliding together. Laura crumpled. While she felt a stab of pain in her hand, it gave her glorious relief; the rest of her arms became cool and painless.

———— ∞ ————

What felt like seconds later she blinked open her eyes. The floor remained as dark and dusty as ever. Cold, too. She shifted and groaned. Her body stiffened as if she'd been there for hours. Her outstretched hand smarted badly. Suddenly it seemed very quiet, and she realized someone had been speaking. A shuffle of clothes came from her other side.

"Careful. Take it very slowly. You're fragile in this state."

"What?" Her tongue felt like lead. She worked at it awhile, frowning.

"That was more magic than a body should take. I'm surprised you survived it."

Something white leaned into her vision. She squinted through the bleariness.

"Grim? Am I dead?"

"Miraculously, no."

Grim focused on her bloodied hand. He turned it over gingerly and she realized glass chunks stuck out of it. That should hurt. She winced more out of obligation than real feeling as he pried the pieces out.

"What happened?"

"You channeled Gin energy through yourself. It's like electrocution in most cases, but you appear to be an anomaly."

"Gin can't hurt other strains," she mumbled. If she crossed her eyes and squinted she could pretend it was Clae in that coat, listing facts. It hurt to imagine. "It recognizes you. Can't or won't hurt you."

"With airborne mist, yes. Treating you as an amulet, however, has consequences." He nodded at the fallen Sweeper. "You only survived by being a conductor. Expelled the magic as soon as you received it."

Memories were a little foggy, but that sounded right.

"I channeled it into him."

"He couldn't redirect it, so it ruined him."

The glass was out. Grim dug through his pockets again before producing a small jar and a roll of bandages. He yanked off a glove with his teeth, scooped something from the jar, and mashed it into her cuts. This time she gave a full-body shudder, straining her jaw to keep from making a sound. Whatever it was stung, and coldness seeped through her hand. He wrapped it all up in the bandage, tying lopsidedly.

"I'm no medic, but that should tide you over until we see a professional. Give me your other hand."

"Why, so you can put more of that nasty stuff on me?"

"We need to regulate your energy. That Gin threw off your natural balance."

Laura frowned but didn't protest as he pulled her into a sitting position. He propped her up, then took her other hand in both of his and closed his eyes. His hands felt cold and rough as if covered in calluses. He didn't seem willing to do anything else.

"What are you doing?"

"Stabilizing. The process is slow with a small point of contact."

She looked pointedly at their hands. "So you want to hug instead?"

"That may be detrimental to both of us."

She wrinkled her nose and regarded him. "Are you a Magi?"

His pale, pale eyes flicked open. "Why do you think that?"

"Isn't it obvious? Strange-eyed guy practicing magic, somehow able to get shot and live? Closest thing I've ever heard to that is Magi ability."

"I suppose so, but I'm not one of them."

"Then what are you?"

"Thracis."

"From *Thrax*?" She laughed. Her ribs ached so she stopped quickly. "Thrax is a ruin."

"So it is."

"Is it Ranger territory now?"

"No. Just mine." He frowned, dropping her hand. "Is it all right if I roll up your sleeve?"

"Sure."

The cloth bunched weirdly at her elbow but she didn't think of that—she was too preoccupied with the state of her arm. The discolored skin had a thin branching pattern, as if a phantom tree spread its limbs to overtake her arm.

"What the—"

"Rangers call them 'lightning flowers.' I imagine it hurts."

Grim shrugged off his coat, rolled up his own sleeves, and pressed his forearms against hers. More chill. Laura hissed and gripped his elbow to ground herself. But this wasn't the same minty *zap* as the medicine. A feeling spread up, like a soothing autumn breeze swirling under her skin. The last of the burning quieted, smoothed out in a graceful instant. The stress eased out of her muscles as the feeling filled her. Warm, cold, neither, both. A perfect balance. Harmony. The room no longer swam but lay before her in perfect clarity.

"Are you the one doing this?"

He nodded and pulled his arms away. The feeling eased out into nothing and Laura felt empty in its wake. She was relieved when he gestured for her other arm and did the same procedure.

"I was afraid to do it earlier," he admitted. "It would balance, but it can soothe too much. I've accidentally lulled a heart into stopping before. The Gin magic ripped your energy out too. You were drained enough that I couldn't risk it."

Laura turned her free hand over, sickened by the color but grateful that it all moved properly.

"I don't understand. You don't have an amulet. Not even Magi can do this, as far as I know. Balance, or whatever."

"I'm special." He pulled away and held out his arms again. Where they'd touched her, something akin to a burn marred the pasty skin, but instead of raised welts and discoloration it gleamed and sparkled, like the surface of Gin but paler, harsher. "I suppose with some crystal, you have to break it open for it to shine."

Crystal? Wait. The breath froze in her lungs. "You're like Clae and Anselm?"

"I take it you mean the child in the river? Not exactly. He was once a normal human. This is how I was born. You could say we crystals are opposites."

"Like opposite magnets? So you don't get along well?"

He nodded. "He has become Gin, which produces magic. His variety of crystal has a different potency, though. It's not a pure stone, but tainted by humanity and the residual emotions. I am not Gin. I am Niveus."

"Like the stone they use to make amulets?"

"Correct." He folded his arms, hiding the glittering patches. "Niveus creates nothing but holds magic in check. Too much magic is a terrible thing. It can destroy the mind, cause mutations, diseases, death. Niveus streamlines and refines it. Niveus is everywhere in the soil, diluting enough for energy to be safely used."

"It calms people down," she murmured.

"It dilutes stress-related energies if someone wears a piece," Grim agreed. "Although—" He nodded at her hand. She looked down, and found only one ring. The Sweeper one rested where it always had, but the Niveus ring from Clae had gone. She looked around frantically, and paused when Grim reached out to pluck something off the floor: a fragment of white. "In contact with large amounts of magic, it becomes overwhelmed and shatters."

The Falling Infestation flickered back to mind: Marshall dipping his hands into the fountain, his frown, *Only one variety broke. It's all the Niveus amulets.* Understanding dawned.

"That's why you looked like you died."

Grim rolled the Niveus piece between his fingers. "Usually there are enough Niveus traces in the soil to outweigh effects of Gin. There must be a balance with Gin and Niveus if you want them to work. That child is smaller than me, but his magic is strong. I didn't have enough mass to cancel it out. He sapped my strength. I almost broke."

"And when he came in contact with you, he calmed down. That's why he'd changed and looked so odd. Crystal doesn't reshape or move on its own, after—Wait. You. You're a talking rock?"

"I thought we'd covered that."

"You're a walking, talking rock."

"Cherry believes I'm an earth spirit," he said, slightly offended. "As a dryad is to a tree, as a sylph is to wind, I am to this stone."

"Are you pulling the religion card on me?"

"Not really. As far as I'm aware, I'm the only one there is."

"Then where did you come from?"

"I woke up in Thrax a little over a hundred and fifty years ago. I don't know why, and I don't know how. I just woke. No one was there. I've tried to find someone to explain it to me, but most of my findings stem from Ranger lore. It's not the most reliable source."

"All alone for that long? Sounds awful."

"Not always. There are many interesting people in the wilds. Rangers like Cherry. Couriers like Okane."

"Rexians, you mean."

"No."

"What do you mean, no?" said Laura. "They're the ones out hunting Rangers and razing satellite towns, and they're descendants of Magi, too."

"Couriers *are* Magi." He pinched the bridge of his nose. "Perhaps it would've been easier to tell you this before, but they are dangerous to speak of. They need to ensure no news of them or their home reaches Rex. They'd sooner murder a Rexian Sweeper than help him. But that isn't our current problem. How do you feel? Ill at all?"

Laura had to snap out of her daze. "What? No. Sore, definitely, but better. Thank you."

"Can you stand?"

"I think so."

Grim held his hands out and she grasped them (fingers of *rock*, she marveled) to help pull herself up. Her legs wavered and she had a little vertigo, but her head cleared quickly. She looked back to take stock of the damage.

The Pit's metal had definitely warped. What little metal remained curled like a wrapper peeled to reveal its contents. A solid pillar of crystal, fusing directly onto a floor of solid Gin, emerged from this wreckage. Old amulets could be glimpsed inside: broken ceramics, figures, sections of larger machines jumbled tight together. Kin treatments were meant to wash out infestations, but Laura never considered what kin did once it arrived at the bottom: evaporate, perhaps, or sink into the ground. The magic must've soaked into the amulets themselves, over and over until the pieces could absorb no more, and then hardened around them. Over 150 years of kin treatments had sent supercharged liquid gold between them, molding the Pit and its contents into a massive magic strain, the purest form of magic that could be found. It shimmered bright, echoing all the colors of sunrise.

"It's beautiful," she whispered.

"It's powerful," said Grim. "But more than that, it's become its own strain, self-sufficiently. No amulets in there are susceptible to infestation."

Laura choked out a laugh. No wonder there had been such a big effect. No wonder there had been so much light. Grim turned and pulled her uninjured arm over his shoulder.

"Let's leave. This area is secure, and it wouldn't do well to linger. I might break after all."

Laura nodded and let him help her back into the mining area. They stumbled back to the battle site. The signs began gradually, some discolored walls and spots of blood giving way to bodies, dropped weapons, craters, and buckling ceilings. A few Rangers lay amid the dead, but the Rexian bodies outnumbered them. The living stepped between corpses, checking this or that in exaggerated silence. All wore drab Ranger gear.

"We won," Laura murmured. Her eyes roved over the crowd. Rangers upon Rangers upon Rexian dead. "Where's Okane?"

"I lost track of him earlier," said Grim.

"He has to be here somewhere. You don't think—"

With a rush of horror she wondered if someone saw his eyes and shot before thinking. Was he lying here among the dead?

"Calm," Grim said evenly.

"We have to find him."

"We will."

"But what if he—"

"Grim!" Cherry leaned out of another passage, waving. "There you are. We've been looking for you."

"I take it everything's been settled?" said Grim.

"What Rexians aren't dead ran away. We've called the upper levels, so the authorities will be here soon. In the meantime, we're treating some of our own."

"Maybe this will get it through their heads," said a passing Ranger, carrying a kit of medical supplies. "Rangers aren't mobs."

"Have you seen Okane?" said Laura. "I haven't seen him anywhere yet, and—"

"Sure I have." Cherry jerked her head at the passage. "He's right over here. Hear that, Okane? She was worried about you, too."

Laura ran to the corner. Okane sat on the floor, arms linked around bent knees while another Ranger squatted to tend to his injuries. Bandages completely hid the right half of his face, but the visible eye was wide and bright.

"Laura!" he yelped, making to stand, but the medic shoved him right back down.

Laura let out a single bark of laughter before her knees buckled. Grim and Cherry steadied her and helped maneuver so she could sit next to him. His eye blinked at her, silver, beautiful as ever. Her own expression probably unnerved him, but she didn't care. She was too busy drinking in a sight she'd been afraid to lose.

"Are - - - okay?" he asked.

"Me? What about you? Please tell me that doesn't feel as bad as it looks."

"It's . . . bad. But they gave me pills." Sure enough, as he spoke his visible skin seemed to pinch.

"That's something at least." She sighed, shaky. "What happened?"

"Someone brought in a machine gun." Okane shuddered.

"It was like shooting fish in a barrel," said Cherry, shaking her head. "We almost thought we'd hit you somewhere in the mix. Good thing you're safe, or I'd never forgive myself. Where did you two run off to?"

"One of them went after the Pit," said Laura.

Okane started. The medic chided him but he whirled about, paler than ever. "They didn't reach it, did they? What's the damage? Is it—"

"I don't think we need to worry about anything."

"Laura killed the invader," said Grim.

"And the Pit?"

"He hit it, but it didn't do him any good," said Laura. "It turns out there aren't any more amulets in there. They all fused. All the washes of kin over the years stuck and made it a strain."

"Wait. We have an entire Pit's worth of Gin?"

"Pseudo-Gin, anyway. It packs a hell of a punch." She raised her hands so he could see the discoloration. "It's so pretty, though! And the Gin won't affect you. The magic flows right around. Clae always said it was because we're strains, but I think it's actually hooked up to the Sweeper rings, like the armory. I have no idea what we could do with it, but—Okane?"

Okane had tuned out the moment he saw her hands. His chest rose in nervous half breaths.

"Laura," he said again, absolutely wretched.

"I'm okay, you don't have to cry!"

"For god's sake, don't force me to change this bandage," said the medic.

"Laura," he whispered. She threw an arm around his shoulders and leaned closer, rubbing his biceps.

"I'm good! I promise. I'm not in such bad shape as you."

He shook his head and bowed over, shoulders shaking. Laura glanced up at the others for help.

"Don't look at me," said Cherry. "I don't know how to handle heartfelt reunions."

"Please check on her injuries too," Grim told the medic, before straightening and tugging Cherry along with him. "We'll give you privacy. Call for us if you need any help. We won't be far."

They retreated into the main tunnel. The medic offered no advice in their stead, just rolled her eyes and dug through her kit for more supplies. Laura pulled Okane back and forth in a slow rocking motion, the way Morgan had held her years ago when she'd been sorted into the wrong class.

"What's wrong? You seemed okay a minute ago."

"I'm just—I was waiting. Now I don't have to wonder. I was afraid."

"Don't worry. Clae didn't teach any pushovers."

"*He* died. If he was so great, how could anyone be safe? Especially someone who hasn't worked the job for a year yet?"

"Are you trying to bring me down?"

"- - - disappeared! One minute - - - were there, and the next I looked and - - - were gone!" He sucked in a breath that rattled in his lungs like an animal's snarl. "I thought, I was afraid, maybe, what if, where could - - - go in such a small space except down with them?" He kicked one leg. A rock bounced all the way to the closest Rexian, her silver eyes locked on them even in death. "I almost lost it when they pulled out the gun!" Now he sobbed, breathing haggard and voice breaking. "I thought - - - were still in there! I never want to be like that again! I don't want to lose anyone else! Not the haven, not Clae, not - - -! Never, never do that again!"

"I thought you saw me going," she mumbled.

"But where to? And when would - - - have come back? The tunnels are a mess if - - -'re not paying attention. - - - could've walked right back into it."

"I'm sorry."

She rested her head on his, at a loss. She'd never seen anyone so upset over her before. Morgan wailed about the future and Clae had hovered relentlessly, but this was uncharted territory. It frightened her. She had to swallow a lump in her throat before speaking again.

"You're going to be stuck with me for a long time yet. And I promise I'll be more obvious about what I'm doing next time. But you have to promise me something too. No more of this 'I'm lucky' bullshit. No jumping off buildings, no making yourself a target. You really scare me when you do that."

He scoffed. "That's different. I'm replaceable."

"Says who?"

"Says my sister." He glared at the dead Rexian.

Laura's stomach twisted. "That's not your sister."

"How would - - - know? How many Sweepers have my blood in their veins because of that paragon? We're gears. We're tiny things in the machine, ready to be swapped out by Rex or Sullivans or—"

She reached with both arms to cradle his head, blocking his view.

"You are completely irreplaceable." Her words were muffled against his head but he stopped struggling. "No one in the world is like you, and that's amazing and it's terrifying. I'm so glad I met you, but if you die I'm never going to find *you* again, and that's one of the worst things I can imagine. If you want me to take care of myself, you have to do the same."

After a moment, he leaned against her. "I know that, but it's one thing to think it and another to feel it. I just . . . I need more time to believe that."

24

JAILBIRDS FLY

Sometimes, Rex's Sweeper breeding program produced duds. They didn't happen often, maybe one in a hundred infants affected, but those children were useless. Magically impaired. They assigned the lucky ones to hard labor, abandoned by the program. Unlucky ones? No one talked about them.

Sweeper 1100106 almost registered as one of those duds. The differences between him and his fellows were obvious. They had luminous eyes; his turned out dark and had to hit the light *just right* to match that luster. They relied on their magic more than muscle for their jobs; while not large by any means, he didn't have the same stick-figure I've-got-a-nasty-trick-up-my-sleeve build, his frame more muscular and his magic sensing not so precise. In fact, he rarely used his magic. He did it enough to get through basic training, and once the handlers stopped monitoring relied on Gin amulets for everything. He wasn't special, but then again, none of them were. Sweepers served as simple pawns on the great chessboard of Rex's advance to glory.

"100087, to the front! 100096, left!"

Two shapes flitted as directed, fast and dark in the fading light. The rest of the group spanned the distance between them, fifteen figures barely visible amid the trees. They'd started out with twenty-five, a month ago.

"1100104, hang left!"

Only one non-Sweeper remained. He rode on a horse near the back of the pack, voice like a foghorn. It wouldn't be surprising if his yelling drew out the monsters.

1100106 ran near the far right of the group, leaping over tangled roots and uneven ground. A young woman sprinted just in front of him; he followed the kingshound crest on the back of her uniform jacket. He felt anxious, but didn't let it show on his face. The monster was close.

The creature appeared on the right flank, an inky shadow spreading fast along the ground and dyeing all it touched pitch black. The formation scattered. All the members sensed it immediately except the man on the horse, who wheeled the animal about in confusion.

1100106 and the woman he'd been following, 1100128, took the same route.

"128." He broke protocol, but it was much easier to say "one-two-eight" than the entire serial number. "Are - - - prepared?"

"My carry-on supply of Eggs is gone," she replied, eyes busy tracking the monster's movement. "I have the blade and some bullet rounds."

"Gun?"

"Functional."

"Good."

He had four amulets, two by his knees and one at each elbow, attached to bracers to help the magic flow. Without pausing he slapped one knee, and magic rushed through the bracers. With the extra power he ran twice as fast, circling around the edge of the darkness.

The infestation rose out of the dark before them, its slippery surface gone solid but wreathed in noxious cloud. The redness caught 1100106's attention first: one ugly red eye larger even than he was, lodged in a socket of seething tar. It had taken the form of a human skull but sharper, nastier, teeth like crooked chunks of broken razors that gnashed with a horrible snap. Rock and earth tumbled as more wrenched itself free, the bend of new blackened bone and phalanges, heaving up so an entire skeleton loomed over the group. It was like an evil god, all the wrath of Kuro no Oukoku come to pass judgment on them. 1100106 froze under its eye.

128 had taken precautions. She ducked her head, eyes on the ground as she wrenched the blade from her sheath and cried, "Forward!"

The amulets of her harness rushed to obey, and she was yanked forward as if pulled in by a fishing line. She landed on another rocky outcrop, twisted, lunged again. Her blade sliced straight through the bottom of its tibia. The foot dissolved into smoke and slime. The leg moved, mauled stump shifting to goo as the whole creature turned and twisted as a true skeleton could never manage. The eye winked out of 1100106's line of sight, and he refocused on the grass, swapped blade for gun.

128 stood on the other side of the creature, still drawing its attention. He managed to land three of his bullets into it, but other Sweepers did the same to no avail. He knelt, popped open the gun, and dug through his pack.

Where the bullets hit, the infestation lost shape, but it didn't seem overly concerned. It swung from side to side in a slow but inevitable shamble, sending slippery blackness spattering over the ground. The Sweepers wisely kept their distance now. They'd lost five others in just this squad to acidic blackness and poisoned air. Only 128 remained in close quarters, skipping around on amulet power with a mask pulled over her face. She cut the other leg. On a human she'd have taken out an entire tendon, but infestations had no need of such things. It gave a long, low groan. The legs bubbled before liquefying. Its arms drooped. Even the skull sagged, the eye slipping to spin in the mess of its jaws before the whole thing vanished into the black puddle.

The handler whooped in victory, but no one relaxed. 128 alighted on more rocks and squinted at its bubbling surface. She jolted in alarm, raised one hand. The larger group had no time to scatter. The blackness surged for them, growing and tumbling over itself before the skeleton surfaced again. They'd adjusted to its slower movement, so its sudden speed threw them off. It caught two Sweepers while the others fled. The first Sweeper didn't last long. A massive hand crushed her, slowly so they could hear the scream and cracking of every bone. The other Sweeper thrashed, arms and equipment pinned as another inky appendage lifted him toward the skull. The jaws opened.

1100106 dug through his pack with renewed urgency. He found a bullet in Sinker crimson, slid it into the gun, and snapped it back into place before aiming. The skull offered the biggest target. He pulled the trigger too late. The Sweeper barely had time to shout before the teeth descended. His legs kicked wildly but blood spurted everywhere before the bullet hit. The Sinker bullet blossomed into a flower of light; sparks flew wide before hardening into shards and swerving right back like a boomerang. This second, brighter volley cut deep and shrieked under the surface. The red eye swirled in its socket. The beast moved again, a low growl rising from its non-throat as magic glittered like boils along its ribs. Once it bit, a Sinker wasted no time. Bare seconds passed before it rooted out the amulet. The growl petered into a whine, and the whole creature burst apart in a shower of red so bright it seemed almost daytime. The infestation vanished in screams and smoke. A rattle and bang announced the amulet's demise too. A piece whistled past 1100106 to clatter on the rocks: the fractured stone of an old cameo pendant, still spitting flame.

128 moved along the edge of the mess, examining the wreckage before announcing, "*Kaibutsu* exterminated."

The verdict made them relax, but not by much. The surviving Sweepers made to move apart in search of amulet shards, but the handler barked, "Stay where you are!"

Tension again. All men frozen. All faces blank. The handler prowled among them, sneered at the creature's remains.

"Who shot that bullet?" Silence. He rounded on them again. "I said, *who shot that bullet?*"

1100106 raised a hand. "I did."

The handler walked to him, stopped only an inch away. His expression made 1100106's insides feel like ice, but he was prime Rexian stock. He didn't show a drop of emotion.

"Why," said the handler, and his breath smelled absolutely rancid, "did you feel the need to waste a Sinker here?"

"I determined the situation otherwise unmanageable," 1100106 replied coolly.

"You *determined*," the handler laughed. "By what standard did you possibly *determine* this?"

It was a hypothetical question, of course. The handler didn't want reasoning, just wanted to grind him into the dirt. But this same handler had no reasoning of his own. The last handler, while cruel, had played the game to win. This man played for the sake of playing and didn't care how many pawns he lost or even, seemingly, whether they made it to the end. He gambled and lived for the thrill of the dice roll and poker tells. He wanted constant action, constant bloodshed, and when Sweepers died the stakes were high, just as he liked it. 1100106 had known many of those Sweepers, even if they never exchanged words beyond orders. The only one he hadn't known was fresh from initial training, barely eleven years old. The newest dead lay in the blackened grass behind the handler, severed halfway down the rib cage so his organs spilled out; the rest of him from shoulders up lay farther on, affected by infestation or Sinker it was impossible to tell, and didn't matter, but he was burned down to raw muscle and bone, the shine of gray eyes the only discernible thing as the wounds wept blood and blackness.

1100106 looked at these gray eyes as they dissolved, felt revulsion and hatred. For the Sweeper's state. For the city that sent them here. For the handler taking pleasure in their deaths.

"My standard is - - -rs," said 1100106, bland but with steel. It was impossible to disguise the harshness of his "you," but while the other Sweepers' eyes narrowed in suspicion, the inflection went entirely over the handler's head. "It is our mission to secure the lowest island for our glorious city, by destroying the *kaibutsu* hive mind and eradicating its lower brethren. For this reason I stepped in to conserve the numbers of our squad, and to eradicate this lower brethren."

"You wasted ammunition we need against the hive itself!" the handler spat.

"We will not reach the hive mind if we have no manpower to reach it with," 1100106 replied. "Besides, every lost Sweeper takes his trove of equipment with him."

The handler's face grew steadily redder; he'd probably never been talked back to by one of his "dogs." "We will reach the hive mind! All you do is break more amulets, making more infestations for our next wave to deal with!"

"Many smaller and weaker infestations are easier to deal with than the intelligent and elderly. Our forces are strong. They will overpower anything we leave in our wake."

There was a moment of silence, and then 1100106 was grabbed roughly by the collar. He stumbled, but kept his expression immobile as the handler seethed, "Are you sassing me, you little shit? Are you questioning my authority, my orders? *Mine?*"

"It is Rexian teaching to never disobey orders, but in this case none were given beyond initial formation."

He really did expect that punch to the head. 1100106 hit the ground hard, his ears ringing. The handler's chest heaved; he cracked his knuckles.

"You want to say that to me again, you shit?"

1100106 pushed himself up again, slow and steady, and faced him. "It is my intention to achieve our goal, with or without shoddy leadership."

Another blow. He had the sense to turn away from it this time so he only staggered instead of fell. The handler screamed something, but the click of a gun's safety lock eclipsed it.

"Rexian code states that Sweepers defying their handlers must be put down," said Sweeper 1100998, aiming her gun at his head. "Does the handler wish to pursue this code to the outcome, in this situation?"

The flicker of rage went out, numbed by resignation. Of course, as much as 1100106's feelings warred over the matter, other Sweepers didn't see it the same way. No use railing against it now. He was alone in that fight. The handler noticed this too, and he seemed pleased, even relaxed as the others took his side.

"Talk back to me one more time," he goaded. "Just once."

1100106 refocused on the mauled Sweeper again. The gray eyes were gone. "I apologize for my rudeness. The *kaibutsu*'s approach provoked irrationality. It will not happen again."

"I'll see to it that it doesn't," the handler laughed. "You. 1100998. I've got another order for you. If you see this one acting up again, put a bullet between his eyes."

"As - - - wish," said 1100998. She clicked the safety lock back into place.

"Do we have anyone else here to complain?" the handler called, spreading his arms and looking around. There was no sound or movement. "Good, because if I get word that any of you even think of doing something stupid like talking back to me, I'll make sure you get the worse end of those *kaibutsu*. Fall in!"

The squad glided together into their ranks, striking the proper form even while gaps remained between them.

"About face!"

They turned. The night sky was barely discernible from the horizon.

"We make camp here!" The handler pointed at the only visible landmark: the slope of a hill with long, swaying grass. "We move now! Get the tents and the rations!"

1100106 had to wonder why they'd bothered with ranks to begin with; probably so the handler could assert his authority again. As they broke out of formation, 1100998 shouldered past him.

"- - - are no paragon," she said. "- - - are not safe from us."

"I know this," he said, and he did. There was nothing else to counter with.

Tents went up, bedrolls unfurled, and rations were passed out from the wagons. 1100106 sat by one of the fires with a tin in one hand and some unidentifiable cutlery in the other.

How bland, he thought as he chewed. Rex didn't waste precious spices on Sweeper fare. So long as it was nutritious and the troops could choke it down, it worked. He didn't even need to chew the mushy concoction, but he worked his jaw anyway and tried to imagine what "sweet" might taste like. Probably bad.

"The night is quiet."

He looked up to see 1100128 standing there, a cup of her own rations in hand.

Despite being two years younger, 1100128 had been his near-constant companion. Small talk might be discouraged among them, but she always sat next to him in their downtime and he found her presence comforting. Everyone in the group admired her; it was hard not to, with the steel of certainty in her vibrant green eyes and formidable Sweeping skill to back it up.

She sat beside him now, surveying the scene with calculated disinterest.

"We would do well not to attract more *kaibutsu*," he replied. "We're far south, after all."

"Closer to the hive," she agreed. She watched him from the corner of her eye. "This excursion is supposed to be special. The one where we strike a killing blow."

He hummed, frowned at his rations, and drank the rest. He couldn't very well say what he thought of the matter, and she knew it. 1100128 was an expert at picking up on his moods, though, so she knew what the silence meant. She looked back at the fire.

"We had an advantage."

"True."

She stabbed at her rations. "What did the stray do with it?"

"No one can truly monitor a stray."

"But one can direct her." Her eyes caught firelight in that Magi way his refused to copy. "Will we die here without that advantage?"

"We would die even with it. The object did not belong to Rex, and chafed at their direction. It would have killed us before any *kaibutsu* had the chance."

"So much knowledge. On what basis?"

"I felt its presence." And what an awful thing it had been. Just the memory made his skin crawl.

She ignored his shudder. "So we will die here, then. It's better than being assigned to the breeding section."

She stirred the contents of her rations, as if such casual mention of her own demise was perfectly normal. But she was a Rex Sweeper. Of course it was normal.

1100106 stood and left the fire to deposit the tin in the food wagon for reuse. Every camp went up on the same layout, so his feet knew where to go even while his head spun. He hadn't thought much of it, pointing Zelda and her companions toward the Wrath of God. So what if they succeeded? Maybe then Rex would see reason. Maybe they'd stay put, not be pigs led to slaughter in a hopeless crusade. But the city remained stubborn as ever, and here they were. If he hadn't helped Zelda, would they be faring better? Would they have lost members at all? If it could just save 1100128 . . .

"Ivo!"

He paused. His hand went for his blade on instinct but he knew this wasn't an infestation. Monsters couldn't talk, and they certainly didn't wear high-end Rexian fashion. Said arm poked around a tree trunk a ways from the campsite, only close enough to be glimpsed in the firelight. After casting around for witnesses, he slinked closer.

"Zelda? What are - - - doing here?"

She simply waved faster, beckoning him in before hauling him back among the trees. She looked rather the worse for wear, clothes torn and spattered with mud, hair hopelessly tangled under a hat he was sure she'd normally not be caught dead in.

"It took forever to find this troop," she griped. "I followed two others before finding out I was in the wrong spot. Couldn't have left me a trail or something, Ivo?"

"That isn't my name. I am—"

"For the last goddamn time, I'm not calling anyone by a number. - - -'re Ivo, so deal with it. Really, - - - ought to be pleased. I did a lot of research on that! Apparently it's the name of some Old Zyran king. Ivo the Tempest!"

1100106 rubbed at his eyes. "Why are - - - here in the first place? I've never seen - - - outside the city. It's dangerous out here."

"No kidding." She sent a scathing glare at the fire. "How many dead so far?"

He thought of gray eyes, of the eleven-year-old. He rubbed at his temples, overwhelmingly tired. "In this group, twelve. Don't add to the count."

"I'm careful," said Zelda. "I may be 'a dud,' but I've got just as much Magi blood as anyone else on this crusade. I'm just here to make sure my favorite Sweeper doesn't join them."

"Really? The stray I know is no fighter."

And Zelda wasn't—she couldn't take so much as a scratch without complaint—but her expression held all the gravity of a veteran's as she said, "I've come to take - - - away."

He laughed. As soon as the sound was out he snapped his mouth shut. Hopefully the camp hadn't heard that.

Zelda snickered. "That was enthusiastic."

"Don't joke about this," he snapped. "Go back to Rex. Disappearing acts don't work on *kaibutsu* or felin."

"But they work on Rexians." He turned to leave, shaking his head, but she blocked his path. "Come on. Just follow me. They'll never find us."

He tried once, twice, to get around her but Zelda was determined. He stopped and scowled. "What do - - - want from me?"

"I want to take - - - away from Rex."

"Let's pretend for a moment that happens. Where exactly would we go?" He pointed at the number under his eye. "We are marked enemies to every other city. The only place we could possibly go is the wilds, and that's obviously not been hospitable."

"We go to Amicae."

Ah, Amicae. The friendly city. Rumor had it that if you ran from something, the best place to go was Amicae with its rabble Quarter and open arms. Of course, that usually got mentioned in conjunction with Thrax's lenient policies, and seeing as how the latter was most definitely a ruin, the ideas must be very outdated.

"Didn't Rex just break in and steal their Gin?" he said. "They won't be forgiving if another set of Rexians turn up on their doorstep."

"Normally yes, but I'm the one who helped them get that Gin and break out of Rex. They already asked me to go to Amicae with them. They said they'd give me protection."

"That doesn't have anything to do with me."

"If they're protecting me, what's the big deal if we add just one more to the mix?"

"A big deal, considering—"

"If informants can move their entire families to keep Rex from catching them, I should qualify too. Who's to know if - - -'re my brother or not?"

He leveled his flattest glare at her, but he didn't quite feel it. The possibility of escaping Rex had always hung high out of reach. A pipe dream. He quashed it down every time it cropped up, denying it any chance to take root. He'd seen others consider it before. He'd seen those same others snatched up from the ranks, never to be seen or heard of again. Zelda often claimed those traitors were melted down into rations; maybe it had been a joke, but her expression always made him queasy. In the middle of the city, capture was an ever-looming threat. But here? Realization dawned. There was no Black Guard, no higher authority watching their every move. The only king here was the hive mind. Sweepers vanished on all sides without a trace. The handler would note their absence, but what clue would an infestation leave behind? There would be no search party. No one would care.

"Now is the best chance," said Zelda. "In the dark of the night, where infestations are at their worst and all the monsters come out to hunt. No one need ever know."

"Surely - - - aren't considering this?"

He jumped. Zelda bit back a curse. 1100128 stood just outside the trees. She frowned at Zelda before turning her gaze on him.

"Desertion is treachery. Rex will hunt - - -."

"Will - - - be the one hunting?" he asked.

Her lips pursed.

Zelda smoothed down her dress, pretending she hadn't been scared. "Of course she will be. Silly little queen bee and her *absolute loyalty*. She'd do anything the handler asks."

"I have no wish to fight against my brother," said 1100128, ignoring her completely. "Come back to the fire."

1100106 took in the huddle of Sweepers and slowly shook his

412 ∾ MIRAH BOLENDER

head. 1100128 made a strangled sound and stepped closer, arm out-stretched.

"106. Please."

His head moved faster as determination swelled in his chest. Now was the time. He couldn't meet her eyes but hell if he was going back.

"We said that we would die here. If that's the case, I'd rather die alone in the wilds than under a force that treats us as dogs."

"Then it's settled." Zelda's expression was smug. "Come along, Ivo. We've got quite a distance to cover. Do us a favor and wait a few minutes before reporting to - - -r owners, 128."

She spun on her heel and marched into the darkness. 1100106 made to follow.

"106," 1100128 said desperately.

He didn't look at her. "I refuse to stay if I have a choice otherwise."

"Is it a wise choice, though?" 1100128 trailed several feet behind him. "How is this not a fool's errand?"

"It is."

"And yet—"

"Call me a fool and be done with it," he snapped.

There was a beat of silence.

"As if *one* could make it all the way to Terual without dying," 1100128 grumbled. Before he knew it she was at his side as if hunting infestations again. She pulled the standard gun from her holster and checked the bullets, feigning nonchalance (terribly) as she continued, "Even Rex knows to have someone watching their backs."

"We're not taking her," said Zelda.

1100128's eyes shifted back to him. He'd opened his mouth to argue too, but something in her expression made him pause. He'd known her long enough not to be surprised when the odd emotion shone through, but he couldn't remember ever seeing this one. It re-minded him of a lost Rexian boy on the main circuit, eyes flicking wildly for his mother but mouth clamped shut in fear.

"She has a point," he said instead.

"What?"

"It will be useful to have another fighter along in Kuro no Oukoku."

Zelda glowered. "This has to be a joke."

"If we wish to arrive in Amicae in one piece, this is a good option."

"I'm not wasting my 'plus one' on her of all people!"

"But it's not limited to one. If agents can take families, Amicae can accept her. Who knows if she's - - -r sister or not? Breeding program."

"I am as much a believable candidate as 106," 1100128 agreed.

Zelda scowled. "Really? Is this really happening?"

"Moaning like that will draw attention even with your ability," said 1100128.

A quick check showed that none of the other Sweepers noted their absence, but he didn't want to push his luck. "We'd best be off now."

Zelda looked tempted to argue but kept her mouth shut. If 1100128 kept him motivated to leave it must not be worth confronting. She stalked into the wilds instead.

"Hurry it up, then."

They jogged after her. A wobbly smile broke over 1100106's face; happiness or adrenaline, he didn't know which. He cast the ration tin aside as they rounded a curve in the deer path. Maybe, some childish thought whispered, if he squinted hard enough he could see the friendly city on the horizon.

In their wake, shadows shifted. The ration tin skimmed slowly left, then right, before dipping down as if into water. An inky black arm rose up, grasped a tree branch, and heaved up the bulk to hang. It shuddered. A crimson eye opened in the very middle, pupil a thin slit.

Sweepers, it decided. Even if they weren't currently slinging around bombs of light, that metal scrap tasted like *King Sweepers. Don't they ever tire of being annoying?* It would tolerate them in its territory up to a point, normally. The Sweepers were generally useless but they brought the others with them: the loud ones, the gossipers. It loved gossipers. Their noise let it cut noise on other fronts.

"We have created a weapon, but it has a drawback," they would say, and this information it would feed to its children, who would use the knowledge mercilessly. This time the gossipers had something better. "The Wrath of God will be the hive's downfall." *Foolish. We are the dark, the quiet. We are the natural state of the world. The light and noise will crumble under us.* "Amicae's Wrath of God." And that made it pause. Amicae. North. Yes. Children whispered of the cities. It knew the cities. Amicae was the one that gave it pause. Wrath. It remembered wrath. Fear. So many children. All together. All gone, so suddenly it could barely hear them scream. All it had sensed was a great anger, and then nothingness. Never before had it known fear. *Wrath of Amicae. Wrath of God. Killer of the dark.* The killer was walking among these King Sweepers? Coming into its territory?

The hive mind shuddered, let go of the branch and seeped back into the shadows, eye winking out. Even then it shook. *The wrath is coming? Here? Here? After my children, after me? Where?* It had sensed nothing from the children here. *Show me. Where is it? Wrath? Where?*

Far away, a child opened its eye. The hive mind looked through it to the sight beyond: a six-tiered city in the shadow of a mountain, shimmering in the dark of near-midnight. *Not this one.* The eye closed. Another opened. Boarded walls, hanging lights, the surroundings scored by battle and humans clamoring down the tunnel. Glass scattered over an earth floor soaked in the gold light of Sweepers. The kin was long absorbed but thrummed with that detestable feeling. The furthest from calm. The worst the hive could think of.

Where is this?

It is Amicae, the child replied. *The un-dark of Amicae, the under, the human amulet quiet until now until the King Sweepers came and the Sinclairs arrived with noise and anger. It is loud. It is detestable.*

"We had an advantage." "Will we die here without that advantage?"

The King Sweepers had known even when the gossipers didn't. The wrath was not here. It was still north. North where these Sweepers were going. But if they had their way the wrath would come back with them, come to stamp out the dark, kill the hive. This could not be permitted.

The hive mind slid along the deer path, moving between shadows seamlessly.

They will lead me to it. I will take my time. I will move to the island with them, as my children crossed before. I will find the wrath. I will destroy it before it destroys me.

Then all will be quiet.